Philip Caveney, bo[...] two-year spell at Manchester's Piccadilly Radio, writing and presenting a weekly film review programme. He is a professional and freelance journalist, and his previous novels include *The Sins of Rachel Ellis*, *Tiger, Tiger*, *The Tarantula Stone*, *Speak No Evil*, *Black Wolf* and *Strip Jack Naked*. He lives with his wife and child in Heaton Mersey.

Also by Philip Caveney

The Sins of Rachel Ellis
Tiger, Tiger
The Tarantula Stone
Speak No Evil
Black Wolf
Strip Jack Naked

Slayground

Philip Caveney

HEADLINE
FEATURE

First published in 1994
by HEADLINE BOOK PUBLISHING

First published in paperback in 1995
by HEADLINE BOOK PUBLISHING

A HEADLINE FEATURE paperback

10 9 8 7 6 5 4 3 2 1

ISBN 0 7472 4418 9

Typeset by Keyboard Services, Luton, Beds

Printed and bound in Great Britain by
Cox & Wyman Ltd, Reading, Berks

HEADLINE BOOK PUBLISHING
A division of Hodder Headline PLC
338 Euston Road
London NW1 3BH

This one, with thanks, is for John 'Marlon' Malam, proof-reader, sometimes-editor and full-time Godfather. And for the staff of Withington Hospital SCBU, July 1993, who helped me through an entirely different kind of thriller.

'When I was a child, I spake as a child, I understood as a child, I thought as a child: but when I became a man, I put away childish things.'

Corinthians 13:11

'Children begin by loving their parents. After a time they judge them. Rarely, if ever, do they forgive them.'

Oscar Wilde

Chapter One

With a casual flick of his hand, Finn McManus wipes out a detachment of Vietnamese foot soldiers. Flames momentarily engulf the section of jungle from which they are emerging. Finn sees their broken bodies flung in all directions, hears their synthesised screams mingled with the roar of the explosion.

He grins, swings the sights of the laser-rifle to take in an approaching tank, the turret turning now in his direction. He is deep into the enemy perimeter and the opposition is fierce. He'll have to use the rocket launcher again but he is uncomfortably aware that he's down to his last three missiles. Just as his finger tightens on the trigger, he sees the little red AMMO symbol floating from left to right across the screen; just enough time to punch one round into it, collect five more missiles, then swing back to take care of the tank. He can see the flicker of fire now as its machine-guns open up on him. Finn knows that he has to hit it dead centre, just under the turret, to take it out completely...

The tank comes apart in delicious slow motion, chunks of twisted metal scattered by the oily, orange eruption of flame. He can almost feel the heat of it on his face. He turns to grin confidently at his mates gathered around the console. He's within a whisker of beating the reigning champ's score, and he knows that they are willing him to succeed.

'Go on, Finny,' whispers Gibbo. 'Stuff the bastards . . .'

Finn returns his attention to *Killing Zone*. Up ahead of him, he can see the blockhouse where the American POWs are held prisoner. His mission is to liberate them. There are machine-gun emplacements lined up in front of the building, but strategically placed concrete blocks offer vantage points from where he can pick the gunners off in safety . . .

The helicopter comes out of nowhere, dropping vertically into view, machine-guns blazing. It's close enough for Finn to see the pilot's grinning face, his squat body hunched over the controls. Finn tries throwing himself hard to the left, firing as he does so – but he is a fraction too late. Blood splatters across the screen and it begins to fade to grey. A perfunctory message informs him that he has just been wounded in action, and will now join the hostages in the blockhouse.

'Fuck it,' snaps Finn. He brings his fist down hard on the console and throws an accusing look at Gibbo. 'That was your fault,' he growls. 'You put me off.'

'Sorry, Finn.' Gibbo looks suitably mortified. At twelve years old, he is a crucial two years younger than Finn and totally subservient to the whims of his leader. If Finn told him black was white, he wouldn't dream of arguing.

Chaz has no such inhibitions. The same age as Finn, he's a good head taller, and over the last few months has been acquiring weight and muscle to go with it. His new-found confidence expresses itself in a tendency to criticise, and Finn is all too aware that one day soon Chaz will be challenging him for the leadership of the crew. Till then he's a useful man to have on the team. He can hotwire a car quicker than anybody and he's pretty handy in a fight. He's studying Finn scornfully now from beneath the brim of his baseball cap, his little blue eyes glinting with mockery.

'If you'd kept an eye on your radar screen, you'd have seen that whirlybird coming,' he says.

'Fuck off, Chaz. You've never even made it to level *two*,' observes Finn dismissively.

'Yeah,' agrees Tommo, thirteen years old, bespectacled, and traditionally the quietest member of the posse. Until recently, Tommo was an altar boy at the local Roman Catholic church but Finn has led him into bad ways. Now he can spit and swear and fight with the best of them. It's just a matter of getting the right training. 'Last time you played, you didn't even make it across the rope bridge to the *swamp*.'

'Yes, I fuckin' well did!'

'No, you didn't!' says Wart. At ten he is the baby of the posse, a skinny, malnourished kid with a thatch of straw-coloured hair and an imitation leather jacket that is several sizes too big for him. He wears a Manchester City scarf knotted around his neck. 'I saw you. You weren't even hit. You just fell in the water with the crocodiles.'

'Shut the fuck up,' Chaz warns him. He's recently discovered an old Robert De Niro film on video, and this is his current favourite catchphrase. He narrows his eyes, adopts an unconvincing American accent. 'Just shut the fuck up, OK?'

Wart sneers, but he wouldn't dare do it if Finn wasn't around to protect him.

Gibbo reaches into the pocket of his jog pants and comes out with a handful of change, which he offers to Finn.

'Play again?' he asks.

'Nah.' Finn shakes his head, turning away from the console. 'It's *boring*.' He takes out a packet of cigarettes and lights one up, ignoring the many NO SMOKING signs that proliferate in the arcade. He stands looking disdainfully around the interior, a gloomy labyrinth of electrical noise and flickering neon, situated on busy Oxford Street in the heart of the city. 'This *place* is boring,' he adds emphatically. 'I don't know why we waste our time here.' He aims an experimental kick at the *Killing Zone* machine to see if it will cough up any of its hoard of coins. It doesn't.

'You're just sore 'cos you didn't rack up top,' observes Chaz.

'Yeah? Listen, pal, I don't think you've got much room to talk. I've seen *girls* that play better than you!'

The younger kids laugh, and Chaz laughs with them, but you can see that he isn't really amused. His eyes remain cold and hard-looking. He takes out his own cigarettes and lights up, ostentatiously using the chunky brass Zippo he lifted from a newsagent's the other day. Finn experiences a stab of irritation. He only possesses a disposable plastic lighter and this is a major loss of face for him. He knows he has two alternatives. He can either take the Zippo from Chaz or steal something flashier. As yet, he hasn't decided which course of action he should take.

Gibbo, Tommo and Wart, feeling somewhat left out, have decided that they want a smoke as well. It's hardly surprising that the concentrated stink of five cigarettes quickly brings the arcade's jobsworth over to remonstrate with them.

'What's going on here?' he protests. He's a fat, ugly man with hair combed forward from the back to disguise his baldness. He has a red, thick-jowled face and a beer belly that threatens to burst out of his *I Love Manchester* T-shirt. He jerks a thumb at the sign above his head. 'What's that say?' he demands. 'Eh? What's that say?'

'What's the matter?' Chaz asks him. 'Can't you read?'

The man's jowls mottle a deeper shade of red.

'Oh, very funny! Come on, you lot, out!'

'All right,' says Finn quietly. 'Keep your *hair* on.' He puts emphasis on that word, knowing how it will wind the fat guy up.

Fats' eyes narrow suspiciously. 'Here, just a minute. I know you, don't I? Haven't I banned you from here already?'

Finn shrugs. 'If *you* can't remember, how do you expect *me* to?' he mutters. He flicks cigarette ash on to the *Killing Zone* console.

'Stop that!' shouts Fats irritably. 'Have you any idea how much that machine costs?'

Finn smiles. 'Who gives a shit? I'm not paying for it.'

'You cheeky little sod. Get out. Go on, get out! And take your friends with you ... Here, stop that!'

Now Chaz is flicking his ash on to the screen. Gibbo, Tommo and Wart immediately follow suit.

'You're like sheep!' snarls Fats, exasperated. He's missing the point; this is a show of solidarity, but the kids oblige him with some bleating noises just the same. Heads are turning all over the arcade to witness Fats' humiliation. He looks like he might be about to blow a gasket, and Finn slips a hand into his jacket pocket to grip the handle of the craft knife he always carries around with him; but he hopes it doesn't come to anything. This isn't worth the effort.

'Calm down,' he advises Fats. 'A feller your size shouldn't go getting all excited. You'll have a heart attack.' He motions to the others with a flick of his head. 'Come on,

5

let's go. There's a bad smell in here. I think somebody just shit himself.'

He moves past Fats and makes a display of flaring his nostrils, sniffing at him suspiciously in passing. The other kids do the same, and then they're all heading for the exit.

'You stay out of here in future!' yells Fats, braver now that he isn't standing face to face with them. 'You hear me? Stay out or I'll get the filth on to you!'

'Yeah, yeah.' Finn stubs the butt of his cigarette out on a flickering screen in passing. It leaves a nice, black smudge.

Out on the street a light drizzle is falling on the litter-strewn pavements. Finn turns up the collar of his nylon bomber jacket and glares sullenly along the length of Oxford Street. Who would believe it was July? Christ. School holidays just started, a Monday afternoon, and the city is *dead*. Across the road, a small queue is forming outside the Odeon for the latest from Tom Cruise.

'Wouldn't mind seeing that,' says Gibbo. 'He's good, him.'

'He's *wank*,' Chaz corrects him. 'What are you, some kind of shirt-lifter or something? You want to sleep wiv' im, do ya?'

There's a pause. Gibbo seems to be considering the question. 'No,' he concludes. 'He just makes good films, that's all.'

'Bollocks, he does,' says Finn. 'Bobby Cooper's the main man. I've seen *No Quarter* eight times. I even bought the video.' Uncharacteristically, he goes into some impromptu dance steps, moonwalking backwards down the street as he snaps out a fair approximation of the black rapper's controversial record, *Nigger With A Gun*.

Well, howdy neighbour, how you doin' today?,
I just moved in to the house across the way.
The brothers and me thought we'd pay you a call,
To give you a little advice that's all.
Don't cross us, don't push us, don't give us no grief,
Don't call me no junkie – don't call me no thief.
If you see me comin' get ready to run,
Cos I'm your worst nightmare – a nigger with a gun!

Gibbo has dropped into his human beat-box routine, the others are providing the repetitive high-pitched ooh-oohs, like on the record. They all think Bobby C. Cooper's about the coolest thing since, well, the last cool thing – and, sure enough, *No Quarter* is a sexy film in every respect, with a higher body-to-bullet ratio than any other movie they can remember.

Then, just as everybody's getting into it, Finn stops abruptly like somebody's thrown a switch, like he's suddenly remembered he's the leader of the crew and he doesn't do this kind of kid's stuff any more.

'Shut it, you lot. You're doing my head in!' he snarls. He thrusts his hands in his pockets and walks decisively off down the street. He looks suddenly thoughtful and then, yes, sure enough, he's taking a pair of leather driving gloves from his pockets and putting them on. Sensing something interesting, the others quickly catch up with him and fall into step.

'Where we goin'?' asks Wart.

'Nick a car,' Finn tells him. 'Save on bus fare.'

'Great,' enthuses Chaz, and he really means it. They haven't stolen a car since last Thursday.

Chapter Two

When Nick Saunders arrived at the office that morning, he found the kid waiting for him on the doorstep. Somehow it contrived to spoil his day.

The kid was maybe fourteen, fifteen years old, wrapped up in a dirty, oversized parka, the hood pulled up to keep out the early morning chill. Greasy ginger dreadlocks protruded from under the imitation fur edging of the hood and there was a glimpse of a hooked nose, a metal stud through one nostril. He was sitting in the doorway to *Futures*, his back against the metal door, his long thin legs drawn up under his chin. In one hand he held a crumpled strip of cardboard. Scrawled on it in blue biro were the words HUNGRY AND HOMELESS. On the floor in front of him, an upturned woollen cap held the grand sum of twelve pence.

Up till this moment Nick had been enjoying an unusually agreeable morning. He had woken early, feeling refreshed after a good night's sleep, and had spent a little time cuddling and talking to his wife, Helen. She was approaching the final month of her second pregnancy, so anything more than a cuddle was strictly out of the question. Their four-year-old daughter Molly had slept later than usual, so Nick had managed to procure the bathroom all to himself for a change. He'd showered himself awake, dressed, eaten a light breakfast of toast and coffee. Then he'd driven his new BMW into town without getting snarled up in any major traffic jams. He'd parked in his own private space at the rear of the PR company he co-owned, and had reflected on his good fortune to be in such an enviable position at the relatively tender age of thirty-two . . .

And then he'd walked around the corner and seen the kid. The effect was much like opening an oven door on a soufflé. His spirits sank.

Of course there was nothing unusual about it. On any given day you could spot half a dozen such youngsters crouched in shop doorways, plying their meagre trade the length of Market Street. Always the same scrawled signs, very often a pathetic-looking puppy beside them, perhaps because these kids knew all too well that, to large sections of the British public, the sight of a hungry animal was a damn sight more compelling than that of a hungry human being.

And, yes, Nick always felt an appropriate stab of guilt at his own middle-class affluence, his own outrageous good fortune. He would invariably attempt to buy absolution, dropping coins into whichever receptacle was proffered to him, then would pass quickly by, unable to look the beggar in the face. Emotive word, *beggar*, but that's what they were when all was said and done.

This time it wasn't going to be quite so easy. Here he stood in the quiet part of Deansgate where *Futures* was located, and this particular kid was sitting slap-bang in his path, leaving Nick with three possible alternatives. He could simply step over the kid as if he was nothing more than some object. He could give him some money and ask him (politely) to move aside. Or he could give him some money and ask him (politely) to leave. Nick was standing there debating the matter, when the kid gazed up at him with eyes that looked as vacant as an empty house.

'Spare us a couple of bob, mister?' The kid's hand extending imploringly towards him like that of some Third World outcast. Nick noticed that the fingers were trembling slightly as though the kid was weak with hunger. His conscience suitably pricked, Nick rummaged in his pockets for change, but found none.

'Look,' he said, 'I'm terribly sorry, but—'

'Please, mister. *Please*! I 'aven't eaten for three days!'

Those hopeless, dead eyes gazing up at him from the thin face. Christ, poor little bastard. Nick reached for his wallet, telling himself that he'd never even miss a fiver ... and then, quite suddenly, the matter was taken right out of his hands.

'Hey! Clear off, you little sod! What have I told you about hanging around here?'

Nick turned in surprise, to see his partner, Terry Littlewood, marching towards him from the direction of the car park. His round, ruddy face was a picture of indignation, and he was holding his metal attaché case in front of him like a potentially lethal weapon.

Nick heard the kid mutter a string of half-intelligible curses; then Terry was bearing down on him, reaching to grab him by the collar.

'Get out of it!' he roared; and began to drag the kid bodily from the doorway. 'Bloody scrounging toe-rag. Bugger off!'

'Take yer 'ands off me!' squealed the kid, clearly astonished by such rough treatment. 'I'll 'ave the law on yer!'

'You must be joking!' Terry gave him a none-too-gentle tap with the shiny toe of an Oxford brogue, and the kid went sprawling on to the pavement, mouthing obscenities. 'If you're still here in five minutes, I'll call the cops myself,' Terry assured him.

Nick had watched the scene in silence. He should have been surprised by Terry's vindictiveness, but somehow he wasn't. Over the last year it seemed to Nick that his business partner had changed almost out of all recognition. When Nick had first met him, he'd been a soft-spoken, amiable sort of bloke: the kind of guy you like to have a quiet pint with on a Friday evening. Married to the lovely Maureen, the proud father of two hyperactive kids, he was just a few months older than Nick and had similar interests. The two of them had founded *Futures* three years ago, and together had worked the small company up into one of the city's foremost PR agencies.

Whether it was the result of pressure of work or some kind of paranoia about losing their reputation, Terry had gradually developed a mean and ruthless streak. These days he seemed unable to tolerate failure in anybody, would hire and fire people at the drop of a hat, and had no interest in any person who wasn't somehow connected to his work. He also had a tendency to suck up to important clients, a habit which Nick was beginning to find extremely irritating. Indeed, he had begun to ask himself how much longer he could continue like this.

'For Christ's sake, Terry,' he protested 'The kid was only—'

'Milking you for your hard-earned cash. Yes, I *saw*.' Terry picked up the hatful of coins and flung it after the kid. 'Little bastard probably earns as much as you do.'

'I doubt that,' said Nick. He watched as the kid got sullenly to his feet, dusting himself down as though he'd actually fallen into some mud. He retrieved his hat and began to move away down the street, shouting back at Terry as he went.

'Fuckin' pillock! I'll get you for this. Just see if I don't!'

'Yeah, yeah, tell me about it.' Terry aimed a casual V-sign at the kid's retreating figure. He ran a hand through his curly hair and straightened his silk tie. Then he turned back to the door, cued a six-digit number into the electronic panel beside it and pushed it open. Nick threw a last regretful glance in the kid's direction and followed Terry inside. The door slammed shut behind them as they strolled into the reception area.

'A bit over the top?' suggested Nick. 'He was only after the price of a meal.'

Terry shook his head, then threw Nick a despairing look, as though he pitied him.

'Poor Nick. You're the original soft touch, aren't you? Kids like that are ten a penny. There's hundreds of 'em hanging around the city centre. Probably on his school holidays, still living with mum and dad, can't be arsed to get a summer job like you and me had to when we were his age.'

'Oh, come on, Terry. You saw his clothes. He must be living rough.'

'They *all* look like that, mate. It's a carefully cultivated image. I'm sorry, but it makes my blood boil. Particularly *that* particular specimen. I called at the off-licence on the way home last night. Guess who was in the queue ahead of me, buying eight cans of Special Brew and two packets of fags?'

Nick stared at his partner. 'You don't mean . . . ?'

'Yes, I do. For somebody who's hungry and homeless, he seems to be enjoying a pretty full social life.'

Nick frowned. 'Well, OK . . . but they can't all be on the

fiddle, can they? I mean, *some* of them must be genuine hard-timers.'

Terry ignored the question. 'Listen, Nick, we've got important clients calling here all the time. How does it look if they find something like *that* squatting on the doorstep? You see any more of 'em, just kick their arses right out of it, OK?'

'Yes, boss,' said Nick, not without a degree of sarcasm. He reflected that this was not an auspicious start to the day. He hoped things would get better before they got worse.

Chapter Three

It takes a while to find the right car. After all, you can't just steal *anything*; there's your reputation to consider. Finn finally spots the Astra GTE parked at a meter on John Dalton Street. It is shiny black, a brand new model, a sexy car in every respect.

'Oh yes,' says Finn quietly. 'That'll do nicely.'

He glances quickly up and down the street. The few people he sees appear to offer no threat: they are mostly wrinklies out shopping for the kind of junk that keeps them alive. He walks across to the car, glances inside to assure himself that there are no wheel or gear locks. No, nothing, not even an alarm – some people are just asking to have their car nicked, aren't they? He reaches into his jacket for the pin-pusher, places it against the glass of the window and applies a steady pressure. The window collapses into tiny fragments, and he is able to reach through and unlock the door. He brushes glass from the seat, then climbs in and unlocks the passenger door. Chaz slips into the passenger seat, reaches under the dash and pulls out a jumble of wires. He sets about hotwiring the car, arranging the contacts with practised precision. By the time Gibbo, Wart and Tommo have piled into the back, the engine is purring like a sleek black cat. Finn leans out of the broken window and winks at an

15

elderly couple who are regarding him doubtfully from a shop doorway.

'Give you a lift somewhere?' he asks them. They shrink back from him in mute fear and he laughs, aware of the adrenalin surging through his veins. He slips the Astra into gear and takes off in a showy handbrake start, letting the wheels spin on tarmac: a smoking shriek of indignation. He pulls out into the street and turns left on to Deansgate.

Chaz has the glove compartment open now, and is inspecting the owner's cassette tapes in outraged disbelief.

'Eric Clapton? Dire Straits? Fuck me, Bruce Springsteen?' He winds down the electric window and flings the tapes out on to the road with a grunt of disgust.

'You wanker!' yells Tommo. 'We could've *sold* them!'

'You've got to be joking. Somebody might think we *listen* to that shit! Get thirty notes for the player, though.' Chaz takes a strip of flat metal from his pocket, slides it in over the top of the tape-player, gives it a half twist and pulls back hard, wrenching the unit free. 'Wart, Tommo, try and get them speakers out of the back . . .'

'No, wait till we've stopped,' Finn warns them. 'We don't have to become a mobile advertisement for the filth, do we?' He crosses a set of lights on amber and hangs a left, heading across town back in the direction of Oxford Road.

Ten minutes later, he's making the right turn that will take them out of the city centre in the direction of Moss Side.

An old woman seems to materialise in front of the car. She is halfway across the road, dragging a loaded shopping trolley behind her. A younger person would make a dash for the safety of the pavement, but she just stands there open-mouthed in astonishment. Finn swears and wrenches the wheel hard to the right. The left front wing clips her trolley, whipping it out of her hand, sending items of shopping tumbling in all directions. The car speeds onwards.

'Silly old cow!' observes Wart gleefully, staring back at her from the rear window. She has recovered from her shock and is shaking a fist at the retreating vehicle. Other traffic is building up behind her, horns blaring, but she seems oblivious to it.

'She was lucky,' says Finn. 'I almost couldn't be bothered to swerve.'

Chaz studies him for a moment.

'Bollocks,' he says.

Finn laughs, acknowledging that, yes, it *is* bollocks; he's only said it for effect. Still, for a moment there, it had occurred to him how incredibly easy it would be to run the old girl down, send her scrawny body hurtling through the air like the Vietnamese soldiers in *Killing Zone*. Over in a moment – and what is her life worth anyway, when you add it all up?

He frowns. Too much thinking gives you a headache. He stamps his foot on the accelerator. They are entering the outskirts of the Merton Estate now, and the chances of encountering the filth have just dropped by about ninety per cent. Not that it makes much difference. Finn's been caught six times for *twocking* and all he ever gets is a good shouting at by the cops; the law won't let them lay a finger on him. Of course, in a year or so, when he turns sixteen, that will be a different story. He'll have to be a lot more careful then. But, shit, he tells himself, by then he'll be away from the Merton Estate and living in the lap of luxury. Get himself a swank place out in Cheshire somewhere, and

17

put alarms on everything except the shithouse. The money he's making now, it doesn't seem impossible.

Finn looks at the dirty grey tenements on the horizon and his spirits sink, as they always do when he gets this close to home.

He turns off the road on to a stretch of rutted waste ground, where the burned-out hulks of two other cars advertise the main use to which this area is put. A couple of passers-by stop to watch as Finn puts the Astra through its paces, riding it around and around in tight circles, letting the car's rear slide about in the soft earth.

After a few minutes, he's bored with it. He gets bored with most things after a few minutes. He lets the car slow to a halt and climbs out.

'Let's 'ave a go,' says Chaz eagerly. He starts to climb behind the wheel but then sees Finn pick up a brick and, turning back, raise his arm to smash the brick against the windscreen. Chaz grabs his radio and, yelling a warning to the others, he scrambles out to safety. The toughened safety glass scars like a spider's web, but Finn isn't content with that. He keeps pounding with the brick until he shatters a hole in it. The few adults who've stopped to watch move quickly away, not wanting to be involved in this, not wanting to put themselves in the dangerous position of being witness to these events.

Tommo and Wart are out of the back now, but Gibbo, sandwiched in the middle, is a bit too slow. He stumbles from the car with a deep gash on his forehead where a sliver of glass has struck him, blood starting to run down his face.

'You all right?' Finn asks him gruffly – but Finn isn't going to apologise. That's a sign of weakness.

'Sure.' Gibbo mops at his face with the sleeve of his

jacket, playing the hard man, shrugging it off. 'I was a bit slow there, Finny. Sorry.'

Chaz isn't so forgiving.

'You arsehole, Finn. I wanted to have a go! You could have knocked my bleedin' teeth out!'

Finn turns to study Chaz. He steps closer to him so that their faces are only inches apart, Finn having to tilt his head back slightly to look him in the eyes.

'I still might,' he says calmly.

Chaz glares back at him. 'What do you mean? What's the problem?'

'Nothing I can't handle.'

Now Chaz looks bewildered. 'I only said you could have hurt me.'

'Yeah. You got a problem with that?'

'Uh?' Chaz looking into Finn's mean grey eyes, trying to understand. 'I don't get it, man.'

Finn staring at the taller boy, giving him that hard-faced glare until he is obliged to look away. Then Finn knows it's over. Almost. He holds out a hand in front of him, the palm uppermost.

'Lighter,' he says.

'Uh?'

'The Zippo. Give it to me.'

Frowning, Chaz slips a hand into his pocket. Hesitantly, he does as he's told.

Finn flips the lid, sparks the wheel with his thumb, gazes for a moment in anticipation at the fierce yellow flame. He is aware that the others are watching him expectantly. He turns away from Chaz and walks to the car. The petrol cap has a lock on it, so he picks up the brick and smashes it open. He motions to Wart to come closer. Now he snaps his fingers.

'Scarf,' he says.

'Oh, eh, Finny, no. Not me City scarf!'

'Give,' says Finn. 'You're gettin' too old for football anyway.'

'Me mam'll kill me!'

'For Christ's sake, we'll get you another one!'

Wart is spoiling the drama of the situation. Finn wants this to be a grand gesture, and Wart is fucking it up. Skriking about his mother, for Christ's sake, like some bloody kid.

Finn reaches out a hand and wrenches the scarf off Wart's neck, making him wince. He pushes it down into the open petrol tank, submerging all but the tip of it. He waits a moment to let the fabric soak through, meanwhile rocking the car to accelerate the process. He glances at Wart and sees there are tears in his eyes. Jesus! Over a fucking scarf that probably cost a couple of quid.

Now he pulls some of the scarf back out, to provide a long fuse. The lighter is still burning steadily. It's a nice lighter, no doubt about it. He lifts the Zippo and holds the flame to the end of the scarf.

He's not prepared for the speed of it. The flame flashes along the length of petrol-soaked material as he turns and runs from the car, seeing now that the others have already scattered. He feels a sudden impact behind him, the fierce heat as the car erupts into flame. He sees Vietnamese soldiers flying across the screen, and then a shock wave of scorching air swats him like a giant's hand, throwing him face down into the mud.

His ears are ringing, but he thinks he hears Chaz yell, 'Fuck!' Glancing up, he sees the others ahead of him. They've turned back; they're dancing delightedly, eyes mirroring the blaze. Finn picks himself up carefully, aware

20

of the smell of singed hair and scorched material, but not wanting to make a fuss about it.

He walks back to join the others and then allows himself to turn and look at the burning car. It looks sexy, like something out of a film. He can feel the heat on his face even from here. Something in him wants to leap and dance and shriek delightedly like the others, but he can't allow himself to do that. He's the leader and he has to show them that this is nothing to him. Nothing.

He is still holding the lighter. He lifts his hand and ostentatiously snaps it shut. Smiling, Chaz reaches out his hand, palm uppermost. Finn looks at him for a moment. Then he drops the Zippo into his own pocket.

'You can keep the radio to sell,' he says.

Chaz glares at him and Finn tenses, waiting for him to say one more thing. But Chaz recognises the danger signals. He bows his head in acceptance and the moment passes.

A thick pall of black smoke is rising above the car. A window shatters with a dull crunch. There's a stink of burning rubber in their nostrils, but already the fire isn't as spectacular as it was a moment ago. Finn wonders if it's worth calling out the fire brigade. Sometimes he enjoys throwing stones at them while they are trying to work. But no, on reflection, he decides he can't be bothered waiting around. Besides, he has things to do.

'Come on,' he says. He moves away and the others trail obediently behind him. They walk on into the estate – and none of them even bothers to look back at the burning car.

Chapter Four

Gail, the fresh-faced young brunette who was the receptionist at *Futures*, greeted Nick and Terry with a cheerful smile. She had worked for them for around six months now, and had already made herself absolutely irreplaceable.

'Morning, Gail.' Terry glanced quickly around the interior of the large open-plan office, as if to ensure that everybody had their nose to the grindstone. Not that there were many noses in evidence. Most of the company's permanent staff were out working on various projects this morning, which left just Bill Philips and Trevor Atkinson, hunched over a drawing-board at the far end of the room. They were currently working on the press launch for a new low-fat spread, but the big news at the moment was the Sanjari account, which Terry had insisted he and Nick should handle themselves.

'Anything we should know about?' he asked Gail.

'Well, Mary Peters phoned from Bristol to say that she and the author have arrived at the book-signing, but there's been a mix-up over the dates . . .'

'That's *her* problem,' said Terry ungraciously. 'Phone her back and tell her to sort it out herself.'

'Yes, but—'

'No buts, Gail! I'm sick of nursemaiding her. If she can't

cut it in PR, then she needs to start looking elsewhere. I've got enough on my plate at the moment.' He glanced at his watch, as if to emphasise the point, and Nick felt another stab of irritation go through him. Why did Terry have to be like this all the time? Mister-fucking-Executive.

'Give me Mary's number,' suggested Nick. 'I'll call her later. I'm sure we can sort something out.'

Gail handed Nick a compliments slip with the new recruit's phone number on it. Terry made an expression suggesting he'd just been stabbed in the back, but refrained from commenting.

'What about the Sanjari account?' he asked Gail.

'The artwork from Domino arrived by courier a few minutes ago – it's in the presentation room. Oh, and Mr Sanjari's PA phoned to say that he'll be here in . . .' She glanced at her watch. 'Twenty-two minutes.'

'Right. Make sure there's plenty of fresh coffee available.' Terry turned and strode towards the glass doors of the presentation room.

'And roll out the red carpet,' added Nick, with a sly wink to Gail, which she acknowledged with a knowing smile. She too knew how adept Terry was at kissing ass. Nick followed his partner into the large, air-conditioned presentation room, threw his briefcase on to the table and watched as Terry got to grips with the carefully wrapped art-boards.

'I pray to God they've got them right this time,' he muttered. 'And by the way, Nick, I can do without you undermining me in front of Gail.'

'I wasn't undermining you. Mary's only been with us a few weeks, so there are bound to be teething troubles. There's no sense in going off the deep end every time there's a problem.'

'Saint Nick!' laughed Terry, but there was no humour in his voice – only derision. He was struggling with the packaging on the art-boards. 'These had better be what we asked for. There's no time to rethink them now.'

'Chill out,' Nick advised him. 'They're only visuals. So long as we've got the right photographer on the shoot, there's no worries. And believe me, Alan Richards is the best.'

Terry didn't look so confident. 'Sanjari isn't sure about him. He was keen to go for a *name* – Bailey, Lichfield, somebody in that league.'

Nick shook his head. 'Duff thinking. Sanjari is a Manchester phenomenon, so where's the logic in bringing in a *southern* photographer? You've seen Alan's portfolio. This is going to suit him down to the ground.'

'You don't have to convince me, sunshine. But I can appreciate Sanjari's thinking. He's spending a cool million pounds bringing Bobby C. Cooper over here. Why cut corners on the little details?'

'A photographer is *not* a little detail,' Nick reminded him. 'And Alan Richards could outshoot any of those so-called major players with his hands tied behind his back. More importantly, he's young and he's hungry.'

Terry grinned. 'You'll be telling me he's homeless next.'

'Very funny.' Nick gestured impatiently to the half-open package. 'For God's sake, let's have a look at those things before his majesty arrives.'

Terry managed to tear away the last of the brown paper. He spread the half-dozen boards out on the table for closer inspection.

Nick thought they looked pretty good: a series of sepia sketches of a muscular black man dressed only in a pair of jeans, standing with his fists raised in the midst of urban dereliction. The ad lines were spelled out in crumbling white letters, as though they too were on the point of falling apart. There were a half-dozen alternative headlines, but all had a similar sentiment:

AJs – TOUGH ON THE STREETS
AJs – JEANS WITH AN ATTITUDE
AJs – WHEN THE GOING GETS TOUGH

Terry nodded. 'That'll do for me,' he said. 'They evidently didn't fall asleep at the brief *this* time.' He was referring to an earlier slagging that he'd given Stewart Anderson from Domino, the agency he'd brought in to handle the visuals. Their first attempt had, Terry told Anderson, resembled a third-rate Benetton reject. 'Looks good,' concluded Terry.

'Good enough for Sanjari, anyway,' said Nick.

Terry studied him for a moment.

'You know, I could swear that you're the tiniest bit jealous of old Ajay. Wouldn't have anything to do with the fact that you were at school together, would it?'

'Hardly *together*. As I recall, he was a couple of forms below me. All I remember about him was that he was widely regarded as the school prat. What reason could I have to be jealous?'

Terry considered for a while.

'Well, let me see now. He's a multi-millionaire at the age of, what, twenty-nine? Started his jeans line for a bit of fun, then turned over his first million in less than a year. He drives a Roller, he's engaged to a top model and ... oh, yes, correct me if I'm wrong, but isn't he an old flame of Helen's?'

Nick glanced at Terry sharply.

'Who told you about that?' he snapped.

'Oh, I picked it up somewhere.' Terry made an expression of exaggerated sheepishness. 'Sorry, didn't realise it was meant to be a secret.'

'It's not. Far as I'm concerned, it's *history*. Listen, what it was, he and Helen had a brief fling when she was working as a fashion buyer for that catalogue company in Ardwick. He was nobody special then, he was just working for his old man. It didn't last more than a few months. Then I came along and—'

'So she left him for *you*?' Terry grimaced. 'Christ, she really missed the boat there, didn't she?'

'Oh, thanks very much!'

'No, really. No offence intended, mate, but, well, you can see my point, surely? She could have wound up married to one of the richest men in Britain.'

'I haven't heard her complain,' said Nick grouchily.

'Relax, I'm just pulling your leg . . . Thing is, if it really is history, why are you so down on the guy?'

Nick frowned. A reasonable question, he supposed, so why did he feel that Terry was probing him more than was strictly necessary? Why did he feel the need to mentally count to ten before he answered? He took a deep breath.

'My reservations are based mostly on my belief that he's employed us for one reason only. It gives him an opportunity to show me how well the school jerk has done for himself.'

Terry looked scornful.' That's just paranoia. *Futures* has an excellent reputation.'

27

'I wouldn't argue the point. But if Sanjari hadn't heard about *my* involvement with it, my guess is he'd have been on the first flight to London. Same principle as his 'name' photographer. Sanjari likes to be *seen* to be successful. That's what this whole exercise is about.'

Terry shrugged. 'Well, it's *his* money, I suppose.' He picked up a potted biography of Bobby C. Cooper and studied it for a moment. 'But let's face it, he's got the right man on his team.' He read a few excerpts from the handout. 'Bobby C. Cooper, born East LA 1965. First single, *Nigger With A Gun*, earned him a gold disc. First album, *Bad Attitude*, went platinum. His first film, *No Quarter*, took forty million dollars at the American box office in its opening week . . .'

Nick listened dutifully while Terry droned on. He wished that he could be so enthusiastic about Cooper's visit. Ever the pessimist, he'd got a friend who worked in a news agency to run a more objective check on Cooper. So he now had his own unofficial bio sheets on the man, and not everything was good news – quite the opposite. Like the banning of his single *Bite The Bullet*, which included lyrics deemed likely to incite violence. It had led to record burnings organised by fundamental church groups all over America, and had put his record company into serious litigation. Then there were two convictions for the possession of narcotics, for which Cooper had received hefty fines and several hundred hours of community service. The general impression was that if he'd been an ordinary joe he'd have gone down for quite some time. Nick had tried mentioning these facts to Terry on several occasions, only to have them brushed away as though they were irrelevant. Cooper was the biggest name that *Futures* had ever handled, and nothing was going to be allowed to spoil it.

'What's our official line,' Nick asked him now, 'if some journalist asks about the drug busts?'

Terry waved a hand as if dismissing the very idea.

'That's old news,' he said. 'Nobody's going to pick up on that.'

'I wouldn't be so sure. It kicked up a royal stink in the States; enough for his studio to postpone the next movie till the heat dies down a bit. I mean, Christ, Terry, why do you think he agreed to come over here to work? Sanjari hit on him at a vulnerable time in his career, otherwise he wouldn't have sniffed at the offer. A million pounds is nothing to him. He probably shoves that much up his nose on a good night.'

Terry sighed, as though he suddenly felt weary. Why, his expression seemed to ask, was Nick intent on spoiling everything? 'So what's your point?' he wanted to know.

'Simply that we're going to have to keep a tight grip on this project. Cooper isn't exactly Mr Clean, and we can't afford to have him getting into trouble while he's here. The target group for AJ jeans is a teenage one, and there are a lot of people eager to point out that he's not a good role model for impressionable youngsters.'

Terry laughed dismissively. 'Since when have kids ever liked anything wholesome? My two have gone through one nasty craze after another. Some of the computer games they play are positively *frightening*.'

'Then you shouldn't let your kids have them.'

'Oh, there speaks the father of a little girl. If the next one's a boy, just come to me in ten years' time and tell me how it's going. Kids wear you down in the end, Nick. In the long run, it's easier to let them have their Nintendos and Segas. I like a quiet life.' He reached up a hand to thoughtfully stroke his moustache. 'Anyway, what are you suggesting we do about Bobby Cooper? We can hardly turn him into a black Jason Donovan.'

'Of course not. But we *can* watch him like a hawk while he's under our care. Once we've packed him back off to the States, he can be as degenerate as he bloody well pleases.'

'Christ, Nick, you can be a right pessimist at times – do you know that? Just what exactly are you worried about?'

Nick was about to answer, but then, through the glass doors, they noticed Ajay Sanjari strolling into reception. Terry was up out of his seat like a trained retriever, bustling through to escort his prize client into the presentation room. Nick stayed right where he was, slumped in his seat, refusing to play that game.

Sanjari entered, and Nick had to admit grudgingly that the man was looking sharp. Tall and lean, his black hair pulled back into a ponytail, he could have passed for one of the male models he regularly employed. As a child he'd been pudgy and plain, but the bastard seemed to get better-looking with each passing year. The loose-fitting electric blue suit that hung so perfectly from his frame looked like Yamamoto, but Nick figured it had probably been run up cost-price in one of his many sweatshops in Cheetham Hill. He nodded to Nick, favoured him with a smug grin and then sank into a chair, crossing one long leg over the other.

'Morning, Nick. How's Helen?'

'Fine.' Nick glowered at Sanjari across the surface of his desk. 'Happily pregnant.' He didn't have the least idea why he'd added that bit. He noticed that Terry threw a glare at him, but he ignored it.

'I'm very pleased for you both. Hey, we recently

launched a big range of maternity fashion wear. I'll drop off a copy of the catalogue next time I see you.'

'Great,' said Nick, without much enthusiasm.

Terry was laying the art-boards out for Sanjari's inspection, handling them carefully as though they were priceless relics. Gail bustled through with a tray of coffee and biscuits. Sanjari sat there, enjoying all the attention; but he was still looking at Nick, smiling that enigmatic smile.

'Here are the visuals for the concept we discussed,' said Terry, waving a hand at the drawings. 'I think they look great, don't you?'

Sanjari allowed his gaze to slide away from Nick and down to the boards, almost as though it required too much effort to look at them. He accepted a cup of black coffee from Gail and took a contemplative sip before answering.

'Not bad,' he admitted. 'But it will all depend on the photographer, of course. This Alan . . . ?'

Pretending to forget the name, Nick decided. Pathetic!

'Richards,' Terry prompted him. 'Oh, he's brilliant, Ajay. Don't you worry on that score. Actually, he's one of Nick's protégés.'

Again, Sanjari was looking at Nick, the ghost of a smile playing around his lips.

'Oh, well then, I'm sure he'll be up to scratch. Nick always did have a good eye for talent.'

Nick flinched and fondly pictured himself planting a thump on Sanjari's aquiline nose. He wondered how cool the man would look with fresh blood squirting down the front of his designer jacket.

'We just need to decide on a location,' added Terry hastily, perhaps sensing the unspoken hostility. He indicated the crumbling, litter-strewn backgrounds depicted in the illustrations. 'There's a few areas we've used before, we can dress them up with some graffiti and garbage, make them look more down-at-heel . . .'

But now Sanjari was shaking his head.

'Moss Side,' he said. 'We'll shoot it in Moss Side. The Merton Estate seems the best bet. Bit of photogenic *squalor*.' He allowed the last word to roll off his tongue, as though he enjoyed the feel of it.

Nick and Terry exchanged wary glances.

'Oh, I don't know about that,' said Nick. 'It's a bit hairy in there these days—'

'Nonsense!' Sanjari waved a hand in dismissal. 'It's the obvious choice, Manchester's own East LA. And it fits perfectly with Cooper's streetwise image.'

'Yes, but it could be dangerous to take him in there,' argued Terry. 'By all accounts, any outsiders are treated as fair game for mugging. You wouldn't want anything to happen to your star attraction, would you? And we could so easily dress up a less problematic location as Moss Side. Nobody would know the difference.'

Sanjari sneered. '*I'd* know,' he said. 'And think of the publicity we'll get taking a gangsta-rap star into the kind of location he sings about. Anyway, you two have been reading too many tabloids. The situation on the Merton Estate has been exaggerated out of all proportion.'

'Think so?' Nick asked him. 'When were *you* last there, Ajay?'

'I go there all the time,' snapped Sanjari unconvincingly. He didn't elaborate on that point. 'Listen, I've just spent a million pounds getting Cooper over here. I'm damned if I'm going to spoil the ship for a ha'porth of tar. Now, if you lads are afraid to do this thing—'

Terry laughed. It was probably meant to sound devil-may-care but, to Nick's mind, it sounded distinctly forced.

'Don't be silly, Ajay! *Of course* we're not afraid. It was simply Mr Cooper's safety we were concerned about.'

'No need to worry on that score. I'm reliably informed that he travels everywhere with two professional body-guards. And a man who was born and raised on the mean streets of East LA isn't going to be worried by anything he sees here.'

'Oh, well then . . .' Terry glanced at Nick. 'Be a bit of a buzz, eh? And Ajay's right, when it comes to getting the necessary image, nothing beats the real thing.'

Nick smiled mockingly. 'You sound like a Coke advert,' he observed. 'And no doubt, Ajay, you'll be attending all the shoots in person as, er . . . creative consultant?'

Sanjari took another sip of coffee.

'Just try and keep me away,' he said tonelessly.

'That's settled then,' said Terry. 'We'll get Alan over tomorrow, spend the day scouting locations, get some images down on Polaroid. Then we'll have everything tied up ready for Mr Cooper when he gets in on Wednesday.'

'Good,' said Sanjari. 'And you're all set up for the press conference at the airport?'

Terry smiled, more confidently this time.

'Relax. Press conferences are our speciality.'

'I hope so. I've put a lot of time and money into this venture, gentlemen. We can't afford any cock-ups. I want the whole thing to run as smoothly as shit through a chicken.' He lifted an arm to glance at a very expensive wristwatch. 'And now, if you'll forgive me—'

'Time is money,' finished Nick, sarcastically.

Sanjari stared at him for a moment.

'Indeed,' he said at last. He set down his coffee cup and got up from the table. 'So, I'll see you at the airport.' Terry escorted him out of the office but Sanjari paused in the doorway and looked back at Nick, with that self-satisfied smile on his face. 'Goodbye, Nick,' he said. 'Be sure and give my love to Helen, won't you? And tell her I'm asking for her.' Then he was gone, heading for the exit and his next appointment.

Terry was back a moment later, looking suitably indignant.

'Well, thanks for all the *help*,' he muttered. 'What's wrong with you? Sanjari is a valued client. You can't go on being so hostile to him.'

'He's an arrogant arsehole,' said Nick flatly. 'You heard that remark: *Nick always did have a good eye for talent!*'

'That's not what he meant!'

'Oh, no?'

'Listen, OK, so he went out with Helen once. That was *years* ago. It's water under the bridge – you said as much yourself. You can't put this deal at risk because you're jealous of the guy.'

'I'm not jealous!' protested Nick. 'I'm just heartily sick of him playing Mr Big Shot all over the place. All that crap about shooting on the Merton Estate. As if it really matters.'

'He's the customer, Nick.'

'And the customer's always right, eh? Well I still don't like it.' He tapped the folder that held the unofficial bio sheets for Bobby C. Cooper. 'Put it together, Terry. Here's a man with two drug convictions; and we're putting him into an area where crack and heroin are the local currency. Now, call me an old worry-guts, if you like, but that sounds to me like a perfect recipe for disaster.'

Terry sat down and poured himself a cup of coffee.

'I wouldn't sweat it. Like Sanjari said, the place isn't as bad as everybody likes to make out. We'll just keep our

American friend on a tight rein and hope for the best.' He sipped at his coffee. 'Besides, he's only here for a fortnight. How much trouble can he possibly cause in two weeks?'

Nick didn't answer that one straight away. He was too busy computing the odds.

Chapter Five

The black man comes lurching out of an alleyway as Finn strolls back to his house. He's an old Rasta man, gaunt and tall and dressed in a ragged khaki rainslicker, greasy grey dreadlocks hanging into his vacant brown eyes. He opens his mouth to speak, giving Finn a grandstand view of his near-toothless jaws. He belches the smell of stale whisky into Finn's face.

'Babylon!' the old man croaks. 'Babylon is a comin'. It's here for us now, walkin' aroun' like it's a judgement. Ain't no hope for none of us no more!'

'Fuck off,' Finn suggests, and tries to step around the Rasta; but now he is clinging to Finn's arm, his long, dirty fingernails digging into flesh. Close up, Finn can see the deeply etched lines in his leathery face, the grey stubble pushing through his skin, the recent scar on his forehead where somebody has got tired of his ranting and has hauled off and smacked him one. And the smell of him! Mingled with the stench of whisky there's something even more unwholesome: a sickly sweet odour of decay. The kind of smell you encountered when you broke into wrinklies' homes: something made up of a hundred different sources – rooms that have gone untended too long, damp papers left to moulder in darkness, soiled mattresses and underclothes, mouse droppings, layers of dust. Finn knows the

37

smell and hates it. He feels his gorge rising and tries to push the Rasta away, but he clings on, as tenacious as an old leech.

'Heed my words, young breddar! The painted whore waits for you to taste her bitter milk. She is building a tower for you. Do not be deceived! Babylon is here and we are but poor sinners. Pray with me, pray for salvation—'

Finn hits him then, in the stomach, and the old man folds like a paper sack, drops to his knees with a gasp of exhaled air. It was the stuff about praying that did it. Finn is touchy where prayers are concerned; too many of his own have gone unanswered. He starts to walk away, but the Rasta's hands close around his left shin.

'Let go,' Finn advises him.

'But ... I'm here to bring you ... the word...' The Rasta man can hardly catch his breath to speak. 'I was a poor sinner and ... he saved me.'

'I told you to let go of me,' Finn warns him.

'Salvation can be yours, too ... if you'll just pray with me. Kneel with me and ask for—'

Finn turns and kicks the old man in the face, snapping his neck back with a crack like a rifle shot. He falls, rolls on to one side, and Finn follows up with another kick into the Rasta's ribs. He feels bones snap beneath the impact and hears the old man grunt.

A middle-aged couple step out of the mouth of the alleyway and walk quickly by, keeping their heads down, trying not to look at Finn, not wanting to get involved. Finn watches them until they turn the corner out of sight, then he stoops to examine the Rasta man's sprawled figure. He's still conscious, his eyes wide and staring, his breathing erratic. There's a thick froth of blood on his lips.

Finn thinks about finishing him. He doesn't like old

people, can't see the point of them. They get past sixty and they are suddenly useless, ill all the time, forever breaking their brittle bones in some poxy fall, endlessly babbling on about how it was *in their day*. They're missing the point. The way Finn sees it, they've *had* their day; but the selfish bastards don't want to step aside for the next generation, give them the necessary space to breathe. That's why he never has any qualms about robbing and mugging wrinklies. To him they are simply non-people – smelly, slow, hopelessly obsolete. And therefore legitimate targets.

He rolls the old man on to his back and considers searching him; but one look at his verminous, piss-stained clothing dissuades him from the idea. Unlikely that he would have anything worth robbing anyway. Finn turns and walks away.

The old man's croaking voice follows him like a bad smell. 'Babylon ... Babylon's all aroun' us! You can't escape the flames, bwoy. Don't even t'ink a tryin' ...'

Finn turns left into the alleyway and strolls on, whistling tunelessly to himself. Around him the crumbling brick walls, the cracked, weed-strewn pavements, the boarded-up windows and doors of the Merton Estate turn a blind eye to his passing. He has lived here all his life, knows every last walkway and terrace, could intuitively find the quickest route through it blindfolded.

He dimly remembers it the way it was when he was a small child – cleaner, friendlier, safer. But that's no more than a distant memory and, unlike many of the adults who live here, he does not pine for those days. Like the estate itself, he has changed and adapted. As his surroundings have lapsed into decay and dereliction, so has that part of him that is still a child.

Games of hide-and-seek played with the other kids have

given way to similar games played with the police and truant officers. Childhood scraps have metamorphosed into savage combat. Where he once traded comics and bubble-gum cards, now he deals in hard drugs. Playground into slayground. Impossible to chronicle the process in any detail. Best to just accept it and get on with his life.

Eventually he comes to an archway that to an outsider would seem like every other archway on the estate; but to Finn it's familiar. He stands for a moment looking at the graffiti sprayed across the wall, searching for any new additions, seeing if anyone has tried to dispute his authority. But, no, his own spray-can monicker is still prominent: three wavy horizontal lines with a curved shark's fin jutting up from the topmost. Jesus, the months he spent perfecting that over the length and breadth of the estate! But that was a year ago when he was still just a kid. These days he never even bothers to carry an aerosol can around with him. These days he has bigger fish to fry.

He turns in through the archway and climbs the concrete steps beyond, not even pausing to try the lift, which hasn't worked for over six months. The gloomy stairway stinks of piss, and as he turns up the next flight he's confronted by three black kids who are waiting for something to turn up. Recognising him, they grin sheepishly and move back against the walls to let him pass. They've all been Finn's customers at one time or another, and doubtless will be again – just as soon as a suitable wallet comes up those stairs. But you don't hit the Candy Man, that wouldn't make any sense at all ... unless, of course, you were looking to take over his turf.

Finn frowns. Just lately he's been worrying about that. There's a new posse encroaching on his territory: older kids, some of them already into their twenties, led by a middle-aged black Yardie called Otis Mason. So far, Yardies are a fairly unknown quantity on the estate, they haven't made the kind of inroads into Manchester that they have in London. Talk is that these guys have found themselves a well-connected supplier based in Warrington, and a couple of chemists working full-time, turning raw cocaine into crack. Talk is that they are already controlling another estate not so far from here. Talk is that they are getting greedy, figuring maybe they should be working a bigger turf. And, inevitably, talk is that they have shooters and aren't afraid to use them.

Finn is reluctant to give these stories too much credence. Often, around here, rumour is just exactly that: people sounding off because they're bored or skint or doing turkey, wanting to take their minds off their own misery. Finn has learned long ago to cross his bridges as he comes to them.

He halts outside number 67 Rembrandt Walk. All the blocks here are named after famous artists. There's a Constable Walk and a Gainsborough Walk and even a Picasso Walk. It's a scream really, because round here art isn't exactly high on anybody's list of priorities. Finn figures it maybe didn't seem so comical when all this concrete was new and gleaming. Now it's like a sour joke.

Taking out a bunch of keys he unlocks the door. He steps through into the bare hallway of the two-storey flat and stands for a moment listening. He can hear the brittle noise of the television set from the sitting room, an American sitcom by the sound of it – some dopey drawling voice saying, 'Honey, I think we've got a problem here!' followed by gales of raucous laughter. Finn glances to his left, through the open doorway of the kitchen. He can see the top of the choked pedal-bin, food scraps cascading down on to the floor where several roaches are feeding happily on the mess. There's a thick stink of grease on the air, mingled with the smell of rotting vegetables.

Finn swears beneath his breath and walks down the hall to the sitting room. He stands in the open doorway looking in at his parents.

It's hard to believe that they are both still in their thirties; they look so much older. They sit huddled together on the sofa, half covered by an old blanket as though they're cold. They are gazing at the television with an abstracted air, not really taking it in. It's just a distraction from the way they are feeling. They'd have sold it by now if they'd thought anyone would give them a couple of quid for it.

Shaun McManus was once a good-looking bloke; Finn has the photographs to prove it. Now his dad's features seem to have sunken in on themselves, especially around the mouth where he's lost most of his teeth. There are dark, weeping sores on his lips. Theresa was a real looker in her teens; she had this beautiful, glossy, black hair. Now it's a coarse lacklustre mess, streaked with grey. Her brown eyes seem too big in the thin face, and the short-sleeved blouse she wears reveals the scarred and pitted skin of her thin white arms.

For a moment Finn actually feels sorry for them. But then he reminds himself that they have built their own traps in life, and that they deserve nobody's pity. For years it was alcohol abuse, as much as they could drink, night after night, pissing their lives against a wall; and finally, when that wasn't enough for them, they'd sought out something even more debilitating. For all that he sells the stuff, Finn has never been stupid enough to use it, not even for the novelty value. He's seen first-hand what it can do to people.

He steps into the room now, and they slowly become

aware of his presence. The big eyes swivel to appraise him, and he can see the naked hope in them. They no longer think of him as their son. He's the Candy Man and he's long overdue. He stands there, gazing back at them, knowing what they want but refusing to make it easy for them. They have to ask for it. That's all they have to do: *ask*. But, no, they still cling pathetically to a last few shreds of pride.

Dad's eyes flicker back to the TV screen. 'Wondered what'd happened to you,' he mutters.

He's trying to sound like he doesn't much care whether Finn comes home or not, but he's failing miserably. There's a slight tremor in his voice, caused by the awful realisation that Finn might not have anything for him. There's still a trace of an Irish brogue. Dad's proud of his ancestry; it was doubtless this that prompted him to give his son the name Finbar. Finn despises his real name; to him it's worthy of a cartoon character in a kid's comic. He can only tolerate it in it's shortened form. None of his friends would ever dare call him Finbar.

'Thought I told you to clean up?' says Finn. 'The kitchen's filthy again. The roaches are back.'

Mum opens her mouth to say something. She thinks better of it and begins to play with her hair, twisting it nervously around her thin fingers. Then she tries again.

'I . . . what it was, I forgot. I'll do it. I *will* do it. We'll both do it, won't we, love?'

Dad looks at her as though she's speaking a different language. Then his dry lips curve into an absent-minded grin, revealing the gaps in his rotten teeth.

'Yeah,' he says. ''Course we will.'

'Get to it, then,' Finn tells them. 'What's the point in me paying the rent on this shit-hole if you let it go down the nick? I'm going up to get changed. I want it done by the time I go out again. I don't suppose there's anything to eat in this dump?'

Now they are staring at him, confused. They look at each other, then look at the floor. He realises that they don't actually know the answer to that one. These days they only ever think of food when they are close to falling down from the lack of it.

'I'll eat out,' he concludes. He turns back to the hallway and starts up the stairs. Halfway up, he hesitates and calls down to them. 'The kitchen!' he shouts. 'You've got fifteen minutes.' He hears the creaking of the sofa springs and then they come lurching out into the hallway, moving painfully like those brilliant zombies in the *Living Dead* movies. In a sense that is what they have become.

Up on the landing, Finn takes out his bunch of keys and opens the four heavy mortice locks that secure the door to his room. Such measures are necessary to safeguard his belongings, not so much from burglars but from his parents who, if they get desperate, are not averse to ransacking his room for items they can sell or trade for heroin. In the end it has become easier to take over supplying them himself. That way he can obtain their drugs at cost price, and make sure it isn't stepped on – cut with anything too harmful. He also realises that if they go without H for more than a few days, all the locks in the world won't keep them out.

He opens the door and steps into the sanctuary of his room. One wall is dominated by a huge black-and-white poster of Bobby C. Cooper, a still from his movie *No Quarter*. It's the climactic scene where Bobby has been cornered in an old warehouse by what seems like hundreds of cops. He stands there defiantly, legs astride, wearing the trademark black leather biker's jacket, the black beret and shades, and he is holding this brilliant gun, Finn doesn't know what it's called, but it's a big mother that fires old-fashioned belt-fed cartridges, and a second barrel slung underneath the first fires these missile things, and though Bobby is wounded in a half dozen places, he just stands there blowing away cop after cop and, like, laughing at them and finally he fires his last shot into this case of explosives and he takes hundreds of cops up with him in this sexy explosion that blows the whole fucking warehouse into little pieces.

Shit! You just didn't get any badder than Bobby C. and that was a fact. Finn hits the Play button on his CD and there's Bobby again, jive-assin' his way through *Show Respect*.

Me brother asked me what was me occupation,
Said I'm the leader in the field of termination,
Don't have to ask because I'm known across the nation,
I'm Bobby C. and I'm a rap sensation!
They show respect,
Jah, brother,
They show respect!

Finn dances across to his wardrobe mirror now, miming the actions he's watched a thousand times in Bobby C.'s videos, crossing his arms, doing that same brooding stare that is another of the man's trademarks. He slides back the door of the fitted wardrobe, revealing the rows of new clothing inside. Earning upwards of five hundred pounds a day, he has very little to spend his money on. He's too young to officially own a car and, besides, why bother when new models are there for the taking every day of the week? He doesn't do drugs, and rarely drinks, since he tends to fall about like an idiot after just a couple of pints.

So most of his money goes on clothes, CDs and tapes. Anything that's left over he gives to Gordie, his supplier, to invest on his behalf. Stocks and shares, Gordie calls them. Finn doesn't exactly understand how it works but Gordie keeps telling him he's making big money now, and he has only to say the word if there's anything he wants.

Finn pulls off all his clothes and throws them into a wicker basket in the corner of the room. He examines his skinny body in the full-length mirror, then tucks his penis between his legs and dances a few steps, wiggling his hips like a woman. He's beginning to acquire a cautious interest in the opposite sex, but is very wary of getting involved with them. From what he can see, girls are just trouble, always saying the wrong thing and getting you into fights, always wanting you to buy them things to prove how much you love them. Bollocks to that!

He picks out some clothes, dresses himself from head to foot in new gear. A purple silk shirt, a pair of black AJs and a black quilted silk jacket. He chooses a pair of red Nike trainers from his collection of forty or so pairs, and adds a red baseball cap with the words 'No Quarter' embroidered in gold across the front. He studies his reflection critically in the mirror, then loops a red bandana around his neck. He poses, arms crossed, just like Bobby on the *Bad Attitude* CD cover. He decides that he looks about right, apart from the colour of his skin, and there isn't much he can do about that.

Now he gets the empty sports bag out of the wardrobe and checks that he has the pair of handcuffs with which he can chain it to his wrist after he has picked up his new consignment from Gordie. He collects his cell phone; everybody in the posse has one, so they can keep in touch at all times. Gordie takes care of the bills, and doesn't quibble about any personal calls that áre made. Finn clips the phone to his belt, then slides his favourite weapon into a leather sheath that he had sewed to the inside of the jacket.

This is a broad-bladed knife with a grip moulded to fit around the fist. An ingenious switch allows the user to jettison the blade inside the victim and use the handle as a knuckle duster. Gordie gave it to Finn as a present on his fourteenth birthday. He's not had occasion to use it yet, though he's come close a couple of times. More often, he has recourse to the shaft end of a two-piece pool cue which he always carries in the sports bag. If he is ever stopped by the filth, he can always claim that he's on his way to a snooker hall.

His dressing complete, he switches off the CD, takes a last glance around his room and goes out, locking the door securely behind him. He walks down the stairs and ducks his head into the kitchen. His parents are making a pathetic attempt to clear up in there; or at least, his mother is. She's on her hands and knees with a dustpan and brush. Dad is watching her, occasionally mustering up the energy to stamp on a cockroach.

'Hopeless,' Finn chides them. 'When I said clear up, I meant do it properly. Hot water, disinfectant, that kind of thing.'

Mum gazes up at him wearily.

'We'll do it,' she assures him. 'Once we've had a fix, we'll do it all . . .'

'But you won't,' Finn corrects her. 'You'll just drop down in front of the telly, like you always do.'

Dad looks suddenly resentful.

'Who are you to tell us to clean up?' he snaps. 'Didn't we clean up after you all those years? Changed your nappy, wiped your face, washed your fuckin' clothes!'

Finn laughs bitterly.

'Maybe *she* did. I don't think you helped much.'

'That's all you know! I did my share, boy. You *owe* me.'

'Yeah?' Finn sneers. 'Seems to me I've been payin' you back with interest lately. Don't forget I pay the rent around here. If I don't come up with the readies, you two go out on the street. I don't think you'd last long, either of you.' He's already getting bored with the argument. 'Anyway, I'm off out. Dunno when I'll be back. See you later.'

He turns and begins to walk down the hall, but his Dad hurries after him.

'Hey, hang on a minute! Haven't you forgotten something?'

Finn turns back to face him and affects an air of puzzlement. 'I don't think so. Lemme see now – bag, clothes, shoes . . . Seems to be everything . . .'

'You know what I mean.'

Dad is twitching now, and Finn can see the thick beads of sweat on his brow. Finn doesn't know why he has to put the poor sod through this routine; he supposes he just enjoys it. He reaches into his pocket and pulls out the little plastic sachet of brown.

'Oh . . . you mean this?' He waves it enticingly and Dad stumbles closer, reaching clumsily for it, but Finn snatches it away from him. 'Now haven't *you* forgotten something?'

Dad licks his lips. Behind him, Mother is stepping into the hallway, placing her feet carefully, as though she's afraid of falling.

'What d'you mean?' croaks Dad.

'The magic word. What's the magic word?'

'Bastard,' whispers Dad. He's looking at his feet now, too ashamed to look his son in the eyes.

Finn shakes his head. 'No, that ain't it! Let's try again, shall we?'

'Just *give* it to me, you evil little fucker!'

Finn sighs. He goes to stuff the sachet back in his pocket.

'Oh well, if you can't say one little word—'

'Please.' It emerges as little more than a whisper.

'Sorry, didn't quite catch that . . .'

'Please!' Now it's a tortured cry and Dad's eyes are brimming with tears. Mum comes up behind him and puts a hand on his shoulder, but he shrugs her roughly away. His eyes focus on Finn, and he holds out his hand demandingly. 'Now give it to me, you little bastard, before I leather you!'

Finn looks at him in undisguised contempt.

'You're a joke,' he says. 'Do you know that? A total fucking joke. Leather me? It's all you can do not to piss in your pants!'

He throws the bag on to the bare floorboards behind Dad. Mum makes an instinctive lunge for it, dropping to her knees in her haste. Then Dad is after it, fisting her roughly out of his way. She falls sideways, bashing her head on the floor. Dad grabs his prize and hurries off into the sitting room, where he keeps his works.

'Leave some for me!' Mum calls after him. She gets to her hands and knees, and then remembers that Finn is still standing there. She gives him a sidelong look, like some dog that has been caught doing wrong.

'Don't move,' Finn tells her coldly. 'I want to remember you just the way you are.'

She looks at him for a moment, and he thinks that he is glimpsing something of the woman she used to be. A flash of defiance lights up her eyes, but it is short-lived. Instead they fill up with tears. She lowers her head and begins to cry, her shoulders moving convulsively, great ragged sobs coming out of her.

For a moment, some part of him wants to go to her, put an arm around those thin shoulders and tell her that everything will be all right. But almost instantly he hardens, remembering all the times he has done this in the past, only to have his words of consolation thrown back in his face. Let the bitch cry her fucking heart out. He knows what that feels like. He knows better than anyone.

'See you, then,' he says brightly. 'Don't wait up. I'll be back late.' He turns away and lets himself out of the front door, slamming it behind him. Revenge is sweet, and he gets to taste it nearly every day of his young life.

Chapter Six

Nick unlocked the front door of his house and stepped into the hallway. He was deep in thought and hadn't expected to be ambushed.

A figure came hurtling down the hallway, then leaped straight at him, to wrap a pair of arms around his neck. He lurched back a step in surprise and let his attaché case drop to the floor.

'Daddy, daddy, daddy!' Molly's freckled face against his cheek, hot sweet breath planting kisses on his face.

He laughed, hugged her to him, marvelling, as he always did at such times, at the sheer devotion he seemed to inspire in his daughter; and by the fierceness with which he returned the emotion.

All through his twenties he'd sworn he'd never father kids; and right up to his daughter's birth he'd felt ambivalent about it. Molly hadn't been exactly planned; she'd just sort of *happened*. But from the moment she'd emerged, bloodstained and bawling, into the world, he'd been a man transformed. Holding her for the first time, he'd sobbed aloud at the wonder of it. This incredible, mewling, crumpled little creature that he and Helen had somehow cooked up between themselves – how was such a thing possible? What good had he ever done in his life to deserve such a precious gift?

He reached up a hand now to push Molly's curly auburn hair out of her big green eyes. She gazed at him with a look that announced to the world that she was in the presence of her greatest hero. Nick thought to himself that it wouldn't always be like this, and he felt a twinge of regret go through him; but he pushed it aside and gave his daughter a smile.

'Hello, princess. Had a good day?'

'You're late,' she chided him. 'Mummy and me were *waiting* – and I've made you a special present!'

'A present? For me? What is it?'

'S'a surprise. It's not finished yet.'

'OK.' He closed the front door behind him, stowed his case under the telephone table, and carried Molly through to the kitchen. 'You're getting too big to be carried,' he observed. 'Almost as big as a . . .' He searched for a suitable simile. 'A rhinoceros,' he said.

She giggled. 'No! Not a 'nocerous!'

'All right then, an elephant.'

More giggles. 'No! Not a 'nellyphant!'

In the kitchen, Helen was stirring cornflour into a chicken casserole. She glanced up as she caught the tail-end of the conversation, and she smiled ruefully.

'Somebody talking about me?' she asked glumly.

Nick moved across and gave her a peck on the cheek. 'Don't be silly,' he assured her; but had to admit to himself that she *was* looking bigger than he remembered her from the last pregnancy. Perhaps the large floral T-shirt worn over stretch leggings served to accentuate the fullness of her belly, as though she'd stuffed a large cushion under the T-shirt for a joke. Her curly auburn hair was tied back from her face. Her green eyes too were just like Molly's. Nick had searched in vain for anything of himself in his

52

daughter's features. Maybe next time, he'd told himself. He patted Helen's stomach.

'Coming along nicely,' he observed.

'Think I'm showing yet?' she asked with exaggerated innocence, and they both chuckled. It was a familiar joke between them.

'*That's* my little brother,' announced Molly gravely. 'On'y he still not ready to come out.'

'It might not *be* a boy,' Helen reminded her, aware that Molly was more keen on the idea of a brother than a sister. She and Nick had decided right from the start to give Molly the basic facts about pregnancy, and she seemed to have taken most of them on board, though she could still come up with some tricky questions when she put her mind to it.

'Can he see me yet?' she asked, peering closely at Helen's stomach. 'Can he peep out of your belly-button?'

Nick smiled. 'No, he can't do that. But he...' He paused, glanced at Helen. 'But the baby can *hear* us talking ... can already recognise our different voices.'

Molly's eyes got big and round. She leaned closer to her mother's swollen belly.

'H'lo, baby! This is your sister, Molly, speaking. You c'n play with my dolls when you come out...' She considered for a moment. 'Well, *most* of them – only not Lucy, 'cos she's *special*!'

Nick and Helen exchanged glances and had to constrain themselves not to burst out laughing. Molly was going through a phase where she easily became self-conscious. Nick set her down and patted her rump.

'Off you go and play,' he told her. 'Your poor old Dad needs a drink.'

Molly looked at him for a moment, then put her hands on

her hips. 'You're an allyholic!' she said brightly; then ran out of the room, giggling at her own audacity.

Nick raised his eyebrows and gave Helen a baffled look.

'Where on earth did she get that from?' he asked.

Helen shrugged. 'God knows. Children's television, probably.'

'Next thing you know, it'll be all over the playgroup. Molly's dad is a . . . what did she call it?'

'An allyholic.' Helen laughed, then broke off with an exclamation of discomfort.

'You all right?'

'I'm fine. Braxton Hicks', that's all. It'll pass in a moment.'

Nick nodded. He knew all about Braxton Hicks' contractions. During the first pregnancy, he and Helen had attended weekly parent-craft classes. As an enthusiastic 'new man', he had been expected to join in with everything that his wife did, including a series of relaxation exercises. Moira, the irrepressibly bubbly tutor who led the sessions, would talk the small group of prone parents-to-be through a ten-minute session, using an intoned chant which described the various areas of their bodies becoming 'soft and floppy'. She would start at the feet and work upwards. Whenever she reached the area that she tactfully referred to as the 'pelvic region', Nick would feel a powerful urge to laugh. He would lie there, his arms around Helen, his whole body shaking with suppressed mirth. This would quickly transmit itself to Helen, and the two of them would be left red-faced and wet-eyed beneath the disapproving, lizard-like stare of Moira, who clearly didn't see her relaxation sessions as a suitable subject for mirth.

Afterwards, driving home, Helen would berate Nick about it. 'I'm warning you, if you ever pull a stunt like that again, I'll leave you at home! Moira was looking *daggers* at us all through that last exercise.'

'I couldn't help it. Where I come from, it's not done to have somebody you barely know discussing your floppy bits!'

Actually, when he was being truthful, he had to admit that he'd learned a lot from the course. Helen's labour had been a slow and painful process. Knowing exactly what was going on inside her had been reassuring for both of them. For a time there it had looked like they'd have to plump for a Caesarean, but Helen had requested a few more minutes, and had used her last reserves of energy to bear down hard, squeezing her first child out into the light of day in the time-honoured fashion. Now it was all coming round again, but the difference, of course, was that this time they thought of themselves as seasoned veterans. It only took one successful birth to achieve that confidence.

Nick removed his jacket and draped it over a chair. He loosened his tie, went to the fridge, and took out an open bottle of Australian Chardonnay. He searched out a couple of glasses while Helen returned the casserole to the oven, stooping with considerable effort to put it in.

'Let me do that,' he suggested.

'No problem. I'm not an invalid.'

'Oh, but you're a proud woman.'

She moved to the kitchen table, pulled out a chair and sat down with a sigh. 'Dinner will be about half an hour,' she announced.

He nodded. 'Gives us time for an aperitif.' He poured two glasses of wine.

'I shouldn't really,' she told him.

55

'Nonsense. One won't hurt. Christ, we gave up smoking. We have to have *some* vices.' He carried the glasses to the table and sat opposite her. He took a large gulp from his glass and smacked his lips in appreciation. 'I needed this,' he said.

'Bad day at work?'

Nick scowled. 'Not particularly. Bit boring, to tell you the truth. Got a visit from your ex-boyfriend, mind you.'

Helen glanced at him sharply.

'You mean Ajay?'

Nick nodded. 'In fine form, he was, swanning about the office, laying down the law. He's got a Roller now with an AJ1 number plate. Oh yes, and a ponytail.'

Helen smiled wryly.

'Why are you telling me this?' she asked him.

He shrugged. 'Thought you'd be interested. Old flame and all that . . .'

'Old flames can't hold a candle to you,' she assured him. It was a line from a dopey old country and western song they both had an irrational liking for. 'Why would I care what he looks like?'

Nick grunted – a sound that lacked conviction. He drained what was in his glass and went to get the bottle. He then replenished his drink, aware that Helen was watching him, awaiting a reply to her question.

'You could have been Mrs Sanjari,' he said at last.

'Who says? It was never that serious between me and Ajay. We went out maybe a half-dozen times. We were both in the trade, so it really was just an extension of business. Tell you the truth, I had half a mind that he was only trying to get me to order more of his products for the catalogue.'

'And did you? Order more products?'

Helen glared at him. 'Hey, what is this? An interrogation?' she asked him irritably. 'You'll have a spotlight in my eyes next. You'll be asking me if I slept with him.'

There was an uncomfortable silence. Nick looked at her over the top of his wine glass, but didn't say anything.

'Oh, for goodness sake!' Helen reached out, put a hand on his shoulder. 'Look, it might have slipped your attention, but I married *you*. I've had one of your children. I'm about to have another. Doesn't that tell you anything?'

He nodded. 'Sure, only . . .'

'Only what?'

'I'd hate to think you regretted it, that's all.'

'Don't be stupid! I'm not complaining. And we're not exactly impoverished, are we?'

'No, I suppose not . . .' He was thoughtful for a moment, turning the wine glass around and around on the table top. He found to his surprise that he fancied a cigarette, something he hadn't even thought about in months. 'Did you ever consider that, Helen? How *lucky* we are? Nice home, lovely daughter, flash car, money in the bank. There was a kid this morning . . .'

'A kid?'

'Oh, some kid sitting in the doorway of the office. Dirty, ragged. He had one of those signs – you know, HUNGRY AND HOMELESS. He was just after the price of a meal, really.'

'Did you give him anything?'

'I was *going* to. Then Terry came along and kicked him out. Literally threw him into the street.'

'Terry?' Helen looked astonished. 'Are you sure?'

'Of course I'm sure. I stood there and watched the whole thing. Oh, Terry said something about seeing the kid buying booze in the off-licence, but . . .' Nick sighed, had another gulp of wine. 'You ever think about what I do for a living? Like, for instance, what utter crap it is?'

Helen raised her eyebrows.

'Oh dear. Something's really got to you all of a sudden, hasn't it!'

He shook his head. 'It's nothing new. It's been creeping up on me for a long time. Seeing the kid this morning, it just crystallised things. I mean . . . you look at this deal with Sanjari. By the time it's over he'll have spent upwards of two million pounds. To do what? Build a hospital or a library, supply a soup kitchen for homeless people? No. To promote a line of jeans, for Christ's sake! And no doubt to generate even more millions in profit. I mean, doesn't that strike you as the tiniest bit *sick*?'

Helen frowned. 'Well sure, when you put it like that. But don't forget, I used to work in a similar field myself. Getting designer clothes run up in Third World sweatshops for pennies, then flogging them for pounds over here. Of course it's corrupt. It's a dirty world, Nick, but that doesn't necessarily make you a dirty person. You're just experiencing the old yuppie guilt trip. Everybody gets a dose of it from time to time.'

'Think so?' He looked at her doubtfully. 'Another thing, Sanjari wants us to do the fashion shoots in Moss Side. "The East LA of Manchester," he called it. He wants a dirty, streetwise look. Burned-out cars, smashed windows, graffiti . . .'

Helen spread her hands in a 'so what' gesture.

'So it's not right, is it?' he continued. 'Bunch of middle-class wankers driving in there with our lights and cameras. Yeah, come on, give us some of that picturesque poverty, that delightfully photogenic squalor. But we forget that some people have to *live* there!'

'Most of us thank God that we don't,' Helen told him. 'You shouldn't start getting all guilty because you haven't experienced life at the sharp end.'

'But I *have*,' he retorted. She glanced at him sharply and he shook his head. 'Well, no, not exactly . . . but I *have* lived in Moss Side.'

'Really?'

'Yes, when I first moved here from Cheshire. I was eighteen years old, freelancing as a copywriter, and I had this crummy little bedsit . . .'

'You've always told me that was in Whalley Range!'

'Yeah, that's what I used to tell everyone. Even then it was deeply uncool to admit that you lived in *that place* – specially if you were looking for an insurance policy. But the Moss Side Community Centre was within spitting distance.'

Helen chuckled. 'Well, there's a few skeletons coming out of the cupboard tonight,' she observed. 'You'll be telling me next you peddled drugs to make ends meet.'

He shook his head. 'The deepest I ever got into that was a few puffs on the occasional spliff.' He smiled, shook his head. 'Of course, the area wasn't so bad then. Oh, my place was turned over by thieves a couple of times, but that was no big deal. In those days I had nothing worth taking, anyway. And, yes, I suppose I *was* always careful walking home at night. If I saw a group of kids up ahead, I'd make a quick diversion, just in case they felt like using my head as a football . . .'

'You'd do that round *here*,' Helen reminded him.

'True enough. But, see, it was also kind of an *adventure* for me. My first place away from my parents, my first bid for a bit of individuality; I had this grotty little room, the size of a postage stamp. Had to share bathroom and kitchen with these other kids, medical students I think they were. I had some great times there, some real laughs ... But even then you were aware that there was something cooking away in the background, something bad waiting to happen ...'

He hesitated, fiddled with the stem of his wine glass.

'Go on,' she urged him.

He sighed. 'The last summer I was there, they had the riots – 1981 I think it was. I was woken up in the night by the sounds of glass breaking, and all this shouting down in the street. I looked out of the window and there was a car burning right outside the house; people running down towards the shops. Well, I didn't hesitate. I got dressed and went outside ...'

'What? You must have been soft in the head!'

'Maybe I was. I don't know. But there was this weird attraction to it, an almost *primeval* feeling. Like bonfire night is for little kids, you know? Anyway, I just kind of went with the flow, not doing anything, just running with these other kids, most of them black, watching them looting stuff from shop windows, turning over cars. In a way I was getting off on the buzz. And then we ran into this line of riot police and suddenly it all got very nasty. They were pushing us back with their shields and batons, and I saw them hitting these kids at the front who couldn't move back. They were trapped by the people behind pushing them forward. The cops were probably frightened by what was happening, their adrenalin was pumping, and they were just hitting out at anything that moved, breaking heads, smashing teeth. And then suddenly I hated them. I saw them as the enemy. It was them or us. People had started throwing bricks and bottles, and I found myself looking for something I could throw, aim for those visors that make the cops look like aliens, smash through to the flesh behind. Only I couldn't find anything to throw. If I had, I might have killed somebody.'

He shook his head. 'Next morning it was as though nothing had happened. There were just a few reminders. A couple of burned-out cars, smashed shop fronts, Black Marias patrolling the streets. And I could see then that it was going to get much worse. Anyway, that was what persuaded me to move to a more genteel area. I couldn't really afford it, but my parents lent me the money. I was lucky: I had somebody to bail me out. A lot of people didn't, and they're the ones who deserve better than to have their neighbourhood used as some kind of cheap-shot publicity gimmick.'

Helen took a deep breath. She looked vaguely stunned by his story, as though she'd just discovered a part of him she didn't know existed.

'How come you've never told me about any of this before?'

'I guess it just didn't come up in conversation.'

'Well, I'm sure Terry would understand if you asked to be excused from this particular project.'

'Are you kidding? He'd throw a fit! As far as he's concerned, this is the best thing that ever happened to us.' He frowned. 'Anyway, I've already agreed to it. Maybe that's why I'm pissed off. Because I didn't have the courage of my convictions.'

Helen patted his hand. 'Oh, come on. It's not such a sell-out. It's just a job, and you're a professional. Think of it as a chance to revisit the scenes of your youthful depravity.'

'You should never go back,' he said bleakly.

'Why ever not? You could look out for that old bedsit of yours. Relive a few memories.'

He grunted. 'Probably burned down by now.'

'Oh, I think the problems there are exaggerated by the media. It can't be as bad as they're making out.'

'Funny, that's exactly what Ajay said. You two been conferring on this?'

Helen was about to give a suitably terse reply, but was interrupted by the arrival of Molly proudly carrying something she had evidently just finished making.

'This is for you,' she told Nick.

He took it carefully from her, lest it fall apart in his clumsy hands. It appeared to be the bottom six inches of a washing-up liquid container, on to which some choice items from Molly's treasured seashell collection had been laboriously affixed with blobs of glue.

'Well, that's fantastic, Princess!' he enthused. He was trying to puzzle out what it might conceivably be used for.

'It's to put your pens in,' explained Molly, as if she'd read his mind. 'You c'n take it to work and put it on your desk.'

'Right. That's what I figured. You know, it's funny, because this is just exactly what I've been looking for.'

Molly beamed with pleasure and Nick reached out a hand to stroke her hair. In that instant, he knew exactly why he went to work every day, why he stayed with a business that sometimes dismayed him. He knew exactly why he would swallow his pride and work on the Sanjari account, and why he would be helping to scout locations in Moss Side the very next morning. For Molly, of course. For Helen and for the unborn child she carried inside her. And because, despite his occasional doubts and his incessant grumbling, he was exactly where he wanted to be – able to provide for his family, to keep them from harm.

God help anyone who tried to interfere with that.

Chapter Seven

Finn walks through the estate in the gathering twilight. After leaving the house, he's stopped off at the Jamaica Pattie Shop for a cheeseburger and fries. The Jamaica is kind of his 'office,' so he's taken his time over the meal, letting a couple of hours slip by while he sits there, picking at his food, chatting to various people who came in, and taking phone orders from his regular clients. He'll get Wart or Tommo to deliver the stuff by bike tomorrow night. Now it's past nine o'clock and he's on his way to Gordie's house, which is located on the other side of the estate.

He turns a corner and sees the group of people waiting for him up ahead. He considers changing his route; but then decides he can't do that. This is his turf – it would be a loss of face. So he keeps walking, studying the group as he draws nearer. They are ranged under the glow of a solitary street light, six of them: four black youths maybe in their twenties, an older black guy and, strangely, one young white woman. They are just standing there watching him, and Finn doesn't recognise any of their faces.

He slips his right hand under his jacket and fits it into the contoured handle of his street knife, but he doubts that he'll need it. If they mean to jump him, they're hardly going to stand around in the light that way.

As Finn gets closer, the older guy catches his attention.

Everything about him – his clothes, his expression, even the way he stands – announces that he is the leader of this posse. He is tall and skinny, barely an ounce of excess flesh on him, but what really marks him out as different is his clothes. He's wearing a full-length black leather coat, a broad-brimmed fedora, flared white trousers and, oddest of all, stack-heeled shoes. As Finn crosses the road towards him, the man lights a cigarette, the flare of the match illuminating his gaunt features.

Standing beside him, the white woman is also dressed oddly in a kind of outmoded punk style. She has on a denim halter-neck top, a tiny black leather skirt with a studded belt, and long black PVC boots that zip up to her thighs. Her hair is peroxide blonde, sticking up in spikes like she's just had an electric shock. She has severe black make-up around her eyes, third-degree burns in the shocking whiteness of her face. It's apparent, by the way she stands beside the guy in the hat, that they are a team.

The other four stand a little apart and behind them, dressed in more conventional leisurewear, arms crossed, giving Finn the old snake-eyed glare. As he covers the last few yards, a couple of them start clicking their tongues at him, a sound designed to intimidate.

It works. Finn feels his heartbeat accelerate but he manages to keep his expression stonefaced, not wanting to give them the satisfaction of knowing that they are spooking him. He has a pretty good idea who these people are, and for once it seems that the local gossip has been accurate.

Now the guy in the weird clothes takes a couple of steps forward, seeming to tower over Finn in his elevated shoes. He grins, and Finn sees that many of his teeth are capped with gold. They glitter dangerously in the streetlight.

'You is Finn McManus, *bwoy*? You is de Yardman on dis piece o' turf?' He sounds slightly incredulous, as though he'd expected somebody bigger. Finn notes that he has an odd accent, a mixture of Jamaican patois shot through with broad cockney, as out of place on the Merton Estate as those weird clothes.

'Yeah. You must be Otis Mason?'

The man's grin seems to spread across his entire face.

'You heard've me! How come?'

Finn shrugs. 'Word gets around. You've been working out of Edge Close.'

Mason nods, takes a drag on his cigarette.

'Dat's where me started,' he says. 'Dere was some kids t'ought they already had it sewn up, but they decide to try their luck some place else.'

'You ain't from round here,' says Finn and immediately feels stupid; it's such a patently obvious remark.

'Nah. From Kingston, Jamaica. But me live some years in Brixton. Me felt like a change of scenery. Den somebody tell me 'bout Moss Side. Deh say it mostly run by little kids. I don't believe it at first, but now I begin to.' He moves closer. 'Me hear you run t'ings aroun' here.' He looks Finn slowly up and down, his lazy eyes mocking. 'How old are you den, star? Fourteen, fifteen?'

'What's it to you?' Finn asks him testily.

Mason laughs. He glances around at his companions, an expression of disbelief on his face. Now the woman steps forward, her pale face a mask of outrage.

'Burn the little fucker, Otis. He's only a bloody kid. Somebody ought to teach 'im respect!'

Mason raises a hand to still her. 'Easy, Carmel. No need feh you to get excited.'

'But he—'

65

'*Calm down!*' Like you say, him just a kid. And every kid deserve de one chance. Even a big-mouthed little twat like dis one.' He turns back to Finn and smiles down on him like some benevolent black saint. 'Now den, Finn ... d'you mind if I call you Finn?'

'Not at all. Do you mind if I call you shithead?'

Mason flinches visibly. Carmel just stares in disbelief. Finn doesn't exactly know why he said that; it just kind of fell out of his mouth. A couple of members of Mason's posse take threatening steps closer, but once again he raises a hand to stop them. Finn notices this time that the fingers of the hand are covered in chunky gold rings. Then Mason laughs, a huffing, asthmatic sound, his shoulders going up and down.

'I'll say dis for you, dread: you's reckless,' he says.

'Yeah,' agrees Carmel coldly. 'What say we break his fingers and see how cocky he is then?' Her voice is so matter-of-fact it's plain she isn't kidding.

Mason shakes his head. 'Not dis time, sugar. If he stupid enough to cross me, mebbe ...' He thinks for a moment, rubbing his chin between thumb and forefinger. 'Awright,' he says at last. 'I'm gonna tell you how it work, and dis time me don't want no interruptions, seen? Your turf now belong to me and me breddars here. I don't want you doin' no business on me turf. You tell Gordie it's time he foun' himself a new location. For his health's sake. You tell him if he doesn't, me gonna give him a nice new necktie ...'

Finn scowls. 'What's that supposed to mean?' he asks.

'Don' worry, star. He'll know what I mean. As for you, bwoy, if I hear 'bout you sellin' so much as a spliff roun' here, I'm gonna burn your ass. And don't t'ink I'm kiddin' you, because I never kid around. *Never*.'

Finn continues to stare right back at him.

'Gordie ain't going to take any shit from you people,' he says.

Mason does a pantomime of looking frightened, rolling his eyes in their sockets, putting his hands up to his face. 'Oh, Lard he'p me. We's dealin' with a hard man here! Me is just about pissin' me pants with fear!' His display is rewarded with a few dutiful guffaws from his crew. Then he sneers. 'Gordie's a piece of yellow shite,' he says. 'Me chase him out of places before now, and me don' 'spect nothin' from him but *skid-marks*, he leave so sudden. So who's gonna stop me, bwoy? You?'

Finn takes a deep breath.

'Me and my posse,' he says quietly.

Everyone laughs at that, but Carmel's screeches of hilarity are louder than the rest.

'The cheeky little fucker! I'm tellin' you, Otis, we should stomp on him now. See how big he talks with his teeth down his throat.'

Mason sighs. His expression seems to ask the world why he ever chose to head up this crew.

'Carmel, we'll do dis my way. Dis soldier deh, him going to take a message to Gordie for us . . . so tonight him under my protection. Don' matter what he say or do.'

'That right?' Finn narrows his eyes suspiciously. 'For all I know, I walk away from here and this lot come after me.'

Mason shakes his head.

'No way, mon. Tonight you got a . . . whatchacallit. An *amnesty*. You got my word on dat. Tonight you're kind of workin' for me. Tomorrow morning, you're unemployed.' He winks slyly. 'Blame it on de recession.'

Finn scratches his head. 'So let me get this straight. None of these people are going to touch me *tonight*?'

Mason nods wearily. 'Dat's what I say, isn't it?'

'Just checking. OK, so . . .' Finn steps forward and hits Mason hard, open-handed across the face.

Mason reels backwards in stunned surprise, almost over-balancing on his platform shoes, his dropped cigarette trailing sparks down the front of his leather coat. He throws one hand up to touch his burning cheek, and his hat falls off, revealing hair cropped close to the skull. There's a deep silence into which the sound of the slap seems to echo.

Things happen quickly then. Carmel produces a craft knife from somewhere and launches herself at Finn with a howl of outrage. He drops back from her, reaching under his jacket for his own knife. Mason, recovering from his shock, jumps forward to restrain his girlfriend, who seems to have gone totally ape-shit, slashing at the air in front of Finn's face.

'Lemme at him!' she screams. 'I'll cut the bastard. I swear I will!'

'Easy now!' Mason soothes her. 'Is all right, baby. Ease up.' He's managing to hold her back only by exerting considerable effort. He turns his attention to Finn and his eyes blaze with bottled-up rage. 'Oh, I'm gwan to get you, soldier. Don't you worry. Tomorrow is open season on you and your posse. You value your life, don' be on dis estate when de sun rises. You hear me, bwoy?'

Finn adopts his best bored tone.

'Yeah, yeah,' he says. 'Suppose so. Tell me, you always rabbit on like this?'

'Jus' walk away, punk,' Mason advises him. 'A'fore I change me mind about dis t'ing. You take me message to Gordie, and then you get de fuck off 've me turf!'

Finn shrugs. He turns slowly and begins to stroll away. His expression remains impassive but inside he is trembling with fear. He keeps his pace unhurried, resisting the powerful impulse to run. Glancing back once, he sees them still grouped under the light. Mason has picked up his hat and is talking to Carmel, clearly still having to restrain her from going after Finn. She is screaming incoherently, and Mason is speaking to her, stroking her face with one gold-encrusted hand.

Finn still can't believe that he's pulled a stunt like that. Hitting a Yardie right in the kisser, Jesus Christ! He must have a death wish or something.

He turns the corner out of sight and really starts going to pieces. His whole body is shaking and he feels acid rising up his windpipe. Finally he can't hold it back any longer. He runs to stand against a wall, leans forward and noisily parts company with a cheeseburger and a portion of fries. He keeps pausing to glance over his shoulder, afraid that somebody will see him vomiting and report the incident to friends. Next thing it will be all over the estate.

Finn was so scared he threw up! Deeply uncool.

He takes out a handkerchief and wipes his mouth clean, then steps away from the mess and hurries on in the direction of Gordie's place, anxious to tell him about what just happened. Clearly, the shit is about to hit the fan. Finn doesn't want to be standing there when it happens.

Chapter Eight

Lights are on in Gordie's ground-floor flat, shining through the narrow slits in the steel-shuttered windows. Few dealers care to live so close to their work, but Gordie's an exception. He prefers to keep on top of things. Not so long ago, other people lived alongside him, but they were persuaded to seek other accommodation. Now their flats stand empty, and Gordie is the undisputed king of the whole block.

Finn approaches the reinforced metal door and taps on it gently. Inside, Satan and Lucifer, Gordie's Rottweilers, start barking, the whole house seeming to vibrate to the deep-throated sound of them. After a few moments, a metal flap in the door slides back and Gordie's suspicious grey eyes peer challengingly out at Finn. They soften in recognition and then there's the sound of heavy locks being unlatched. The door swings open and Finn steps inside, Gordie slamming it shut behind him. Satan and Lucifer are sitting obediently in the hallway now, and Finn reaches down to stroke each of their heads. Funny things, Rotties, they can be as gentle as lambs till Gordie gives them a certain command. Then . . .

Gordie turns back from the door and grins a welcome. 'All right?' he asks.

He's pretty old, Finn thinks: maybe in his late thirties, a

thin, grizzled hippie type with a sparse goatee beard and curly brown hair, receding at the front. He wears a silver cannabis-leaf earring, blue dungarees and a red bandana knotted around his skinny neck. His bare arms are heavily tattooed with the names of ex-girlfriends and archaic rock groups, and he looks more than anything else like a refugee from the Glastonbury Festival. If it wasn't for the Rolex chronometer on his wrist, you'd be forgiven for writing him off as a New Age traveller – but Gordie's preferred method of transport is a Mitsubishi Shogun; and when he's away from home, he tends to make camp in the nearest five-star hotel. Some hippie.

He slips an arm around Finn's shoulders and leads him through into the lounge. Satan and Lucifer trail dutifully after their master, and take up guard at the doorway. At a word from Gordie they'll happily chow down on anything that moves, including Finn.

'Drink?' suggests Gordie, and seems surprised when Finn asks for a glass of brandy. 'Christ,' he says. 'That's not like you, kid. Gettin' a taste for the good life, are we?'

He moves across to his cocktail cabinet and prepares a couple of drinks, brandy for Finn, tequila sunrise for himself, his balding head nodding rhythmically to the loud music that's pumping from the speakers of his Nad stereo system – some kind of jazz-fusion experiment, Finn decides: wailing saxophones and clattering percussion. Gordie really has shitty taste in music. Now he's turning back to face Finn, motioning for him to sit on one of the two leather sofas, but Finn shakes his head. The way he feels just now, he prefers to stand. Gordie shrugs and sits down himself. He reaches for a half-smoked joint in an ashtray on the coffee table, and watches Finn gulp down his brandy in one swallow, then give a grimace of disgust.

'You're drinkin' like you're in a hurry,' Gordie observes. Finn coughs, nods.

'I think we've got trouble,' he says.

Gordie raises his eyebrows. 'Oh?' He lights the joint, filling the air with fragrant smoke. 'What kind've trouble?'

'I was given a message for you tonight. Black dude called Otis Mason. Heads up a posse from Edge Close?'

Gordie thinks about it for a moment.

'Yeah, I know him. What's he say?'

Finn's pacing up and down on the deep-pile carpet now, a lot of unused adrenalin jolting through his system.

'Only that he's taking over our fuckin' turf. Starting from tomorrow.'

Gordie frowns. He inhales on the joint, holds the smoke in his lungs for a few moments, then lets it out in a thin stream.

'Bollocks, he is. Guy's all talk.'

'Yeah? He said that he's run you out of places before. Says you're a piece of yellow shite.'

Gordie looks amused. 'Does he, now? Well, well.'

Finn, still pacing up and down, his hands jammed into his pockets, remembers something else.

'Says he's gonna give you a nice new necktie.'

Gordie looks momentarily startled by this information. Then he sneers. 'Same old Otis. Man's a gobshite – always has been. Don't sweat it.'

'What's all this stuff about neckties?'

'Macho bullshit, that's what it is. He's been watching too many gangster movies.'

Gordie doesn't elaborate on this and Finn finally stops pacing.

'But you *do* know him?'

'Sure. I knew him down in the Smoke. Brixton. We used to work neighbouring turfs.'

'Till he chased you out of it?'

Gordie laughs. 'Of *course* not. I ... I just decided to leave, that's all. Heard there were better pickings up north.' He shakes his head. 'So Otis Mason is back on the scene, is he? He still dress like a reject from a *Shaft* movie?'

'Uh?'

'Before your time, I suppose.' Gordie indicates the vacant part of the sofa. 'Will you, for fuck's sake, sit down and *relax*?' he mutters. 'You're enough to make anyone nervous.' He waves the joint. 'Should take a coupla tokes on this. Might calm you down a bit.'

'I don't do drugs,' Finn tells him primly; but he does sit down beside Gordie.

'So, Otis Mason. Who was with him?'

'Four black guys. Never seen any of 'em before. Oh, and this one skinny white girl, looked like something from a Halloween party. Right hard-faced cow, she was doing more giving out than *he* was. Wanted to cut me with a craft knife, only he wouldn't let her.'

'A woman?' Gordie looks intrigued. 'That's funny. From what I remember, he was never interested in chasing tail.'

'What, you mean he's a shirt-lifter?'

Gordie shakes his head. 'Don't think so. Just not interested in sex, period. Bit like yourself really.'

'Get out of it. There's nothing wrong with me!' Finn thinks for a moment. Gordie seems to be playing down the incident, but Finn senses an underlying nervousness in him. 'Mason said: from tomorrow night this turf is his. Said if he caught me sellin' anything, he—'

'Ah, bollocks, he was just trying to psych you out. You'll carry on as normal. There's the concert tomorrow night at the Nile Club. We'll take a fucking fortune.'

'Yeah, but—'

'Look, since you're worried, I'll draft in a few heavies to keep an eye on you – just to put your mind at rest. If Mason so much as shows his face, they'll kick his skinny arse all the way back to Brixton.'

Finn frowns. 'I heard that their posse have all got shooters.'

'You don't want to believe everything you hear, mate.'

'Well . . . couldn't you give us some, too, Gordie? Just in case?' There's a long pause while Gordie considers the question – a pause punctuated by the wailing of brass instruments. To Finn it sounds like a cat being tortured, a procedure he is not unfamiliar with.

'Christ, what a row,' he mutters. 'Can't you turn it down?'

'You fuckin' philistine! That's Miles Davis!'

'Yeah? Who are they then?'

'It's not a "they", dimbo. It's a "he". And that's bloody genius you're listening to.'

'Oh aye, yeah. When do the lyrics start?'

'Lyrics? Jesus!' Gordie slaps himself on the forehead in exasperation. Then he sighs, acknowledging the subject that they've been discussing earlier. 'It's like this, Finn. I can't tool you and your mates up. You're only kids. Who knows where that would end? I'm sorry, mate.'

'What, just because I didn't like your fuckin' music?'

'It's nothing to do with that! It would be a pointless exercise, that's all.'

'But if Mason's posse come after us with shooters—'

'That's not going to happen. Believe me, Otis Mason is

just a mouth on legs – thinks he's stepped out of an Isaac Hayes song.'

'Who?'

'Oh, never mind! He hasn't got the balls to come in here and take our turf, no matter what he told you. But just in case, I'll put some gorillas on to it. If he so much as gets his *dick* out tomorrow night . . .'

'And will *they* have shooters? These gorillas?'

'For Christ's sake, what's all this shit about guns? There's no need for any of that, we've managed to work this system for years with just knives and baseball bats. People start shooting each other, and who knows where it fucking well ends? No, we'll do it the way we've always done it. A little physical persuasion, that's all it takes.'

Finn shrugs. 'Well, all right. If you're sure.'

'Trust me,' Gordie tells him. 'Have I ever fucked you over?' Finn has to admit to himself that Gordie never has. If he says something is going to happen at a certain place, at a certain time, it always does; or at least it always has up till now. On reflection, Gordie is probably the one adult Finn trusts in the entire world. Well, him and Bobby C. Cooper anyway.

Gordie stubs out the roach of his spliff and leads Finn over to the other side of the room. They each take one end of the sofa and move it away from the shuttered window, revealing what appears to be an ordinary stretch of wall below the wooden sill. Gordie takes a couple of metal handles from his pocket and inserts them into tiny metal lugs located in the plaster. He gives each of them a half-turn anti-clockwise, and then pulls downwards. The wooden windowsill and the section of wall beneath it hinge smoothly forward, revealing a long, deep recess within. This is Gordie's supply store, installed by a joiner friend of his, who's been handsomely paid to forget that he ever constructed it.

The interior is packed with plastic packages of heroin and cocaine, cannabis and marijuana, phials of crack, bottles of ecstasy tablets, speed, acid, you name it. Here too are his precision scales, his bongs and other implements of oblivion: syringes, spoons, tourniquets. But for the moment Finn is more interested in the contents of a canvas toolbag lying in one corner.

'What's this, then?' he asks, prodding the bag with his foot. He hears something metallic clank inside.

'Never you mind,' Gordie tells him dismissively.

'It's shooters, isn't it?'

Gordie rolls his eyes to the ceiling.

'You're getting obsessed with this, Finn. For Christ's sake, change the fucking channel!'

Finn scowls.

'Maybe if you just gave *me* a gun. I wouldn't tell the others.'

'Read my lips, Finn. *No*! If you want a shooter, there's plenty of places you can buy one. You could pick up a handgun for, what, fifty notes?'

Finn nods. 'Maybe I will,' he says.

Gordie is filling Finn's sports bag with produce.

'Now, you know all the prices? I'm going to give you plenty, and I don't want to see you coming back from that gig with any left over. Also, absolutely no credit.'

'Supposing it's a friend, and you know they're good for it?'

'I don't give a shit, Finn. We've lost too much that way already. So you don't do anybody a favour, even if it's your best friend – even if it's your mum and d—' Gordie winces, gives Finn an apologetic glance. 'Sorry, mate,' he says. 'I wasn't thinking . . .'

'That's all right. It ain't your fault. You don't make 'em buy this shit, right?'

'Right.' Gordie sighs, runs a hand through what's left of his hair. 'You know, kid, it's *people* that are to blame, not the drugs. I mean, drugs are like bricks, right? You can use them to smash somebody's head in, or you can build a wall with them.'

'Yeah.'

Finn hates it when Gordie starts talking like this. He never has the slightest idea of what the man's on about. The standard cosmic hippie bullshit, he supposes. Or maybe just trying to justify to himself what he does for a living. Finn can't see the point in it. He has no such qualms about himself, he knows that he's scum. The thing is that he doesn't give a flying fuck about it. Being scum is better than being poor; and better by far than being nobody.

Gordie is warming to his theme.

'Like, you know, I've seen some good people go down over the years, and that's because they let the drugs control *them*. And then, for some reason, there's other people who learn to use their bodies as *channels*, let the drugs open the doors of their perceptions. And those people are the most sussed human beings you'll ever meet in your life – and, of course, I'm talking here about the hallucinogens, you understand. Acid, hashish, peyote . . . the *good* drugs.'

'Oh, yeah, the good drugs.' Finn smiles bleakly. 'Pity we can't just sell those ones, isn't it? Pity we have to sell crack and heroin as well.'

Gordie grins sheepishly.

'Got to take your profit where you can find it these days.'

'Yeah, right. That it, then?'

'That should cover you for now.' Gordie zips up the sports bag and watches as Finn chains the leather handle to his left wrist. 'So,' he concludes, 'you get along to that gig tomorrow. And don't worry about Mason and those other wankers. I'll sort it.'

'Thanks, Gordie.' Finn gets to his feet, while Gordie locks up the remains of his stash. 'By the way, how are my stocks and shares doing?'

Gordie turns back to face him, a big grin on his face.

'They're doin' great, kid. You just tell me when you want your cash. You saving for something special?'

'Yeah. I plan to retire to the country when I'm twenty.'

Gordie laughs. 'If you live that long,' he says.

Finn laughs too; but he will reflect on those words before very much longer, and then they won't seem quite so funny. In fact they won't seem funny at all.

Chapter Nine

The next morning, Nick, Terry and Alan Richards piled into Terry's BMW and drove into Moss Side to scout locations. The weather had changed dramatically. It was a clear, hot July day, not a cloud in the sky. The interior of the car was uncomfortably sticky and Nick and Terry were soon sweating in their work suits, despite the open windows and sunroof. Alan had brought his 35mm Nikon, and had attached a Polaroid unit to give him instant results. He sat in the back of the car, fiddling with the various shutter speeds and apertures, experimenting with a series of filters he had brought along.

'Typical,' he complained. 'The one time in my life I actually *wanted* miserable Manchester weather, it comes on like the bleeding Costa del Sol!'

Nick studied Alan in the driving mirror. He was a tall, skinny individual, still only in his early twenties, who always arrived for work dressed in uncompromising grunge fashion. This morning, he sported a tie-dyed grandad vest, a handmade Indian waistcoat and (*typical*, thought Nick) a pair of baggy indigo AJs. An embroidered pillbox hat perched on his close-cropped head, a miniature silver skull dangled from his left ear, and a soft leather shoulder-harness, strapped to his lean frame, held the various accoutrements of his trade:

light-meters, filters, spare film and eyeglasses.

'You got a gun tucked away in that rig?' Terry asked him jovially. 'Only, by all accounts, we might be needing one before the day's over.'

Alan laughed dismissively.

'Ah, no sweat, man! I've been here more times than you've had hot dinners. Listen, all the best ragga parties are in Moss Side!'

Nick smiled. He knew that Alan liked to project a loutish, streetwise image, but behind it all he was as middle-class as they come, operating his business out of a twinky detached cottage in a leafy South Manchester suburb. Oh, he'd probably been to *some* ragga parties around here, but Nick figured that they'd be very few and far between and, even then, in the company of friends who'd back him up in any trouble.

Terry turned the car on to a familiar road and Nick found himself peering out of the open window in anticipation. The BMW cruised past the three-storey Victorian house where Nick's first bedsit had been located. He felt a shock of disappointment go through him as he registered the fact that all the windows were boarded up. Slates had come off the roof, guttering had broken away, and what he remembered as a carefully cultivated garden was now a jungle of weeds. He registered it all in a flash, and then the car was moving on, leaving this small chunk of his past behind him.

'That house back there . . .' he started to tell Terry.

'Yeah, a real eyesore, but we can do a lot better than that. Ajay wants the Merton Estate, and that's what we'll give him.'

Nick looked at his partner for a moment and considered pressing the point, but decided against it. What had he been about to say, anyway? *Hey, see that building? When I was nineteen, I lived there. In one little room up on the first floor, I had my first real experiences of life. I smoked dope, learned to cook and fend for myself and, most importantly, I got laid. Christ, did I ever get laid!*

He had a hazy recollection of what seemed like an endless procession of young women climbing the stairs to that scruffy little room to take coffee with him, to listen to his records, to share a spliff – oh, all manner of excuses to get them there – but sooner or later each of them would succumb to his advances, climb into his narrow bed to get better acquainted. How exciting it had all seemed then, how *dangerous*, though, of course in those relatively AIDS-free times, a good deal less dangerous than it would be now. And it wasn't that he pined for those days; he saw them as an inevitable part of growing up. And he *had* grown up: he'd matured into a happy, responsible family man. He had no regrets on that score.

It was simply that whenever he saw that building, it would be forever associated with a phase of his life when everything in the world was there for the taking; and seeing it boarded up and deserted seemed to him to be a profoundly sad state of affairs. There should be another nineteen-year-old living up in his old room, Nick told himself. Discovering a new-found freedom. Learning what life was really all about. And getting laid, of course.

The car was approaching the Merton Estate now. The streets seemed largely deserted here. They passed a couple of old black men standing disconsolately outside a pub, as though they were waiting for it to open. A young kid on a mountain bike cycled alongside for a moment, staring in at them with open curiosity. A thin girl of around fourteen was pushing a baby buggy along the pavement. Nick saw that she had dark clusters of love bites around her neck. Alan leaned out of the open window and shouted to her, then snapped her photo as she glanced up. She stared indignantly at the car as it cruised onwards.

Alan collected the square print as it slid out of the unit at the back of the camera, and tucked it under his armpit to speed up the developing process.

'Just testing,' he explained.

'That's some set-up you've got there,' observed Nick. 'I assumed you'd be bringing an *old* Polaroid.'

Alan sneered.

'You must be joking. Wait till you see the kind of definition this gives us!'

'Yeah, but it must be worth an arm and a leg.'

'Relax. Everything's insured.' Alan examined the exposed print. 'Image is coming through now,' he said, handing the print to Nick. 'Here, take a look at that.'

Sure enough, there was the young mother, staring straight at the camera with an outraged expression on her face. The image was still faint but, as Nick watched, the colours gradually intensified and he could see that the definition was sharp enough to show those purple smudges on her neck.

'Excellent,' he said. 'Christ, Terry, how old would you say she is? Fourteen, fifteen?'

Terry glanced at the picture, shrugged.

'Around that, I guess.'

'Kind've sad, isn't it? To be a mother at that age . . .'

'You don't *know* she's a mother,' Terry reminded him. 'Could be she's just taking her baby sister for a walk.'

'Could be.' Nick tapped the photograph. 'Except that she's wearing a wedding ring.'

Alan leaned forward over the seat, grinning proudly.

'Now *that's* definition!' he said.

Terry turned the car right, into the outskirts of the Merton Estate. 'Abandon hope all ye who enter here!' he quipped. Then: 'Christ, look at that!'

On a stretch of waste ground off to their right, the burned-out shells of three cars stood like pieces of modern sculpture in the fierce sunlight.

'Nice one,' said Alan. 'Stop here a minute, Terry. That's worth getting on film.'

Terry obligingly brought the BMW to a halt. Alan got out of the car, snapped off a couple of frames, then jumped back in and tapped Terry on the shoulder.

They drove on into the estate, grey concrete rearing up on either side of them. Up to fifty per cent of the flats seemed to be boarded up or vandalised beyond habitation. Graffiti covered virtually every surface they could see. Off to their left was the twisted metal frame of what had once been a phone-box, its panes of glass long since smashed to smithereens. Clumps of straggly weeds were growing up from cracks in the pavements.

Then they reached a point where the road ended, and they were obliged to park in a layby, alongside the rusting hulk of an ancient Datsun saloon up on bricks and seemingly stripped of every movable part. The open bonnet yawned like the toothless jaws of an old man. Beyond this point, interconnecting walkways led into the very heart of the estate.

Alan jumped out of the car, and the two older men followed at a more cautious pace. They watched as Alan snapped off a couple of frames at the looming grey tenements up ahead. Nick felt that he was looking at the dry, sunbleached carcass of a dinosaur slowly rotting in the heat of the sun. The hair on his neck prickled as he got the distinct impression that he was being watched.

'Mind yer car for yer, mister?'

Nick turned in surprise. The kid seemed to have appeared from nowhere: a skinny, under-nourished youth with a thatch of unruly hair and a Manchester City scarf wound tightly around his neck, despite the heat. He was walking towards the newcomers, one arm held out as if in supplication.

'What do you mean?' growled Terry.

The kid looked at him as though he was stupid. He was maybe ten years old, Nick decided, or eleven tops. Looked like he hadn't eaten a square meal in months.

'I mean, I'll look after yer car, right? For...' He appraised the three men for a moment, studying their clothes, the posh car, figuring out what they were worth to him. 'For a fiver,' he concluded.

'A fiver!' Terry looked suitably horrified. 'To do what?'

The kid shrugged.

''Ang around 'ere. Keep the other kids off 've it.'

Nick was just about to observe that there *weren't* any other kids, but then he noticed a couple of older youths strolling towards the car. A few moments later, a couple of black teenagers on mountain bikes appeared, as though summoned here by some kind of secret signal.

'You from the telly?' the first kid wanted to know. He was eyeing Alan's camera with interest. 'You come to make a documentary or summing? We gerra lot of them just lately. Making films about 'ow bad this place is.'

Alan laughed, shook his head.

'No, we're not from the telly. We're here to scout locations for Bobby C. Cooper. You heard of him?'

''Course I heard of him. The Rap Terminator! I got a

friend who's mad about Bobby C. But what does he want photies of this place for?'

'No, no, these are just test shots. Bobby's going to come here in a few days time and—'

Terry coughed a warning and Alan broke off, realising that he was giving away too much. In communities like this, such news was liable to spread.

Anyway, the kid seemed to doubt the story.

'Bobby Cooper coming here? Bollocks!' he said.

'Yeah, maybe so.' Alan turned away and began fiddling with the camera. 'I was just testing you out.'

'Want me to show you all the best places? I'll do it for fifty notes.'

Alan laughed at him.

'Fifty notes? You must be joking!'

The kid scowled up at him, his good humour suddenly evaporated. He made a gesture with his clenched right fist. 'Hey, man, show me respect!' he said. 'You want me to look after the car – yes or no?'

Nick reached into his pocket and came out with a couple of coins. 'Here,' he said. 'It's all the change I have.'

The kid inspected the money in apparent disbelief.

'Two quid?' he moaned.

'Maybe you could keep *one* eye on it,' Nick told him.

'You don't think much of your car, do you, mister?'

'It's not *my* car.' Nick pointed to Terry, who was securing the central locking system and activating the alarm. The kid moved over and yanked at Terry's sleeve. 'Come on, mister, that's another three quid.'

'Bugger off and stop pestering me!' Terry turned back to his friends and pointed along one of the walkways. 'Come on, let's try down here.'

They began to walk deeper into the estate. Glancing

back, Nick saw the kid glowering after them, and he had misgivings. He nudged Terry gently.

'Hey, you sure you haven't got a couple of quid?' he muttered. 'That BMW's a bit of an easy target.'

'No way,' said Terry. 'You can't let those little toe-rags hold you to ransom, Nick. If you do that, they've won.'

Nick shrugged. He had a bad feeling about this, but there wasn't much he could do about it. So, with a sigh of resignation, he followed his two companions into the dead grey heart of the Merton Estate.

Chapter Ten

Nick followed Terry and Alan along the walkway, moving between the tenements. Scenes of squalid dereliction lay all around them. Through the open doorway of a ground-floor flat, they could see a litter of rubble, rusting Coke cans and discarded hypodermics. Graffiti on the smashed-in door read *More Drugs* and *Paki Cocksuckers*. In a rubbish-strewn alleyway, a pack of mangy-looking dogs were scavenging from torn-open bin bags, snapping and stripping their teeth at each other in their haste to secure the best scraps of food.

'Fuckin' brilliant!' enthused Alan. He was shooting off frames left, right and centre, tucking the Polaroids into an empty compartment of his leather shoulder-harness. 'This is good stuff,' he said.

Nick found it hard to raise any enthusiasm. What he saw here, he found profoundly depressing. That people should be obliged to live in an environment like this. Jesus! He thought of his own house, the spacious rooms, the tasteful furnishings, the carefully tended garden, and he felt like cringing with shame.

'What a dump,' he heard Terry say. 'The people here want locking up for letting it get into this state.' He kicked a hypodermic off the pathway with the polished toe of one shoe. 'They're no better than animals,' he added.

Nick was about to challenge the statement but, on reflection, he decided it would be a waste of time. You could hammer on at somebody like Terry for hours without ever getting him to change his views. Still, he was now seeing a side to his partner that confirmed how much he'd changed over the past year.

They had reached an intersection: a point where four paths converged. Up ahead of them, taking up the whole end wall of a block of flats, was a truly stunning piece of graffiti or, depending on your view, a genuine work of art. It was dominated by a spraycan image of a naked Rastafarian, one arm raised in a Black Power salute. A halo of fire seemed to radiate outwards from his body, and emerging from the flames was a whole host of other images: exploding cars, huddled people holding out their arms in supplication, a crucifixion, a huge gun, stacks of blazing money, mounds of white powder. The vivid reds, blues and yellows were the only bright colours they had so far seen on the estate.

'Jesus, look at that!' exclaimed Alan. 'Must have taken them months to finish it. Hey, we could get Cooper to stand right underneath that – echo the pose. Whaddya think?'

'Maybe,' said Terry. 'It's not exactly what Ajay had in mind, but . . .'

'It'd look bloody brilliant!' Alan assured him. He was standing in the very centre of the converging paths now, focusing his Nikon on the image.

Then there was the sound of rubber on stone.

Nick turned in surprise and a mountain bike shot close by him, a black kid crouched low over the handlebars, a bandana tied across the lower half of his face. He was making straight for Alan. Nick turned, a shout forming on his lips, and then he saw the other bike, coming from a different direction – this one, too, aiming for Alan and doubtless the Nikon which he was virtually holding out like an expensive chunk of candy.

'Alan, watch out!' Nick yelled, but it was already too late; the bikes were scything past the photographer, on either side of him, one slightly in advance of the other.

The first rider didn't go for the camera, though. He reached out a hand and Alan yelled in agony as the silver skull earring was ripped right out of his lobe, blood spurting down his neck. He let go of the camera, reached up to claw at his torn ear, and in that instant the second biker grabbed the camera strap of the Nikon and pulled hard. It snagged briefly around Alan's neck, jerking him forward off balance, and then he was falling face down on to the pavement, the bike accelerating away along the path.

Alan made a desperate grab at the trailing strap, but missed by a mile.

Nick and Terry, stunned by the suddenness of the incident, ran to Alan and helped him to his feet. He came up with a curse, one hand vainly trying to stem the flow of blood from his ear.

'My camera!' he yelled. 'Come on, don't just *stand* there!'

He took off after the second bike, and Nick and Terry followed. They could see the biker up ahead of them, his legs pumping madly as he quickened his pace.

An alleyway opened to their left, and Alan waved Nick down it. 'Try and cut the little bastard off,' he roared. 'Don't let him get away!'

Nick pounded obediently up the intersection, reflecting

that it hadn't been a great idea to wear his suit on this expedition. He was still shocked by the speed with which the theft had occurred and was – he had to grudgingly admit – rather impressed by the military precision with which it had been accomplished. He turned right around a corner and began to run along the narrow walkway beyond, thinking now that he was moving parallel with his two friends, the long run of a row of flats between them, another row off to his left. He was rather out of condition, and was soon panting and sweating, his heart thumping like a piston in his chest.

A hundred yards further on, a high brick wall bisected his path and, as far as he could tell, that of the biker too. He would have the choice to turn left or right, and if he turned left . . .

Sure enough, the mountain bike came out of the mouth of an alley up ahead, the biker doubling back on himself. He came straight towards Nick at speed. Nick stopped running. He took up a defensive stance, crouched in the walkway, like a goalkeeper, his arms spread out to cover the width of it.

The biker seemed to register Nick's presence and he skidded to a halt. He glanced over his shoulder, just in time to see Terry and Alan bursting out of an opening behind him, cutting off his retreat. The pair of them yelled triumphantly and closed in on the youth. He seemed to come to a decision. He lowered his head and started pedalling hard straight at Nick.

Nick gritted his teeth. *Kid's trying to bluff me out*, he thought. *Thinks I'll jump aside at the last moment. He's wrong.*

The bike rushing at him now, the noise of the tyres echoing in the narrow walkway, the oiled chain whirring.

Nick hunkered down, braced himself, kept his gaze fixed resolutely on the kid's eyes.

Come on, then, he thought. *You won't get past me, sunshine*.

The bike uncomfortably close now, close enough for him to see that the kid was wearing an LA Raiders baseball cap, that the bandana around his face was a rich red paisley, that there were little beads of sweat on his forehead. He was obviously scared now, frantic at the thought of being cornered.

Come on, I got you, I got you . . . He'd told himself that he'd just step neatly to one side at the last instant, wrap his arms around the kid's neck, wrench him backwards off the speeding bike. It was just a question of timing, no need for anyone to get hurt—

And then suddenly, almost magically, the rider bucked in his seat and the bike seemed to fly, leaving the pavement in a steep arc, the front wheel aimed straight at Nick's chest. And he couldn't help himself; instinct took over and he threw himself backwards away from the impact, to crash full-length on the pavement with a force that jarred his bones. He saw the bike soaring over him in what seemed like smooth slow motion; slow enough for him to note the Puma logo on the soles of the youth's trainers and that the rear tyre was descending towards his face, the black rubber still spinning madly. He closed his eyes, waiting for the crushing impact against his skull.

Then the rear tyre hit the pavement just inches behind his head, the thud of it like an explosion in his ears, the wind of it ruffling his hair. He opened his eyes and watched the biker speeding crazily away, upside down, heading now for the heart of the estate where there was no hope of catching him.

Nick groaned, rolled on to his side. As he struggled wearily to his feet, Terry and Alan came pounding up to him.

'What happened?' yelled Alan in disbelief. 'You had him cold! How could you let him get away?'

Nick glanced at him scornfully.

'What was I supposed to do? Stand there and let him drive his bike into my *mouth*?'

'Yeah, but Nick, that camera's worth over a thousand quid!'

'Well, excuse me all over the place, but I value my life a little higher than a fucking Nikon, OK?'

'Shut it you two . . . calm down. There's . . . no sense in arguing about this!' Terry was desperately trying to coax his breathing back to normal. His chubby face was dripping with sweat. He took a handkerchief from his pocket, about to mop his brow with it, but then he thought better of that and handed it to Alan, making him hold it against his ear. 'That looks pretty bad,' he observed. 'We ought to get you . . . to the hospital.'

'Never mind the hospital,' growled Alan. 'The police station would be a better idea. I need to report the theft as soon as possible. My insurance—'

'Fuck the insurance!' snapped Terry. 'It's more import- ant to—' He broke off in mid-sentence, a look of astonishment on his face. 'Oh no, I don't bloody believe it!' he cried.

The other two looked at him, not understanding.

'Listen!' he yelled.

They listened. Now they were aware of it, a high- pitched, warbling sound, rising and falling on the hot summer air.

'My fucking car alarm,' added Terry, just in case they

were in any doubt. And then the three of them were running again, retracing their steps through the estate, back to where they had parked. It took them maybe ten minutes to get there – though it seemed longer.

As they approached the layby, they slowed to a halt, staring in dismay at what they saw. Terry opened his mouth to say something appropriate but all that came out was a feeble 'Oh God'.

The red BMW had been magically transformed, from a sleek, shiny beast to a pitiful wreck; a very expensive wreck, as it happened, but it now looked a suitable partner for the old Datsun that stood beside it.

Every window was smashed, without exception. The doors and wings had been kicked all out of shape. If you looked carefully, you could see the imprints of toe caps up and down the length of it. The tyres had been slashed, the radio cassette ripped out of its housing. The lock on the boot had been jemmied open and whatever contents had been within had been stolen. As a final indignity, the words RICH CUNT had been scratched deep into the paintwork of the bonnet, with something like a screwdriver.

There was a terrible silence then. Terry walked slowly around the wreckage of his car, staring at it intently, as though he was trying to take in every detail, or maybe just looking for one item that had been left intact. Then he turned away with a gasp and Nick could see that his eyes were brimming with tears. Nick put an arm around Terry's shoulders and moved him away from the car, knowing that the BMW had been his pride and joy – that this was deeply upsetting for him, almost on a par with having a member of his family beaten up. He glanced at Alan, who was glumly mopping at his ear, the once white hanky already a sodden

95

red rag. At least he'd stopped moaning about his bloody camera.

'The bastards,' he heard Terry mutter. 'The fucking little bastards.'

'Come on,' said Nick gently. 'There's no point in hanging around here.' He began to lead Terry and Alan away from the spot, heading for the edge of the estate and the main road, where they might at least stand a chance of flagging down a taxi.

Terry resisted at first, as though reluctant to leave the car behind, but after a few moments he capitulated and allowed Nick to walk him out of there. He was mumbling under his breath, a long string of vicious expletives, and Nick told himself that neither Terry nor Alan would be quite so flippant about the Merton Estate the next time they paid it a visit.

When they reached the main road, Nick glanced back and saw that the kids had reappeared, a half dozen of them now. They were standing around the wreckage like it was a spoil of war, something they'd taken in battle. The little kid with the Manchester City scarf had the BMW's radio cassette tucked under one arm, and with his free hand he made a familiar two-fingered gesture at the departing strangers.

Nick said nothing, knowing that if he mentioned this to Terry, the man would fly into a rage, would pursue the kids back into the unfamiliar labyrinth of the estate. Perhaps that was what they wanted. After all, it was their home ground: a place where they would always have the advantage. They'd taken a car and a camera – God knows what else they might take before they were finished.

One thing was for sure. If Ajay Sanjari still insisted on

doing the fashion shoot here, then the next time they came, they'd have to be a damn sight better prepared.

Nick kept right on walking and he didn't look back again. He was afraid of what he might see.

Chapter Eleven

When Finn gets to the Nile Club later that night, the place is already rocking. He can feel the deep sonic-boom of a ragamuffin bass line shaking the ground beneath his feet well before the club's modest entrance comes into view. The featured act tonight is Jah Lion, a sound system from Kingston, Jamaica, so the club will be packed to the rafters. There are crowds of people standing around the entrance, talking, smoking, doing deals, many of them just waiting to make a connection. Over eighty per cent of these people are black, but that doesn't worry Finn. He pretty much thinks of himself as an honorary black anyway, and people with racist notions wouldn't last very long on the Merton Estate, where white faces are definitely in the minority.

Chaz and Gibbo are waiting for him in the forecourt. As he reaches them, they turn and fall into step, one on either side of him.

'Packed out in there tonight,' Chaz tells him.

Finn grunts. He unzips his sports bag and hands each of them their individual packs of drugs. He has already divided out another package of stuff for which he has taken phone orders. This he will get Wart and Tommo to deliver on their bikes. The rest he can handle himself.

'You see Gordie last night?' Chaz asks him.

Finn glances at him irritably.

'Sure I saw him! Where d'ya think all this shit came from?'

Chaz looks sheepish, but presses on with his point.

'He say anything about this new Yardie – what's his name?'

'Otis Mason,' says Gibbo helpfully.

'Yeah, guy from Edge Close. It's just that there's been a lot of talk, Finny. People are saying he's a *star*.'

Finn sneers.

'An *arsehole* is what he is. I met him last night.'

'You met him?' Chaz looks astonished. 'Where, at Gordie's?'

'Of course not at Gordie's, you tithead! In the street. He stopped me for a rap. Him and his posse.'

'Christ! So what did he say?'

Finn makes a dismissive gesture. It's important to play this down, assure his crew that it's all under control. He stops, takes out his cigarettes and lights one up with the brass Zippo, taking his time, aware that Chaz is studying the lighter sullenly as he does so. Then Finn blows out smoke and slips the lighter back into his pocket.

'Tried to freak me, didn' he? Gave me a lot of shit about how he was going to take over our turf.'

'What?' Gibbo looks worried.

'Ah, forget it, man. It's just talk. Gordie says the guy's always mouthing off about something. He used to know this Mason back in the Smoke.'

'Yeah, but I heard tell he chased Gordie out,' says Chaz glumly. 'Said he was gonna burn 'im if he stayed.'

'Ah, bollocks! You should see the guy. He dresses like something out of the Oxfam shop. He's got these shoes, right – they've got heels *this* high!' He holds his hands a foot apart to give them the general idea. 'Worse, he's got this

slag called Carmel goes round with 'im. More or less tells
him what to do. He's a joke, man, a real joke.'

The other two are lighting cigarettes now. Both of them
look reassured.

'Anyhow,' continues Finn. 'Gordie said he'd put some
heavies on to it. If anyone tries to pull anything tonight,
they'll step in and sort it.'

Gibbo is looking anxiously around.

'Heavies? What heavies?'

Finn shrugs.

'Well, I don't know, do I? Somebody at the gig, I
suppose, watching out for us. We don't need to know who
they are, do we?'

'Suppose not,' mutters Gibbo.

'Finn! Finny!'

Finn turns at the sound of his own name, and sees Wart
cycling frantically towards him, waving an arm to attract
attention. He brings the mountain bike around in a showy
rear-wheel skid, to stop alongside the others.

'Wha'appen?' Finn demands.

'Nothin' . . .' Wart is a bit out of breath. 'I been tryin' to
ring you on the cell phone. Kept gettin' the engaged tone.
Finn, you heard who's comin' to Moss Side?'

Finn shakes his head.

'Go on, see if you can guess! Somebody really big!'

Finn shrugs. 'I dunno. The fuckin' Pope?'

Wart laughs. 'No, Finny, somebody who *matters*. Somebody you really *like*. Somebody who . . .'

'Look, Wart, you wanna just tell me? I'm gettin' a bit
bored with this.'

Wart nods, but he still pauses for dramatic effect.

'Bobby C. Cooper,' he says.

'What?' Finn stares at him. 'Piss off!'

'No, honest, Finn, straight up! He's coming.'

'To Moss Side? I don't believe it.'

'Not just to Moss Side. To *our* estate.'

Finn's eyes narrow suspiciously.

'You been smoking draw?' he mutters.

'No, see, there was these three guys came around this mornin'. Two suits and this weird-looking guy with a camera. They was takin' pictures around Merton – doorways, broken windows, shit like that. Rich fuckers too, they came in a new model BMW. An' this one guy who was takin' the pictures, he told me that Bobby Cooper was goin' to be having his picture taken there in a few days. Said they was . . . scout locators or somethin'?'

'Get away,' says Finn.

'Honest, Finny, that's wha' he tol' me. And what made me believe it was right, this other guy, one of the suits, he tried to shut the first guy up, like he was talkin' too much. That made me think there was somethin' in it.'

'Then what happened?' Gibbo wants to know.

'Oh, then I asked 'em for a fiver to mind the car; but they gave me two quid and a lot of lip. So, when they went off, me and some mates trashed the BMW. Made a right fuckin' mess of it. I got fifty notes for the radio cassette down The Sports.'

'Expensive trip for them,' observes Finn. 'Well, maybe there's something in it. One thing's for sure, if the Rap Terminator's coming to our turf, we gotta meet him.'

'Did I do good?' asks Wart hopefully.

'Yeah, you did all right.' Finn punches him affectionately on the arm. Then he reaches into the sports bag and hands Wart the deliveries package, together with a handwritten list of addresses. 'Divide the list up between you and Tommo,' Finn instructs him. 'Tell everybody it's strictly cash – no exceptions. I'll meet up with you at the Swamp, tomorrow mornin'.'

'OK, Finn.' Wart transfers the pack to his own rucksack and slips the list into the pocket of his AJs. 'What do you think, Finny? You think Bobby C.'s really comin'?'

'Maybe. You push along now, dread. There's a lot to do.' He watches as Wart's diminutive figure pedals furiously away across the forecourt. Then, taking out his handcuffs, he locks the leather handle of the sports bag to his wrist. He nods to Chaz and Gibbo, and turns back to face the club entrance. They walk across to join the crowds of people milling around the doorway, Finn acknowledging the greetings of many of his regular customers.

'Wha'appen, Finny!'

'Hey, mon, you got any of that good wash-rock wid you?'

'Boo yacka, star! Me t'ink you never come!'

By the door, he sends Chaz and Gibbo around to the alley that runs alongside the club. It's his intention now to walk through the length of the place to advertise his presence, then go out through the exit doors and into the alley to start trading.

He pushes, elbows, jostles his way through the crowds in the foyer. Occasionally some hot-headed young dread spins around to look at him challengingly, but most of them nod apologetically when they see who it is; and even the ones who don't know his face can see by the red bandana around his neck that he's a Candy Man, and therefore beyond retribution.

He reaches the swing doors of the dancehall itself and the bouncers wave him through without hesitation. He pushes his way inside, and the combined heat, sounds and smells of the packed club wash over him in welcome. Close up, the sound system is powerful enough to shake his insides, and he finds himself moving to the beat as he makes his way across the packed dance floor. The thick sweet smell of ganja fills his nostrils and makes him feel slightly light-headed as he steps his way closer to the DJ's podium.

The Jamaican operator is a thick-set man with a spectacular mane of dreadlocks. He's wearing a Caribbean shirt that's every bit as loud as his music. Standing beside him is Robbie, the resident DJ. He spots Finn approaching and leans over to shout something in the operator's ear. The big man nods and cues in his microphone.

'Step it up, breddars. Now de party really begin, seen? Dis one feh de young Yard Man with de magic potion!' He segues into a radical remix of Junior Murvin's *Police and Thieves*, the drums and bass punched right up in the mix, and the dancers respond, swaying and skanking to the infectious rhythm.

Finn nods his thanks to the podium and moves on, acknowledging the various signals he gets en route: hand gestures, nods of the head, winks, grins and blown kisses; everyone has their own way of displaying their interest. Drawing nearer to the emergency exit, he glances over his shoulder and sees that a lot of people are trailing after him. He grins. It always put him in mind of a story his mother used to tell him when he was a kid, before she really started fucking herself up with drink and drugs.

It's about this guy called the Pied Piper and how he rids a town of rats by getting them to dance along behind him. Sometimes Finn thinks he knows just how the guy must have felt – except of course, in the story, he doesn't get paid, and he makes all the kids in town follow him the fuck out of there. Finn, on the other hand, always gets paid; his customers can't seem to give him the money fast enough. And for what? To get high for a few hours, maybe even for just a few minutes. Any way you look at it, it doesn't make any sense, but it *works* and you can't argue with that. When you think of all the stupid arseholes who slave their guts out all their lives for some lousy take-home pay and a roof over their heads, it makes you wonder why anybody bothers.

He pushes back the metal bar of the exit and the doors swing open, letting in a welcome rush of fresh air. Outside, Chaz and Gibbo are already dealing. Finn sets his back against the wall, hangs the sports bag around his neck, and he's open for business.

Crack is currently the biggest earner. With a street price of two hundred thousand pounds a kilo, it means he can shift the tiniest bits of wash-rock for twenty quid a go; and Finn knows that people who try it once usually want it again, at any price. But he's got all the other bases covered. A lot of these Rasta men are happy with ganja, and since they consume a lot of it, they buy it in massive quantities.

In a matter of minutes, the contents of the sports bag have diminished by half, and the wad of money Finn is holding has grown out of all proportion to it. Finn has a money-belt around his waist, into which he periodically stuffs the cash, knowing only too well that some dumb arsehole might try and make a grab for the loot and do a runner. It's happened once before, but Gordie saw to it that by the next day the culprit was in no condition to run anywhere; indeed, a full six months after the event, he's still hobbling around the estate on crutches. Retribution like that dissuades other hotheads from trying their luck, and makes Finn's job a whole lot easier. But you always have to be prepared for the unexpected . . .

His first indication that something is wrong is the

unnatural silence that suddenly descends on the alleyway. Where a moment before there was a low hum of conversation mingling with the muffled boom of music from the dancehall, now he's aware of the sound of traffic moving along the main road several hundred yards away. Finn glances up and sees that his queue of customers is breaking up, heading back through the open doors and into the club, as though they've taken fright. His first thought is that the Old Bill are making one of their rare raids, and his instinct is to follow the punters inside, lose himself in the crush on the dance floor; but then he sees Mason and a couple of members of his posse approaching him along the alley.

He glances wildly around. Where are the heavies Gordie has promised him, the guys who are supposed to prevent Mason from coming anywhere near him? Chaz and Gibbo have realised that something is wrong. They move across to stand on either side of Finn, as the last punters disappear through the emergency exit, slamming it shut behind them.

Mason comes to a halt a short distance away. He just stands there grinning at Finn. In the harsh glow of the safety light above the exit, his face looks positively skeletal. Three of his soldiers are ranged behind him.

A movement at the other end of the alley tells Finn that there's no point in making a run for it. Mason has got people in position there, too. It's a bad feeling knowing that he's surrounded.

'Wha'appen, dread?' asks Mason, enjoying the moment. 'Seems to me, bwoy, you don't listen so good. I seems t'recall sayin' that I didn' want you sellin' no shit on me turf.'

Finn glares at him for a moment, telling himself that he must play for time till the heavies get there.

'It ain't your turf,' he replies calmly.

Mason laughs, that weird huffing sound again, his narrow shoulders going up and down.

'Heh heh! You is one funny mudderfucker, seen? But I is here to tell you, bwoy, dis *is* my turf. And I'm taxin' you. Hand over de money-belt.'

'Or what?' Finn prompts him. He reaches under his jacket for the knife, still hoping against hope that Gordie's heavies will appear out of nowhere, like the Seventh Cavalry in an old John Wayne movie.

'I already tell you wha's gonna happen if'n me find you roun' dese parts.' Mason reaches into his own coat and comes out with the gun: a big, squat automatic. He aims it at Finn's chest. 'Now, mudderfucker, you wan' to throw me dat belt?'

Finn swallows hard. He glances at Chaz and Gibbo, sees the looks of fear on their white faces, knows that it is pointless to argue. He reaches down, unbuckles the belt and throws it at Mason's feet. 'De odders too,' says Mason. He waggles the gun impatiently and Chaz and Gibbo hurriedly comply with his request. Mason smiles bleakly. He keeps the gun pointed straight at Finn.

'OK, you taxed us,' mutters Finn. 'Gordie will see to it we get that money back. Every penny.'

Mason shakes his head. 'Ah, I don' t'ink so, bwoy. Me is the Yard Man now. Me already explain dat to Gordie. He see it my way in de end.'

'Well, then, we'll just leave.'

Again, Mason shakes his head. He looks kind of sad, Finn thinks, like he has genuine regrets about what he's doing. 'Las' time me talk wid you, you don' show me the proper respect. An' me warned you what would happen if'n I laid eyes on you again. You had de chance to get out, bwoy, an' you should a took it.' He raises the gun slightly

107

and makes a sucking sound with his teeth. 'No hard feelin's, but I believe I'm gwan' to have to kill you.'

Finn's eyes widen in shock and his heart gives a sudden kick in his chest. Mason is going to burn him! Quite calmly, in front of two witnesses, he is going to blow him the fuck away. Finn can't really believe it's going to happen, but the look on Mason's face doesn't suggest for one moment that he's kidding.

There is a terrible instant which seems to last forever. Finn stands there, cold and numb, with the adrenalin pumping through his system, staring down the barrel of Mason's gun, watching his finger whiten on the trigger, knowing that he should run, or throw himself to the side, or dive forward on to the floor. But every muscle in his body seems locked rigid with terror. His heart is thudding fit to explode in his chest. It's like that moment when the helicopter dropped into view on the *Killing Zone* screen, Finn knowing that he isn't going to make it. Only this time it's different: this time it's for real.

And then it happens. Gibbo throws himself in front of Finn, just as Mason fires. Finn will never know why he does it – whether it's purely instinct or a conscious attempt to save his leader's life. At any rate, Gibbo takes the bullet full in his chest, the impact punching him backwards as powerfully as any right hook, slamming him hard into Finn. The two of them reel against the wall, Finn grabbing instinctively at Chaz, and then the three of them go down in a heap. Finn feels the breath driven out of him, his shoulder burning where it grazes against the bricks. Gibbo arches his body and looks back over his shoulder at Finn, his eyes wide, his mouth open as he emits a horrible croaking sound. He's trying to say something, his hands clawing at the bloody hole in his chest.

Finn tries to push Gibbo off him but his body seems to be made of lead, and then there's another shot. The bullet ploughs into the side of Gibbo's head, snapping it sideways against Finn's face, making stars dance in front of his eyes and spraying him with a warm, pulpy wetness. Finn screams, lying there helpless with Gibbo's dead weight on top of him, aware now that Mason is moving closer, the gun held out in front of him. The red tip of his tongue protrudes between his white and gold teeth and he looks vaguely irritated, like he's trying to thread a needle without success.

'Hol' still, mudderfucker,' he growls.

And then someone throws open the exit door, the heavy wooden frame catching Mason's gun hand a glancing blow. There's the abrupt muzzle flash of the shot, the spanging of a ricocheting bullet bouncing off concrete. Finn hears Mason curse as the gun flies out of his hand and goes clattering into the darkness of the alley.

Finn seizes the moment, throwing Gibbo's heavy body off with an almost superhuman effort. He begins to scramble towards the doorway on his hands and knees. He's just getting to his feet when Chaz vaults over him, knocking him flat again. He sees his friend run headlong into the dancehall, pushing past the astonished Rasta who has just opened the door. Finn is up and after Chaz in an instant, horribly aware of movement in the alley behind him, the sound of Mason barking angry commands to his posse.

He plunges into the scattering crowds inside the club, people who a moment before treated him like some demigod and who now seem very reluctant to stand beside him. A young woman is too slow in making room and he slams against her, sending her sprawling across the polished wooden floor, but there's no time to stop and apologise.

Ahead of him, he sees Chaz disappearing through the swing doors into the foyer, and he follows, aware now of footsteps thudding on the wooden dance floor behind him as Mason's soldiers give chase.

It occurs to him, only now, that he is running for his life.

He crashes through the doors into the crowded foyer. They can't have heard the shooting back there, but they have just seen Chaz race by them and must know that something bad is going down. People duck back against the walls as Finn runs full-tilt for the main doors. He nearly makes it too but, just at the last instant, somebody grabs hold of the sports bag that's still trailing from his left wrist. His forward flight is abruptly interrupted and he's snapped back with a force that almost dislocates his shoulder.

He bellows in pain, but spins around to face his adversary, reaching for the knife with his free hand as he turns. One of Mason's soldiers has caught up with him and is reaching into his jacket for some weapon, a knife or a gun maybe. No time for finesse. Finn uses his own momentum, throwing himself forward and butting the man in the face with his forehead. He feels the man's nose flatten under the impact, hears him grunt in mingled pain and surprise as he sinks to his knees. Finn pulls out the knife and the man's eyes widen in shock. Finn slashes downwards with the broad blade and the man flinches, but Finn is merely cutting through the leather handle of the sports bag. He hears the man give a gasp of relief.

Then Finn is turning away, easily evading the instinctive grab that's made at him. He leaves the sports bag in the man's clutches, and runs out through the main entrance.

He races down the three steps to ground level, and across

the forecourt. Chaz is already long gone, and Finn runs in the direction he imagines Chaz must have taken: into the dark but familiar labyrinth of the Merton Estate. It's the first time in his life that he's eager to get back to it. He hears shouts behind him and, glancing back, sees a couple of dark figures coming out of the club. He hears the crack of a pistol shot but it already seems half-hearted, even when he hears it whining off a brick wall up ahead of him.

He plunges into cover and allows himself to slow his pace a little. Only now, with time to think about it, does it fully occur to him what has happened to Gibbo. Poor stupid, hero-worshipping Gibbo is gone. He has crossed over the line once and for all. That warm sticky covering on Finn's face is all that's left of the kid's brains.

What the fuck? What *happened* back there? Where were the heavies that Gordie promised him? He's been left totally on his own. How have Mason and his soldiers been allowed to walk right in and humiliate Finn in front of everybody?

As he trots along, he keeps turning automatically – left, right, right, left – until he feels sure that Mason and his men won't be able to trail him. In his mind's eye he keeps seeing Gibbo's astonished face, as he looks over his shoulder at Finn, the wide eyes and open mouth seeming to say, 'Christ, look what they've done to me, Finn! They've fucking well *killed* me!'

Finn slows to a walk now and thinks about his humiliation, the total loss of face he's just suffered. *On his own turf*, for fuck's sake! Made to run like some pathetic kid!

It's this more than the thought of Gibbo's death that makes his eyes fill up with tears. And then he's crying like he hasn't cried since he was nine years old, slipping into the dark shadow of a block of flats in case anybody should see him. He crouches down in darkness, buries his face in his hands and weeps uncontrollably, and it takes him some time to get hold of himself.

In the end, he simply thinks of Bobby Cooper in *No Quarter*, what *he* would do in a situation like this, and he knows that Bobby wouldn't waste any time in planning his revenge. That helps. He gets back to his feet and wipes his eyes on the sleeve of his jacket, feeling a little better now. Yeah, be cool like Bobby, who always knows what to do. OK, so he's taken a licking, but one battle doesn't win the war, and he's not finished yet – no way.

He leans over and spits on to the pavement. Then he walks on and begins to draw up his plans.

Chapter Twelve

Standing in the crowd by the arrivals barrier, Nick reminded himself that this wouldn't exactly be the first time he had set eyes on Bobby C. Cooper. He'd watched him performing his latest hits on various TV programmes over the past year or so, and had even gone so far as to hire a copy of *No Quarter* from his local video store. That was an attempt to learn something about the man whose visit he would soon be handling, but he hadn't liked the movie much. Oh, he'd understood why it had been so successful, but he had found Cooper's performance smug and over-bearing, and had thought the film's violent message totally reprehensible. Still, he'd told himself, Cooper was simply playing a part; it didn't necessarily follow that he was the same macho, misogynistic thug that he portrayed in the movie – did it?

And then Cooper came strutting into the terminal, and Nick had some terrible doubts on that score.

A roar of approval came from the mouths of hundreds of young fans fenced off behind safety barriers and held back by harassed-looking policemen. God knows how the kids had got wind of this – Nick and Terry had done their best to keep a tight lid on it – but Cooper's fans had been arriving since the early hours of the morning, and it had soon become apparent that extra security would be needed.

113

Bobby Cooper paused to acknowledge the mass greeting, raising one fist in a Black Power salute. He was a big, beefy individual, heavily muscled around the arms and shoulders. He wore his hair cropped close to the skull, giving himself a distinctly bullet-headed appearance. His eyes were hidden behind the inevitable designer shades, and his wide mouth seemed fixed in a perpetual sneer.

He was dressed in the impeccably casual style that only the very rich seemed able to achieve: a grey marl tracksuit under a black silk hooded bomber jacket. On his feet were the expensive basketball boots he currently endorsed, and an even more expensive travel bag in crocodile skin was slung carelessly over one shoulder. He had no accessories unless you counted the two bodyguards who flanked him, massive guys who stood head and shoulders above the man they were paid to protect. They too wore shades, and were glancing all around them as they approached the barriers, as though expecting an attack at any moment.

Behind them, as if in deliberate contrast, walked a small, tubby white man in a grey silk Armani suit. He seemed almost dwarf-like compared to his companions, his torso and legs unnaturally short, so that his arms hung almost to his knees. His hair was confined to a few grey curls clustered around the sides of his head and the place where his neck should be. Since the latter was virtually non-existent, his large, pugnacious face appeared to sit directly on his narrow shoulders. For all his lack of height, he gazed around Terminal Two like he was thinking of buying it, his mouth working rhythmically around a wad of chewing gum.

This, Nick decided, was Gabe Rothman, Bobby's manager – the man who had sold Cooper to the movies, and consequently sent an already successful career hurtling into the stratosphere. By all accounts, Rothman was a difficult customer, and Nick's recent phone conversations with him had confirmed that. Nick had spent a lot of time persuading the little man that his client would have nothing but the best for his stay in Manchester. The Midland Hotel? Certainly! A whole floor for the exclusive use of Bobby and his entourage? Yes, of course, something would be arranged! Fresh flowers in the rooms, changed daily? A fully stocked drinks cabinet? Supervision of all food by Bobby's personal chef? No problem! Nick had found himself wondering if Ajay's bill wouldn't hit *three* million by the time Rothman was finished.

Behind Rothman trailed the half-dozen individuals (all male) who comprised Bobby's 'posse' and accompanied him everywhere: the aforementioned chef, his personal fitness trainer, his personal assistant, his hairdresser, his wardrobe assistant, and his biographer. Looking at this motley collection of scruffs pushing luggage trolleys in their employer's wake, Nick reflected wryly that 'Bobby's mates' might be a more accurate description of them. Why would a man with a crewcut need the services of a hairdresser, for Christ's sake? And watching Cooper as he prowled through the barriers towards him, Nick told himself that this didn't look like a man who cared too much about having fresh flowers in his hotel room.

Nick held up the card neatly printed '*Mr Cooper and Entourage*'. This had been Terry's idea. He'd pointed out that since the Americans had never laid eyes on their hosts, Nick would need something to distinguish him from all the other punters waiting around at the air terminal. 'Don't want his bodyguards jumping on you, do you?' Terry had added. At the time, Nick had laughed but, looking at those two guys face to face, it didn't seem quite so funny now.

Gabe Rothman spotted the sign and darted past Cooper to shake Nick's hand. His own hand, though plump and childlike, had a surprisingly powerful grip.

'Welcome to Manchester, Mr Rothman. I'm Nick Saunders from *Futures*.'

'Pleased to make your acquaintance.' Rothman beamed up at Nick. He had a deep, rasping voice with a marked Bronx accent.

'Good trip over?' Nick asked him.

Rothman shrugged, made a dismissive gesture with his free hand.

'We left, we got here,' he said gloomily. 'The food was lousy, we'd already seen the inflight movie, and the air hostess had herpes. What else can I tell ya?' He released Nick's hand and then, taking a step back, he cleared his throat. 'But now, Mr Saunders, let me introduce you to the man you've been waiting to meet.' He said this with an exaggerated, theatrical tone, as though somebody had just turned a spotlight on to him. 'Mr Saunders, here's the homeboy, the Sultan of Soul, headmaster of the High School of Cool, the Rap Terminator himself . . . Mr Bobby C. Cooper!'

He stretched the last word out as though he was a ringmaster at the circus, as though Cooper was actually waiting out in the wings rather than standing right behind him. Nick felt decidedly embarrassed by the routine, and was relieved to see that Cooper didn't respond to it with a series of cartwheels. He just shuffled forward and grunted something that Nick didn't quite catch. Then his huge right fist closed around Nick's hand and exerted what seemed a ludicrously inappropriate amount of force. Nick couldn't see Cooper's eyes, but he thought he felt them appraising him from behind the shades.

Nick hissed a welcome through clenched teeth. 'Nice to meet you.'

'Yeah, it must be,' said Cooper, with no apparent hint of irony. He jerked a thumb at the two muscular giants behind him. 'This here's Amos 'n' Andy,' he said, and Nick wasn't sure if these were (by some appalling coincidence) their *real* names or simply a derogatory alias that Cooper had invented for them. He suspected the latter. Amos was tall, lean and predatory, built like a basketball player. Andy was big in a different way: shorter by six inches but heavier by maybe ten or fifteen stone.

'A pleasure.' Nick held out his hand to shake but the two men kept their massive arms folded across their chests. They were studying Nick as though they suspected he might be carrying a concealed weapon.

'Er, yes, well we've a half-hour or so before the press conference. We have a room all fixed up across the way and we thought you might like a bite to eat and a drink before we go in to talk to the press. My partner Terry Littlewood is there and, of course, Ajay Sanjari . . .'

'San-jar-ee?' Cooper looked amused. 'What kinda name is that? Sounds like something you'd order in a Vietnamese restaurant.'

Rothman laughed, but Nick noticed he didn't look particularly amused.

'Mr Sanjari is the gentleman who brought us over here,' he explained. 'The gentleman whose jeans you are going to model.'

'Yeah, no shit?' Cooper gave Rothman a look like it was the first he'd heard of that. Then he shrugged, and slapped Nick on the shoulder with a force that nearly dropped him to his knees. 'Where's this drink then, homeboy? Let's see some of this British horse-speet-alitee that I keep hearing about!'

Nick gestured questioningly at the members of Cooper's entourage, but he made a dismissive gesture. 'Oh, don't worry about them, Nick-O-Las. They's just dumb niggers. Ain't no need for a nice white boy like you to shake hands with trash like that. Besides, they'll follow us to hell and back for a free drink. Come on, let's get to it. My tongue is just about dried out!'

Nick turned and led the way across the terminal.

'What about your fans?' he asked. ' Perhaps you'd like to say a few words, sign some autographs...'

Cooper grimaced. 'Say what?' He looked at Nick as though he wasn't quite right in the head. 'Are you kidding me? I don't do that kind of shit any more. I got too big for that. Hey, watch this!' He lifted a hand and waved to the kids as he walked by – and they went wild, beginning to jostle the line of police that was holding them back. Many were shouting out to Cooper and waving their autograph books at him. He winked at Nick. 'See, that's all you got to give 'em. The bare minimum.'

'Very economical,' said Nick. He dropped back a little to walk alongside Rothman.

'Not a very big turnout,' observed Rothman, nodding at the crowd.

'I'd say it's surprisingly big considering we didn't tell anyone it was happening. Christ knows how they found out.'

Rothman grinned.

'Oh, fans are peculiar animals, Mr Saunders. They've got ways of finding out stuff. Most probably some security guy who works here mentioned it to his kid, and that kid went out and told all his friends, and they went out and told all *their* friends ... me, I worry when a thing gets too low-key. After all, those are the people who put Bobby C. where he is today. A star of his magnitude can't afford to be too long out of the public eye.' He glanced slyly at Nick. 'I take it you've warned the press off asking certain questions relating to Bobby's ah ... misunderstandings with the American legal system?'

Interesting way of putting it, thought Nick.

'It isn't quite as straightforward as that, Mr Rothman. British journalists have minds of their own. But obviously we've done our best to persuade them to concentrate on the reason he's here: to promote AJ jeans.'

'Well, I guess we'll just have to see how it pans out.'

Up ahead there was a sudden commotion. Nick saw that a teenage girl had somehow managed to scramble over the crash barrier and elude the policemen who were fronting it. Now she was making a run for Cooper, her hands outstretched to grab at him. But she'd reckoned without his bodyguards. Amos threw out a hand the size of a catcher's mitt and grabbed her around the waist. She squawked indignantly as she was lifted clear of the floor. Then, with an almost leisurely motion, the man half turned and threw her headlong back the way she had come. She went sliding across the polished floor in an ungainly sprawl, and crashed heavily against the barrier. She was immediately pounced on by a couple of policemen, who manhandled her back over the rails.

Nick caught a glimpse of her face as she sank into the rest of the crowd. She looked stunned, but whether from the suddenness of the incident or whether she had hurt herself when she hit the barrier, it was hard to tell. Nick hurried forward to confront Amos.

'Was that strictly necessary?' he asked. 'She was only after an autograph or something.'

The big man glared down at Nick, as though deliberating whether he should receive similar treatment.

'She gettin' too close to Bobby C.,' he growled in a slow voice that suggested he didn't have an over-abundance of working brain cells. 'She coulda hurt 'im.'

'Yes, but really, she was only a *kid*!'

'Hey, chill out, Nick-O-Las!' Cooper was moving back now to slap Nick on the shoulder, a habit that was already becoming very annoying. 'Don't you be givin' Amos no grief, now. Boy's just doin' what I pay him to do!' He and Amos did a little routine: banging their clenched fists together, then slapping each other's palms. 'Respect,' said Cooper. He slipped an arm around Nick's shoulders in an unconvincing show of bonhomie. 'Now, which way is this hospitality room, bro?'

Scowling, Nick pointed to a doorway on the other side of the terminal, which was flanked by a couple of bored-looking security guards.

'Through there,' he said.

'OK, what say we walk along together while Bobby C. puts you straight on a few things.' Cooper began to move and Nick was obliged to go with him. 'Point *numero uno*, these two niggers are paid to look after me. They do a good job; I ain't got no criticisms. So I'd appreciate it if you'd keep your nose *out*, you dig?'

Nick glared at him. 'My only point is that he was being a little heavy-handed. As one of the people who have to organise your visit, I don't think it's a good idea to get off on the wrong foot. If that girl had been injured—'

'Nicky, baby, *listen* to me!' Cooper was still smiling, but there wasn't much humour in his voice. 'A lot of bad shit's gone down for me over the las' coupla months. When somebody gets this big there's always people wanna see him fall. I did a gig in Detroit a while back and a little girl no older than that one come at me with a fuckin' *knife*. And you can bet I was real glad that I had Amos 'n' Andy on my team that time. I've kind've evolved my own way of doin' things and I'd 'preciate it if you'd just let me get on with it, OK?'

'No, it's not OK! I've been paid to act as your PR while you're here, and that means—'

'That means doodly-squat, as far as I'm concerned. Look, we're gonna get on just fine, Nick-O-Las, long as we're clear on one point. I don't need no fuckin' wet nurse, right?' He waved a hand at the entourage behind him. 'Those guys back there are like family to me, they take care of me, keep me up and runnin' like clockwork. All I need from you is times and locations. Stick to that and we'll get along just fine.'

They had reached the doorway now. Cooper paused and turned back to give his fans a last Black Power salute, eliciting a roar of enthusiasm from the kids he'd all but ignored. Then, grinning, he pushed through the swing doors into the hospitality room, followed closely by Amos and Andy and Gabe Rothman.

Nick was left standing there, wondering if he would get through the next two weeks without suffering a nervous breakdown. With a sigh, he turned back to organise Cooper's entourage and their baggage. No sense in kicking against the pricks, he told himself. He was just going to have to make the best of it; but he suspected that the next two weeks were going to be very hard work indeed.

Chapter Thirteen

By the time Nick made it to the hospitality room, the initial introductions had already been made. As he entered, Terry was just reaching the final stages of the lengthy welcoming speech he had prepared. Cooper was standing beside Gabe Rothman, hands in pockets, looking faintly bemused by it all.

The rest of his entourage had congregated around the cloth-covered table where drinks and a cold buffet had been laid out. They were laying into the provisions like hungry wolves, as though they hadn't seen food or drink for weeks. Nick managed to rescue a glass of wine for himself, and went to stand beside Alan Richards, who was watching the proceedings from the other side of the room. A large white surgical dressing covered most of his right ear, so he needed to crane his head about in order to pick up any conversation.

'. . . so it only remains for me, on behalf of *Futures*, to welcome you to Manchester and to add that I hope you have a fruitful and rewarding visit here,' concluded Terry.

Polite applause rippled through the room.

'Fuckin' A,' muttered Cooper. He began to make a move towards the refreshment table, but at that moment Gabe Rothman cleared his throat loudly, and Nick saw him pull a sheet of paper from his jacket pocket. The manager put on a pair of gold-rimmed glasses and began to read his reciprocal speech.

'On 6 September 1620, the *Mayflower* sailed from Plymouth Ho to America. At last here's our chance to return the favour . . .'

Nick resisted the impulse to groan, but instead laughed obligingly with the rest of the crowd. He took this opportunity to look around the packed room and see who else was there. It seemed to be the usual rent-a-mob invariably pulled in for such occasions – actors from the local TV soap opera, some alternative and not so alternative comedians, prominent businessmen and their wives, prominent businesswomen and their husbands, club owners, cinema managers, town councillors, and a few professional liggers already the worse for wear after too much alcohol. For the moment the journalists were safely locked up in the adjoining room, with their own supply of food and drink, awaiting the start of the press conference.

Nick spotted Ajay Sanjari standing just off to one side of the group comprising the reception committee, one arm ostentatiously draped around the narrow waist of Maria Sweeny, a tall photographic model of some notoriety. She had a mane of blonde hair, dazzling teeth and long legs that disappeared into a little black dress and appeared to terminate somewhere in the region of her thorax. Though not yet a household name, she was nonetheless successful, had recently modelled for the cover of *Elle* and had just signed a contract to promote a new range of cosmetics. For some reason, she always put Nick in mind of a racehorse – a notion reinforced whenever she laughed. She was currently sipping at a glass of Perrier water in an exaggeratedly theatrical manner, as though she was auditioning for a part in some Greek tragedy. The way Sanjari was posing beside her suggested to Nick that Maria was really just another of his acquisitions, like the Roller with the AJ1 number plate. He reminded himself that Sanjari had lost Helen and instead gained a celebrity model, but Nick was in no doubt that Ajay had got the worst of the deal.

'...and finally,' said Gabe Rothman, 'to use one of Bobby's own catchphrases, "if the mother ain't busted, why fix it?"'

There was a puzzled silence as the crowd absorbed this no-doubt useful piece of information, expecting perhaps that Rothman might go on to explain what that had to do with the price of bacon. But, no, he'd clearly finished, folding his sheet of paper and beaming at his audience like a bespectacled little Buddha.

Nick handed his glass to Alan, and dutifully led the applause. After a few seconds, others joined in.

An anticipatory silence followed, and all eyes turned expectantly to Bobby Cooper himself. He frowned, glanced quickly around. 'Yeah, well,' he muttered. 'I ain't no speech-maker. I go along with what Gabe said. Now, what does a guy have to do to get a drink around here? Go down on the fuckin' waiter?'

The embarrassment was palpable, but Cooper didn't seem to notice. In the ensuing silence, he pushed his way towards the refreshment table. Rothman's face had reddened, and he gave Terry an apologetic shrug as if to say, 'There's the situation, what can I do about it?' Eventually the hubbub of conversation returned but, even over that, Nick could hear Bobby Cooper complaining loudly to the barman.

'Hey, homeboy, you got any beer? I don't drink this shit! *Lager*, what's that? You got any American beer? Schlitz, Budweiser, somethin' like that? ... Yeah, yeah, gimme one of those. Hey, this is warm. Whatsa matter, you don't serve *cold* beer in this country?'

Nick glanced at Alan and grimaced. 'Oh, this is going to be fun,' he observed drily.

'He's not exactly mister congenial,' admitted Alan, returning Nick's glass of wine.

'You haven't heard the half of it. I just had a pep-talk out there about keeping out of his way. Keeps calling me Nick-O-Las. Christ! I've only known him ten minutes and already I feel like punching him in the mouth.'

'Maybe he's jet-lagged,' suggested Alan.

'Hmm. And maybe he's just an arsehole. I strongly suspect the latter.'

Ajay Sanjari and Maria Sweeny glided across to join Nick and Alan.

'Well, he seems OK,' said Sanjari brightly, leaving Nick unsure if he was being ironic or not. 'A man of few words.'

'Yeah, but very *intense*,' said Maria who, despite her exotic looks, had an accent that could only have originated in Manchester's Wythenshawe district. No wonder that in her upcoming TV commercials she wasn't actually required to say anything. 'I think people like that actually don't 'ave to say *nothing*, right, 'cos it's all in their body language, ennit?'

Nick glanced across at Cooper, whose body language currently seemed to be telling him to drain a bottle of beer in a single swallow, his Adam's apple chugging rhythmically.

'Oh, he's poetry in motion,' said Nick.

Terry was talking intently to Cooper, doubtless trying to persuade him to circulate.

Nick realised that he should be trying to help his partner but, just at this minute, he didn't feel inclined.

126

'You been introduced yet?' he asked Sanjari.

'Not yet.' Sanjari smiled dismissively. 'I don't want to crowd him. There's plenty of time.' He then made an exaggerated display of looking around the room. 'Helen not here, then? Thought you might have brought her along to this one – to meet a genuine Hollywood star?'

Nick looked into his glass for a moment and mentally counted to ten. 'Believe it or not, an eight-months-pregnant woman isn't over eager about crowded gatherings like this one. Besides, I'm sure she wouldn't be remotely interested.'

Sanjari shrugged. 'Nick and Helen are about to have a child,' he told Maria, rather unnecessarily.

'Our second,' Nick added.

Maria pulled an expression suggesting she had just been told that Nick and Helen liked wallowing in dog shit.

'Ooh, I just *couldn't*,' she said. 'I mean, I think kids are sweet n' all, but . . . to get all swelled up out of shape and have somethin' moving around inside you . . . like in *Alien*, you know?'

Nick glared at her, but was prevented from saying anything appropriate by the arrival of Terry, who was virtually dragging Bobby Cooper along with him.

'Now then, Bobby, here's somebody you've been wanting to meet . . .'

'Hey, yeah, way to go!' Cooper seemed suddenly very animated. Sanjari held out his hand to shake, but Cooper stepped smartly past him and took Maria's hand instead. 'Hello, baby! Where've you been all my life?' he purred.

Nick stood back a little to enjoy the spectacle of Sanjari's crestfallen look quickly masked behind a stupid grin that tried – but didn't quite succeed – in hiding his displeasure.

Maria wore an embarrassed smile, her face colouring up, though you could see that really she *loved* this, flattered by his attention.

Alan tried not to laugh, clearly wishing he'd had a camera to capture this moment for posterity.

Terry's face was an absolute picture, his mouth hanging open, his eyes bulging as if he'd just made some *faux pas* of gargantuan dimensions.

Only Cooper remained oblivious to it all, pressing his attentions on Maria with unabashed enthusiasm.

'Holy Jesus, you're a tall gal, aintcha? Shit, you could be a fashion model, you know?'

'I am, actually,' protested Maria.

'Yeah, yeah. Get a little more meat on your bones, you'd do all right. I like a woman's got a little more to grab hold of, you get my meaning?'

Judging by the expression of outrage on Maria's face, she got his meaning all right.

Terry, sensing imminent disaster, made a desperate attempt to intervene.

'Er, Bobby, let me introduce you to Ajay Sanjari, the man responsible for bringing you to Manchester!'

'Yeah, sure. Just hold your hosses, homeboy. I'm trying to get acquainted with this young lady, here.'

'But I'm *with Ajay*,' protested Maria feebly.

'That a fact?' Cooper glanced at Sanjari scornfully, then turned away as if dismissing him. 'You know ... Sorry, I didn't catch your name ... ?'

'Maria.'

'You know, Maria, now I come to think of it, I've seen your face someplace. A magazine, somethin' like that? Let me ask you a serious question: you ever thought about makin' movies?'

'Oh, I don't know if I'd have the talent.'

'Honey, you've got more than enough, if you know what I mean, and I think you do! Maybe we oughta have a word with Gabe over there – see if he can think of a way to cut you off a slice of the action.'

'Well, I . . .'

Sanjari was now glaring at both Terry and Nick, in a silent appeal for help. He looked about to cry.

'Well,' said Terry, 'Bobby, perhaps we'd better think about getting you and Ajay into that press conference, now – hmm?'

Bobby waved a hand at him.

'Gimme a minute, will ya? Me and the lady are talkin' *business* here.' Now he leaned forward and started whispering right into Maria Sweeny's ear – a big leering grin as he spoke.

Maria's face passed through several shades of red, her eyes wide as though she couldn't quite believe what she was hearing. She took a step back and stared at him in apparent disgust.

'How *dare* you!' she cried at last.

'Hey, now, come on, honey. That was a *compliment*. Be nice. You know you *want* to be nice.' He slipped an arm around her shoulders, one hand casually cupping her left breast. She just stood there with an expression suggesting she didn't believe it was happening. At this point, even Sanjari was prompted to intervene.

'Now look here,' he said pompously. 'I think you've gone far enough!' He stepped forward and grabbed Cooper firmly by the arm.

Nick had just started thinking this might not be the wisest move in the world, when there was a commotion in the crowd behind him. For such big men, Amos and Andy moved with surprising speed: Sanjari was jerked backwards by a huge hand on the collar of his stylish jacket. His back hit the carpet with an impact that drove the breath out of his body, then Andy was pinning him down, one hand around his throat, the other massive fist raised to strike once the order was given. Amos had turned to face Nick and Terry, his arms held out from his sides as though anticipating that they might try to back Sanjari up.

A deadly silence fell on the room, in which the only sound was an audible gulp from Sanjari.

'For Christ's sake,' he spluttered, 'I was only . . .'

Andy raised his fist threateningly, and Sanjari abandoned his attempt to explain. In the silence, they heard footsteps as Gabe Rothman hurried over, a look of irritation on his face.

'Bobby, what have I told you about this kind of thing, for Jesus' sake?' He nudged Nick in the ribs. 'Who is that?' He pointed at the prone figure.

'That's Mr Sanjari,' said Nick, trying hard not to sound too smug.

'Oh my God!' Now Rothman was slapping Andy around the head and shoulders, attempting to pull him off Ajay. 'Let him up, you gorilla! Let him up, this is the man who bankrolled this whole deal! Bobby, for Chrissakes, how could you let this happen? How could you? Haven't I warned you about keeping these guys under control?'

Now Rothman was helping Sanjari to his feet, was actually mopping at his jacket with a serviette, where he had spilled a drink on himself.

'A thousand apologies, Mr Sanjari! What can I tell you, these boys, they're so goddamn *protective*!'

'No problem,' muttered Sanjari. 'A misunderstanding, that's all.'

But Nick could see that he was absolutely blazing, humiliated in front of everyone, and by the very person he'd spent a fortune flying over. Worse still, Cooper didn't seem to be very sorry about the whole business. Hands on hips, he just stood there, grinning insolently at Sanjari.

'Hey, homeboy, kinda ruffled up your feathers a little, huh? Those boys've mine are always on a hair trigger. Might be advisable to keep an eye out for 'em in future.'

'I'll remember that,' said Sanjari coldly. He turned and stalked towards the exit, closely pursued by Terry, Gabe Rothman and – after a moment of indecision – Maria Sweeny.

Cooper looked at Nick and Alan, feigning an expression of wide-eyed astonishment.

'Shit, that boy looks *upset*,' he observed. 'Think it was somethin' I said?'

Nick worked hard to keep from smiling. Against all his expectations, he was surprised to discover that some small part of him was definitely warming to Bobby C. Cooper.

Chapter Fourteen

Gibbo is lying across Finn, and Finn can't push him off. His skinny body seems to have turned into a crushing dead weight. Finn feels his breath being squeezed out through clenched teeth; he can feel his ribs cracking under the pressure, and a thick, acrid sweat bathes his body. Mason is coming closer, but instead of a gun he carries an axe. His muttering is so low that Finn can't make out what he's saying.

Now there's a creaking sound as Gibbo turns his head to look over his shoulder – at Finn. His forehead is split open like a ripe watermelon, blood and brains trailing down across his face, yet he looks quite happy with the situation. He thrusts out a hand, palm uppermost, and Finn sees that it's full of coins. They glitter enticingly in the gloom of the alleyway.

'Play again?' Gibbo asks him.

Finn shakes his head. He is trying his utmost to throw Gibbo off him, but his sweaty hands can't seem to get a purchase on the slippery body. He realises that both of them are naked, and that comes as a real surprise to him.

'What's wrong, Finny?' asks Gibbo. 'Don't you love me any more?'

'You're crushing me,' gasps Finn. 'Get off me.'

'Play again, Finny? Play again?'

Gibbo cranes his neck forward and kisses Finn full on the lips, filling his mouth with the coppery taste of warm blood. Finn gasps, tries to pull away, but the back of his head is already grinding against the wall, and Gibbo is kissing him harder now, pushing his tongue into Finn's mouth, and Finn can't breathe. He can't get away from that foul taste—

Blood, it's his blood and brains, I can't . . .

—choking him, and Gibbo's hands are around his neck, in his hair, mouth like a vacuum now, a terrible numbness spreading outwards from those slippery lips as the shadow of an axe rises above them . . .

Finn jolts awake at the sound of a key in the door. He lies there a moment, wrapped in the sleeping bag stretched out on the old, soiled mattress, staring wildly about him at the unfamiliar interior of the Swamp. This is what the kids call their current hideout, a derelict fifth-floor flat in Van Dyke Plaza. They keep a few things here for emergencies – and last night's disaster certainly falls into *that* category.

Finn has decided not to go back to his parents' place, as Mason is sure to come looking for him there. Finn is fairly certain that the Yardie doesn't know about the Swamp.

Only, there's that sound again: somebody coming in through the front door now, and moving quietly along the hallway towards the door of the back room – where Finn is lying.

He unzips the sleeping bag and slips cautiously out of it, reaching for the handle of the knife. It's morning, and light is streaming in through the grimy French windows that lead out on to a rickety wooden balcony, so he's able to place his stockinged feet accurately on the rubble-strewn floor as he tiptoes through its covering of discarded chocolate wrappers, Coke cans and building rubble. He takes up a position beside the still-closed door, his back against the wall. This makes him think of his recent dream, but he feels ashamed and pushes that away from him. He's no shirt-lifter, so he can't figure out why he would have a dream like that; and he's also horribly aware that when he woke up, just for a moment or two, he had an erection, and that worries him more than anything, like he *enjoyed* Gibbo kissing him or something. But who could ever figure dreams, anyway?

He listens intently. Whoever is now approaching is taking his time, trying not to make much noise. But the warped, unseasoned floorboards of the hallway betray every step. Finn draws the knife silently from its leather sheath. He tenses himself as the door slowly opens and a figure appears in the frame.

Finn jumps forward, throws an arm around the newcomer's neck, and pulls him headlong into the room. He slams him up against a wall, holding the blade of the knife against his throat.

'Jesus, Finn,' gasps Chaz. 'It's only me!'

Finn stares at him for several moments before he speaks. 'Yeah, I remember you. You're the cunt who ran off and left me last night.' Finn doesn't relinquish his hold.

Chaz's eyes bulge in disbelief.

'Hey, come on, Finn. It was every man for himself!' he protests. 'You'd have done the same!'

'Think so?' Finn glares at Chaz for a moment, then snorts, releases his hold, turns away. 'One thing you always do in a rumble: look after your mates.'

'Like you looked after Gibbo, you mean?' sneers Chaz.

Finn looks down at his bare feet. 'There was nothin' I could do about that. He just jumped in the way...' He makes a small, dismissive gesture with one hand. 'I never asked him to do it, did I? He just ... pitched in.'

'Fuckin' hell, Finn, the bastards *killed* him.'

135

Finn nods, goes across to sit down on the mattress. He begins to put on his trainers.

'I *did* notice,' he says. He takes his time lacing up the trainers. 'Question I keep asking myself is what happened to the hired muscle Gordie promised us?'

'It was bollocks; that's what happened! He just told you what you wanted to hear. Bastard didn't give a shit what happened to us.'

But Finn is shaking his head. 'It ain't like him to lie. He's never done it before. And besides, he wouldn't want to risk losin' all that money, would he? I need to talk to him, find out the score.'

'And what are we supposed to do in the meantime, eh? They took our turf. They ... they just took it.' Chaz is standing there, his hands on his hips. The look on his face says that he can't believe it has really happened. 'You see the telly this morning?'

Finn gestures around the empty room and gives Chaz a scornful look. 'See a TV anywhere?' he asks.

'It was on the news, wasn't it? Cameras outside the Nile Club, filth crawling all over the place. Said a boy of twelve was killed, but it didn't mention Gibbo's name or nothin'. Police was appealin' for witnesses.'

Finn laughs. 'They'll be lucky! Nobody ever sees nothin' round here. Gibbo'll be just another dead dope dealer. Cops ain't gonna lose much sleep over that.'

Chaz moves closer, hands on hips.

'But Finn, what we gonna do? They had shooters, just like everybody said. People tried to warn us, but—'

'Shut it, will you! You're doin' my head in.' Finn is desperately trying to think his way through this one. If Gordie had only given him the gun when he asked for it, at least they'd have had a chance. Mason's all talk, he said,

136

but that bastard pulled the trigger without batting an eyelid. Now Finn has to find a way out of this mess . . .

The key turns in the lock and footsteps come pounding along the hallway. Wart and Tommo burst into the room, in a state of high excitement. Wart has a nasty-looking bruise on his cheek.

'Finn, Finn, we just been taxed!' he yells.

'What?' Finn scrambles up off the mattress. 'What you talkin' about?'

'Me and Tommo, they was waiting for us, the bastards. They had a car an' they got everything. I tried to stop 'em but we couldn't, Finn. They said it was their turf and—'

'Shut up!' Finn slaps Wart hard on the side of the head – silencing him. Then he glances at Tommo, knowing that he's the less excitable of the two. 'Talk,' he says.

Tommo pushes his spectacles higher up his nose, with his index finger, an habitual gesture.

'I called at Wart's house this morning,' he says. 'We were going to bring you the money we collected last night. These black guys were waiting for us around the corner, dragged us off our bikes before we knew what was happening. They took our money-belts . . .'

'Jesus,' says Chaz. 'Oh, that's just great, isn't it? Now we've got *nothing*. Those bastards have taken the lot! Shit, shit, shit!' He wheels around and aims a kick at the wall, bringing down chunks of plaster. He's steaming.

'There weren't nothin' we could do,' insists Tommo. 'They had a shooter. Said they were goin' to count to ten, and if we didn't hand 'em the dosh . . .' He makes a familiar motion, drawing his index finger sideways across his throat.

'I gave 'em some lip,' announces Wart defiantly. 'One of

'em hit me, see?' He points out the bruise on his cheek. 'Anyway, we got back on our bikes and fucked off out of there.'

Finn has a sudden panic. He grabs Wart by the lapels of his jacket. 'They didn't follow you, did they?' he asks.

Wart looks at him, uncomprehending.

'Uh?' he grunts.

'Wart, tell me they didn't follow you! We can't let them know about this place!'

'It's all right,' Tommo assures him. 'They were in a car. We came a route they couldn't follow.' He's staring at Finn, worried by this unfamiliar display of fear from a leader who's always seemed so much in control.

Finn relaxes a little. He lets go of Wart and tousles his hair, trying to mask his funk with a display of affection. Wart is looking around the room now, as though he's just missed something.

'Where's Gibbo?' he asks Chaz.

Chaz laughs bitterly and points at Finn. 'Ask *him*,' he suggests.

Wart looks puzzled. He turns to face Finn. 'What does he mean?'

Finn decides there's no point in beating about the bush. 'He means that Gibbo's dead.'

Wart and Tommo exchange bemused glances. Tommo breaks into a smile – but the smile fades when he sees Finn's expression remain grim.

'Dead?' echoes Wart, trying the unfamiliar word for size, and not having an awful lot of fun with it. 'You mean, he—'

'I mean *dead*,' snarls Finn irritably. 'What the fuck do you *think* I mean? They shot him last night, after you left. Robbed us and . . . and killed Gibbo. Me and Chaz made a run for it.'

Wart still doesn't seem to comprehend. 'You mean, *really* dead? Like he's not coming back again, not ever. Like ... like my Grandad?'

'That's what he means,' says Chaz. 'It was on the telly this mornin'. Didn't you see it?'

Wart shakes his head numbly. 'Well ... where is he now?'

'How should I know?' snaps Finn. 'The fuck difference does it make? He's dead, right. Otis Mason shot him. He'd have shot me too, if he'd been any quicker.'

'Or you'd been any slower,' Chaz reminds him.

'You ... you *ran*?' Wart is taking time to absorb all this. It has never occurred to him that Finn McManus is capable of being beaten – not by anybody.

'Sure we ran! What did you expect us to do? He had a gun, we only had knives, and we'd just seen him blow Gibbo's head off. Anybody would have run. *Anybody*!'

There's a silence now, the four of them standing there in the empty, rubble-littered flat, trying to come to terms with the enormity of what has happened. Wart groans. He walks across to the mattress and sits down heavily. His face has gone very pale. He puts his head between his knees. After a few moments, his shoulders start to move up and down, and they hear the muffled sounds of his sobs. The older boys ignore him.

Tommo is the first to ask the inevitable question. 'So what happens now?'

Finn shrugs. 'First thing, I've got to talk to Gordie, tell him what's happened. I think I can get him to give me some shooters. He's got some stashed up at his place. After that we'll see about taking our turf back off those bastards.'

'They've got more people than we have,' Chaz reminds him.

'S'OK. Gordie can recruit some more soldiers.'

'Yeah? Like the people he sent us last night?'

'I already told you, there must have been some kind of cock-up. Gordie wouldn't drop us in it – not on purpose.'

Chaz doesn't look convinced by this.

'He's like every other one of 'em: just lookin' after number one. And poor bloody Gibbo—'

'Dead?' repeats Wart. He's got his tears under control now but is still desperately hoping he's misunderstood it all.

Chaz glances at him scornfully.

'Be told,' he says.

Tommo raises the point they've all been thinking about.

'We're skint,' he announces.

Everybody looks at him.

'Well, *think* about it. I don't know about you guys, but my old man ain't going to be very happy about losing a hundred quid a week.'

Finn narrows his eyes.

'A hundred?' he mutters.

'That's how much I tell him I get. But it don't matter. If I go home and say there's nothing for him to drink with, an' put on the gee-gees, he's gonna go ape-shit.'

Finn frowns. He's thinking about his own parents, knowing that they'll go ape-shit too, but for entirely different reasons.

'Tommo's right,' says Wart. 'My mum's bought loads of stuff on the drip: furniture an' that. I take care of the payments ... least, I *used* to. I got a few quid put by, but that's all.'

Everyone looks at Chaz, but whatever money problems he has, he's keeping them to himself.

'We're *fucked*,' he says quietly.

Finn waves a hand dismissively. Deep down he's on the

edge of panicking, but he can't let them see that. They're looking to him to keep his head, and lead them out of this.

'Money's no problem,' he tells them. 'We can always get money, one way or another.'

'Yeah?' Chaz looks at him with interest. 'How we gonna do that, then?'

'Well, soon we're gonna get our turf back, right?'

'OK, but supposin' that takes a bit of time? What do we do till then?'

'Plenty of things we can do.'

'Such as?'

'You name it. Ram-raiding, car ringing, robbing shops and houses . . .'

Everybody exchanges glances.

'It ain't as easy as dealing,' observes Tommo nervously. 'I mean, with dealin', everybody's queueing up to give you their money. *Taking* it from somebody, that's a different story.'

'What, you scared?' Finn asks him.

'I didn't say I was scared! It's just . . . not as easy, that's all. Takes a bit more bottle.'

Finn shrugs. 'Maybe it won't come to that,' he says. 'I'll call and see Gordie tonight, maybe he can sort it for us.'

'Oh yeah,' gloats Chaz. 'Sure. All Gordie has to do is wave 'is magic wand and everything's back the way it was. You saw that mad fucker last night. He blew Gibbo away without turnin' a hair. He's a psycho, Finn. Think he'll take any notice of what Gordie does?'

Finn rounds on him suddenly, grabbing him by the lapels of his jacket. He pulls him up close so he can stare right into his face, aware that Chaz's constant moaning is infecting the others.

'You got a better idea?' he demands. 'Eh? You got any

useful suggestions about what we should do? 'Cos I'd love to hear 'em.'

Chaz shakes his head, struggles to get free.

'No, I ain't got any suggestions. I just think—'

'I don't give a shit what you *think*! I'm still in charge here and I'll do the thinkin'.' Finn pushes Chaz back several steps, then turns to confront the others. 'Either of you got anything to say?'

Tommo spreads his arms in a gesture of appeal.

'Look, what I said before. I was only—'

'Yeah, I heard you! And you're right: it ain't gonna be so easy from now on, not till we get our turf back. I know that. But I'll tell you what we *don't* do – we don't give up. Whatever we gotta do to get money, we'll do it. I'll take care of things. And, like I said, tonight I'll go see Gordie. If we're gonna take on Mason and his posse, we'll need to be well tooled up. Gordie can organise that.'

'Supposin' he's left town?' says Chaz. He's pacing backwards and forwards on the bare boards, chunks of rubble crunching under his boots. 'Supposin' he's run out on us?'

Finn reaches into his jacket and Chaz stops pacing, goes on the defensive. He stands poised, arms spread to brace himself for an assault, but Finn's hand emerges holding nothing more deadly than a ten-pound note.

'Go and get me some breakfast,' he tells Chaz.

'Huh?' Chaz stares at him. This is the last thing he expected.

'Breakfast. A bacon buttie and a cup of tea.' He moves closer and stuffs the tenner into Chaz's breast pocket. 'Get yourself one, too, if you're hungry.'

Chaz looks at Finn. Finn can see his thoughts working the muscles just under the skin of his face, knows that he's thinking about telling Finn to go get his own fucking breakfast. Finn bunches his hands into fists.

One word, he tells himself. *One wrong word . . .*

There is a long silence; but then Chaz thinks better of it. With a shrug he turns and goes out of the room.

'And make sure you ain't followed back,' Finn shouts after him.

The three boys hear Chaz's footsteps going down the stairs. When he has left the building, Finn looks at the others.

'About Gibbo,' he says. 'We don't know nothin'. He went to that gig alone. We never saw him. We never met up with him. Anybody asks you, doesn't matter if it's the filth or your best mate, that's the story, OK?'

Tommo nods but Wart looks thoughtful. 'Couldn't we just tell the filth that it was Mason topped him? Get him put away?'

Finn shakes his head. 'You're missing the point, dick-brain. How could we know who shot him? We weren't there, right?'

'Yeah, but—'

'We weren't there! Say it.'

Wart nods. 'We weren't there,' he says quietly. 'But I was thinkin' like an *'nonomous* call. A tip-off.'

Finn looks disgusted. 'What's the matter with you?' he wants to know. 'Grass somebody up? To the filth? No way, man.'

Wart sighs. He knows that that is a kind of unspoken commandment around here, but this seems a special case.

'But Finn – Otis Mason! I mean, he's a piece of shit, right? He killed Gibbo, and—'

'Anyway, why give the filth all the fun?' interrupts Finn. 'I'll pay Mason back myself, with interest.' Finn's feeling a lot better now, more in control of the situation. The kids always did respond to big talk, and from now on he'll need to do a lot more of it, and be prepared to back it up with deeds. He sits down beside Wart on the mattress and gets out his cigarettes. He lights one up and blows out a cloud of smoke.

The two younger boys are looking at him now, waiting for him to speak.

'I'll see to it personal-like,' he says. 'Might take a bit of time, of course, but what's the big hurry? Let him think he's running things around here. Let him think he's the Candy Man. Then, one night, just when he's not expecting it . . .' He raises two fingers to the side of his head and makes a sound from between pursed lips – the sound of somebody being blown away.

It seems very loud and very satisfying in the silence of the empty flat.

Chapter Fifteen

Nick's big mistake, he decided, had been to hang around the Midland Hotel too long. After seeing Cooper and company safely installed in their various rooms, he had repaired to the Octagon Bar for a couple of fortifying snifters, before heading back to the office. It was here that he was eventually collared by the desk clerk. Only a young man – barely out of his twenties, Nick supposed – he had that squeaky-clean look about him: short black hair immaculately trimmed, pink skin scrubbed and shining, the effect marred only by a discreet smattering of spots around the chin. His thin lips currently sported a smug smile, which Nick found particularly irritating.

'I'm afraid you'll have to do something, sir. We've had several complaints.'

'Already? For God's sake, they've only been up there fifteen minutes!' Nick glanced at his wristwatch, as if to verify that fact.

'Quite, sir. But it's the music, you see. People on the floor below phoning to complain. If you could see your way to—'

'Yes, yes, sure. I'll handle it.'

Nick got up from his seat, collected his attaché case, and stalked out of the bar and across the lounge to the lifts. He was fuming. *Typical*, he told himself. He still hadn't properly recovered from the fiasco of the airport press conference, during which Bobby Cooper had made himself about as welcome as a dead mouse in a loaf of bread. He'd treated fifty per cent of the questions with flippancy, forty per cent of them with indifference, and met the remaining ten per cent in a scowling silence. He had repeatedly embarrassed Ajay Sanjari by pretending to be unable to pronounce his name, and had feigned complete ignorance of the product he was here to promote.

Finally, when a desperate interviewer from the *Evening News* had touched on his two drug convictions, Cooper hit the roof and had to be physically restrained from hitting the journalist. A lot of flashbulbs had gone off during the altercation, and Nick could just picture the kind of coverage this would get in the papers the following day. Even Terry was beginning to have second thoughts about this 'dream account'.

Now, to cap it all, a mere fifteen minutes after checking Cooper and entourage into the top floor of the Midland Hotel, there was already a problem.

As Nick rode up in the lift, it quickly became apparent that any complaints were justified. He could hear music booming and thudding as he approached the sixth floor. When the lift doors slid open, the noise intensified, swamping him with a force that was almost physical. No need to ask who the featured artist was. That arrogant, sneering rap could only come from the mouth of Cooper himself.

> Cut the crap, motherfucker, move to the beat.
> Listen to the lessons that they teach onna street.
> You gotta duck an' dive,

If you wanna survive,
Get the first punch in if you wanna stay alive!

Nick strode down the corridor to Cooper's suite, and saw Amos standing guard outside. He went to step past, but Amos intercepted him, placing his huge body between Nick and the door, pushing him back firmly but gently.

'Mr Cooper don't wanna be disturbed,' he rumbled in a voice that was almost subsonic.

Nick glared at him.

'Is that right?' he said. 'Well, the other guests in the hotel don't want to be disturbed either. We're getting complaints about the music. I just want to go in there and tell him to turn it down.'

Amos shrugged. 'That's too bad,' he said. ''Cos' he tol' me, no visitors.'

'All right then, supposing *you* go in there and tell him?'

'Me?' Amos considered this for a moment, then shook his head. 'Cain't do it,' he said. 'Mr Cooper's resting right now.'

'Resting? With that racket going on? Jesus!' Nick attempted to push past Amos, but found he was as solid and unyielding as a rock. 'Look, this is ridiculous!' he snapped. 'We'll have the police here in a minute. Where's Mr Rothman's room?'

'Down the end there.' Amos nodded along the corridor. 'Las' one on the left.'

Biting back a curse, Nick swung around and strode along the corridor, livid now. He hammered on Rothman's door, but got no reply. He tried again, louder this time, and, after what seemed an age, the door opened. Rothman glared out

147

at him, then softened when he saw who it was. He was in his shirt sleeves and his collar was unbuttoned.

'Mr Saunders, come in, come in. Have a drink with me!'

'Never mind that, we have to do something about—'

Rothman held up a hand to interrupt. He reached up and pulled two plugs of cotton wool out of his ears. Nick stared in disbelief. Rothman smiled sheepishly.

'Only way a guy can get any rest around here,' he explained. 'The boys are liable to keep that up for hours.'

'That's what I came about. We're getting complaints, and that big ape down the hall won't let me into Bobby's room.'

Rothman sighed, nodded. 'I guess they *are* piling it on a little. OK, we'll fix it. Coop isn't going to like this, though.'

'That's tough. We have to consider the other guests. Unless, of course, we can go from room to room, issuing them *all* with earplugs.'

That had been meant as sarcasm, but Rothman looked like he was actually weighing up the possibility. Then, sighing again, he stepped back into his room and, for some reason, put on his jacket and did up his tie. Then the two of them proceeded back along the corridor.

'It's ridiculous me not being allowed in to talk to Bobby,' grumbled Nick. 'I mean, I'm handling the PR for this visit. I need to have regular access to him.'

'Of *course* you do.' Rothman looked sympathetic. 'I'll have a word with Amos and Andy. Those boys are just too *literal*. Bobby tells 'em no visitors, and they take him at his word.' As he approached the door, he waved Amos aside impatiently. 'You hear that, Amos? Mr Saunders here has special clearance. I don't want you boys giving him any more trouble, you understand?'

Amos grunted but he looked far from convinced. He continued to stand there with hands on hips, glowering at Nick.

Rothman opened the door and they stepped inside. The effect was like being whacked over the head with a shovel. The volume in the room was awesome. Cooper must have brought in his own hi-fi equipment, Nick decided; the hotel's modest stereo system wasn't capable of delivering this kind of power. The curtains had been drawn against the afternoon sunlight, and silk scarves had been draped over the bedside lamps, giving the room a gloomy, subterranean feel. The next thing that hit Nick was the smell: a fragrance he remembered from the parties of his youth; the heady, sweet aroma of hashish.

Cooper was stretched out on the sofa, wearing a red silk kimono. He was smoking a huge, Rasta-style joint. Andy was sitting beside him like a faithful Rottweiler on guard duty. Other members of the entourage were sitting, standing or lying around the room. The television was on, and somebody was aimlessly flicking through the channels with the remote control. Cooper's personal assistant, Lionel, a small, effeminate man with fuzzy hair and a pencil moustache, was sitting cross-legged on the floor, rolling another joint. A sizable pouch of dope lay on a coffee table beside him. He had also taken a mirror off the wall and had laid out several lines of cocaine on it.

The room itself was in a state of disarray – furniture pushed back against the walls, lamps overturned, crumpled beer cans and crushed potato chips ground into the carpet, clothing lying about in heaps. It didn't seem possible for it to have got into such a mess in such a short space of time.

Nick stared around, open-mouthed in astonishment. He glanced at Rothman – but the man hadn't so much as raised an eyebrow. Presumably he had seen far worse than this.

'Hey, Nick-O-Las, my man!' yelled Cooper over the din of the music. He had the lazy-eyed look of somebody who was already well en route to oblivion. 'Come lookin' to shake some action?'

'No, I . . .' Nick had to adjust his voice to make himself heard. 'The music!' he yelled. 'You've got to turn it down.'

'Say what?' Cooper was grinning now, playing a dumb-ass role, cupping one hand behind his ear. 'Sing out, brother, I cain't make out a goddamned word!'

Nick looked at Rothman hopefully. The manager nodded. He walked around the sofa to the state-of-the-art, miniature hi-fi set standing in the middle of the carpet. Stooping, he punched the volume down to a more respectable level.

Cooper sat up, a peeved expression on his face.

'Aww, come *on*, Gabe. I was enjoying that,' he protested.

'I'm sure you were. Unfortunately, the other hotel guests don't share your taste in music. Nick here says there've been complaints.'

'Complaints? Like from who? We've got this whole fuckin' floor man.'

'Complaints from people on *other* floors,' Nick explained.

'Fuck 'em! We paid for these rooms. We can do what we want.'

'Correction,' said Rothman. 'Mr Sanjari paid for the

rooms. And as I keep reminding you, Bobby, we're ambassadors for America here, so we don't want to go treading on anyone's toes. This ain't the fuckin' Dakota building.'

'You can say that again!' Cooper handed the joint to Andy, to allow himself the opportunity to cross his arms in a gesture of disgust. He looked suddenly like a petulant child denied his favourite toy. 'Oh well, then, let's just turn the music right *off*. How would that be? If these tight-assed Brits are gonna make a fuckin' case out of it, let's have no goddamned music whatsoever! Let's just sit here and get bored out of our tiny minds, whaddayasay?'

Rothman rolled his piggy eyes towards the ceiling. 'Bobby,' he said. 'Bobby, Bobby, nobody is asking you to turn the music off – just *down*. See, there's this thing called a volume control, you turn it anticlockwise and, hey, you won't believe this, but the music's still there, only at a volume so you can hear yourself *think*. Do I really have to have this shit every place we go?'

Cooper sneered, but he seemed to concede the point. He uncrossed his arms and snapped the fingers of his right hand. Andy handed back the joint. Nick noticed that the big man hadn't inhaled on the thing: had simply held it politely till his boss had further need of it.

Cooper took a big toke and held the smoke in his lungs for a few seconds, before expelling it through his nostrils. He grinned and offered the joint to Nick.

'No thanks.'

'Oh, I get it. Clean-livin' dude, huh? So what are your vices, Nick-O-Las? Everyone done gotta have vices, ain't that right?'

Nick shrugged. 'I take an occasional drink,' he said. 'In fact that's just what I was doing when the desk clerk complained about the noise. I gave up smoking dope years ago.' He gestured at the mirror on the coffee table. 'And I never was stupid enough to give *that* stuff a whirl.'

Cooper grimaced, then lapsed into a hopelessly inaccurate cockney accent. 'Gor blimey, guv'nor, do me ears deceive me or do I detect a note of criticism?'

'Actually, I *was* wondering how you managed to get your hands on all that stuff so quickly. I mean, you've only been in the country a few hours.'

Cooper gave him a scornful look. 'Get *real*! We brung it with us, man.'

'You...' Nick couldn't believe it. He glanced at Rothman, who spread his arms in a 'what can I do?' gesture. 'You brought that stuff through customs?'

'Relax. Not me personally. Lionel carried it through. Shit, everybody needs a little R 'n' R, don't they?'

'Jesus Christ!' Nick shook his head. 'That was unbelievably stupid. If you'd been *stopped*...'

'Then Lionel woulda had a longer stay here than the rest of us.' Cooper grinned across at his PA, and the man just laughed. 'See, we've got an arrangement between us. He's my *mule*, he takes the heat, I pick up the tab. The day he gets busted on my behalf, he becomes a very rich man.'

'A pity you didn't think to use the same method those other times,' growled Rothman disparagingly.

'Yeah, well, I wasn't so organised them days.'

Nick didn't know what else to say on that subject, so he moved to another one.

'Well, while I'm here, I guess we may as well go over your schedule. Think we could do that?'

Cooper frowned. 'The whole two weeks? I dunno ... say, supposin' we do it on a day-to-day basis. Like, for now you jus' tell me what's happenin' tomorrow. How would that be?'

'I suppose we could do it that way,' said Nick reluctantly.

'If you two boys will excuse me, I'll go back to my room and try and get some shuteye,' said Rothman. He gave Cooper a meaningful look. 'Don't forget, Bobby, Mr Saunders here is on our team. I want you to show him every consideration, OK?'

'Sure thing, Gabe,' said Cooper. 'We's gonna get along just fine, ain't we, Nick-O-Las?'

Rothman nodded to Nick and went out of the room, closing the door behind him.

Cooper studied Nick in silence for a moment. Then a big, mischievous grin split his face. 'Well now,' he said. He inhaled the last of the joint and flicked the roach in the general direction of an ashtray on the floor. It careered off, scattering a trail of sparks and landed, still smouldering, on the carpet. Andy helpfully ground it into the deep pile with the heel of a huge basketball boot. Nick tried not to wince.

'Come and sit down,' Cooper told Nick, a mockingly obsequious tone in his voice now. 'Andy, move yo' big ass. Make some room for my man, here. Hey, and get the guy a drink! Whaddya say, Nicky baby, what's your poison?'

Nick was about to refuse, but he told himself not to be standoffish. 'I'll take a whisky and dry ginger,' he said.

'Absolutely. You want ice with that?' Cooper leaned forward, as if to confide a secret. 'By *ice*, you understand, I mean frozen water, not the amphetamine-based substance that grown men have been known to kill for!'

'I'm relieved to hear it,' said Nick. 'Yes, ice, please.'

Andy got up and trudged dutifully across to the drinks cabinet. Nick took his place on the sofa. He opened the attaché case and took out some papers.

'Say, Nick, tell me. I'm interested. What's a guy like you do for entertainment? You listen to music, do ya?'

'Yes, sometimes.'

'What kinda music? Brass bands – all that tiddly-pom stuff? Or, what's it called, Gilbert and Sullivan? That kind of thing?'

Nick laughed dismissively.

'Of course not! I listen to *rock* music!'

'Yeah?' Cooper looked impressed. 'For instance?'

'Oh, I don't know. U2, REM . . . Elvis Costello . . .'

'Who?' Cooper was looking blankly around the room at his entourage. 'El-vis Cost-yellow?' He repeated the words back as though they were in some foreign language. 'Anybody heard a dat cat? The only Elvis I know ate thirty burgers, swelled up and *died*!'

Andy came over with Nick's drink, the tumbler looking like a glass thimble in his huge hand. Nick took it and had a sip. He tried not to grimace. If there was any ginger ale in there, it must have been added with an eye-dropper.

'You don't listen to black music?' Cooper asked him.

'Well, I'm quite fond of Prince . . .'

'Prince? Shit, man, I said black music, not fag music! What about rap – you don't listen to rap?'

'I'm not what you'd call an expert.'

'Hot damn! I don't know if I approve. I mean, shit, maybe you *oughta* be, runnin' round doin' my R 'n' R and all.'

'That's PR,' Nick reminded him. 'And maybe we could just get down to these—'

'Tell you what I'm gonna do, Nick-O-Las. Gonna give you a whole bunch a tapes to take home and listen to. Want you to be able to tell your Public Enemy from your Ice T, you know what I'm sayin'?'

154

'OK, fine.' Nick tapped the sheets of paper impatiently. 'Tonight at seven there's a fitting. The stylist and her assistant will come here to help you select the jeans you'll be wearing tomorrow . . .' Nick glanced around the room and made a mental note to warn the women to bring a couple of minders with them. Otherwise, the experience might be akin to stepping into a cage full of hungry lions. 'Then, tomorrow morning at six a.m. . . .'

'Say what? *Six* a.m.' Cooper looked horrified. 'Nothin' happens at six a.m., man, 'cept people sleep and sometimes dream.'

Nick pressed on gamely.

'At six a.m. a couple of limousines will call to pick up you and your entourage – to take you to the shoot.'

'It may *arrive*, Nick-O-Las, that I do not dispute, but it ain't gonna depart with my ass inside of it – not at that time o' the mornin'. I tell you what I do at six a.m., boy, I *sleep*, and I do a damn fine job of it. You tell 'em to come for me at midday, I'll be up and functioning by then.'

'But we can't do that! The photographer needs to take full advantage of the light.' Nick thought for a moment. 'What about when you were shooting *No Quarter*. I'm bloody sure you didn't get a midday start then.'

'Shit, no, but that was a thirty-million-dollar movie, and I was on a percentage. I don't mind gettin' out of bed for that kind of dough.'

'But not for a mere million pounds, eh? Well, tough. You've signed a contract, you've agreed to our terms, and we want you ready to start at six. I'll book you an alarm call.'

Cooper looked at Nick as though seeing him for the first time. 'Hey, and I thought you was some kind of candy-ass!' He smirked, thought about it for a few moments. 'OK, respect to that,' he conceded. 'But I sure hope you ain't got a lot of these early starts lined up.'

'Just three of them, spaced out through the two weeks. We're shooting several different locations. For the interviews and public appearances, you mostly won't be required till after ten.'

'Well, that's somethin', I guess.' Cooper looked vaguely distracted for a moment. He glanced over at Lionel, then beckoned to him. 'Hey, boy, bring me that mirror will ya? I need a lift.'

Lionel got up and brought the mirror across to the sofa. He kneeled and held it out in front of Cooper, like a vassal offering his king a tray of refreshment.

Cooper took a gold tube from the surface of the mirror and snorted two lines, one for each nostril. He sniffed, tilted his head back, then waved the mirror away.

'Good shit,' he muttered. He looked at Nick and the pupils of his eyes suddenly looked like two blobs of black tar. 'You don't know what you're missing, Nick-O-Las.'

'I'll live with it,' Nick assured him.

'Thing is, with all these early starts I'm gonna be needin' me a good supply of this stuff. Now, I figure you're in charge of that department, so . . .'

'I beg your pardon!' Nick glared at him. 'I hope you're not suggesting that one of my responsibilities is to supply you and your friends with—'

'Hey, hey! Lighten up, m' man! No reason to get all overheated. All I'm sayin' is that one of your concerns must be the health and well-bein' of your guests, right? And we *are* guests in your country, ain't that so?'

'Yes, but—'

'So, you know, me and the brothers here, we like to get into a party vibe most nights. Hey, we don't mind payin' for our pleasures neither. First thing we do when we hit town is cash some big traveller's cheques. Already taken care of that in the *bureau de change* downstairs.' He glanced up, snapped his fingers. 'Hey, Andy, fetch that case for Nick to have a look at, will ya?'

Andy waddled across to a dim corner of the room, and returned a moment later with a black attaché case. He unlatched it and held it out so that Nick could observe the contents. It was full of piles of neatly stacked twenties, each one with a paper band around the middle. Nick couldn't help gasping. He didn't know how much was there, but it was probably more money than he'd ever seen together in one handy pile.

'Look on it as us helpin' out the Manchester economy,' said Cooper smugly, waving Andy away. 'What we like to do is maybe score a little home-grown produce, get introduced to some friendly local girls, you know, sample the city's *poontang* . . .'

Nick was horrified by this latest suggestion.

'What d'you think I am? Some kind of pimp?'

This initiated laughter from Cooper and the others.

'Hell, no! For one thing you dress too sharp. Need maybe to add some gold chains and a full-length leather coat!' He spread his hands in a gesture of helplessness. 'You see my point, though. We're just innocents abroad. *You've* got all the contacts.'

'Not those kind of contacts,' Nick told him icily. 'I work for a respectable company. I'll be damned if I'll go that far to make you feel at home.'

More laughter. Nick couldn't be sure if they were just winding him up or were serious about this. Actually, he suspected the latter. 'Aww, come on,' pleaded Cooper. 'Don't be like that, blood. We'd make it worth your while.

Naturally I'll expect to pay you some kind of commission. Hey, what about that broad from the airport? Skinny-shanked girl that was hangin' out with old Sanji-Panjie? Thought to myself, now there's a chick knows how to do the horizontal boogie! Maybe you could get her over here. I'd like to give her my autograph, know what I mean?'

Cooper's speech was getting faster and faster as the cocaine fired up inside him. His entourage now seemed to find every word he said unbelievably funny. Nick recognised this condition as a side-effect of smoking hashish. There was suddenly an air of absolute insanity in the room.

'I mean, what's he doin' with a chick like that, right? I mean, I'm the star of this show right? It's like I told 'em in *No Quarter*, the star gets the chick, right, and they said, no, the bad guy cain't get the chick. What kind of a message is that givin' to the world? I told 'em, I got a message for the world, an' they said, oh, what's that, an' I said the message is: kiss my black ass!' He threw back his head and screamed with laughter.

'Listen,' said Nick. 'You already told me you don't need a wet nurse; and it's not up to me to tell you how to behave. All I ask is that you turn up for your appointments and do your best to keep out of trouble ... any extracurricular activities you get up to—'

'Any what? What's that? Extra *what*? Speak English, man!'

'Any ... any unofficial pleasures you indulge in may not be my business, but I would be professionally compromised if—'

'Will somebody *please* translate what this dude is saying to me!' screamed Cooper.

'He's saying drugs fuck you up!' offered Lionel, and everyone started laughing again.

Nick could feel his temper rising. He told himself that he mustn't lose his rag. He folded his papers and put them back into the attaché case, but plodded gamely on to his conclusion.

'Let me put it simply. Do your own dirty work. I don't want to be involved.'

'Shit, man, anyone would think I'd asked you to go down on me. All I want is for you to make a few phone-calls. Christ, in Hollywood all I had to do was click my fingers and some suit would show up with a case full of snow—'

'This isn't Hollywood!' roared Nick, and suddenly nobody was laughing anymore. 'You're in my country now. We do things differently here. You want drugs and call-girls, you just make your own fucking arrangements! Understand?'

'Well, now, Nick-O-Las...'

'That's another thing! My name is Nick. Not Nicky-baby, not Nick-O-Las, but Nick plain and simple. I would *really* appreciate it if you'd remember that.' He lifted his whisky glass and slugged it down in one. He fought off an impulse to cough, and just about got away with it. Then he stood up and glared down at Cooper. 'Tomorrow morning,' he said. 'Six a.m. I'll be calling for you. Don't be late.'

He turned and strode across to the door, leaving a stunned silence behind him.

Nick went out, slamming the door and found himself standing beside a suspicious-looking Amos. He gave the big man a cold stare, as if challenging him to say something – but he didn't. Nick pushed past him and walked along the corridor to the lift. He punched the button and the door opened immediately. Stepping inside, he hit the ground-floor button. The doors closed and the lift descended.

'Oh, the wonderful world of show-biz,' he said bleakly.
   He had descended maybe half a floor when he heard the
music crank up again.

Chapter Sixteen

Shaun McManus sat in front of the television set and tried to concentrate on the programme. Maybe if he could get really interested in it, he could forget about the awful, crawling sensation on his skin, the sickening cramps in his stomach, the impression that the skin of his face was shrinking – tightening across the contours of his skull until it threatened to tear down the middle.

He and Theresa had finished the remains of the heroin last night, and had confidently expected more when Finn got home; except that he didn't come home – still hadn't – and now it was mid-afternoon. Theresa was up in the bathroom; Shaun occasionally heard the sound of her muttering as she shuffled around on the bare floorboards. A bead of sweat popped on Shaun's forehead and ran tickling down his brow. His gums were itching. He took a cigarette from his pack and lit it. There were three cigarettes left in the packet, and he'd no money for any more till his dole cheque came tomorrow.

He furrowed his brow and tried to home in his concentration on the TV screen. Oprah Winfrey was interviewing couples who'd abused their children. She had these guys and their wives sitting in leather chairs on one side of the studio, and among the audience sat their respective children, most of them grown up now and, boy, were they asking some shitty questions! Shaun couldn't figure out what it was about the Yanks: they seemed to love hanging out their dirty washing in public.

The fathers all had that solid, no-nonsense look about them: crew-cut hair, short-sleeved plaid shirts, chino trousers. One of them was bearded, but the beard was immaculately trimmed. They sat there in a row, arms crossed to a man, doing their best to provide answers. And they looked totally unperturbed by it all, like they were answering questions about their favourite holiday destinations.

Beside them, their wives looked furtive, haunted, a couple of them wearing dark glasses, some with the mottled, saggy features of habitual drinkers. One woman was sobbing, reaching in under her glasses to dab at her eyes with a handkerchief, but her husband looked unrepentant, even when his twenty-year-old daughter said that she wished he would die of some horrible disease.

A pain jabbed through Shaun's side, like somebody had stuck the blade of a blunt knife in there. He hunched forward on the sofa, and then he couldn't concentrate any more. He was thinking about Finn's room, that triple-locked door, and he knew where he could get his hands on a crowbar . . .

No, no, can't start thinking like that!

He remembered, the last time it happened, Finn had lost his rag, came close to pasting his old man. Imagine, the little kid whose nose he used to wipe, now so in control of himself and pulling down more dosh in a week than Shaun had earned in his entire life.

'You kids gotta 'preciate,' said one of the TV fathers, 'that I couldn' he'p what I did t' you. I was sick n' outa control. Now I've found the Lord and I've got my life back on course, I pray every night for the strength to stay with it.'

Shaun sneered. Maybe that was what *he* needed: the help of the Lord. There was a time when he and Theresa were strong Catholics, never missed mass on Sunday, even when Saturday night had vanished into an alcohol-fuelled blur. Yes, and they'd had one of those Sacred Heart gizmos: the portrait of Christ with an eternal (electric) candle flickering away in front of it. It had been a wedding present from relatives in Ireland and they'd always sworn that, no matter how bad things got, they'd never part with it. You could still see the lighter patch on the wallpaper where it had hung, and the bare wires that had connected to the candle. Shaun had got ten quid for it last winter, when he'd been really desperate for a fix. Theresa had cried when he told her what he'd done, but she'd taken her share of the skag, just the same.

'You're a bad father!' One of the kids was talking now: a girl, voice cracking as she confronted her old man. 'I used to lie awake at night and pray for you to die! I can't ever forgive you for what you did to me!'

Shaun thought about that. Fair play to her, she was bloody angry. He'd never abused Finn, at least that was one thing. Oh, clipped him across the ear a few times when he was smaller, and once ... only once, mind you, tanned his arse with a leather belt that time he set fire to a neighbour's shed. But he'd never had any thoughts about him *like that*. No, Shaun was fairly sure that the only abuse he'd ever initiated had been directed squarely at himself.

Theresa trudged into the room, her arms wrapped around her own body as though trying to keep warm. She looked at the television screen with dead eyes.

'What's on?' she muttered, but the question was a formality. You could tell she didn't much care either way. There was a dark bruise on her cheek where Shaun had hit her the other day, when they were scrambling for the packet of dope. At least Shaun thought that he'd hit her. He couldn't be sure. She might just have fallen and knocked herself; it was hard to remember now. She slumped down on the sofa beside him. 'What's happened to Finn?' she asked him.

'Fuck knows. I expect he'll show up sooner or later. It ain't the first time he's stayed out.'

'I know, but . . .' She reached up a hand to scratch at the bare flesh around her neck. 'He knows we're not supplied. Wouldn't you think he'd consider us once in a while . . . ?' She broke off guiltily, knowing she was being unreasonable. She reached for the cigarette packet and Shaun looked at her, watched as she took one of the last three fags. But there was nothing he could say; it was her money that bought them. Theresa lit up, blew out smoke. She knew she was just substituting one drug for another, but it would make her feel better for a minute or two, dull the edges of the various strands of pain that were colliding in her body.

'I thought of suicide,' announced one of the TV mothers. 'Many times I was *that* close to it.' She held out a thumb and forefinger to demonstrate exactly how close she was. Only an inch away, it seemed.

'I know how she feels,' muttered Theresa, nodding at the screen.

Shaun looked at her then grinned mockingly, showing the dark gaps in the rotting ivories.

'Bollocks! You'd never do that. It's a mortal sin, ain't it?'

She smiled sadly. 'Oh aye, and us the big Catholics now!'

She glanced up at the lighter-coloured rectangle on the wallpaper, and Shaun felt a stab of irritation lance into him. She always did that, not saying anything but letting him know that she resented him selling the Sacred Heart. He'd asked Finn to buy her another one the other day, but Finn only sneered and said that there was no God other than money, and what was the point of him exchanging the one God for another, less powerful one? Smart-arsed little bastard, these days he had an answer for everything.

'I been thinkin',' said Shaun, making an attempt to steer the conversation in a different direction. 'Harry Curtis tells me they're takin' on casual workers over at the Crescents – help with the demolition, like. Well, maybe I could moonlight for a few weeks, huh? They aren't askin' for cards or nothin', so I could still be signin' on. Maybe bring in an extra hundred a week – what d'you think?'

Theresa gazed at him impassively. She was used to these fantasies of his, and knew, just as he did, that no foreman was ever going to take him on. You could see by just looking at him that he hadn't the strength to use a screwdriver, let alone a sledgehammer. Still, she didn't challenge him. She wasn't feeling strong enough to handle an argument just at the moment.

There was a knock at the door. Shaun and Theresa looked at each other, their hopes rising.

'Maybe that's him now,' said Shaun.

'But Finn has a key.'

'Maybe he lost it.' Shaun got up from the sofa and went out of the room. It crossed his mind that it could be the filth. Maybe Finn had got himself arrested and they were bringing him home. Bad news if that was the case, because then he'd be cleaned out of supplies. The Old Bill would be out selling it themselves.

Shaun unlatched the door and peeped out. An unfamiliar black face peered back at him from beneath the brim of a fedora hat. 'Mr McManus?' the face enquired politely.

Shaun nodded. 'Yeah. Who are you?'

'A friend a Finn's. He aroun'?'

Shaun shook his head. 'Sorry.' He tried to close the door but it was intercepted by the shiny black toe of a platform boot.

'Hey, ease up, mon! What's de hurry? Finn ask me to drop off somethin' for him, seen?'

'Yeah?' Shaun perked up a little at this. 'What exactly?'

'Some supplies.' The black man grinned, displaying gold-capped teeth. 'Don't t'ink me criticisin', dread, but me ain't wantin' to stand around out here wid hot merchandise in me pockets.'

Shaun nodded. 'No . . . no, of course not.' He opened the door and Mason stepped into the hallway, closely followed by Carmel. Shaun looked at her suspiciously. 'Who's this?' he asked.

'Me mudder,' said Mason and laughed, a strange huffing sound, his shoulders going up and down. Now Shaun could see him properly, he wondered if Finn really *would* have a friend like this.

Mason indicated the staircase to the punky-looking girl and motioned her up it. 'Check out up dere,' he said.

'Hey, now, just a minute!' said Shaun. 'You've no right to—'

Mason slipped a long arm around Shaun's shoulders. 'Jus' a precaution, mon. Make sure de bwoy's not hidin' from us.'

'Hiding? Why would he hide? You said you were—'

'A friend.' Mason steered Shaun towards the lounge. 'Well, less say more a business partner, know wha'a mean?

Me have some unfinished business wid Finn de other night.' He pushed Shaun into the sitting room and smiled at Theresa, who was starting to get up off the sofa. 'No, no, missus, me don't wanna interrupt nothin'. You jus' go on wid what you's doin'.' He motioned Shaun to sit beside his wife, and then dropped into a vacant armchair. He put his big feet up on a Formica coffee table, crossing his legs at the ankles.

'Who's this?' Theresa asked Shaun indignantly.

'Says he's a friend of Finn's.'

She stared at him as if he was stupid. 'Why . . . why did you let him in?'

'He said he had some merchandise.' Shaun licked his dry lips nervously. He was only just realising that he might have badly miscalculated. He could feel jolts of panic mingling with the withdrawal pains that were currently slamming around inside him, but the lure of a potential fix was still stronger than his fear.

Now Mason was looking at the TV screen. 'What you watchin'?' he asked. 'Anyt'ing good?'

Now one of the fathers had finally started to break up. 'I tried to stop myself,' he muttered. 'God *knows*, I tried – but I just couldn't he'p it.'

The camera cut to Oprah, nodding thoughtfully. 'Seems like you regret what you did,' she observed. 'But does a leopard ever really change its spots?'

'Oh, it's dat Winfrey woman,' said Mason. 'Me don' much care for her.' He took his feet from the coffee table and got up. He walked over to the television and stood there a moment like he was going to switch it off. Then he seemed to think better of it. He aimed a kick at the screen, tipping the ancient set backwards on its spindly metal legs. It crashed to the floor and erupted in a flash of electrical

167

fire. The screen collapsed with a dull crump and black smoke billowed up from it, leaving a dirty patch on the flaking ceiling.

Shaun and Theresa sat there, stunned, hardly believing what had happened.

Mason shrugged his shoulders. 'Dat woman talk too much,' he said. He went back to his seat and resumed his position, like nothing had happened.

Shaun and Theresa stared at the scorched place on the floorboards, where the TV had exploded. The room was filling up with an acrid stink.

They heard footsteps on the stairs. Carmel entered the room and perched herself on the arm of Mason's chair. She shook her head. 'Not there,' she told him. 'One room's locked, mind you. Got more locks than the fuckin' Bank of England. Could be hidin' in there, I suppose.'

Shaun shook his head. 'That's Finn's room,' he told them. 'But he ain't there, I swear to you.'

Mason nodded. 'I b'lieve you,' he said. 'T'ing is, if he ain't here, den where is he?'

'We don't know. He didn't come home, last night ... Listen, what's going on? Who *are* you?'

'Me's the new Yardman in dese parts. Me takin' over Finn's turf. Him ain't no more de Candy Man, seen? Like I say, me got some unfinished business wid him, so, is wonderin' mebbe if you can tell me where he's hangin' out?'

Shaun sneered. 'Why would I tell you?' he wanted to know. 'You're taking over his turf? Says who? Listen, I think you better leave.'

Mason waved a hand in dismissal. 'Nah, nah, breddar. Take it *easy*! No reason t' go shootin' off at de jaw. Ain't nobody pushin' you on de matter. We's just rappin', is all.'

He slipped a hand into his pocket and brought it out holding a cellophane packet of fine white powder. Shaun's eyes got very big. 'I hear tell you people got a taste for dis produce,' said Mason. 'See here now, dis is quality merchandise, purest Colombian.' He tapped the package against his fingertips, and it made a seductive rustling sound. 'Dis ain't de kind o' shit you's used to, dread. Dis is like kissin' a virgin's ass in de dark.'

Theresa grimaced. 'I hope you don't think we'd give you information in exchange for *that*,' she said primly.

Mason gave an unpleasant laugh. 'Oh, me don't *t'ink*, honey. Me *know*. People like you I seen before. You give anyt'ing if you go wid'out long enough. And lookin' at you, I'd say you gone some time aweady.'

'Get out,' said Theresa, but her voice lacked conviction. She, too, was staring at the package in his hand. She didn't want to, but she couldn't seem to stop herself.

Carmel brought her hands together in a mocking burst of applause. 'Nice speech,' she observed. 'But it's bollocks, and you know it.'

'What about your man dere?' asked Mason. 'He ain't sayin' nothin' an', lookin' in his eyes, me see he give anyt'ing I want feh dis shit. Like, s'pose I ask him to give me *you*, bent buck-nekked over dat table? You t'ink he gwan to say no? Lady, he hold me coat while I do it!'

Theresa's eyes widened in panic and she threw a furtive glance at Shaun, but he hardly seemed aware of her. All his attention was focused on the packet of heroin.

'Relax,' Mason told her. 'Me ain't lookin' for no squeeze. No, all I want in exchange for dis...' he jiggled the package temptingly '...is a little information. Supposin' we get started? Where's Finn?'

Shaun shook his head.

'Honestly, we don't know. It's like I told you. He just didn't come home last night.'

'Any idea 'bout where he might be stayin'?'

'Umm . . .' Shaun was now tapping his fingers on the arm of the sofa, barely able to sit still. 'Friend's house, maybe.'

'Shaun!' Theresa warned him – but he ignored her.

'Friend's house. Good. How 'bout names, addresses?'

Shaun didn't know any addresses, but he haltingly supplied names and approximate locations of all the friends he could remember. Among them was Gibbo. Shaun didn't know that the boy was no longer alive.

Carmel had produced a notebook from her pocket, and busied herself in taking down the details in slow, laborious handwriting. It took maybe half an hour to get everything down, by which time Shaun and Theresa had started to tremble with anticipation.

'Any place else you can t'ink of?' asked Mason.

Shaun shook his head.

'D'wan forget, your bwoy is finish aroun' here. From today he can't get a hold of so much as an asprin wid'out I say so. An' I gwan to look after me friends, seen? Mebbe you had an arrangement wid Finn, he bring home de stuff you need? If you ain't on de list of me friends, den you gonna have to pay wid de rest. An' dis shit don' come cheap, y'nah wha'a mean?'

Shaun swallowed with difficulty.

'The Swamp,' he whispered.

'Come again?'

'I don't know where it is. I heard Finn talking on his mobile phone to some kid or other, and he said, "Meet you at the Swamp".' Shaun spread his hands in a gesture of helplessness. 'That's all I know. I swear.'

Mason and Carmel exchanged puzzled glances.

'Hideout, maybe,' suggested Carmel.

'Mebbe. We can ask aroun'. Some mudder might recognise it.'

'What are you going to do to Finn – when you find him?' asked Theresa fearfully.

'What d'you care, woman? He no use to you, no more. Him jus' been demoted back to de bottom of de shit pile.'

'He's still my son,' Theresa informed him.

Mason laughed, the brim of his fedora bobbing up and down.

'Do me a favour, lady! A son's a luxury you can't afford n'more.' He sucked noisily on his teeth, then threw the packet of dope on to the coffee table. Shaun grabbed it. He lifted a cushion of the sofa and brought out the Jiffy bag in which he kept his works. He shook them out on to the table top, picked out a candle and a soot-blackened spoon from the debris. He lit the candle then sorted through his battered collection of hypodermics, selecting the one with the sharpest needle.

'I gwan to leave you me mobile phone number,' Mason informed him. 'If de bwoy show up here, you give me a call an' dere's a whole ounce of dat shit wid your name on it. Fix a whole passle of good dreams wid dat much.'

Shaun nodded eagerly. He tipped some powder into the spoon and added a splash of vinegar from a bottle on the table. He held the spoon over the candle flame. His hands were shaking so badly, he was in danger of dropping it. Theresa watched him anxiously.

'Go easy, breddar,' Mason told him. He watched the proceedings with an air of amusement.

The spoonful of powder had melted now. Shaun dropped a small piece of cigarette filter into the spoon and managed to suck the liquid into the syringe without spilling too much. Theresa picked up a leather belt from the table top and helped him strap it around his left arm. He pulled it tight with his teeth, upended the hypo, and flicked out the air bubbles.

He searched out a place on his arm with the blunt needle, seeking a section of vein that was relatively uncorrupted. He found a spot, sank the needle into flesh and shot up. He released the belt and pulled the needle from his arm. Then the rush hit him, snapping his head back and making his eyelids flicker. He flopped back against the sofa, his eyes staring sightlessly up at the ceiling.

'Yeeeessss,' he whispered. Then he was out, and already dreaming of the full ounce that Mason had promised him.

Now Theresa was sprinkling powder into the spoon. Mason grinned, realising that she had virtually forgotten him. He slapped Carmel on the shoulder, and the two of them got to their feet.

'Now, dwan forget,' he said. 'A full ounce in exchange for de bwoy. You ain't gonna get anodder offer like dat.'

She didn't answer him. She was wiping the needle of the syringe on her dress, a token gesture to cleanliness. Mason watched as she drew up a sizeable shot for herself, then looked doubtfully at her sore-encrusted left arm. Instead she lifted her skirt and pulled her knickers to one side, not caring that she was exposing herself to this stranger. She plunged the needle into her femoral vein, and shot up.

'Sweet dreams,' said Mason. He and Carmel headed out to the hallway, laughing to themselves. But Theresa had the drug in her bloodstream now and, occupied as she was, she didn't even hear the front door slam.

Chapter Seventeen

After the trials of the day, going home was like an escape to paradise. Nick arrived back a little later than usual, to find Helen and Molly curled up in front of the television, watching a video of *Chitty Chitty Bang Bang*. It was Molly's favourite film; she must have watched it at least a dozen times, even though it frightened her in some respects.

The scenes she had problems with were those involving the Child Catcher: a thin, cadaverous gentleman in black clothing, who went around enticing youngsters with lollipops and sweeping them up in his net. This character exerted a powerful fascination for Molly – she was simultaneously perturbed and intrigued by him. Whenever he appeared on screen, she would cling for dear life to whoever was sitting beside her, but any attempt to fast-forward to some less disturbing scene was greeted with yells of protest. Nick and Helen assumed this was just a phase their child was going through – something she would eventually resolve for herself.

Molly, already in her pyjamas, was pretty sleepy by the time the video ended, so Nick carried her straight up to her room to tuck her in, while Helen saw to dinner. As Molly snuggled under her dinosaur-print duvet, she lay gazing solemnly up at her father with lips pursed.

Nick sensed there was something on her mind, and sat down on the edge of her bed.

'What's wrong, Button?'

She shook her head. 'Nuffin'.'

'Yes, there is,' he insisted. 'There's something bothering you. Come on, tell me what's wrong?'

She sniffed, then whispered, 'It's him.'

'Him?'

'That man . . .' She lifted an arm to make a scooping motion with an imaginary net.

'Oh, *him*. He still worries you?'

She nodded. 'He . . . he won't come for me, will he?' she asked in a tiny voice. This was a puzzling development. Though the Child Catcher character had worried her for some time, she had never before expressed a fear that he might actually exist.

'Of course not! He's not real – only pretend. We talked about that before. The things in that film don't happen in real life.'

She still seemed unconvinced. 'But children *do* get taken, don't they?'

'Well, sometimes, yes. But not by him. He's just a character that somebody made up.'

'Only I heard on the telly, there was a girl from near here, and *she* was took from her home. An' they don't know who did it, do they?'

'Well, no, they don't. But that was done by some sick person – somebody who's very ill and needs help.'

'Not the Child Catcher?'

'No, not him. Don't you remember we told you that Mummy and me would never let anyone take you away from us?'

'Yes, but . . .' She was still searching his face for

174

answers. 'It's jus' that you didn' have another baby, before.'

He stared at her. 'Another baby?' he echoed.

'Yes and ... well, when the baby comes, maybe you won't care so much about *me*. An' if that happens, *he* could come wiv' his big net and take me away. An' you and Mummy not even notice.'

It might have seemed amusing, but wasn't – not one little bit. Nick felt a stab of concern that she should consider the possibility of such an occurrence, and that it terrified her. He reached out to stroke her hair.

'Button, that could *never* happen. We wouldn't let it. It doesn't matter how many babies we have, you'll always be special. We'll always be there to keep an eye on you.'

'You promise?' she whispered.

'Of course, I promise.'

'Cross your heart n' hope to die?'

'In a cellar full of rats,' he assured her. 'See, Molly, when the baby comes along, it might seem like we care more about him ... or *her* ... it could be a little girl, remember.'

'No, a boy! I want a *brother*!'

'I know you do. We'll just have to see what we get. But listen, this is important. It might just seem like we care more about the new baby, because he's so small and helpless, and because he won't be able to do anything for himself at first. You were like that, too, not so long ago.'

Molly giggled. 'Was not!' she protested.

'Yes, you were. Everyone was – me, Mummy, everyone. But then we grow up and learn to do things for ourselves. What I'm saying, Button, is you mustn't be jealous of the new baby, even if it seems we spend a lot more time with him. Will you try not to be jealous?'

She thought about it for a moment, then nodded gravely.

''Kay,' she said. 'An' the man wiv' the black clothes won't never come n' take me? You promise?'

'I swear to you, darling. Nobody's ever going to do that. If anybody ever tried, I'd . . . I'd *stop* them. You do believe me, don't you?'

She nodded. Then she sighed, blinked, snuggled deeper under the duvet. 'An' if he *did* take me . . .'

'He won't.'

'Yes, but say he did. You'd come and get me back, wouldn' you?'

He smiled. 'I'd go to the ends of the earth – that's another promise.'

She returned his smile. With that off her mind she was suddenly ready for sleep. Amazing creatures, children, thought Nick. They could carry so much worry around inside their little heads, and then, reassured, as if at the flick of a switch, they were gone. Nick stroked her face gently, then leaned forward and kissed her on the cheek.

'Good night. Sleep tight,' he whispered.

The reply was barely audible as she drifted towards dreams. 'Don' let . . . the bedbugs . . . bite . . .'

As her breathing became steady, rhythmic, Nick reached out and switched off the bedside lamp. Getting quietly to his feet, he went out of the room, leaving the door slightly ajar. Downstairs in the kitchen he found Helen preparing a spaghetti Bolognese.

'Everything all right?' She asked the question automatically, but when he hesitated in replying, she glanced up from the stove.

176

Nick frowned. 'She's not a happy little girl tonight. Seems worried about the Child Catcher again.'

Helen grimaced. 'That damned film. Whenever she asks for it, I'm in two minds about letting her watch it. Buying a copy was one of the worst moves we ever made.'

Nick went over to the cupboard and took out a bottle of Scotch. 'It's more specific this time. She figures that when the baby comes, we'll lose interest in her. Then the Child Catcher can creep in and take her away.'

Helen stared at him. 'She said that?'

'Yup.' He poured a generous measure of whisky into a tumbler. 'It's OK. I had a little talk with her. But we're going to have to be very careful when that baby comes – be sure to make an equally big fuss of Molly.' He splashed a modest measure of ginger ale into the tumbler, then went to the fridge-freezer for ice-cubes. Once again he experienced the powerful desire for a cigarette to accompany his drink. He tried to shrug the urge off, but it remained with him, nagging away. 'You like anything?' he asked Helen.

'No thanks.' She glanced at him in mock disapproval. 'You hitting the bottle again?'

'After the day I've just had, who can blame me?'

She raised her eyebrows. 'That bad?'

'Worse. That Cooper character...' He did a mime of strangling an invisible adversary. 'If there was ever a more self-centred, arrogant, obnoxious berk, I've yet to meet him.'

Helen smiled slyly. 'Funny. I thought he'd made quite a hit with you. You even phoned me from the airport to describe how he'd insulted Ajay...'

'Yes, well, that was a very short-lived enthusiasm, I'm afraid. He then went on to insult just about everybody else in sight, including me.'

'Oh *dear*. Don't tell me he made a play for one of your girlfriends, as well?'

Nick took a large gulp of whisky, and smacked his lips. 'Worse than that,' he told her. 'He suggested I go out and score some cocaine for him ... oh, and arrange a little female company while I was at it.'

Helen was staring at him now. 'I hope you're joking.'

'He genuinely seemed to think such activities fell within my brief. Told me that was the kind of treatment he gets in Hollywood.'

'The cheeky sod. He should bugger off back there!'

'Quite.'

'Did you, er ... mention this to Terry?'

Nick shook his head. 'Listen, if I had done, Terry would probably have driven straight off to fix it for him.'

Helen grimaced. 'No! You're too hard on Terry. He'd never get involved in anything illegal like that.'

'Love, you don't know the half of it. That man has *changed*. Oh, I know whenever you meet him, he still seems the same affable old fluff, but you don't see him in a work situation. For a client of Cooper's importance, he'd probably be prepared to *kill* to keep him sweet.'

'You're exaggerating.'

'No, not at all!' He considered what he had just said and thought better of it. 'Yes ... sure, a bit. Only ...'

Helen moved closer to him, with genuine concern in her eyes. She opened her arms and he set down his drink, then stepped gladly into her embrace. 'But something's really getting to you, isn't it?' she continued. 'I've noticed it over the last couple of weeks. You're *not* happy.'

He sighed. 'For the first time in my life ...' But he found he couldn't continue. With a sound of exasperation, he shook his head.

'No, go on,' she urged him. 'Tell me. Is it *me*? Is it something *I've* done?'

'God, no! It's nothing to do with you! I mean...' He tried again. 'For the first time in my life, I'm beginning to question what I'm doing.'

'Go on.'

'Well...I keep asking myself, do I really see me working at *Futures* for the rest of my life – or even in PR, come to that? I want...I want to do something *real*.'

'What do you mean, real?'

'I don't know. Something I can see and touch and appreciate. Making furniture or something.'

There was a pause, then Helen stifled a giggle.

'What's so funny about that?' he demanded.

'Nothing, I...I was just thinking about the time you tried to put up those shelves in the living room.'

He grinned sheepishly, remembering hours of curses, injured thumbs and crumbling plaster – and somebody swearing they'd never get involved in DIY again. 'Yes, well, I know I couldn't really make furniture. That was just an example of what I mean.'

'A very bad example,' she pointed out. 'But don't worry. I do understand what you're saying. You have other talents you don't feel able to exploit?'

He sighed. 'Yeah. Trouble is, I don't have a clue what these bloody talents *are*!'

'That's ridiculous.'

'No, it's not, love. I've been involved in PR virtually since I left school, so I can't seem to remember how to do anything else. And that's what fills me with absolute panic: the thought that if it does get to be more than I can handle, there's really nowhere else for me to go.'

'Hey.' She gently patted his back. 'There's *lots* of other

things you can do. And if you need to train for something, it's not too late for that either. You're not exactly ready for the scrapheap yet.'

He frowned. 'I suppose not.'

'And remember, whatever decision you make, I'll back you.'

He pulled away a little, so he could look into her eyes. 'You would, too, wouldn't you?' he murmured. He thought for a moment. 'I don't know, Helen. We've got a mortgage to pay, a kid to raise ... soon *two* kids ... and that needs a regular income.'

'I appreciate all that. But you can't let it compromise your happiness. We only get one life to live, so we owe it to ourselves to be happy.'

'And what about you?' he asked her. 'Are *you* happy?'

'Deliriously.' She glanced at him slyly. 'Despite missing the golden opportunity to become Mrs Ajay Sanjari.'

He grinned. 'I guess I asked for that,' he said. He kissed her fondly on the cheek. 'You know, maybe all I really need now is a holiday. Get out from that bloody office for a couple of weeks.'

Helen patted her stomach. 'Not exactly a good time to be going away from home,' she reminded him.

'Oh, that doesn't matter. I'd be happy just to potter about here. Read a few good books, drink a few bottles of wine, leave the bloody answerphone on ...'

'Oh, that reminds me. Terry phoned for you just a few minutes before you arrived. Wants you to ring him back tonight. He's got some ideas he wants to go over with you.'

Nick made a sound of irritation. He turned back to the work surface to replenish his glass. That nagging desire for a cigarette was with him again, a dull, throbbing ache at the back of his throat. Tomorrow was the first fashion shoot, and his spirit sagged at the very thought of it. He found that he really didn't want to ring Terry; he resented having to devote some of his precious free time to discussing work. He gulped down another mouthful of whisky.

For Christ's sake, what's happening to me? he asked himself. He glanced guiltily at Helen, but she had turned away and was busying herself at the stove again. He drained the glass, and quickly topped it up to the brim again. *Get a grip*, he warned himself. *If you let this thing take hold of you . . .*

The thought didn't progress any further. It was interrupted by the ringing of the phone in the hall, its shrill tone jangling his nerves. Nick took another slug of whisky.

Helen glanced at him inquiringly. 'Want me to get that?' she asked.

He shook his head. 'No, I'll get it,' he said. 'That'll be Terry. Too bloody impatient to wait for me to ring him.'

'Well, tell him I'm just about to serve dinner.'

Setting his glass down carefully, Nick turned and walked a trifle unsteadily into the hall.

But it wasn't Terry. It was Bobby Cooper. Nick recognised instantly the deep, arrogant tones spilling out of the earpiece.

'Hey there, dude, how ya doin'? I was just wonderin' if you'd had a chance to think about my little proposition.'

'How did you get my number?' protested Nick.

'Easy, man. Just looked you up in the book. Now listen, I'm sure we can do some kind of deal on this. You just tell me how much you want to make all the arrangements and I—'

'I've already told you, I'm not interested,' Nick interrupted him. 'Now, if you'll excuse me, I'm very busy. I'll see you tomorrow at six a.m.'

Cooper started to protest, but Nick put the phone down on him. He stalked back to the kitchen, bristling with indignation.

Helen glanced at him. 'That was quick,' she observed.

'Wrong number,' he said. Reaching for the whisky bottle, he filled his glass to the brim, again.

Chapter Eighteen

Finn slowly covers the last hundred yards to Gordie's flat, holding himself ready to run if he needs to. He's left it till after midnight, wanting to be sure he's in no danger of being observed by passers-by. There's a full moon tonight, and it provides more illumination than he is comfortable with, so he hugs the shadows of walls and fences, checking out everything thoroughly before he makes each move.

Now he's just across the road from Gordie's place, and everything looks normal – the steel door and the window shutters buttoned up tight against the outside world. But no light shows through the rectangular slit of the letterbox, which seems odd. If Gordie's in there, then he's sitting in the dark.

Finn frowns. He slips one hand under his jacket to grip the handle of his knife, and that makes him feel a little more confident. He originally planned to walk right up to the front door and knock, but now it seems far too well illuminated. He'll try around the back instead.

He doesn't walk across the road, but doubles back along a series of interconnecting walkways, and approaches the flat from the rear. There's a wooden fence surrounding a small plot of land that originally served as a communal garden for the whole block, but now it's effectively Gordie's back garden. Finn approaches the fence, glances quickly left and right, then scrambles over into the shadows beyond.

The soles of his Nikes hit the grass with barely a sound, and he crouches down beside the fence while he studies Gordie's back door. He can see instantly that something is wrong. The heavy metal door stands slightly ajar, badly buckled across the middle where considerable force has been applied. A crowbar, Finn decides. He feels a shiver of apprehension ripple through him, and then that's replaced by a sense of indignation. Somebody has broken into Gordie's place! Finn has always thought of the flat as unassailable, the one safe haven in an unpredictable world. For an instant, he thinks about running away, leaving it right here, but from somewhere inside him a determination quickly asserts itself. He rises and moves towards the door, putting on his driving gloves.

He stands listening for several minutes before reaching out a hand to push the door open wider. The damaged hinges squeal in protest, and the back of Finn's neck crawls with fear. Calming himself, he steps into darkness, one hand searching the wall for a light switch. His fingers find what they're looking for, and he pushes the switch to the down position. Nothing happens. He is beginning to get a very bad feeling about this.

Then he becomes aware of the sound of breathing: slow, stertorous, coming from somewhere up ahead of him. It doesn't even sound human, and he's just on the point of freaking when a low rumbling growl alerts him to the fact that it's *not* human. He moves forward, peering into the gloom, and then, in the pale wash of moonlight streaming in through the open back door he makes out Lucifer stretched on his side in the hallway.

The animal's not a pretty sight. The lips are curled back

to show his teeth, and his tongue lolls obscenely, coated with thick yellow foam. The dog's eyes look imploringly up at Finn, as if beseeching his help, while the huge chest jerks convulsively as he fights to keep breathing.

Finn crouches beside the dog and strokes his head helplessly. There are scraps of regurgitated meat on the floor beside Lucifer's head, and it doesn't take a genius to conclude that he's been poisoned – doctored steaks pushed through the letterbox. It's one of the oldest tricks in the book, and Lucifer has fallen for it. He gives another convulsive heave and lets out a long, wet fart. The hallway fills with an unholy stink and Finn, stifling a curse, gets back to his feet and moves on. The tortured sound of the dog's breathing follows him.

'Gordie?' He whispers the name, not daring to raise his voice in this unearthly half-light. The door to the lounge is closed, and Finn is now sure that Gordie is in there, probably waiting with a gun to get the bastards that poisoned his dog. Finn rests his back against the wall, and reaches out to rap on the door. 'Gordie, don't shoot,' he calls out. 'It's me, Finn.' Silence. Finn swallows. He takes hold of the handle and tries to open the door – but feels resistance. There is something, or somebody, on the other side, trying to keep the door shut.

'Gordie, that you?' he hisses through the narrow gap. 'It's me, Finn. You OK?'

No answer.

Finn now puts his shoulder to the door and pushes harder, aware of a thick sweat of terror breaking out on his neck and chest. Inside the room, something shifts, and the door opens wider. There's just enough room for him to push his way inside . . .

Something heavy falls across his feet, and he nearly

screams. Looking down, he sees Satan's hideously distorted face, the jaws wide open in a rictus of pain, the foam dried to flecks on his bloated tongue, his dark eyes glazed and vacant. He must have died there, slumped against the door – his last conscious thought being a desire to protect his master. Now Finn becomes aware of a smell in the room: a yeasty, rotten smell that seems to kick him in the pit of the stomach. He heaves and makes a valiant attempt to hold down the impending vomit. He tells himself there's no point in hanging around here, something is badly wrong and he should get the fuck out of it; but part of him is still reluctant to leave before he knows the full story.

Finn reaches out a hand and flicks on the light switch. Again nothing happens. The power must have been turned off at the mains. He takes a deep breath, squeezes his eyes shut, then opens them again. He is gradually adjusting to the darkness and now he can dimly perceive a figure slumped in a chair on the other side of the room. He can just about make out the thick mop of curly hair, the thin white face, the familiar grin.

'Gordie!' Relieved, he steps over Satan and strides into the room. 'I've been worried sick about you. I thought maybe . . .'

His voice trails off. Gordie has made no move to acknowledge Finn. He is sitting in the leather easy chair, his thin arms stretched out on the padded rests, only . . . only something is wrong. Gordie's jeans and underpants are down around his ankles and there seems to be an enveloping blackness in his lap – a blackness that seems to have spread all across the seat of the chair.

'What the fuck?' Finn steps closer, scared but fascinated at the same time. He takes the Zippo from his pocket and strikes it, holds it out to get a better look.

Now he can see that Gordie is dead. His eyes gaze blankly back at Finn, holding the dancing reflection of the lighter's flame. His thin arms are tied to the rests. What, in the dark, appeared to be a grin, is something infinitely more horrible. The teeth are clenched as though he is still in terrible pain. You can see where he's bitten through his lips, and where black blood is matted into his beard. Finn keeps on staring. He doesn't want to, but somehow he can't help himself, as if he needs to record every detail of this. He sees now a wide splash of dried blood down the front of Gordie's T-shirt; it almost obliterates the *Save The Rainforest* slogan on the front. Most puzzling of all, Gordie seems to be wearing some kind of a tie, a stubby, lumpy little necktie that hangs a few inches below the neck of his T-shirt.

Finn remembers Mason saying something about that. *Tell Gordie, I'm gonna give him a nice new necktie to wear.*

And sure enough, Gordie is wearing one, but it's like no other tie Finn's ever seen. It's more like . . . more like . . .

Oh my God, no, it can't be, please don't let it be!

Finn recoils in terror. It's like he's been hit in the chest with a baseball bat, the breath swatted right out of him.

He's just recognised what it is he's looking at. That's not a necktie. It's Gordie's penis. Somebody's cut it off, and somehow attached it to his throat, so it hangs down. This is Otis Mason's idea of a joke.

The vomit fills Finn's mouth before he can even draw breath. He half turns, and sprays the contents of his stomach into the darkness of the room. His eyes fill with tears of shock, and he drops to his knees. He heaves convulsively, and the liquid shoots out of him in thick spurts, the acid stinging his throat. He moans, and wipes his eyes on the sleeve of his jacket.

For a moment Finn is lost. He cannot grasp the enormity of what has happened. Gordie is his stability: the one adult he can rely on. He can't be dead, he just *can't* be! Finn has to force himself to turn and look again at the silent white face staring out of the darkness.

Gordie, for fuck's sake, what is this shit?

He needs Gordie. Gordie is his lifeline, his employer and, Christ . . . moving to more practical matters now, his *bank*. What about the money Gordie's invested for Finn? All his savings? What happens about that?

Kneeling there, Finn allows himself to cry for a while. After all, it's dark here; there's nobody to see him. Whoever did this to Gordie (Otis Mason, who else?) is long gone. Nothing's going to happen to Finn if he just stays put for a moment. Besides, he needs to *think*. What's he going to do? He's told the others that Mason doesn't scare him, but after what's happened to Gordie – *my God, look at his throat, the blood* – how is he going to convince them to stay together? How are they going to *survive*, for Christ's sake?

Finn flicks the wheel of the Zippo again. His gaze moves about the room, noting that it has been ransacked, stripped of all items of value. Gordie's prized hi-fi system is gone, along with most of his CDs. The stash of dope which usually lay carelessly on the onyx coffee table is gone too – naturally.

Then Finn looks at the sofa, and notices that it doesn't seem to have been moved. A glimmer of hope springs into his mind.

Maybe they didn't find the main stash!

He stands up and pulls the sofa away from the wall, revealing the stretch of unblemished panelling beneath the false window.

Yes! Now all he has to do is find the keys . . .

He remembers that Gordie always kept the keys somewhere on him, so he'll have to search the body. Finn's not sure he's up to that, but tells himself he must. Maybe there's money hidden in there, or more dope that he can sell. And guns – maybe there's guns?

OK, I can do this.

Finn takes several deep breaths, and then approaches Gordie's body. He holds the lighter close to the dead man's face. Up close, you can see how the necktie trick's been achieved: a short horizontal slash across the windpipe, and the pouch of the scrotum pushed inside it. Finn hopes that Gordie was already dead when they did that, but the expression on his face suggests he wasn't. Finn crouches down beside the body, noticing that it already exudes an unpleasant odour.

This killing must have happened sometime yesterday, he tells himself. That's why the promised back-up never arrived at the Nile Club. If he'd still been alive, Gordie would have sent them. This makes Finn feel a lot better about his former employer.

He reaches gingerly into Gordie's jeans pockets, but somebody has already cleaned them out. He tries the pockets of the embroidered Indian waistcoat, but has no luck there either. He's about to give up his search, and look for a crowbar instead, when he suddenly notices the unusual ring that Gordie has inserted through his left ear – with two tiny keys threaded on to it.

Finn instantly feels cheered by this. He thinks of Mason's posse tearing the place up in their search for Gordie's treasure – not realising the solution was right in front of them all the time. A hollow victory, but at least it's something.

Finn reaches up to tug at the earring and Gordie's head

hinges backwards, widening the ugly cut in his throat. His penis drops into his lap with a dull plop, as though trying to return to its original home. Finn grimaces, fumbles the earring open, and manages to hang on to the keys with his shaking fingers. He takes them over to the wall and opens up the secret recess. Setting the lighter down on the floor, he looks inside Gordie's hiding place.

There's no money in there, just a few leftover packages of cocaine and a couple of phials of crack. But the long canvas holdall he saw the last time he came here is still tucked away at the back. Finn reaches in and drags it out. It's heavy and the contents clatter as he pulls it closer. Unzipping the bag, he examines the guns with interest. There are two heavy-looking pistols: a .38 Smith and Wesson revolver and a Glock 9mm automatic. There's a sawn-off Remington pump-action and, best of all, a sexy little Uzi machine-pistol. There are boxes of ammunition and magazines for the automatic weapons.

In the semi-darkness, Finn gives a nod of satisfaction. OK, it's not much, but it's a start. If shooters are going to be the new currency on the estate, well at least now he's got enough to open an account. He pictures himself putting a bullet between Otis Mason's eyes, and the anticipation is so strong he can almost taste it. But he mustn't be in a hurry, he warns himself. Got to wait till the time is right. Go rushing in there all unprepared, and he'll just be asking for a pasting.

He zips up the bag and gets to his feet, testing the reassuring weight of it in his grasp. He picks up the lighter and takes a last look at Gordie. His head's tilted back now, so he's grinning up at the ceiling. The slash in his throat curves like a spare smile.

'Should have let me have these before,' murmurs Finn,

rattling the armoury in the holdall. 'Maybe then you wouldn't be in this fucking mess.'

He stands in silence for a moment, wondering if there's something else he should say, over the body. Like a prayer or something. He's seen that in movies. Only he doesn't believe in prayers, and wherever Gordie was headed, he must be well installed by now, maybe already looking for a new scam. One thing for sure, it won't be harps and halos he's flogging; more likely charcoal and pitchforks.

Finn shrugs. He snaps the lighter shut and goes out of the room, closing the door behind him. He pauses to look at Lucifer, but the dog's clearly past saving, his massive chest barely rising and falling. So Finn walks out into the night, lugging the holdall along with him.

It's early morning now, a light rain is falling, and he's never felt so lonely in his life.

Chapter Nineteen

The problem was, Bobby C. didn't like the jeans. They didn't feel right, he said. Sure, he understood that these were the exact same jeans he'd OK'd at the fitting the previous evening, but something must have changed since then. Maybe he'd put on a couple of pounds in the night; he had this weird metabolism that could do that to him. But, anyway, something must have happened because the jeans were *pinching* him. He just didn't feel comfortable in them, he needed to have bigger jeans brought in, and meantime he'd just go sit in the trailer and read the newspaper, how would that be?

Nick stood there and watched it happen and wondered how good a chance he had of getting Cooper on his own and throwing in one good punch at his nose. Sure, it would be the last thing he ever did; Amos and Andy would be down on him like two brick shithouses but, boy, would it be worth it. Glancing at his watch he saw that it was already gone ten a.m. The film crew had been here over five hours already and, so far, not one shot had been taken.

They were all assembled in a godforsaken area of the Merton Estate. Arc lamps illuminated the stretch of graffiti-sprayed wall where Cooper was required to strut his stuff. In addition to the photographer, Alan Richards, a whole regiment of people stood around waiting glumly for

193

something to happen: an art director, a stylist, a hair and make-up lady, two photographic assistants, not to mention the half-dozen burly security men specially recruited by Terry since the last disastrous visit to this estate. If you added to this the light police presence, the driver of the trailer, and the large crowd of onlookers that had gathered to watch the proceedings, it all added up to an awful lot of people waiting for Cooper to get his act together.

It had not started promisingly. Nick and the limousine driver had arrived at the hotel at six on the dot, knowing full well that the photo team had been setting up from first light, and would not want to waste any more time than was strictly necessary. Nick had found Cooper and his entourage still fast asleep in their respective beds, and had the very devil of a job to prise them out. He'd gone to Gabe Rothman's room in an attempt to enlist a little support, only to discover that Rothman had left early with the intention of doing some sightseeing. Nick was soon wishing that he'd joined him.

Cooper had insisted that he eat a substantial breakfast before he set foot outside the premises. So Nick was left to pace around the foyer in impotent fury while Cooper and company dined on food specially prepared by his personal chef, Marco. Nick had finally got Cooper – along with Lionel, Amos and Andy – into the limo at about eight o'clock. Various other members of the entourage piled into a second limo, and at last they were off. They had made it to the location by eight thirty-five, whereupon Cooper wasted fifteen minutes inspecting the trailer, and another fifteen complaining about its various shortcomings.

It wasn't as big as he would have liked, the radio system was – to use his own description – 'shit', and just where was Marco supposed to prepare the vitamin drinks and wholefood snacks necessary to get Cooper through the day? So Marco was despatched back to the hotel to prepare said drinks and snacks, while a skinny, hyperactive youth called Boots was despatched to pick up the sound system.

For his next trick, Cooper made a pass at Anna, the young hair and make-up girl, which almost resulted in her walking off the set – 'Hey, whatsa matter, babe? Cain't you take a goddamned *joke*?' – and then the jeans were produced, and the final bombshell was dropped.

Now, as Nick stood watching in silent disgust, Cooper was disappearing back through the open door of the trailer. Since his late arrival, Nick figured he had only come out of it twice, for less than five minutes on each occasion.

Alan Richards shuffled over, a fed-up expression evident on his face. He was wearing a leather flying helmet, its sheepskin earmuffs down, not so much against the cold, Nick decided, but to hide his bandaged ear. Alan was smoking a cigarette, and Nick found he couldn't take his eyes off the glowing tip of it. Just one wouldn't hurt, surely?

'What we supposed to do now?' muttered Alan. 'The light's perfect, but it ain't gonna stay like this for long.'

Nick nodded. He gestured to Alan's cigarette. 'You got a spare one?' he asked.

'Sure.' Alan reached for the pack, then hesitated. He glanced at Nick doubtfully. 'Thought you gave up,' he said.

'I did. But it's a good day to start again, wouldn't you say?'

Alan shrugged, handed him the pack. Nick took out a cigarette, put it between his lips and accepted the light that the photographer offered him. He inhaled deeply, blew out smoke. A powerful dizziness swept through him and he shook his head to dispel it. Then he ran a hand through his hair, pushing it out of his eyes.

'It'll take us ages to get hold of more jeans,' said Alan.

'I know. Fuck it. Those ones fitted him fine last night. I'll go and have a word with him.'

'Well, don't lose your rag. It'll only make things worse.'

'Thanks for the advice,' said Nick gruffly. He made his way through the crowd of waiting people, and walked across to the door of the trailer. Amos stood by the entrance, inscrutable in shades and aggressive black leather. He held out a hand to Nick in an effort to discourage him from entering, but today Nick was having none of it.

'Get out of my way!' he snapped and Amos stepped back in surprise. Nick climbed up the steps, and in through the open door of the trailer. There he found Cooper, Andy and Lionel sitting around the built-in table, playing cards for loose change. Despite the close proximity of the police, Cooper was casually smoking a joint. He glanced up as Nick entered, and gave him a lazy grin.

'Hey, what say, my man? How goes it out in the real world?' He noticed the cigarette in Nick's hands and frowned his disapproval. 'Whoah dere, dude. Don'tcha know those things are *baaad* for you?'

Nick fixed him with a scornful look. 'I'd say you're the wrong person to be giving a lecture on that subject, wouldn't you?' he snarled.

For a moment Cooper studied him thoughtfully. 'Now I could be wrong,' he said in an exaggeratedly camp voice. 'But I *swear* I detect a trace've hostility in you.'

'More than a trace,' Nick assured him, doing his best to hang on to his temper. He stepped closer to the table, leaned one arm on the edge, and spoke with controlled venom. 'Would you mind telling me exactly what the *fuck* you're playing at?'

Cooper glared at Nick for a moment. Then he glanced at his companions. 'Shee-it,' he said. 'This man is *pissed*!'

'I haven't touched a drop,' retorted Nick, misunderstanding.

'No, man, I mean you's angry. Me, I'm askin' myself if it could be anything *I've* done.'

'You?' Nick laughed bitterly. 'Jesus Christ, as if!' He inhaled on his cigarette, blew out smoke, then pointed at Cooper. 'A word in private, if you don't mind.'

Cooper frowned, as if considering the wisdom of such a move. Finally he shrugged and threw down his cards. 'What the fuck, I had a lousy hand anyway. OK, boys, why don't you go out and get yourselves a little fresh air? Let me and Nick have some space, whaddyasay?'

His companions got obediently to their feet and moved across to the exit, the vehicle swaying beneath the weight of Andy's massive frame. They descended the steps into the open air, and closed the door behind them.

Nick sat down opposite Cooper. He was aware that his heart rate was up, and that he was about an inch away from losing his temper, so he made an effort to calm himself before he spoke again. When he did, it was in a quiet, toneless voice.

'This can't go on, Bobby,' he said.

'Say what?' Cooper looked puzzled. 'You seem to be all het up, Nick. Need to chill out a little – stop takin' everything so goddamn serious.'

Nick shook his head. 'I'll tell you what I need, Bobby. I need you stripped to the waist and wearing nothing but a pair of AJs.'

Cooper waggled his eyebrows, adopting a camp voice.

'Ooh, Nicky, *sugar*! This is kind of sudden. I gotta decide how I *feel* about this!'

Nick didn't crack a smile. 'No jokes,' he warned. 'We're getting a little tired of the jokes. And we're all fed up to the back teeth with the fucking prima donna routine as well.' He jerked a thumb over his shoulder. 'Outside that door are a bunch of professionals waiting around for your input. They're not asking you to *do* very much: just stand there and strike a few silly poses. In return for that you're being paid a sum of money that many people won't earn in their lifetime . . .'

'Hey, don't try hittin' on me with that jive. You're talkin' about the neighbourhood I came from! Shit, when I was a kid . . .'

'Bobby.' Nick leaned forward across the table and silenced Cooper with a look. 'Do me a favour, will you? Just for five minutes, shut the fuck up and *listen*.'

Cooper sat back as abruptly as if he'd been slapped in the face. His jaw dropped. He looked like he couldn't believe what he was hearing.

'I don't *care* where you come from,' Nick told him. 'I don't care that you've earned a thousand dollars a minute or that you've got a penthouse full of platinum discs. I don't much care that you think the rest of the world should hang on your every word and, frankly, I couldn't give a flying fuck what you think of me. As far as I'm concerned, you're here for one reason only. To do a job. And I would *really* appreciate it if you would get up off your indolent arse and do it.'

Cooper sat there looking at Nick.

'You finished?' he asked, at last.

'That'll do for starters,' Nick told him.

Cooper let out a long whistle from between his teeth. 'Boy, did I have you figured wrong,' he said. 'You got a tongue can cut to the bone, when you's in the mood, don'cha? See now, all I said about those jeans was, you know, that they pinch a little aroun' the crutch . . .'

'I don't care if they have you singing with the Vienna Boys' Choir! Get them on and get outside.' Nick glanced at his watch. 'I'm giving you ten minutes,' he fumed. 'If you're not outside by then, I'll come in here and drag you out myself.' He got up from his seat, and was about to leave, when he hesitated. 'One more thing,' he said. Reaching out a hand, he took the joint from Cooper's lips and ground it into an ashtray on the table. 'We'll do this by the book now. When you're back at the hotel, that's one thing. When you're working, I expect you to stay within the law. Understood?'

Cooper smiled. 'Absolutely,' he said. And Nick even thought he sensed genuine respect in the other man's tone.

'Ten minutes.' Nick tapped his watch. 'Don't forget.'

He walked to the door and let himself out into the fresh air, where another wave of dizziness went through him. He took a last regretful drag on the cigarette, then dropped it and ground it under his foot. Amos and Andy lounged against the side of the trailer. They gave him suspicious looks but he ignored them and headed back towards Alan Richards, who was making some final adjustments to his camera set-up.

He looked at Nick hopefully. 'Well?' he inquired.

'Ten minutes,' Nick assured him, and hoped he sounded more confident than he felt. He realised that if Cooper didn't put in an appearance at the appointed time, then he'd be forced to go in there and attempt to carry out his threat. At which point, Amos and Andy would almost certainly put him straight into intensive care. But Nick appreciated that the one thing he couldn't do was back down on this. Do that, and Cooper would continue to treat him as a joke for the rest of his stay.

Nick offered up a silent prayer to the gods of reason, and settled down to wait.

Eleven minutes passed with what seemed like indecent haste. The second hand on Nick's watch had performed another half revolution, and he was steeling himself for a confrontation, when the trailer door swung open and Cooper emerged, dressed only in jeans. There was a sudden flurry of activity as the make-up lady, stylist and art director converged on him.

Nick breathed a sigh of relief and Alan patted him on the shoulder.

'All *right*,' he said. 'Let's get this show on the road!'

After that, the shoot seemed to go well. Nick retreated to a safe distance to watch the proceedings. The cigarette had left a stale taste in his mouth, but he noted with a trace of concern that he still fancied another one.

Cooper, duly made up and sprayed with moisture to make his physique glisten, took his position and followed the instructions given to him by Alan and the art director. Nick noted that, divested of his top, Cooper wasn't quite the same magnificent physical specimen that had appeared in *No Quarter*. He was beginning to run to flab around the waist and upper arms, and had to suck in his belly for each shot. The final picture might well require a little judicious retouching with an airbrush.

Turning away, Nick surveyed the crowd watching the proceedings from the other side of the police barriers. There were maybe a couple of hundred of them, the majority of them black, doubtless wondering if the shoot would ever become more interesting than this. Uniformed policemen were placed at strategic points around the perimeter of the shoot, playing down their presence, desperately trying to look like they belonged. The security men that Terry had hired paced around muttering into walkie-talkies. They all wore matching red sweatshirts and baseball caps, and seemed determined to give the impression they were earning their fee; though they'd only be doing that if there was some kind of trouble to contend with.

A couple of kids on mountain bikes wheeled slowly past the edge of the crowd. Nick thought they looked like the same two who'd stolen Alan's camera, but he couldn't be sure, and anyway what could he hope to do about that now?

Then Nick noticed Lionel standing in the midst of the crowd, chatting to a couple of men. He started taking notice, mainly because those two guys looked like trouble – particularly the tall, thin individual dressed like something that had escaped from a bad-taste party. He stood a head taller than Lionel, grinning down at him from beneath the brim of a black fedora. When he said something, Lionel started talking excitedly. The man in the hat put a hand on Lionel's arm, a gesture of obvious familiarity, and Lionel beamed back up at him. Next thing, Lionel was leading the two of them through the crowd towards the barrier. There he had a word with the policeman guarding that access point, showed him his laminated security pass, and gestured to his two companions. The policeman shrugged and nodded them through, and the three of them began to stroll towards the shoot.

Nick found himself moving forward to intercept them. He wasn't exactly sure why, but something didn't seem right.

'Lionel?' he called out, and the three men turned to look at him. 'What's going on?' he demanded.

Lionel looked startled. Then he smiled sheepishly. 'Oh, Mr Saunders, hi. I'm just takin' these two boys over to the trailer. They wanted to meet Bobby, and I told them I'd fix it. They're *fans*.'

'Is that right?' Nick looked at Lionel blankly. Then he waved a hand in the direction of the crowd. 'But *they're* all fans, aren't they? What's so special about these two?'

Lionel pondered the question a moment. 'Well, er, they've . . . they've come a very long way to see him. And they've, er . . . yeah, they've got this idea for a film, they think Bobby might be interested in.'

'Really?'

The man in the hat flashed Nick a dazzling, gold-studded grin. 'Relax, star,' he said. 'Me jus' wanna sound de man out on a few ideas!' Then he laughed, making noises like the dog in the old *Wacky Races* cartoons.

Nick scowled. This situation stank of an imminent drugs deal. He moved in a little closer and spoke quietly. 'Here's what we'll do,' he said. 'You two turn around and get back to the other side of that barrier. If Mr Cooper wants to talk to you, he can do it in his own time.'

The man in the hat looked distinctly amused by this.

'We', now, sport. Me t'inkin' dat dis is a free country. Was' stoppin' me and me breddar here from gwan see de man dere? You? You gwan stop us?'

Nick smiled back at him. 'Me, the police and the security men if necessary. I didn't come down with the last shower, you know. And I've already had words with Bobby about the kind of merchandise you're selling.'

The tall man looked affronted. 'Sellin'? Me no sellin' nuffin'!'

'Yeah,' said Lionel. 'Like I said, Mr Saunders, they've got this screenplay idea. You ain't got no right to come here makin' accusations like that.'

Nick moved a step closer and fixed the tall man with a look. 'A screenplay idea, huh? Perhaps you'd like to tell me about it?'

The tall man looked momentarily irritated. Then he masked it with a laugh. 'OK, sport, why not?' He paused for a moment as though thinking how to start. 'Dere's dis real tough breddar, runs a powerful posse, seen? Den 'long come dis skinny white mon, wid more mouth dan sense, start shootin' off at de jaw . . . you follow me so far?'

Nick nodded. 'I think so,' he said.

'Good. We', de next t'ing you know, de breddars get a little bit tired of bein' tol' what to do by dis prick. Dey t'ink he done overstay his welcome. So dey come round his place one dark night and stop his clock—'

'OK,' interrupted Nick. 'I've heard enough.'

The tall man looked wounded. 'You na like me story?'

'Not really. Too far-fetched.'

'Oh no, sport. Me'd say she dead realistic.'

Nick stared at him for a moment. 'Get back behind the barriers,' he said, 'or I call over the security men. It's up to you.'

The tall man made a sucking sound with his teeth. Then he turned abruptly away, motioning to his companion with a flick of his head. 'Come on, Linton, less split. Me not gwan to stand aroun' listenin' to some dick in a suit!' The two men began to head back towards the barrier.

'Hey!' Lionel shouted after them. 'What about the screenplay?'

The tall man spoke back over his shoulder. 'You kna' where to fin' me.'

Lionel grunted. He threw an accusing glare at Nick. 'Thanks,' he muttered. 'I finally find me a live one and you scare him right off. You know somethin', you got a real attitude problem, man.'

'Yeah?' Nick shrugged. 'Better than having a coke problem, wouldn't you say?'

They began to head back towards the shoot.

'Bobby is gonna *shit* when I tell him about this,' said Lionel glumly.

'I'm sure he will. But it's as I already told you: if you boys are going to fool around with that stuff, you do it when there's nobody from my company there to get involved.'

'Oh, so it's OK when we're back in our hotel?'

'I didn't say that! As far as I'm concerned, I don't want to see or hear *anything* about it.'

As they neared the camera, Nick saw that Cooper was warming to his new role of male model: hamming it up for the crew, throwing a few muscle-man poses, flexing his biceps and pulling goofy faces. The results would hardly be usable, but Alan was dutifully shooting off a few frames to keep the star sweet.

The sudden loud bang took everybody by surprise, and it made Nick's heart jump in his chest. But he was worried only for an instant, quickly identifying the noise as a car backfiring. Yet he was really intrigued to see Bobby C. Cooper's reaction.

The big man looked instantly terrified. His jaw dropped open, his eyes bulged, his hands gestured involuntarily – and he very nearly jumped out of his skin. For an instant, he looked as though he was about to fling himself to the ground in terror, but then the relieved laughter of the crew signalled it was a false alarm – and it must have simultaneously occurred to him that all eyes were still fixed upon him. He clapped both hands to his chest, staggered a few steps, and crumpled slowly to the floor with a groan. The whole thing was over in an instant, and it seemed to have fooled the crew. They reacted with polite laughter and a smattering of applause. Cooper sat up, grinning heartily, then he noticed Nick eyeing him intently. His expression faltered as he realised that Nick had seen through his little pantomime.

Who are you trying to kid? thought Nick. *You were scared, boy. You nearly shit yourself!*

It was a small incident, all over in a matter of seconds, but it was Nick's first indication that Bobby C. Cooper might not be quite what he seemed.

Chapter Twenty

Finn crouches behind the brick wall, watching the archway that leads up to his parents' flat, and trying to pluck up the courage to approach it. Gordie's death has him scared shitless, he doesn't mind admitting it – and he now knows exactly how far Otis Mason is prepared to go to claim this piece of turf. Finn hasn't told the others about Gordie's death. He's merely announced that Gordie wasn't there when he called around, which isn't exactly a lie. The others are already demoralised, so news like that would send them running in all directions like headless chickens. Finn needs to salvage the situation, hold them together, show them other ways to survive. By the time they hear about Gordie's death – and it's only a matter of time before somebody discovers the body – they've got to have become a working unit again.

Finn has his eye on a newsagent's shop in nearby Rusholme; he figures that might be a good place to start putting the pieces back together.

Meanwhile, he has his own problems. He's afraid that Mason and his posse might be staking out his parents' place, waiting for him to show. But there's no getting away from it, after just a couple of nights sleeping at the Swamp, there are things that Finn badly needs – the emergency cash that's stashed in his room, his portable CD and some decent sounds, a good hot bath and, most importantly, a change of clothing.

The walkways seem deserted. Finn can put it off no longer. He gets to his feet and approaches the arch, reaching into his jacket for the keys but holding himself ready to run at the first glimpse of an unfamiliar face. He steps inside and glances up the bare staircase, knowing that if there is to be an ambush, this is probably where they will lie in wait for him. But everything looks normal. He climbs the steps slowly, setting his feet down with care, not wanting to alert anyone to his approach. He gains the first-floor landing and walks along to the door of number 67. Inserting the key into the lock, he opens the door and steps inside.

'Shaun?' His mother's voice, sounding anxious. 'That didn't take long, did you get—?' She breaks off just as she appears in the sitting-room doorway, staring at Finn like she hasn't seen him for years. 'Oh,' she says at last. 'It's you.'

He sneers at her. He can see that she's hurting; she's probably gone without H for a couple of days now. 'Nice welcome,' he observes. 'I can see you've missed me. Where's Dad?'

'He's ... he's gone out.' There's something evasive in her tone. She seems to realise it, and offers more information: 'He went down to the shops.'

'Yeah?' Finn isn't convinced. OK, so it's dole day, but that lazy bastard never went to the shops in his life. More likely he's out looking to make a connection, blow the whole wad on the price of a couple of fixes. He steps past his mother into the sitting room, and glances suspiciously about. He notices the television lying on its back, the black scorch marks on the floorboards and up the wall. He gives his mother an enquiring look.

'Somebody came looking for you,' she explains. 'A tall black guy with funny clothes. He said...' She picks nervously at a loose thread hanging from the sleeve of her cardigan.

'What?' Finn prompts her.

'He said he'd taken over from you. That you're finished around here. Wanted us to tell him where you were.'

'And what did you say?'

'What *could* we say? We didn't know where you were, did we? And even if we had...'

Finn laughs bitterly. 'Oh, sure. You two would never grass me up, right? Not unless he made it worth your while.'

She stares at him. 'That's not fair,' she protests. She makes an effort to soften him up a little. 'I'll make you a nice cup of tea, shall I? And... I think there's some soup in the cupboard.'

'Forget it. I'm not staying long.' He prods the dead television with the toe of his trainer. 'So *he* did this? Otis Mason.'

'Is that his name? He just put his boot right into it. It was your Dad let him in. The bloke said he was a friend of yours. How were we to know he was up to no good?' She frowns, looks at her feet. 'Finn, I don't suppose you're carrying?'

He shakes his head. '*He* took it all, didn't he! The bastards had shooters...' For a moment he's back there in the narrow alley behind the Nile Club, seeing the muzzle flashes of the pistol lighting up Otis Mason's grinning face, feeling Gibbo's body jerk as the bullets punch into him...

Finn takes out his cigarettes, offers her a smoke, then

lights them both with the brass Zippo. They stand there smoking in silence for a moment. 'Did you hear about Gibbo?' he asks her at last.

She frowns. 'That kid you knock about with? What about him?'

Finn looks at her for a moment in disbelief, then realises that it isn't so unusual. His parents never buy newspapers, and the telly's in no condition to broadcast the information. They have no friends left they don't owe large amounts of money to, and round here that's as good as having no friends at all. Still, you'd have thought that somebody on the estate would have told them about it. No doubt the cops would soon be sniffing around and asking questions. Finn doesn't feel like talking now; he's reluctant to rake over those particular coals, so he just shrugs.

'It's not important.' He turns to the door. 'Anyway, I'd better not hang about. Need some stuff from my room.'

'No, Finn, wait!' Her hand on his arm now, trying to restrain him. 'What's the hurry? Let me heat up a can of soup for you. You must be starving.'

He studies her for a moment. She's as jittery as a bedbug, and he's not sure that it's all just withdrawal symptoms. She seems distinctly nervous about something.

'What's going on?' he asks.

'Nothing!' The reply seems too quick, too forced. 'It's just, you know, you've been away a couple of nights and I . . . I'm *worried* about you.'

'Bollocks,' he says. 'Since when did you turn into Florence fucking Nightingale?' He heads out into the hallway, and she follows him, tugging at his sleeve like a little girl.

'We could sit and talk, just the two of us, the way we used to – what d'you say?' He notices that her gaze keeps flicking towards the staircase, there's something up there that she doesn't want him to see, and a powerful suspicion takes hold of him. He gives her a shove in the chest, pushing her back a couple of steps, and then he runs up the stairs.

Theresa calls after him. 'It was your Dad's idea, Finn! The giro cheques didn't come this morning and . . . I told him not to do it. I said you'd come back and get mad, but he wouldn't listen to me! He was desperate, you see! We both were! You can see that, Finn, can't you? Finn? Finn?'

He is up on the landing now, looking at the remains of his bedroom door. The four powerful locks have been jemmied until the wooden frame has collapsed upon itself. It must have taken some time to do this. Finn kicks open the shattered door and looks into his desecrated room. He sees instantly that his hi-fi is missing; there's a square patch on the dusty shelf where it previously stood. Drawers and cupboards are open and their contents strewn across the room, as if burglars have been at work. Looking around, he begins to miss other things. His portable CD player. His laptop computer. Even his Bobby C. Cooper albums, for Christ's sake!

He just stands there, looking around the room in mute disbelief. He hears his mother coming slowly up the stairs, and she's talking ten to the dozen now, almost as though she's afraid of what might happen if she stays silent.

'You've got to understand, Finn. We were doing turkey. We were counting on those dole cheques. When they didn't come, well, we panicked, didn't we? And your Dad couldn't help himself, see? But we've been talking about it, right? We're going to get ourselves registered down the clinic – yeah, start getting methadone, clean up our act. Should have done it years ago really, but we . . . we'll make it up to you, Finn, really we will.'

He shakes his head. He doesn't want to listen to any more of her pathetic excuses, he's liable to blow his top and hit her. He finds a sports bag lying amidst the debris and throws it on to the bed. He begins to stuff things into it, not taking much notice of what they are, just grabbing handfuls of clothes and ramming them into the bag.

She sees what he's doing and dares to come into the room.

'Finn, listen to me! What were we supposed to do? That fellow who came here, he told us you were finished. He said you wouldn't be coming back.'

Finn turns on her, feeling his anger burst like a hot balloon in his chest. 'Oh, and you were ready to believe that, weren't you! Finn ain't comin' back, so let's see what he's got we can sell!'

'It wasn't like that! You don't know what it's like. It's as if your whole body is *screaming*!'

'Yeah, well, that ain't my fault, is it? I mean, I didn't make you a junkie, did I? I didn't ram the stuff into your veins.'

'No, but . . . but you made it easy for us to get it, didn't you!' She's angry, too, her voice rising in a shrill, indignant squeal. 'You were the one who always brought it back for us, like some kind of treat. Maybe if it had been harder to get, we wouldn't be in this mess!'

He glares at her, astonished by her ingratitude.

'You . . . you're blaming me?' he cries. 'I don't believe this. You're blaming *me*!' He turns away from her, has to, otherwise he's going to punch her in the face. 'You rotten bitch,' he says. 'I helped you, that's all. If it hadn't been for me, the two of you would be dead by now from jacking up kitchen cleaner or some other shit. And don't lay that crap on me. You two were addicts long before I started dealing.' He paces about for a moment, shaking his head. He can't believe she just said what she did. 'Well, fuck you,' he concludes. 'Let's see how the two of you get on without me.'

'No, Finn, don't be like that!' Anxiety back in her voice now as she realises that she has gone too far – that this time he really does mean to go. 'You're right, I shouldn't have said that. I'm doing turkey; it makes you say things without thinking.'

She watches as he kneels down and prises up a section of loose floorboard in one corner of the room.

'What are you doing?' she asks, but he doesn't answer.

He reaches into the gap and pulls out a small roll of banknotes: a couple of hundred quid that he's tucked away for an emergency.

'Jesus, Mary and Joseph,' she says.

He grins up at her. 'Didn't know about that, did you?' he gloats. 'Could have gone right out and bought what you wanted, 'stead of havin' to flog all my gear first.' He stuffs the money into his jeans pocket. 'Well, too late. I've got it now.'

'Finn,' she pleads. 'Don't go. Not like this.'

'How would you like me to go?' he asks her. 'In a taxi?'

'No, please don't make jokes. This is serious. We need to stick together now, the three of us.'

He laughs bitterly. 'Christ, that would be a first! You two've held me back all my life. Now I'm gettin' shut of you, and do you know what? It's a good feeling.'

'No, Finn, listen to me. We have to talk this over. We

have to—' She breaks off at the sound of the key in the front door. She opens her mouth to shout a warning, but Finn grabs her and claps a hand over her mouth.

'Theresa?' Dad's voice down in the hall. 'Theresa, I got the stuff. Where are you?'

They can hear him shuffling around downstairs, looking for his wife, eager to show her the deal he's made.

'Seventy quid for the hi-fi, thirty for the computer, twenty for the other stuff. Then I looked out one of those black kids in the Sports. Tell you what, he was OK – made me a good deal . . . Theresa? You upstairs?'

His footsteps now coming up the bare wooden steps, his voice still talking excitedly. 'Hey, listen, I got something else for you. A surprise! Saw it in the market-hall. It's second-hand, but you can't tell. Might even be the same one! Theresa, you in here?'

Shaun steps through the doorway. He's grinning like a kid, and he's holding a framed picture of the Sacred Heart. Jesus looks sorrowfully out from behind grimy glass. His curly hair and beard make Finn think of Gordie.

Shaun sees Finn and Theresa standing there and the grin slips off his face.

'Finn,' he says tonelessly. 'I can explain.'

Finn isn't aware of crossing the short distance between himself and his father, isn't even aware of hitting him in the face – though he must have, because an instant later Shaun is sprawled against the bannisters, blood pouring from his open mouth, and the knuckles of Finn's right hand are skinned raw.

Shaun still hangs on to the picture, as though it's some kind of a life preserver.

'Enough,' says Theresa, but Finn isn't anywhere near finished. He steps from the room and snatches the Sacred

Heart picture from his father's hands. He looks at it for a moment.

'Very nice,' he says. Then he hits Shaun with it, swiping him sideways across the head – once, twice, three times.

The glass shatters and Shaun is crawling away, whimpering, hands up to shield his face, but Finn keeps hitting him until the picture splinters to matchwood in his hands.

Shaun has reached the top of the stairs now, his face streaming blood from a dozen cuts. 'Please,' he groans. He gets up on his knees and holds out his hands in supplication. 'Please, Finn . . . I'm your Dad . . .'

Finn places a foot against Shaun's chest and pushes hard, tipping him backwards down the stairs. He slides down on his back, his spine jolting against every ridge, before coming to rest spreadeagled on the floor.

'You've killed him!' gasps Theresa, but Finn shakes his head. Shaun is still moving and ragged moans come from his broken mouth.

Finn spits down at the sprawled figure, then strides back into his room to collect the bag, while Theresa scrambles down towards her husband. She is bending over him, sobbing, when Finn comes down the stairs after her. She glances up at him wildly.

'Finn, he's hurt bad! Call him an ambulance.'

Finn nods. 'OK,' he says. He bends over his father and looks him straight in the face. 'You're an ambulance,' he says.

Theresa stares at him in total incomprehension.

'This is serious! He could die.'

'Think so?' Finn considers this, shakes his head. 'I couldn't be that lucky.' He steps over his father and heads for the door. 'Anyway, I'm off. Remember, the rent's due today. Hope he kept a bit of dosh back to cover it.'

'Finn, don't go! Please!'

'Too late,' he tells her. 'Way too late. It's time the two of you learned to fend for yourselves. From now on I'm going to be busy looking after number one. See you around.'

He goes out of the door, slamming it behind him. Then he walks quickly away – without looking back.

Chapter Twenty-One

Standing beside Otis, Carmel looked up at the towering, spotlit façade of the Midland Hotel, feeling decidedly overawed by its magnificence. She had already walked past the place a few times since her arrival in Manchester, and had once paused to watch a uniformed flunky guiding an elderly VIP into his waiting limousine. To her, the Midland seemed the very epitome of glamour and sophistication. Now here she was about to pass through its hallowed portals, and she had never felt more self-conscious in her life.

She glanced at Otis uncertainly. 'I can't go in there,' she told him.

He made a sucking sound through his teeth. 'A 'course you can, girl! We got us selves an invitation from de main man, didn' we?' He shrugged his shoulders, hefted his attaché case, and took Carmel's arm in his own. 'Dis' is just de start. In a coupla months' time, we won' t'ink nuffin' a gwan in a place like dis one. We gwan to be stayin' here all de time.'

'Think so?'

'I *know* so. Dis' a genuine Hollywood star, don' forget. Big time soon come. All we gotta do is show de man a good vibe, an' pick up de tab for the first party. Den he be eatin' outa me hand.'

'But he's only here for two weeks.'

'Sure, but dis bwoy got dollars fallin' outa his ass. Me t'ink de price o' me merchandise gonna rise pretty steep after tonight.' He chuckled. 'An' mebbe he put de word aroun' for any of his friends dat come visit de city. It's all about gettin' a better clientele, girl. Dem people don' care what dey pay, seen?' He huffed gleefully, then gave her a sly wink. 'Come on, den. Less check out de premises – see if deh's up to scratch.'

He led her in through the arched entrance. A tailcoated flunky was waiting beside the revolving doors. He gave them a suspicious look, but Otis just grinned at him.

'Evenin', star. How's she hangin'?'

The man looked nonplussed. Otis and Carmel moved on, pushing through the doors into the hotel reception. Carmel gazed around, and reminded herself not to let her mouth hang open. She had not been prepared for the scale of this. The foyer was massive, surmounted by a magnificent glass roof and lit by gigantic crystal chandeliers. On a raised area off to her left, people sat drinking and chatting at a series of rattan tables. Up ahead, and away to her right, stretched the long, polished reception counter, behind which uniformed staff were waiting to greet visitors and guests. As they approached the desk, Carmel got the impression that every eye in the place had now turned to inspect her, and she felt the colour rise into her cheeks. Glancing at Otis, she saw that he was apparently unconcerned by it all.

This man was amazing, she decided. He could walk into Buckingham Palace in his underpants and not turn a hair. Carmel had even made an effort to dress more soberly than usual, putting on a plain black Lycra tube dress and a leather coat that lacked the various studs and badges of her everyday gear. She'd assumed that maybe Otis, too, would make some concessions to the sophistication of this venue, but, no. When he'd arrived at her flat in his flash red Chevrolet, he was gaudily dressed in a gold foil-effect shirt, black velvet bell-bottoms, and a full-length coat in purple suede. His stack-heeled boots were black patent leather.

When she'd originally met him, back in Brixton, she thought he looked like a bad joke. Then he'd explained to her how, as a kid in a dirt-poor suburb of Kingston, he'd spent all his free time at a local fleapit cinema, watching the 'blaxploitation' movies currently coming over from the States. *Shaft*, *Superfly*, *Cleopatra Jones* – the young Otis Mason had lived and breathed movies like those. Together with homegrown classics like *The Harder They Come*, they'd formed the blueprint for the kind of style he would adopt as soon as he was old enough to buy his own clothes – regardless of any subsequent changes in fashion. He'd brought the same look with him when he moved to Brixton in the late 1980s, and had refused to compromise it ever since. On occasion, people had made fun of the way he looked, but they only ever did it the once. Afterwards they were usually too busy learning to cope with their new crutches.

Carmel had developed a lot of respect for Otis, quickly learning that he was the kind of guy who didn't take shit from anybody. He had a ruthless streak a mile wide, and came down heavily on anyone who crossed him. They had been stepping out together ever since she'd first met him at a ragga club in Brixton eighteen months ago. And when he had urged her to accompany him to Manchester, she hadn't hesitated. It wasn't that they were in love, or anything dumb like that. Otis never laid a finger on her. That seemed strange to her at first, but once he'd explained the situation she understood why he needed to take his pleasures in other, less obvious ways. Now there was a closeness between them: an understanding that Otis was going to claw his way right to the top, and was going to take Carmel along for the ride. As for his clothes, she'd got used to those. Dressed in any other way, he simply wouldn't have been Otis.

But the young desk clerk clearly wasn't used to such fashions. He was staring at Otis as though he doubted the evidence of his eyes. Noting the ghost of a smirk on his face, Carmel wondered if he realised the risk he was running.

'Yes, sir? Can I help you?'

Otis grinned across the counter, showing all his teeth. 'We', now, sport. Me t'ink so. We's here to meet Mr Bobby C. Cooper. He say feh me to ask at de desk. He gwan to leave me name.'

'Which is?'

'Say what?'

The young man smiled. 'What *is* your name, sir?' He spoke slowly, as if to a retarded child. Carmel had a momentary vision of Otis reaching across the desk and smashing open the man's skull with the butt of his pistol – she'd seen it done several times – but today Otis was on his best behaviour and wasn't even packing a shooter.

'Otis Mason. Dis' here is me assistant, Carmel Brody.'

The young man consulted a sheet of paper and nodded. He seemed satisfied. 'Mr Cooper and his entourage are up on the sixth floor, Mr, er ... Mason. I'll phone to announce you're on your way. If you'd like to go up, sir?'

'Yeah, me like to go up.' Otis turned away and Carmel heard him mutter, 'Up your arse wid a blow torch,

mudderfucker.' The two of them exchanged a con-
spiratorial smile. They walked over to the lifts and rode up
to the sixth floor.

There was a brief moment of confusion when the lift door
they had come in by – and were facing – stayed shut, and the
door *behind* them opened instead. Turning, they stepped
out into the corridor and were met by the hulking slab of
flesh that was Andy.

'I believe you're here to make a delivery,' he growled.

Otis grinned. 'Dat's right, breddar. Take me to your
leader!'

'Hold up a second. First, I gotta check you out. Stretch
out your arms.' Otis obligingly put down the case and
extended his arms, while Andy frisked him expertly. 'I
need to look in the case,' Andy told him.

'Sure t'ing.' Otis kneeled and unlatched the case,
showed Andy the contents. Andy's eyes got big and
round.

'Holy shit,' he said. 'You came loaded, didn'cha?'

Otis shrugged. 'Mr Cooper's man said he likes to party
down. Ain't no kinda party widout de jelly and ice-
cream.' He closed the case, and Andy eyed Carmel
thoughtfully.

'Gonna have to search you too,' he announced.

'I thought you'd never ask,' she said. Smiling at him, she
held her arms out and kept eyeing him as his hands moved
up and down the curves of her body, seeming to take a little
more time than was necessary. 'Find anything you liked?'
she asked him when he finally stepped back.

He grinned, and motioned them to follow him along the
corridor. 'Less go see the man.'

As they headed down the corridor to Cooper's suite,
Carmel glanced at Otis and saw he was swaggering along

like he owned the place. The glamorous surroundings clearly didn't phase him one little bit.

They stopped at a door and Andy rapped with his knuckles. He waited a moment, then opened it and went inside, Carmel and Otis following. The room was gloomily lit by scarf-shrouded lamps and, peering around, Carmel could see three men sitting there – another big, heavily muscled stooge, a small effeminate guy with fuzzy hair and a half-hearted moustache, and there, reclining on a plush sofa in the very centre, was Bobby C. himself, dressed in a red silk kimono. He grinned happily when he saw the new arrivals. It was that same infectious grin she recognised from his movie and videos.

Though she had never thought of herself as star-struck, Carmel felt a thrill of excitement go through her. It was going to be fun making a play for this guy, she decided.

'Hey, I was beginning to think you wasn't going to show! Come in, sit down, make yourselves at home! Lionel, get some drinks for my friends here!' Bobby was studying Otis with an amused expression, and Carmel hoped to God he wouldn't comment on the clothes.

'Now, it's er . . . Otis, ain't it?'

'Dat's right, Mr Cooper. Dis here's Carmel.'

Cooper nodded at Carmel, but for the moment he seemed more interested in her companion. He gestured the two of them to vacant armchairs, and Lionel noted their drink orders like they were somebody special.

'Well, whaddya say?' asked Bobby at last. 'How's it goin'?'

'Pretty good, t'anks.' There were a few formalities to be observed before they got down to business. 'Me jes' like t' say I'm a big fan of yours, Mr Cooper. Me got every las' one o' your recuds.'

Carmel knew this was a lie. Otis had no interest in any music post-1979. The last album he'd bought had been Isaac Hayes' *Greatest Hits*.

'Well that's real nice of you to say. Listen, why don't you call me Bobby? Only my accountant calls me Mr Cooper!'

Otis grinned. 'Whatever you say . . . Bobby. How's t'ings in Hollywood?'

'Uh . . . good. Pretty good.'

'Hey, next time you're dere, mebbe you can give me regards to Richard Roundtree?'

Cooper looked puzzled. 'Richard who?' he muttered.

'Roundtree. He was de main man in *Shaft*, you nah? Big movie star. Me watch ever't'ing he ever done, seen?'

Cooper nodded slowly. 'Yeah . . . well, I'll be sure and look out for him.' He watched as Lionel brought over his guests' drinks, and waited impatiently while they took their first sips. Carmel noticed how his gaze kept flicking to the attaché case at Otis' feet, but Otis was deliberately playing it cool, she realised – waiting for Cooper to bring up the subject first.

After a few more minutes of listless waiting, he did so. 'Well . . . Otis, my man, I believe you done brought us a few samples.'

Otis set down his glass of Southern Comfort, picked up the case and laid it on the low coffee table standing in front of him. Slowly he unlatched it, opened it up.

Cooper gave a low whistle. The interior of the case was packed with large plastic bags of cocaine, a half-pound block of hashish, and bundles of plastic pipes containing nuggets of crack.

'Holy shit,' said Cooper quietly. 'It's medication time!' Then he glanced at Otis warily. 'You want to fix a price list first?'

Otis shook his head. 'Dis is me treat,' he said. 'If'n you gennlemen enjoy me wares, you put in a big order and *next* time you pay de goin' rate. Whaddya say? Me talkin' fair or wha'?'

'Most fair,' agreed Cooper. 'And if that shit's as good as it *looks*, we'll be putting in the biggest order you ever had.'

'Good.' Otis glanced at Carmel. 'Start layin' out some lines for de gennlemen, girl. Me t'ink it's time we got dis show onna de road.'

An hour later the party was warming up nicely. Carmel had her jacket off now, ready to go to work. A rap album was playing – one of Bobby's own records, she thought – but the volume was kept at a reasonable level in case anybody came along to complain. Everybody was feeling nicely mellow. They had started with draw – big Rasta-style joints that Otis had rolled himself; progressed to lines of pure white Colombian; and had now started on the crack. Only Otis had showed any restraint, but Carmel knew he never used anything stronger than ganja.

Cooper looked particularly smashed. Reclining on the sofa, his bare legs stretched out the length of it, he was staring at Carmel from beneath heavy-lidded eyes, clearly more interested in her now that his other appetites had been satiated.

Carmel glanced over at Otis, who still sat in his armchair, presiding over the proceedings like some emaciated Roman emperor at an orgy. Carmel gave him a questioning look and he replied with a barely perceptible nod. She picked up a crack pipe from the table, stood up from her place on the floor, and went over to sit beside Cooper on the sofa.

'Hey there, baby,' he said, his voice husky like he'd just emerged from sleep.

'Hey, yourself.' She offered him the pipe and he slipped the end of it into his mouth. She produced a lighter and held it close to the other end while he inhaled. The tube filled with white smoke, and the hit rocked his head back, his eyelids flickering. He released a thin stream of diffused smoke through his nostrils with a contented sigh.

'Oh yes,' he whispered. Then his eyes gradually focused on Carmel's arm, noticing that several thin, silvery weals crisscrossed the darker skin of her wrist. He lifted a hand and traced one of them with a fingertip.

'Didn't have you down as a suicide jockey,' he said.

She laughed. 'I'm not,' she assured him. 'I used to cut myself sometimes when I was bored.' She put a hand on to Cooper's thigh, just at the point where the red silk of his kimono bordered the dark brown flesh of his leg. He glanced down in surprise and swallowed hard.

'Bored?' he echoed.

'Yeah. Like you do – you know?' She smiled playfully. 'I've got other scars. You want to see them?'

He considered that for a moment, then grinned.

'Sure. Why not?'

She reached up her hands and peeled the tube dress down to her waist. She wasn't wearing a bra, and Cooper was staring at her small but full breasts as though he had never seen a naked woman before. There were scars on her breasts, too: long curving ridges of slightly raised flesh, paler than their background.

'What it is,' explained Carmel, 'when I was a kid I really wanted to be a boy. When my breasts started growing I used to try and disfigure them. But I never went very deep with the knife.' Now she was tracing a scar with her own forefinger. 'See?' she whispered. 'Want to feel for yourself?'

The last track on the CD ended, and it was suddenly very quiet in the room. Carmel was aware that the other four men in the room were watching her intently, but she enjoyed the sense of power this gave her. Keeping her body angled to provide Otis with the best view, she reached out and took both Cooper's hands at the wrists, guiding his fingertips to stroke the scar ridges.

'You ... you did this to yourself?' asked Cooper, his voice hoarse now, his eyes agog.

'Sure,' she told him. 'A girl's gotta have some hobbies, ain't she?'

'Yeah, but ...' Cooper glanced sideways at Otis, who sat in his armchair, watching impassively. 'Hey, man, this OK with you?'

Otis shrugged. 'S'OK wid me. S'OK wid you?'

'Uh ... yeah, but what I mean, man, isn't she *your* woman?'

'Yeah, she my woman. But she gotta mind've 'er own. You got some problem wid dat?'

Cooper seemed bewildered. 'Weirdest Goddamned arrangement *I* ever heard of,' he said.

Otis was skinning up a new joint now, using a record cover on his lap. The chunky rings on his fingers glittered as he crumbled hash on to the papers. 'Chill out, man. *Enjoy.*'

Now Carmel was sliding her hands up under the hem of Cooper's kimono. 'Funny thing about wash-rock,' she said. 'Always makes me feel horny. What about you, Bobby? You feelin' horny?'

'Pretty much.' Cooper seemed mesmerised by her. Now Carmel was undoing the tie of his kimono, allowing the folds to fall back, to reveal that he was wearing nothing underneath but a white silk posing pouch currently straining to contain his erection.

Carmel put out her tongue and began to lick her lips.

'The other thing that happens is, for some reason, I get the munchies. You know that feeling, Bobby?'

He nodded. Beads of sweat were breaking on his forehead now.

Carmel leaned slowly forward. She eased away the fabric of the pouch and went down on him. Cooper's eyes got very big, and his mouth opened in an O of surprise. The atmosphere in the room was now electric.

'Jesus,' said Amos. 'That gal's quite a performer.'

Otis lifted the joint and traced the tip of his tongue along the gummed edge of the paper. 'She got stayin' power too. Mebbe if you is patient, she get around to you also.'

'Yeah?' Amos looked intrigued at the prospect.

Cooper gasped suddenly and lifted Carmel's face out of his lap. Her dark red lipstick was smeared across her cheek. It was clear that she had taken him close to the point of no return.

'Let's go in the bedroom,' he suggested.

She shrugged. 'What's the matter, Bobby. You shy?'

'I work better without an audience,' he told her.

'OK, whatever you want.' She got up and sauntered towards the door of the bedroom, glancing around the room as she did so. 'Relax boys,' she told the others. 'There's plenty to go around.'

Cooper hauled himself up off the sofa, holding the kimono closed in front of him to hide his excitement. He hesitated, glanced suspiciously at Otis. 'This going to cost me anything?'

Otis took out his Ronson and lit the joint. He inhaled, then blew out a cloud of fragrant smoke.

'Like I say before, star. Everyt'ing is free tonight. Nex' time you pay, seen?'

'Fuckin' A,' said Cooper. He hurried into the bedroom.

Amos and Andy took his place on the sofa, and immediately took on the demeanour of a couple of patients in a doctor's waiting room. Only Lionel seemed uninterested in what was happening next-door. He had himself a fresh pipe, and seemed happy enough to stick with that.

There were sounds coming from the bedroom now, the creaking of bedsprings mingled with grunts and gasps of pleasure.

Amos eyed Otis scornfully. 'Man, listen to that! You honestly don't *mind*?'

Otis chuckled. 'Why me mind, sport? Me always brought up t' believe in share 'n' share alike, you nah?'

'Yeah, but—'

In the bedroom things came to a climax. They heard Cooper give a long groan. Then silence descended for a moment. Otis inhaled, blew out smoke. Amos and Andy were looking towards the door now, waiting for an invitation. After a few minutes, it came. And it was Cooper who summoned them.

'Amos ... Andy ... you wanna come in here? There's somethin' she wants to try.' The two men were off the sofa in seconds, unbuckling their belts as they went.

'Have a nice time,' Otis called after them, smiling, as he sat there toking on his spliff. It was top-grade shit and he was getting a real buzz.

Now Lionel came over to sit on the recently vacated sofa. Otis glanced over at him in surprise. 'Don' tell me you's waitin' feh a turn also?'

Lionel shook his head. 'Oh, I ain't no pussy-hunter,' he said. 'I guess you and me got somethin' in common there.'

Otis frowned. 'T'ink so?' he muttered.

'Sure. You're like me: you get your kicks in other ways.' He reached out across the gap and placed a hand on Otis's knee. 'Whaddya say, you wanna come to my room and watch some videos?'

Otis made a sucking sound between his teeth. 'Bwoy, you better take your mudderfuckin' hand off've my knee, afore I break it off and shove it up yo' ass – fingers first!'

Lionel flinched away as though he'd been smacked in the face. 'Christ, sorry,' he said. 'I just thought . . .'

'You thought *wrong*, sport. Me ain't no fudge-packer!'

Lionel sank back in the sofa as though trying to push himself through it. He held up his hands as if surrendering.

'Hey, no offence intended, bro. I guess I just kinda assumed . . .'

'You got one t'ing right. I do get me kicks in udder ways. But dere was a time when me chased cooz jes' like all de rest. Shit, mon, me *lived* for it!'

Lionel looked puzzled. 'So, what happened?'

'Back in Kingston, when I was in me teens, me 'ave quite a reputation as a ladies' man, y'nah? Me t'ink me can get away wid' murder. Started fuckin' dis gal who was in real tight wid de biggest Yardman on my piece o' turf. Him was like, y'nah, de godfather where I was raised. Anyways, him find out what me doin', an' he don't exactly take it as a big compliment, seen? So him an' his bwoys, dey fix me.'

'*Fix* you? What does that mean?'

'It means dey treat me to a necktie party.'

Lionel shook his head.

'I'm sorry, I don't get it.'

'You know what dat is, don' you? Ah shit, I *show* you what it means.' He dropped the joint into an ashtray, stood up and unbuckled his trousers. He let them fall, then hooked his thumbs into his jockey shorts and pulled them down too.

Lionel stared. 'Jesus H. Christ,' he murmured.

'Not pretty,' Otis admitted. 'Dem bwoys do a very professional job, didn' dey? Still, for all dat, I was lucky.'

'Lucky?' gasped Lionel. 'How do you figure that?'

Otis grinned. 'Some friends a mine got to de place where dis was happenin', and rescue me. Blew dat Yardie and his posse outa dere fuckin' socks.'

'Yeah, but they got there too late.'

'No, mon, dey got dere jus' in time.'

'I don't get it. The man cut your dick off.'

Otis nodded. 'Sure nuff. But when me bwoys got there, he was jus' about to make me *eat* it.'

Lionel slumped back against the sofa. Under his dark skin he looked quite pale.

Otis did himself up and retrieved his joint from the ashtray. He took another big toke and held the smoke in his lungs for a long time.

'So, how . . .' Lionel struggled to find the right words. 'I mean, what do you *do*, man? You know to . . . to get off?'

From the bedroom, the chorus of grunts and groans was resuming, the creaking bedsprings settling into an urgent rhythm.

Otis smiled sleepily. 'Man, dere's still t'ings I can do. Mostly, I just likes to *watch*.'

'Watch?' murmured Lionel.

'Sure.' Otis moved across to the sofa and drew Lionel to his feet. He slipped an arm around the man's shoulders and guided him towards the bedroom's open door, so that they both had a clear view of the four sweating figures grappling on the bed. 'See ah dat?' he whispered. 'Ain't she beautiful? Isn't she somet'ing, breddar?'

Lionel didn't answer. Maybe he didn't know what to say.

The two men stood there, arms around each other like lovers, watching in silence as the four on the bed moved towards their individual climaxes. That was going to take some time but, then, for the moment at least, neither of them had anything better to do.

Chapter Twenty-Two

Finn and his posse sit in the stolen Sierra and stare across the road at the entrance of the newsagent's shop. It's raining quite heavily, the drops hammering urgently on the car's roof. There's been a flurry of activity over the last ten minutes but now it seems to have gone quiet. They're all tooled up and ready to go, but Finn is worried that they've not spent enough time on preparation. Necessity has demanded quick action on this, they're all skint and need to see an instant resolution to their problems. Otherwise, Finn will lose them; he senses that.

He's chosen to hit this place in a busy suburb of south Manchester because he figures the owners will be unprepared for anything like this. When he checked it out yesterday, he noticed that they don't even have video cameras installed. They're just asking for trouble. Finn's in the passenger seat, and he has the sawn-off Remington tucked under his coat. Tommo has the Uzi, and Wart has been entrusted with the .38 pistol. The real fly in the ointment is that they're going to have to leave Chaz behind the wheel of the car, since he's the only one, apart from Finn, who can drive.

Finn's not sure about Tommo, about whether he'll be able to cut it in there, and as for Wart – Christ, the kid's only ten! He just hopes they'll measure up OK. Back at the

Swamp, when Finn was outlining his plan to them, they seemed confident enough, but now, sitting here in the car, they're pale and nervous. They look like they're ready to bottle out at any second.

'We just gotta keep real calm,' he tells them for perhaps the fifteenth time. 'There's only one old bloke in there – a Paki he is. I checked it out. He'll probably shit himself when he sees the guns. Anyway, I'll take care of him. Tommo, what do *you* do?'

'Uh?' Tommo glances up in surprise, like he's been lost in thought. 'Oh, er . . . I cover the door. If anybody comes in I tell 'em to get down on the floor.'

'Good. Wart?'

'I cover the Paki while you get the dosh from the till.' Wart's words come out in a tumble. He's so nervous he can't stop fidgeting; he's twitching and scratching like he's got ants in his pants.

'Right. Remember, if we keep our heads, we'll be OK. It's like football: it's teamwork. If everybody does their bit, it'll go like a charm.'

'I don't like it,' mutters Chaz. 'I should be comin' in with you.'

'I already told you, I need you behind the wheel wiv' the engine runnin'. It's gonna be OK.'

'I fuckin' well hope so,' growls Chaz. 'Hey, 'ang on a minute, somebody's goin' in!' They watch as an elderly man steps in through the open doorway of the shop.

'Right,' says Finn. 'As soon as he comes out, we go in. OK?'

A silence.

'OK?' Finn says again, more forcefully.

Nods. Nervous shuffling. Finn is scared too, but he can't let them know that. His stomach is fluttering and he feels a powerful desire to have a crap, but he has to show the others that he can handle this, that he's in control. He's horribly aware of the time ticking away.

Tommo fumbles out his cigarettes but Finn spots him in the driving mirror.

'Not now, you pillock!' he growls.

Tommo reddens, puts the packet away. The rain comes down harder, bouncing up off the windscreen in a thick spray.

'Eh up,' says Chaz. The old man is coming slowly out of the shop, shuffling along on arthritic legs. There's a rolled-up newspaper stuffed under his arm. He lingers by the shop door, studying the personal adverts in the window.

'Come *on*,' whispers Finn. 'Stupid old git!'

The old man glances up as though somehow he's overheard the remark. He stares blankly towards the car for a moment, then looks up at the sky as though he's only just noticed it's raining. He pulls up the collar of his grey raincoat, and shuffles away along the street. Finn notices that he's wearing tartan carpet slippers.

His feet are gonna get soaked, he thinks, then feels foolish – is glad he didn't say that out loud. What would the others think of him, the hard man, waiting to do a bit of GBH and worried about the state of some old man's feet? He waits until the figure in the raincoat is a good distance off, and then he turns to look back at Tommo and Wart.

'Let's do it,' he says.

He takes the latex fright mask from his pocket and pulls it over his head. This was his idea; he figures it's better than using stockings. He's bought four of the masks from *Toys R Us*, all identical, and he reckons that the only thing any witnesses will remember is these three wizened old faces running out of the shop.

He takes a deep breath and opens the car door. 'Come on,' he says. His vision is limited in the mask – he hasn't considered this – so he can't be sure that the others are following him. He just hopes to God they are, he's going to look pretty stupid going in there all by himself . . .

As he crosses the pavement, he's pulling the Remington from under his coat, and he's aware of his heart pounding in his chest. He hears Tommo say something to Wart and, reassured, steps in through the doorway of the shop, holding the gun out in front of him. Through the slits in the mask he can see the shop-owner's face staring back at him across the counter. Wide-eyed and open-mouthed, the old man looks frightened, and Finn reckons he has every right to be.

He gestures with the shotgun, aiming it straight at the man's chest.

'Don't fuckin' move!' snaps Finn. 'Give me everything that's in the till or I'll blow your fuckin' head off!'

Nick couldn't rid himself of the craving. It had nagged at him all through breakfast and he kept thinking how he used to love the first cigarette of the day, the nicotine mingling with the caffeine from his coffee: the two stimulants kick-starting him into some semblance of wakefulness. Sure, he still had the caffeine, but somehow that didn't seem enough this morning, not anywhere near enough.

Now, driving into town, through the pouring rain, to handle a series of magazine interviews at the Midland, he kept thinking about stopping off somewhere to pick up a packet of fags. After all, where would be the harm? If he just got a packet of ten, it wouldn't be like he was starting again in earnest, would it? Smoke two or three of them today, maybe the same tomorrow, and when the packet was empty it wouldn't necessarily mean he'd run straight out and buy another one . . . would it?

His local newsagent's shop loomed out of the blur of rain that hammered against his windscreen, and he considered stopping there. But no, the owner knew him too well, and was bound to comment on his sudden lapse, might even mention it to Helen. Nick drove on, telling himself that this was stupid. He had the willpower to say no, didn't he? Of course he did! But when he saw the next newsagent's coming up, he began to slow down and indicate he was stopping.

That wasn't to be. There were double yellow lines along the stretch of pavement outside the shop, and the heavy goods vehicle behind him flashed its lights as if to warn him that he'd better not even *think* of trying to stop there . . .

Nick frowned, pressed down on the accelerator again, got his speed back up to thirty. Damned right, he told himself. *Pathetic!* Had to use his willpower here, show that he wasn't a slave to his urges. He punched the button on the radio cassette player and got the tail end of a rap record: the sneering, self-aggrandising vocal all too familiar. Cooper ranting on about life on the street, poverty, drugs and violence, a whole host of subjects he claimed to be an authority on. Nick was about to punch to another pre-set when, thankfully, the record faded down and the DJ came in with a slick, moronic voiceover.

'Hey, hey, coming up to nine-ten a.m. here on *Metrosound*, and that was Bobby C. Cooper with his latest hit, *Show Respect*! Bobby, of course, is right here in Manchester even as I speak. We're planning to have a live interview with the man they call the Rap Terminator on Ray

Wood's Saturday Show tomorrow morning at ten-thirty, so miss that at your peril! Now ... it seems that sex is on its way *out*! In a recent survey of fifteen to twenty-five year olds, people were asked what they would rather have – a steamy, all-night sex session with their favourite movie star or a nice cup of tea. An amazing eighty-four per cent said that they'd rather—'

Nick punched the off button with a scowl. It seemed to him that *Metrosound* had really gone down the tubes over the past six months. A lot of people blamed the big scandal that had erupted there just over a year ago, when a talk-show DJ had got himself mixed up with a very scary character. *Metrosound*'s head honcho, Sir Gareth Parker, had subsequently axed virtually everything of a serious nature, and what was left seemed to consist of the charts interspersed with an occasional snippet of infantile trivia.

Of course, for a visit from a celebrity of Cooper's stature, they were going to make an exception. Nick figured he ought to go down well there, provided he could keep his language clean. He pictured Cooper hunched and scowling in front of a microphone, relaying his thoughts to thousands of listeners, and immediately his spirit sagged. And there was that craving again, stronger than ever.

'Fuck it!' he snarled. He thumped a fist on the dashboard, and almost instantly saw an illuminated sign for Silk Cut come gliding out of the drizzle – like a rescue beacon in the midst of a storm. There were no yellow lines here, and there was a convenient spot just behind that red Sierra ...

Making his mind up, he indicated, changed down, and brought the BMW to a halt outside the newsagent's. He'd buy ten cigarettes, for Christ's sake. After all, it wasn't a

capital crime, was it? He stepped out of the car and locked
the door behind him. Cold spots of rain peppered his head
and shoulders and, turning up his collar, he ran across the
pavement towards the open doorway.

The shop-owner is scared, he's standing there behind the
counter and looks like he's going to have a heart attack. His
hands are held out in front of him, and he's moving his
plump face from side to side.

'No, no, no,' he keeps saying. 'Please, you go now.
Nothing here for you.'

'Shut up!' Finn barks at him. He jerks the double barrels
of the shotgun meaningfully. 'Empty out the till, quick!'
He glances at his companions, who just stand there,
wizened old-man faces staring.

Finn waves a hand towards the door. 'Shut that,' he tells
Tommo, and the boy moves to obey him, but slowly, like
he's half asleep. He fumbles the cardboard sign around to
the CLOSED position and begins to shut the door – but it's
suddenly intercepted by a hand.

It swings open again, and a man steps into the shop. He
stands there looking at the three boys, his mouth open in
surprise. He starts to smile, then stops when he realises this
isn't some kind of Halloween prank.

'Tommo, the door!' snaps Finn and immediately feels
like biting his tongue off. Didn't he tell the others not to use
any names, and here he is shooting off at the mouth like
some amateur. Tommo reacts by kicking the door shut and
jabbing the stubby barrel of the Uzi at the newcomer.

'Get on the floor,' he says, but there's no urgency in his
voice. He might as well have added 'please'. The man just
stands there, staring at Tommo like he can't really believe
this is happening to him, like at any moment Jeremy Beadle

is going to pop out from behind a curtain and tell him he's on *Beadle's About*.

'You heard him!' yells Finn, half turning to face the newcomer, swinging the barrel of the shotgun around to intimidate him.

Wart, doing as he's been told, drops into a crouch and trains the .38 on the newsagent, holding the gun two-handed like they do in the movies.

But the newsagent must think the smaller boy is less of a threat, because that's when he reaches down to punch a button under the counter. An alarm bell goes off, a shrill, unearthly clamouring. As the shopkeeper bobs up again, Wart fires the gun, the sound of the shot deafening in the enclosed space. The bullet misses the man's head by a few inches, blowing down packets of cigarettes from the display behind him.

Spooked by the gunfire, the newcomer turns suddenly back towards the exit and Finn goes after him, crossing the short distance that separates them in a fraction of a second and bringing up the butt of the shotgun to strike him across the side of the head. The man gives a grunt of surprise and goes down like a poleaxed steer, his arms gesticulating, his fingers still clutching for a door handle that's no longer within reach. He hits the floor hard, and doesn't move.

As Finn turns back, Wart fires again, and Finn sees the impact blow a cloud of dust and shreds of fibre out of the shopkeeper's padded jacket. He reels back against the shelves of cigarettes and he screams something, seeming angry more than anything else. The old man starts to come around from behind the counter and Wart hesitates, not knowing what to do.

Finn is thinking, *It's all right, it's all right, I'll put him down with the rifle butt, he's not badly hurt*, but, before he can even move, Tommo is stepping past him with the Uzi and—

NO, TOMMO, DON'T, DON'T!

—the shots seem to reverberate through Finn's head as Tommo pulls the trigger, spraying the shopkeeper with automatic fire. The man's body jerks as the bullets punch into and through him, hammering into the merchandise ranged behind him. For an instant he's like a demented puppet dancing in the midst of a blizzard of shredded paper, broken glass and shattered plastic. Blood sprays like a dark blessing across the display behind him, and he drops out of sight behind the counter.

But Tommo keeps right on firing, his own body shaking, his mask riding up over his eyes so he can no longer see where he's aiming, the bullets smashing bottles of boiled sweets now, puncturing cans of Coke and kicking up splinters of wood from the surface of the counter.

Then suddenly the Uzi's magazine is empty, and they're back to the relative silence of the alarm going off. It's eerie that such a racket can now sound subdued, but nevertheless it does.

They stand there in the silence that is not a silence, and the shock settles over them, cold in their guts. Their masked faces betray no emotion.

Finn forces himself to move, though his limbs feel like lead. He goes across to the counter and peers fearfully over at what looks like a heap of blood-soaked rags on the floor. The old man's face is partially obscured by the folds of his jacket, and there is a hole in his cheek the size of a fifty-pence piece. No way he can be alive – not looking like *that*.

Finn swallows hard, reaches out a hand and pushes the SALE button on the till. The drawer slides open to reveal the price of this man's life: a thin bundle of notes and a plastic bag full of pound coins. Finn stares down in shock and disappointment. How can there be so little, a busy shop like this? The man must have a safe somewhere, but there's no time to look for it now. Everything here has just turned to shit. He scoops up the notes and thrusts them into his pocket, then grabs the bag of coins. It's probably his imagination, but the alarm seems to be getting louder.

He turns to his companions and waves them back towards the door. They need no second bidding. Tommo flings the door open and runs out of the shop, holding the Uzi in plain view, making no attempt to hide it. Wart follows.

Out on the street, Chaz has the engine running.

Finn is about to follow them, but he hesitates as he nears the other man's prone figure. On impulse, he kneels beside him and reaches into his inside jacket pocket. His hand emerges holding the man's pigskin wallet, and he transfers this to his own pocket. He starts to rise, and that's when the man comes suddenly awake, throwing up his arms to grab Finn around the neck – wrestling him down to hold him on the floor.

Finn curses, struggles to free himself. He's still holding the shotgun in one hand, both barrels loaded, but for the moment it's trapped under the weight of his own body. He's dimly aware of a car horn blaring, Chaz warning him that they daren't wait much longer.

Desperate now, Finn lashes two quick punches into the man's stomach, feels the grip relax slightly. He slides backwards out of the man's hold and his mask comes off, but he manages to retain his grasp on the gun. He rolls backwards, scrambles to his feet and starts for the door.

But the man is tenacious; he grabs hold of Finn's right leg and hangs on tight, stopping him where he stands.

Finn swings around and jabs the barrel of the shotgun into the man's face.

'Let go,' he says with a calmness that surprises him. 'Let go or they'll be scraping your fucking head off the floor.'

There is a moment of silence that seems to last an eternity. Finn stands looking down at the man, and the man stares back defiantly, and for a moment, Finn thinks that he's going to have to pull the trigger, blow the guy's skull wide open. But then the man's eyes widen in the realisation that Finn isn't shitting him, that he will do it if he has to.

Maybe the man's got a wife and kids at home or maybe he's just realised that he's got the rest of his life in front of him. At any rate, he releases his hold and Finn runs out of the shop.

Chaz is totally freaked by now; he starts accelerating before Finn is properly in the car. For a terrible moment, Finn hangs half-in, half-out of the moving vehicle, then swings himself inside, seconds before the door crashes against the rear right wing of a parked Nissan Cherry. The door slams shut with an impact that smashes the window, showering Finn with broken glass. Chaz is swearing rhythmically as he coaxes the car up to speed, steering wildly to avoid a couple of pedestrians who almost step into his path.

Then they are away from there and heading in the direction of home, and only now does the full enormity of the cock-up slam into Finn.

Everything has gone hideously wrong. Now they are killers. It's no longer a game they're playing. He glances over his shoulder into the rear of the car. Wart and Tommo are taking off their masks. They are both of them grey-faced and close to tears.

Chaz glances at Finn, puzzled by the dark atmosphere.

'For fuck's sake,' he mutters. 'What happened back there?'

But for the moment, nobody answers him. They are only just piecing it together for themselves.

Chapter Twenty-Three

Detective Inspector Willis was a small, dark-haired man who looked like he carried the weight of the world on his narrow shoulders. He sat beside Nick's bed in the small cubicle at Accidents and Emergencies and tried repeatedly to get Nick to run through the whole sequence of events from start to finish.

Nick didn't feel much like talking. The whole left-hand side of his head was a dull throb of pain and from time to time a powerful wave of dizziness would wash through him, making his stomach heave. The young consultant who had attended him didn't think there was any real damage, but had urged Nick to go home and get to bed – something he intended doing just as soon as Helen arrived to collect him. He had used his mobile phone to ring *Futures* and arrange for Terry to take over his duties for the day; but meanwhile he still had Inspector Willis to contend with.

Willis seemed duty-bound to question every little detail that Nick gave him, his mournful brown eyes narrowing as he considered all the possibilities. His glum demeanour and world-weary sarcasm suggested that he'd rather be in any other line of work than this one but, since it was his profession, he was damn well going to make a thorough job of it.

'So, Mr Saunders, you stopped at the newsagent's at nine o'clock . . .'

'Maybe a little after that. Say ten past, I can't be certain. Yes, I seem to remember a time check on the radio.'

'Indeed. Nine-ten a.m. And why exactly did you stop there?'

'For, er . . . for cigarettes. I was on my way to the Midland Hotel and I . . . I just fancied a smoke.'

'Hmm.' Willis looked as though he was considering the information. 'But what made you stop *there*. It's not your local shop, is it?'

'No, I live a few miles further down the road. It was just an impulse, really.'

'Odd.'

Nick looked at him sharply, then winced as a fresh jolt of pain kicked him in the head. He wished the painkillers he'd been given would hurry up and take effect. 'What's odd about it?' he demanded.

'Hmm? Oh, only that we're all creatures of habit, Mr Saunders. Now, you take me. I'm a smoker. Always buy my fags at the same shop, my local Spar. Wouldn't dream of setting off for work unless I had a fresh packet on me. So are there no newsagents closer to home?'

'There *are*, yes, of course. But I drove past them.'

'I see.' Willis looked at him. 'And why is that?'

'No particular reason. I just . . . well, I suppose I was just resisting up to that point.'

'Resisting?'

'Yes, you see, I've given up smoking.'

Willis smiled sourly. 'But you just told me you went in to buy *cigarettes*!' he said, as though he'd hit on a significant point.

'I know. I know I said that. You see, that was when the

246

craving got too much for me. So I stopped and went in.'
Nick spread his hands in a matter-of-fact gesture. 'And
then, when I went in there—'

'Yes, excuse me, I'm still not clear on this point. What
made you choose this particular newsagent?'

Nick stared at him. 'I didn't choose it. It was simply the
next one I came to.'

But now Willis was shaking his head. 'No, Mr Saunders.
I'm very familiar with that stretch of Wilmslow Road.
There are other newsagents between your local one and the
one you stopped at. Not to mention a couple of garages,
which, correct me if I'm wrong, do sell cigarettes, even to
people who've given up; and who would offer more
convenient parking than the place you actually visited.'

Nick looked at Willis for a moment in total bewilder-
ment. He wondered what the punishment was for assault-
ing a police officer, and whether he should just go ahead
and risk it anyway.

'Inspector, I don't know *why* I stopped there. It was
chosen completely at random.'

Willis nodded. 'It's significant, though, isn't it? The one
shop you chose to stop at was the one shop in that area
where a serious crime was in progress. Makes you think,
doesn't it?'

Nick sighed, shook his head to dispel a feeling of
mounting dizziness. 'Is there some point to this?' he asked
tetchily. 'Only I've got the worst headache in history and I
would be very grateful if we could cut this short. Do you
think that would be possible?'

Willis frowned. 'Just a few more questions, Mr Saunders,
if you don't mind. Let's not forget that a man has been
murdered, and it's my job to see that justice is done.'

Then God help us all, thought Nick.

'Now, I believe you said your assailants were children.'

'That's right. Teenagers, I'd say.'

'Hmm. School holidays,' muttered Willis.

'Pardon?'

'It's the school holidays, Mr Saunders. Crime rates always soar at this time of the year. The kids get bored, you see, and the next thing you know, there's trouble.'

'Christ, I used to scrump apples when *I* was bored. This was a bit more serious than that.'

'Quite. Now, they were all wearing masks.'

'Yes, but one of them did lose the mask when I struggled with him. I'd say he was the oldest—'

'Why would you say that?'

'Well, he was the biggest.'

'Doesn't necessarily follow, Mr Saunders. I've got two sons myself: one eight, one twelve. Would it surprise you to learn that the eight-year-old is several inches taller than his older brother?'

Nick was experiencing a strong urge to weep. 'Please, get to the point,' he urged Willis. 'I feel like shit at the moment.'

'Is that a fact, sir? How very unfortunate. Now, you've said that these young hooligans were armed.'

'Yes. They each had a gun of some kind. At first glance, I thought they were toys.'

Willis snorted. 'Some toys!' he exclaimed. 'The interior of that shop looks like they held World War III in there. An automatic weapon, I'd say – quite definitely. That shopkeeper had enough lead in him to start a pencil factory.' He paused, as though anticipating a laugh, and looked vaguely disappointed when he didn't get one. Then he continued, 'You saw what happened?'

'No, I was unconscious by then.' Nick indicated the dark

mass of bruising that covered the left side of his head down to the cheekbone. 'There was something, though. Just before I got hit, one of them spoke to the kid guarding the door, called him "Tommo".'

Willis frowned. 'Tommo? Funny sort of name . . .'

'Well, I assume it's an abbreviation. Maybe the kid's surname is Thompson or Thomas, something like that? I know it's not much to go on, but it's the only thing that sticks out in my mind. After that, I don't recall anything else until I woke up, and the eldest of them . . . the *tallest* of them was going through my pockets. I grabbed hold of him. We fought.'

'A very stupid thing to do, if I may say so. I'm not keen on these have-a-go heroics.'

Nick shrugged. 'I didn't even think about it. I just acted instinctively. Then his mask came off and I got a look at his face . . .'

Willis perked up considerably at this news. 'You could identify him?'

'Maybe. I don't know. He looked just like any kid off the street.'

'Yes, well, we'll get you some time with an Identikit artist, then show you a few photographs.'

'Not today,' Nick told him flatly.

'No, no, of course not. When you're feeling ah . . . up to it. For the record, how old would you say that boy was?'

Nick frowned. 'Hard to say. Fourteen, fifteen? Old enough, anyway. Little bastard stood there with the shotgun pressed right to my head, and told me to let go of him or he'd kill me. At first I didn't believe him, but then I looked him in the eye and I could see he meant it. He would have done me and not turned a hair. For a minute I really thought . . .'

Nick's voice trailed off as it snagged on something that lay just beneath the surface of his composure. His eyes filled with moisture and he lifted a hand to shield them. 'I'm sorry,' he said. He was shaking now, as the full terror of the situation slammed into him.

Willis cleared his throat self-consciously. He seemed embarrassed by Nick's reaction.

'It's a terrible thing,' he announced to nobody in particular. 'Children, mere babes in arms, running wild, holding society to ransom. What kind of a world is it when that can happen? And you know who's to blame? The parents, that's who! Lack of parental discipline. I'm sure you're familiar with the old saying, Mr Saunders. Show me the child of seven and I will show you the man. We're getting more and more of this kind of thing and believe me, we—'

'Inspector,' Nick interrupted him. 'I wish you'd fuck off now and leave me alone.'

'Er ... yes, well...' Willis got to his feet, looking aggrieved. 'Understandable, I suppose. Terrible thing, it's clearly been a shock for you. We can talk about this in more detail when you've had a chance to ... ah ...' He shrugged, turned away. 'I'll be in touch,' he concluded and stepped out of the cubicle, leaving Nick to his own devices.

Nick cried. It had been some considerable time since he had last done that, at Molly's birth four years ago – and this, of course, was quite different. This was a powerful outpouring of emotions, as though his unexpected brush with mortality had opened the floodgates deep inside him, releasing pent-up doubts and fears that he must have been carrying around with him for years. Eventually he stopped fighting it, and gave in to his emotions. After just a few minutes of uncontrollable weeping, he felt better.

By the time Helen got there, he had managed to compose himself, and the tears had long since been wiped away. He even managed a weak smile for her as she hesitated in the curtained entrance to the cubicle, staring fearfully in at him, as though she didn't quite recognise him.

'Hello, sweetie,' he said.

'Nick!' She hurried over to fling her arms around him, making him wince as her cheek brushed the injured side of his head. She was close to tears herself. 'I got a phone call at home. I'd just got back from dropping Molly at the nursery,' she explained breathlessly. 'They said you'd been involved in an accident, but they wouldn't give me any details.'

'It wasn't exactly an accident,' he told her.

'Oh, I know what happened, now. I've just been talking to that Detective Inspector Willis.'

Nick rolled his eyes towards the ceiling. 'Lucky you,' he said. 'Manchester's answer to Hercule Poirot!'

'He said you'd walked in on an armed robbery. A newsagent's in Rusholme?'

'Yes, that's right . . .'

'Only I can't understand what you were doing there! I thought you were driving to the Midland.'

'I was. But I stopped for . . . for something I needed. There were these kids with guns. One of them knocked me out.'

'Kids? Nick, for Christ's sake . . .' She paused for a moment, frowning. She pulled away a little so that she could look at him. 'So what was it you needed from the newsagent's?'

'Oh, a . . . a bar of chocolate,' he muttered.

She looked unconvinced. 'Since when did you start

251

eating chocolate?' she protested. 'You don't even *like* chocolate!'

'Well, maybe I just fancied some for a change.' As she still looked unconvinced, he began to bluster. 'Look, don't *you* start! I've just had Inspector bloody Willis in here giving me the third degree, and he seemed to think I had some dark ulterior motive for going into that shop. It was like I told him, I just got unlucky, that's all!'

'OK. OK. Calm down.' She took his hand and squeezed it tightly. 'Willis said somebody was killed.'

Nick nodded. 'They ... they shot the guy behind the counter. Knocked me out and took my wallet. I woke up just as one of the kids was lifting it. I tried grappling with him but...' He paused and glanced at Helen, realising it wasn't a good idea to give her the full story. 'But he got away,' he concluded. 'I didn't even know the newsagent was dead until I went to look over the counter. An old Asian, he was. They must have shot him twenty times or more.'

'My God, Nick, it could so easily have been you.'

He didn't know what to say to that. They hugged each other again, and Helen buried her face in his shoulder.

'I couldn't bear it if anything happened to you,' she murmured. 'I think I'd want to die myself.' She thought for a moment. 'Listen, we'd better not mention any of this to Molly. Let her think you just had an ordinary accident.'

'OK. They say I can come home with you now,' he told her. 'My car's still back at that shop. We'll have to arrange to pick it up later.'

'Forget the car. You're more important.' She disentangled herself from his grasp and got up from the bed. 'I'll go find a doctor and get you discharged. Then straight home to bed.' She hesitated on seeing the dazed expression on his face. 'You all right?' she asked him.

He was staring up at her white-faced.

'I can't get over it,' he said. 'Helen, they were *kids* . . . just bits of bloody kids and they were armed to the teeth. I mean, what's happening to the world? What kind of a place is it going to be by the time Molly's reached our age?'

She looked at him helplessly. Clearly she didn't have an answer to that right now. 'I'll find the doctor,' she said finally.

But as she started to leave he called after her. 'Helen?'

She turned back to him. 'Yes?'

'It . . . it was cigarettes. I went into that shop for cigarettes.'

She smiled back at him. 'I figured as much. I could smell smoke on your clothes when you got back from the shoot last night. You didn't have to make a big secret of it, you know.'

He nodded, frowning. 'I'm sorry. I guess I thought you'd be disappointed in me.'

'I'm a big girl now,' she assured him. 'I can take disappointments much better than I can take secrets. I'm just glad that you're safe. Now I'll go and get you discharged . . . unless you've any more confessions to make?'

He smiled. 'Only that I love you.'

'That's a *nice* confession,' she said. She pulled the curtain aside and went out of the cubicle to look for a doctor.

Chapter Twenty-Four

Back at the Swamp, Finn and the others are morosely holding a postmortem of the disastrous holdup. It's just a few hours after the event, and Finn is only now beginning to realise how badly it all went. There's a part of him that wants to blame Wart or Tommo, but he knows that he can't really do that. *He's* the leader, so it's up to him to carry the can at a time like this.

Wart hasn't said a word since they left the newsagent's. He sits slumped in a corner now, his face shockingly pale, like he's going to throw up or something. Tommo isn't much better. He's spoken only a word or two in answer to the occasional question. The two youngest members of the gang seem stunned more than anything else, like they can't believe that they've really killed a man. It wouldn't seem so bad if it had been a member of Otis Mason's posse, someone they had a genuine grudge against, but this was just some old shopkeeper. There's no real reason for him to have died.

Chaz is pacing restlessly up and down, occasionally going to peer out through the grimy French windows, like he's expecting the cops to show up at any minute. But Finn doesn't think that's going to happen. They've dumped the car well away from the estate, and set fire to it to ensure that they left no tell-tale clues behind them. Also, they've no

previous form for armed robbery, so they won't be the first
names that spring to mind when the coppers look for
suspects. But just the same, Chaz keeps pacing nervously
about, and Finn feels like telling him to sit down, as he's
making everyone jumpy.

'I don't believe it!' Chaz tells Finn. 'I don't fuckin' well
believe it! A doddle, you said. Just stroll in there with
the shooters and he'll hand over the money. Now we're
fuckin' killers! Every scuffer in Manchester will be lookin'
for us.'

Finn gives Chaz a warning look. 'Not for *us* specially,'
he corrects him. 'For the people who pulled that robbery.
There's a big difference there. Now, give it a rest, will
you?'

'Oh yeah, you'd like that, wouldn't you! And let you off
the hook. But it's gotta be said, man, you fucked up. You
planned it, you laid it all out. We just went along, didn' we?
And the next thing I know, there's all this shootin' goin'
on!'

'Shut your fuckin' mouth!' yells Tommo, with such
uncharacteristic venom that even Chaz stops to take notice.
'It weren't Finn's fault,' protests Tommo. 'It ain't fair to
blame him.' His eyes are bulging now and his voice rises to
a shriller tone as he recalls the terror of what happened to
him back there. 'It was me and Wart, we ... we lost it in
there. Couldn't cut it. Wart shot the Paki once and it ... it
looked like he was comin' out from around the counter!'
He shakes his head in sorry disbelief. 'I dunno what
happened then. I must've panicked. I meant to shoot just
once ... you know, like a warning shot, but the ... the
fuckin' gun I had, it just seemed to shoot all by itself. It ...
it just kept goin' off in my hands, you know ... ?' His voice
dissolves into tears and he takes his glasses off, wipes his

eyes on the sleeve of his jacket. Wart begins to cry, too, like he was just waiting for the signal, shoulders hunched, his mop of hair hanging into his face.

Finn and Chaz exchange glances, and Finn sees that Chaz has a triumphant half-smile on his face, like some part of him is enjoying the sight of Finn's leadership going down in flames.

'How much did we get?' he asks now, and it's the moment that Finn has been dreading. He's been horribly aware of the paltry sum of money in his coat pocket ever since they left the scene of the crime; has been putting off the moment when he has to share that knowledge with the others.

'Not as good as we hoped,' he admits.

Chaz sneers, glances around at the others as though seeking their support. 'Not good, as in *bad*?' he suggests.

Finn scowls. 'The Paki must have had a safe tucked away somewhere. If we'd stayed cool, we could have got him to tell us the combination . . .'

'Only by then, you'd wasted him, right?' Chaz begins pacing again, his hands on his hips. He's enjoying this new role, Finn can tell. 'So how bad is it? You gonna tell us, or are we supposed to guess?'

Finn sighs. He takes the thin bundle of notes from his pocket and throws them on to the bare floorboards. Then he takes out a bag of pound coins and adds that to the collection.

Chaz stares at the money in disbelief. He crouches down and counts the notes. 'Thirty-five quid?' he says. 'You killed somebody for *thirty-five quid*?'

Put like that, it does sound pretty damning, Finn has to admit. He looks around at the others' faces, and they're staring at him in silence. This is a bad moment for him: the moment when he senses that if he says one more wrong thing, they'll walk out of the door and have nothing more to do with him ever again. It's time to play his trump card. He reaches into his pocket and takes out the wallet.

Chaz looks at it suspiciously. 'What you got there?' he asks.

'Dunno yet. I took it off that guy who walked in on us.'

'I seen him before,' says Wart. It's the first time he's spoken since the robbery, and they all turn their heads to look at him.

'Where?' asks Finn.

'On the estate that time. He was with the photographer: the one that was talking about Bobby C. Cooper. Remember, I told you, we trashed his car? A BMW. That guy's a friend of Bobby C.'s!'

Finn sneers. 'You mean, he *says* he is. Christ, Wart, anyone could say that. Doesn't mean it's true.' He opens the wallet and takes out the money he finds there. 'Another seventy quid, cash,' he announces, throwing it down on to the pile.

'Oh, great, we can all retire,' says Chaz, and Finn throws him a warning look.

'You're a bit fuckin' mouthy today,' he observes 'Gettin' tired of livin', are you?'

Chaz avoids his gaze and Finn returns his attention to the wallet. A large selection of credit cards, which he tells himself have probably already been cancelled. Some fancy business cards featuring an address on Deansgate, and several phone and fax numbers. 'Nick Saunders,' mutters Finn. '*Futures.* I've seen that in town, swank-looking place. He must be worth a fortune.' Finn pulls out a folded letter and, look there, the man's home address printed at the top of the page! This is getting more interesting by the minute.

Now he finds another business card and he raises his eyes when he's read it, because this one belongs to a Gabe Rothman of Rothman Representation Incorporated, and the address is La Cienaga Boulevard, Hollywood, and it's funny, but Finn *knows* that name. He's heard it somewhere before ... but where? Where?

'A hundred quid,' grumbles Chaz. 'Twenty-five notes each. Now that's what I call big-time.'

'Shut it!' Finn warns him. 'I'm tryin' to think here.'

'I bet you are! While you're at it, you'd better think about a quick way to leave town, 'cos that's what I'm gonna do.'

'What are you talking about?'

'You came out of that shop without your mask. That guy must've seen your face!'

'So what? He'd had a whack in the head. You're not telling me—' Finn breaks off. Suddenly he knows where he's heard about Gabe Rothman. He does a quick flashback to a TV interview with Bobby C. Cooper on *Rock Of America* some weeks ago. Bobby C. lounging on a leather sofa, grinning into the camera.

'Gabe Rothman is more than just a manager, he's the guy that taught me about respect, you know. Said to me, "Bobby, I'm gonna put you into the year's hottest movie", and that's just exactly what he did!'

So Wart's right, that guy back at the shop *does* have some connection with Bobby C. It's just like he was saying the night Gibbo was killed ... Christ, that seems so long ago now; hard to believe it's, what, only a couple of days. So much has happened since then, so much compressed into such a short stretch of time. Finn feels like he's aged twenty years. Maybe he has.

But now lightbulbs are flashing inside his head as he senses a possible way to redeem himself. OK, so this guy *must* be big-time; and, shit, Finn's got his home address right here. So what he does is, he nicks a van and drives it up there; he breaks in and . . .

And then Finn finds a photograph tucked away at the back of the wallet. There's the guy from the shop; he's sitting beside a good-looking woman – got to be his wife. It's one of those pictures you take with a delay timer, both of them smiling at the camera, and sitting in the woman's lap is this little girl, maybe two or three years old, and she's smiling too. She's holding this doll up like maybe she's just been given it as a present. Sure, see, it's Christmas, there's the decorated tree tucked away at one side of the shot! The picture's been taken with one of those cameras that give you a printed date in the corner. Just last Christmas, so the little girl won't be much older now . . .

And suddenly Finn is beginning to see a way out of this mess. Big-time, mind you – a lot more serious than breaking and entering, but in some ways a lot simpler and, hey, what the fuck, they're big-time now anyway. They've just killed somebody, haven't they?

Trouble is, it won't be easy to get the others to go for it, not after what happened today. They're fed up, scared, quickly losing their faith in his abilities as a leader. Chaz is acting up more than ever, got to be put back in his place again before Finn can take this any further. And if it's going to be done, they'll have to act soon. But that makes sense. Do it, then split for good, before the scuffers can home in on them. Maybe try their luck out in the sticks, where the natives are slower and the pickings are easy. Be able to set themselves up nicely if they get it right this time . . .

He realises that the others are all watching him, as though they know that he's planning something. Even Chaz is paying attention, the know-all smirk gone from his mouth, and Finn realises that, for all his bluster, Chaz is as freaked out as the rest of them. Well, let them sweat it a little bit longer, then they'll be more receptive to his idea.

Finn takes out his cigarettes and lights one up, warming to the plan now, thinking of little refinements to help it all go smoother. Oh sure, he's seen movies about things like this, and the characters spend *months* planning it in every detail: drawings on blackboards, stopwatches, shit like that. But Finn and his crew don't have that luxury – got to get in there, hit and run. With the cops on one hand and Otis Mason on the other, they've already overstayed their welcome in this city.

'Well?' Chaz finally prompts him. 'What's goin' down? What you thinkin' about?'

'Another job,' says Finn. He blows a cloud of smoke in Chaz's direction.

'I'd say we've done enough already,' growls Chaz. 'What we want is sensible ideas.'

'Is that right?' Finn smiles. He gets to his feet. 'You're shootin' off at the mouth a lot today, Chazzer. You got anythin' else you want to say?'

Chaz pushes his jaw out defiantly. 'Maybe,' he says. 'Yeah, maybe I have. Maybe I'm not so sure if you're the right person to be callin' the shots around here. Maybe I should go see Gordie, have a word with him about this.'

Finn laughs. 'That would be worth watching,' he says.

'What's that supposed to mean?'

Finn moves closer, fixing Chaz with a mean look. 'It means that Gordie's dead.'

'What?' Chaz is staring at him now. 'What you talkin' about?'

'You heard me. He's dead. Mason had him burned. I found his body when I went over the other night.'

'You're lying!' protests Chaz.

'Think so? Run over to his place and take a look if you don't believe me. They broke in there and killed him and his dogs. Not a pretty sight.'

'But . . . you didn't say anything before!'

'Yeah, you know why? Because I figured you'd shit in your pants and go runnin' to your mum.'

Chaz's eyes widen in indignation. 'You what?' he yells. 'You can't talk to me like that!'

'No?' Finn flicks his cigarette into Chaz's face.

As Chaz yelps and throws up his hands to shield his eyes, Finn leans in under his guard and punches him in the mouth. Chaz goes down hard, his shoulders slamming against the bare floorboards. He lies there unmoving for a moment, staring up at the ceiling in dull surprise. Then he groans, spits out a tooth. Finn stands over him, fists raised but Chaz doesn't try to get up.

Finn turns to glare at the others. 'Anybody else think I shouldn't be leader?' he asks. Nobody answers.

He glares down at Chaz a moment longer, then turns aside. He spits emphatically on the floor and returns to his place, sitting down with his back to the wall.

'So now you all know,' he says. 'We're on our own. No Seventh Cavalry to the rescue. This time we have to wipe our own arses. So . . . we do one more job.'

Chaz sits slowly upright, one hand clamped over his

bleeding mouth. Finn glances towards him, then looks at the others.

'One *easy* job which will bring in enough dosh to take care of everything.'

Tommo snorts dismissively. 'You said that about the newsagent,' he growls.

'Yeah, I know. And, OK, so we fucked up. It happens. And you've already said that wasn't my fault. Fuck, it wasn't *anyone's* fault! But, listen, supposin' I told you how we can get hold of guaranteed big money? Without havin' to rob anywhere? No guns, no violence, no risks – not if we use our heads. Fix it so the scuffers don't even find out.'

Chaz stares at him blankly. 'That would be a fuckin' miracle,' he mutters, his smashed lips slurring his words. But he doesn't sound half as cocky as a moment ago. Finn decides that he's learned his lesson and still wants to run with the gang.

'Just a case of usin' this for a change.' Finn taps the side of his head with his index finger. 'We'll be able to name our price, and somebody'll come and hand it to us on a fuckin' plate.' Finn snaps into a quick Tommy Cooper impression, gesturing with his hands like a magician. 'Just like that!'

'Bollocks,' says Chaz. But he's intrigued now, you can tell. He's already forgotten the skirmish; he'll go back to toeing the line for a while.

Tommo, too, looks interested. Even Wart has raised his gaze from the floorboards and is studying Finn intently, waiting to be told what to do.

Finn smiles. He has them now. He can make them do anything. Anything at all.

'Listen,' he says. 'This is what we do . . .'

Chapter Twenty-Five

Nick sat at the breakfast table and tried to ignore the dull throb of pain in the side of his head. He lifted a forkful of scrambled egg to his mouth and chewed without enthusiasm.

Opposite him, Molly lifted a spoonful from her own plate and copied his pained expression as she munched. Glancing up, Nick spotted her and gave her a look of mock disapproval, which made her giggle.

'Daddy's in a grump this morning!' she told Helen.

Helen sipped at a glass of orange juice. Early on in this pregnancy, she had 'gone off' tea and coffee, and was now drinking copious amounts of juice to make up for it.

'It's because he bumped his head,' she told Molly. They had fabricated an accident to explain the dark bruise on Nick's cheek. 'I keep *telling* him he should go back to bed.'

Nick frowned. 'I can't, love. There's a live interview on *Metrosound* this morning and Terry isn't available to handle it. Everybody else at *Futures* is tied up with other projects.'

'Surely they can manage without you just for one day.'

'What, let Bobby Cooper loose in a radio station on his own? That's an open invitation to disaster. No, I'll have to be there to co-ordinate.'

'Co-orbirate,' said Molly helpfully. 'Daddy gonna be on the radio?'

Nick smiled. 'Not me, Button. Bobby C. Cooper.'

'Is he famous?'

'Yes, I suppose so.'

'Will you get me his orby-graph?'

'His autograph?' Nick was horrified. 'What do you want that for?'

'Linda c'llects famous orby-graphs.' Linda was her friend at playgroup.

'Er . . .' Nick glanced at Helen, noticing her smile. 'I'll see what I can do.'

'Imagine,' said Helen. 'Working on a *Saturday*.'

'I often work on a Saturday.'

'Yes, but not the day after a serious accident.'

'N'accident,' parroted Molly, around a mouthful of scrambled egg. 'A serial n'accident.'

'I'll be fine,' insisted Nick. 'Honestly, I feel a lot better this morning.'

'That why I saw you swallowing a handful of paracetamol just now?'

'A bit of a headache, that's all.'

Helen shook her head and gave him a disparaging look. 'I don't understand you sometimes. One minute you're telling me how much you hate that job, how you'd like to pack it in; the next, I can't even persuade you to take a flipping day off!'

'It's just bad timing, that's all. Terry was pretty hacked off about having to cancel all his appointments yesterday.'

'Well, that's tough! If he puts his business above the health and wellbeing of one of his best friends, maybe it really *is* time you told him to stick his job right up . . .' She glanced at Molly warily. 'Right where the sun don't shine,' she concluded.

'Right up his bum-bum!' added Molly, and she squealed with laughter.

'Molly, that's not nice,' said Helen, trying hard not to smile, but failing.

Nick made an effort to change the subject. 'So what are you two doing today?' he asked.

'Going shopping,' Helen told him. 'I promised Molly a new pair of shoes.'

'We's goin' on the bus!' announced Molly excitedly.

For some inexplicable reason, she loved travelling by public transport. This was just as well today. They were normally a two-car family, but Helen's Citroën was currently in the garage, undergoing repair. Nick's BMW was, so far as he knew, still parked outside the newsagent's in Rusholme.

'We're goin' to sit upstairs,' enthused Molly. 'Lucy's coming too!' Lucy was her favourite doll, a scruffy-looking plastic thing currently down to her last few strands of blonde hair.

'What kind of shoes will you get?' Nick asked her.

Molly thought for a moment. 'Yellow ones,' she said.

Helen looked at her daughter with a 'we'll see about that' expression.

Nick glanced at his watch. 'I'd better order a taxi, to go and pick up my car. I hope to God it's still there. My briefcase is locked in the boot, with all my papers in it.' He stood up, wiping his mouth on a serviette.

'You haven't had enough breakfast,' observed Helen.

'It was lovely, but I just don't have much of an appetite this morning.'

'If that headache gets any worse, come straight home.'

'Yes, mum.' He leaned over and gave her an affectionate peck on the cheek.

'Me too!' Molly prompted.

'As if I'd forget.' He stepped around the table and leaned forward to kiss her gently on the forehead. As he straightened up again, he had the strangest sensation, a feeling of presentiment. Molly was still smiling up at him, her mint-green eyes sparkling, and he thought that she looked terribly, terribly vulnerable. He was suddenly afraid that something awful was about to happen to her.

'Take care in town,' he warned her. 'Keep a tight grip on Mummy's hand.'

Her freckled face took on a solemn look. 'Yes, Daddy. Shall us bring you a present – to make you better?'

He reached out a hand to stroke her hair.

'I don't need a present,' he said. 'I've got everything I need.' The bad feeling was slowly dissipating, and he could only put it down to the sense of anxiety that the incident in the newsagent's had kindled in him. He told himself not to be silly and, turning away, walked out into the hall to phone for a taxi.

Wart and Tommo were standing in the phone-box across the road from the imposing Victorian semi. Tommo had the receiver against his ear and the two boys were trying to look like they were making a call, but really they were keeping a close watch on the house's front door. They felt decidedly uncomfortable in this prosperous suburb. The smart houses and carefully tended gardens seemed to be sneering at them, as though recognising them as outsiders hailing from a rough part of the city, and they felt oddly out of their depth.

Wart was depressed. He hadn't spoken much since the

robbery, and there was a movie playing in his head: a constant slow-motion replay of the newsagent's body jerking as the bullets slammed into him. Awake or asleep, the film was the same; he couldn't seem to shake it. He knew that he didn't actually kill the newsagent – that was Tommo – but he *did* shoot him the first time and that had made Tommo pull the trigger, hadn't it? So he was as bad as a murderer, and murder was a mortal sin; everybody knew that. He glanced at Tommo, sensing that he too was disturbed by what had happened, only he was doing a better job of coping with it. But that was Tommo for you, straight down the line, never gave much away.

'What d'you think about this?' Wart asked him.

'About what?' Tommo seemed startled by the sudden sound of Wart's voice.

'This new idea of Finny's. Think it's gonna work?'

Tommo shrugged. 'Maybe,' he said. 'I dunno.'

'Supposin' it goes wrong? Like the robbery.'

Tommo made a gesture with his free hand. It seemed to say 'Fucked if I know'. Then he reached up and pushed his spectacles higher on to his nose. 'You believe what Finn said? About Gordie?'

Wart thought about it. 'I suppose so. Why would he lie?'

'I don't know. Sometimes I think Finn would say anything to keep bein' the top man in the outfit. But this new idea he's got, 'bout leavin' Manchester and startin' up somewhere else, I ain't sure about that. I always lived in Manchester. I don't know if I could handle bein' anywhere else.'

'But what else can we do? Wait around till the scuffers get us? Or Otis Mason? I dunno which'd be worse. You heard what Finn said about Gordie? You know, havin' his dick cut off?' He swallowed with difficulty. 'At least the cops wouldn't do *that* to us.'

Tommo laughed bitterly. 'No, they'd just bang us up and throw away the key.'

'But they couldn't do that: we ain't old enough.'

'Don't kid yourself. Murder ain't the same as robbin' and takin' cars. They put you away. Oh, it ain't called prison – you don't go *there* till you're older. But it ain't a fuckin' health farm neither.' Tommo sighed. 'Anyway, whatever we do, we're gonna need some dosh. I just wish there was an easier way of gettin' it. If I'd only thought to put a bit aside when I was earnin' . . . You just don't think it's ever gonna change, do you?'

Wart looked wistful. 'My old man pissed most of mine away,' he said. 'He played hell last night when I only had twenty-five quid to give him. I think he thought I was holdin' out. Gave me a week to come up with another hundred to pay off an IOU. He's been playin' cards again—'

'Eh up!' said Tommo. 'What's this, then?'

A taxi had pulled up outside the gates of the house. The driver sounded his horn impatiently, like he'd already been kept waiting for some time. After a few moments the front door opened and a man stepped out. It was the guy from the shop, all right. Wart could see the big purple bruise across the left side of his face, where Finn had hit him with the shotgun butt. *Just like that*, thought Wart, and recalled Finn doing his Tommy Cooper gestures the night before.

The man paused in the doorway and turned back to kiss the good-looking but visibly pregnant woman who was seeing him off.

Great, thought Wart, *so now we know she's in there too*.

The man turned away from the door and walked to the

taxi. Wart instinctively lifted a hand to shield his face, but the man wasn't even looking. He opened the door of the taxi and climbed in. It pulled smoothly away from the kerb, and Wart and Tommo exchanged glances.

'Now what?' asked Wart.

'Well, that's him out of the way. Now we—'

They were startled by a rapping on the glass, and they turned in surprise to see an elderly lady standing there. She was wearing a tweed suit, a little hat with a feather in it, and tan leather gloves even though it wasn't particularly cold. Her red jowly face held an irate expression.

'Are you boys going to be there all day?' she demanded to know.

Tommo opened the door a few inches and studied her calmly through the gap. 'Could be,' he said.

'Well, please hurry it up. I've an important call to make!'

'No use,' Tommo told her. 'The phone's out of order.'

'What are you talking about?' She pointed to the receiver in Tommo's hand. 'Weren't you just using it?'

'No, it's broken.'

The woman peered at it suspiciously. 'It looks all right to me,' she said.

'I'm tellin' you, it's broken.' Tommo lifted his arm and brought the end of the handset down hard against the main body of equipment – once, twice, three times. Plastic shattered and metal components fell out of the ear-piece. 'See,' said Tommo. 'Completely fucked. We only came in here for a piss.'

The woman looked like she was about to suffer a massive coronary. Her face turned purple and her eyes threatened to pop out of their sockets.

'Why you filthy little brutes! You *vandals*! I've a good mind to call the police!'

'Be my guest,' said Tommo. He held the broken handset out to her. He laughed and the woman retreated from the laughter, as though afraid of being infected by it. The two boys watched her stride away down the street, muttering to herself.

'Silly old cow,' said Wart. 'Think she *will* tell the police?'

'I don't care,' said Tommo. Wart looked at him in surprise and saw that he was telling the truth. 'I'm a killer,' said Tommo flatly. 'We *both* are. It doesn't matter what happens to us now.'

Wart didn't like the sound of this. It was dangerously close to the way he felt himself.

'Finn won't let us down,' he said. 'He'll look out for us.'

Tommo shook his head. 'He can't help us. Nobody can. We're damned. I can't even go to confession now because Father O'Rourke warned me never to show my face at St Kentigern's again.'

Wart was impressed by this. He'd never heard tell of such a thing. 'What did you do?' he asked.

Tommo shrugged. 'It was when I was an altar boy. I nicked a bottle of Communion wine and got rat-arsed. Then I threw up in the sacristy. Father O'Rourke found me sleeping it off in there.'

'Jesus.' Wart was even more impressed. He knew the priest well and wouldn't have dared cross the cantankerous old bugger. 'I bet he *shit* himself.'

'Near enough.' Tommo frowned. 'And all that crap he gives out about forgiveness. He wasn't very bloody forgiving to *me*, I can tell you. It's funny, it all seemed pretty cool at one time. Church 'n' stuff. Father O'Rourke said I had a vocation.'

'What, you mean, like a job?'

'I suppose. But then I fell in with Finn. The Father told

me I'd come to no good if I hung around with him.' He looked down at the broken phone in his hand, as though he was surprised to find it there.

'You sayin' it's his fault?'

Tommo frowned, shook his head. 'No, not really. It's just ... there's somethin' about him. You want to, like, *please* him. You want him to think you're OK. Know what I mean?'

Wart nodded. 'Yeah,' he said. 'I know.'

'And it's like he's always pushin' you that bit further. Gettin' you to do things. I mean, that newsagent's – the robbery. I wouldn't have even *thought* about doin' somethin' like that before I met Finn. He just makes it seem like a good idea. You know, now I think of it, it was him gave me the idea of stealing that wine. He said that's what *he'd* do if he was an altar boy. And me, I just went for it, you know? Now, this new thing—'

'You sayin' you don't wanna do it?' Wart tried to keep the note of hope out of his voice. He wasn't strong enough to say no himself, but maybe if Tommo made a stand with him ...

Tommo frowned. He pushed his glasses higher up his nose. 'I dunno. Maybe we're too deep in the shit now. Maybe we've *got* to do it. It's like Finn says, it's the only way out of this mess.'

Wart sighed. He felt like crying, because he knew now that he was lost. They were going to do this thing for Finn; they were going to walk on that last mile with him to the end of the road. It was like a fairground ride he'd climbed on, and the guy at the controls wouldn't turn it off, wouldn't even slow it down enough for Wart to jump clear. It was like ...

The front door of the house opened again and the woman

273

stepped out, closely followed by the little girl from the photograph. They were both wearing coats and the woman had a straw shopping bag slung over her shoulder. She turned back and locked the door.

Tommo reached into his coat and took out his cellphone. He dialled a number and the call was answered immediately.

'Finn, it's Tommo. The woman and the kid have just come out of the house. They're walkin' up to the gate.' Tommo watched as they opened the gate and stepped out on to the pavement. 'Now they're headin' off down the street. Looks like they're goin' shoppin' or somethin'.'

He listened for a moment, then nodded. He folded the phone and put it back into his pocket. He glanced at Wart. 'Finn says to follow them,' he announced. 'Report back every ten minutes. Him and Chaz have got a car, they're on their way.'

'Right,' said Wart, but his voice was flat and unenthusiastic.

Tommo opened the door of the booth and the two boys stepped out. Keeping a safe distance between themselves and their quarry, they started to follow them along the street.

Chapter Twenty-Six

Nick's headache was getting steadily worse. He glumly acknowledged this fact as he stood in the control room of *Metrosound* radio, gazing through the glass partition into Studio Two. Beside him in the control room were Gabe Rothman and a tubby sound engineer called Steve Acton, who was there to handle the phone-in they'd be having later in the show. On the other side of the glass, behind a mixing desk, sat DJ Ray Wood; and opposite him, seated at a green baize table, were Bobby C. Cooper and Ajay Sanjari. They were due to go on the air in a matter of minutes, just as soon as the current crop of advertising cartridges had played through their sequence.

Cooper had been his usual arrogant self when first introduced to Wood, and Nick feared the worst for the broadcast. His anxiety must have showed on his face.

'Relax,' Rothman advised him. 'Bobby's a natural for radio. He'll be just fine.'

Nick sipped at the paper cup full of tepid coffee he had been handed and grimaced. 'I'd feel happier if it wasn't live,' he said. 'Your boy can be somewhat unpredictable.'

Rothman waved a chubby hand in dismissal. 'Don't sweat it. I had a little pep talk with him before we left the hotel. I told him strictly no expletives, and he's to treat every question *seriously*. You wait and see: he'll do good.'

'I hope so,' murmured Nick. It had been another wearing day for him. It had started reasonably enough when he'd discovered that his car was still where he'd left it, unharmed, with the attaché case safely locked in the boot. And since Gabe Rothman had accepted the responsibility of getting Cooper to the radio station on time, Nick had at least been spared any of that bother. But, once at *Metrosound*, Bobby had started to kick up the traces in his own inimitable fashion. He'd been horrified to learn that Amos and Andy would not be able to accompany him into the cramped studio, but were expected to wait for him out in the reception area.

'For Christ's sake, man, these guys go *everywhere* with me!' he'd protested. 'I'll be *defenceless* in there!'

'Who are you expecting?' Nick had asked him testily. 'Lee Harvey Oswald?'

'Man, you just never know. You'll find this hard to believe, but there's a lot of people out there who've got it in for me.'

'Imagine,' muttered Nick under his breath.

After lengthy arguments, a compromise was reached. Amos and Andy would be issued with passes, and would take up a position by the swing doors just outside the main entrance to Studio Two, where they would be able to intercept any would-be assassins who happened along.

Next, Cooper had announced that he was thirsty and he wasn't going to be fobbed off with a cup of coffee from the machine. No, he wasn't going to put that poison into his body; he wanted a bottle of mineral water – and not just *any* water. It had to be Volvic because that was the only brand his delicate system could tolerate this morning. A *Metrosound* minion was dutifully despatched to scour the city for some

Volvic, returning with it just a few minutes before the transmission began.

Now, as the final seconds ticked away, everyone was in position. Cooper, mineral water at the ready, sat behind one microphone; Sanjari behind the other. Since their skirmish at the press conference, the atmosphere between the two had been decidedly strained.

Nick almost felt sorry for Sanjari. By now he had doubtless realised he had made a terrible mistake in bringing Cooper over, but was obliged to make the best of a bad job. Cooper continued to treat the Asian businessman with ill-disguised contempt but, then, that was how he treated most people.

Ray Wood opened up his studio channel to announce that they were coming up to time. Wood was a tubby, balding little man whose suave, rather smug voice was strangely at odds with his homely appearance. He slipped on his headphones, cued the cartridge that held his jaunty intro music, and came in with a bubbly voiceover.

'Hello, hello! It's Saturday. It's ten o'clock. It's time for the Ray Wood Radio Show! In today's special show a live interview with the man they call the Rap Terminator; and with the Manchester entrepreneur who's just paid a cool million to bring him to the Rainy City! But first a word from the Sultan of Cool himself. Here's Bobby C. Cooper with *Show Respect*!'

Wood hit the play button on the CD machine, and the familiar strains of Cooper's most recent hit thumped out of the big studio speakers.

Wood relaxed, slipped off his headphones. He leaned forward over the desk to have an informal chat with his two guests. Nick couldn't hear what he was saying, but he noticed that only Sanjari bothered to make any kind of reply. Cooper sat there looking distinctly bored and, Nick thought, rather tired. His eyes were red and puffy and he had a dazed look about him.

'Bobby looks like he could use an early night,' Nick told Gabe Rothman. 'Perhaps you should suggest it to him?'

'You kidding?' Rothman chuckled. 'It'd be easier to get Yasser Arafat to sing "Hava Nagila" at a bar mitzvah! I long ago stopped trying to make that boy do anything other than keep his business appointments. Christ, you saw the trouble I had in the hotel just to get him to turn down his stereo. Bobby sees his personal life as his own affair. He doesn't take kindly to being ordered around.'

'So I noticed. It beats me how you put up with it.' Nick realised he was hardly being professional in saying this, but was past caring. 'What makes you stick with him?'

Rothman gave Nick a look that verged on pity. He made the familiar gesture of rubbing his thumb and forefinger together. 'A whole mountain of dough, that's what! Whatever my personal feelings towards Bobby, that boy is my biggest meal-ticket. In a coupla years, I'll be able to retire to a four-hundred-acre ranch in Wyoming and tell the world to kiss my ass!'

Nick smiled. 'Somehow, I can't picture you riding the range.'

'No? Well, picture me doing it in a Jeep Cherokee. Maybe that'll help.'

Ray Wood allowed the music to fade down, and came in with his opening line: 'Bobby C. Cooper, welcome to Manchester!' He paused to allow Cooper to reply, but the guest just sat there behind his microphone, studying Wood as he might consider some lesser form of animal life. Unphased, Wood steamed in again without losing momentum. 'So, Bobby, this your first trip to our own fair city?'

'Uh . . . yeah.'

'So, what do you make of the place?'

Cooper seemed to consider the question for an unnecessarily long time before answering. 'Well, now, I don't make nothin' of it, Ray. What do you make of it?'

Wood laughed as though Cooper had cracked a brilliant witticism. 'I think it's an absolutely mega-stupendous place, Bobby. After all, Manchester has the best clubs, theatres and cinemas in Europe!'

'That right?' Cooper looked genuinely surprised. 'If that's the case, man, how come they won't give you the Olympics?'

In the control room, Nick winced. Even long after the event, this was still a touchy subject around the city. Trust Cooper to put his big foot in it.

'Well, er, Bobby, that's an interesting question. The reason we lost our Olympic bid seems to be largely political—'

'Political, my ass! You wanna know why you keep gettin' passed over? It's your *weather*!'

'Our . . . our weather?'

'Sure, you got what has to be the worst weather in the world here. Can you imagine trying to guarantee two weeks of decent weather for the Olympics? I mean, shit, man, this is supposed to be summer, right? It ain't hardly stopped rainin' since I got here!'

At the mention of the word 'shit', Wood's confident grin slipped momentarily off his face, but he pressed on like the battle-hardened veteran he undoubtedly was.

'Ha, ha! Yes, we do have quite a reputation in that field, don't we? But luckily we have plenty of good things to make up for it.'

'Yeah, like what?'

'Er...' Wood was probably beginning to wonder who was interviewing who here. 'Well, there's a brilliant Indie-music scene, for a start.'

'You kiddin' me? I heard some of that stuff on the radio, man; that sounds like Sixties American pop to me. What was that bunch of kids used t'be on the TV? The Monkees! Yeah, that's what it is, man – goddamned Monkee-music! And then you got these white rap acts everyone says are so good, but like, you know, white men cain't rap for shit. It's embarrassing watchin' 'em try to cut it. There were these guys on the TV yesterday afternoon, Manchester band, they said – Jesus, they just about stunk up the screen!'

Wood made a valiant attempt to resume control of the situation. 'So ... what have you been doing for entertainment, Bobby? Have you been to the Hacienda?'

'You kiddin'? I'm too famous to put my head out on the streets, man. There'd be a riot. 'Sides, I'm an old-fashioned kinda guy. Like to make my *own* entertainment, if you know what I mean.'

'Well, let's take last night, for instance.'

'Last night? Last night we had ourselves a party.'

'Oh right, jelly, ice-cream, paper hats, that kind of thing?'

'Say what?'

'You know, all good clean fun?'

'Clean ain't got nothin' t'do with it. There was this one chick last night and she—'

'Ha ha! Moving right along, Bobby, I'd like to bring in Ajay Sanjari, the young Manchester businessman whose inspiration it was to bring you over here. Hey, Ajay, how's it going?'

'It's going just fine, Ray. And may I say what a pleasure it is to appear on your programme? I'm a big fan.'

In the control room, Nick tried not to feel nauseous. Sanjari was almost as smug and obsequious as Wood himself. They made a great team.

'Ajay, you are, of course, the genius behind the AJ Jeans phenomenon, currently up there competing with the major American brands. How do you account for your success?'

'Well, Ray, I'd put it down to hard work, dedication, and the courage of my convictions. I knew I had a good product and instead of playing down my Manchester connection, I decided to make a virtue of it. You know, on every label it says *AJ Jeans, Manchester, England*. I'm proud of this city and I'm getting tired of listening to people put it down.' Sanjari glanced scornfully at Cooper.

'But some critics have questioned your use of an American performer to launch your latest range. They're bound to say: if you're so proud of Manchester, why not use a Mancunian?'

Sanjari gave an oily smile. 'Well, that's a fair point, Ray. But you see, AJ Jeans are now an international success. So when I started looking for somebody to promote my new range, it seemed to me that Bobby had the kind of image that would complement AJ Jeans perfectly.'

'Yeah,' said Cooper. 'He thought I was cheap, shoddy and totally without style!'

Nick groaned. He shot an accusing look at Gabe Rothman, who merely made his by now familiar what-can-I-do gesture.

Sanjari was making a feeble attempt to laugh off the last remark.

'It's a constant delight to work with Bobby,' he said. 'He's always making jokes.'

'Who's joking?' asked Cooper, dead-pan.

'Er . . . so . . . so how did you get him to agree to the trip?'

'Well, I contacted his manager, Mr Rothman—'

'And offered to go down on him!' finished Cooper, gleefully.

'No, I . . . I simply made him a very attractive offer.'

'Yeah, like I said. He offered to go down on him!'

Even Ray Wood's unerring professionalism was starting to crumble under this onslaught. He made a desperate attempt to steer the conversation into safer waters. 'Bobby, you're perhaps as well known in England for your film work as for your records. Your last movie, *No Quarter*, was a massive success. Are we going to be seeing you in another film soon?'

'Well, Ray, I was doing some filming just last night.'

'You were?'

'Yeah, that chick I was tellin' you about? She was really hot for it, right, so we got out this camcorder and—'

'Yes. I think this would be a good point to play another track from Bobby's latest album. This one's called *Citizen Cocaine* . . .' Wood panicked as he realised he'd just announced a track that was banned from the station's playlist. He did some frantic rejigging of the buttons, interrupting the song after just a few bars, and wound up playing *Show Respect* a second time.

As the music track punched in, Nick could see that some pretty terse dialogue was being exchanged between the three men in the studio. He turned to look at Gabe Rothman.

'That was some effective pep talk you had with Bobby,' he observed.

'What can I tell ya? The kid's got a mind of his own.'

'He's also got another twenty minutes to fill, and we can't have him filling it with smut like that. We'll have to talk to him.'

'Correction,' said Rothman. '*You'll* have to talk to him. I already gave it my best shot.'

'Oh, well, thanks. Thanks a lot!' Nick headed for the swing doors of the control room, aware that his headache was coming back with renewed force. He strode the short distance to the next room, angled left, and pushed through the double set of doors into the studio.

As he entered, he caught the tail end of a remark from a very unhappy Ray Wood.

'. . . but with respect, Mr Cooper, we do have a responsibility to this programme's audience.'

'Yeah. Who gives a shit what *three* people think, anyway?'

'Bobby!' snapped Nick. 'A word in private, if you don't mind.'

Cooper rolled his eyes towards the sound-proofed ceiling. 'Aww, come on, Nick-O-Las! Get off my case, will ya?'

'Up to you, Bobby. You can accompany me out to the corridor, or we can have words right here. It's all the same to me.'

'Jesus, man.' But Cooper got to his feet and followed Nick out into the corridor. Then he stood there, his back against the wall, his hands in his pockets, looking for all the world like a naughty child.

'What's the big idea?' demanded Nick.

'Aww, fuck man, I was just havin' a little fun, is all. Goddamned two-bit radio show, what's the big deal?'

'The point is you're supposed to be a professional! The switchboards here will be jammed with people calling to complain about you. For God's sake, Bobby, it's ten a.m., Saturday. Most of the listeners will be kids, and you're going on about filming sex sessions and giving people blowjobs! You've compromised the station, you've embarrassed Ray Wood, and you've made Mr Sanjari look like a complete jerk.'

'He *is* a jerk!'

'That's your personal opinion, but it has no relevance here.' Nick started pacing up and down, aware of the resentment building up like an electrical charge inside him. His head felt like it was going to burst. 'Did you ever in your life stop to consider somebody besides yourself? Are you so fucking selfish that you can't see past your own over-inflated ego?'

Cooper bristled. 'Yeah, well who the fuck are you to be mouthing off to me, mister? You're just a two-bit PR man. I snap my fingers and you're off this project quicker than greased shit!'

'Really? Under the circumstances that sounds pretty enticing.'

'It's easily fixed, boy. No problemo! You seem to forget, *I'm* the star around here. I'm the one with the *talent*!'

Nick sneered. 'I'm not sure that a talent for being a prize arsehole is anything to be proud of.'

'There you go again, man, mouthing off at me. Just who the fuck d'you think you are, huh? Ain't no wonder people want to beat the shit out of you.' He pointed at the bruises on Nick's cheek. 'For two pins I'd give you some more of that.'

Nick laughed at this. 'You? That's a good one! Maybe you forgot, your two trained gorillas aren't here to back you up.'

'Don't need no gorillas,' growled Cooper. 'Could take you with one hand tied behind my back. Hey, know what I heard, Nick-O-Las? It was a coupla kids beat you up. Itty-bitty little kids!'

'That may be so, Bobby, but I guarantee each and every one of them acted more mature than you do. At least they weren't throwing tantrums every time something didn't go their way. Next to you, they seemed *mature*!'

'I'm warning you, man.' Cooper gave Nick a shove in the chest. 'Get off my case, before I lose my temper!'

'Come on, then, big man.' Nick made beckoning gestures. He just didn't care any more. He'd had as much of this as he could take. 'Let's see what you're really made of, when you're not hiding behind that phoney image of yours . . .'

Cooper's eyes widened in a sudden rush of anger. He lunged forward, swinging a fist at Nick's head. Nick ducked a little too late and the punch glanced a stinging blow against his ear. He retaliated by leaning in under Cooper's guard and popping his right fist hard into the man's gut. Cooper doubled over with a grunt of mingled pain and surprise. He slumped back against the wall a moment, fighting to catch his breath; then launched himself head-long at Nick, driving him back against the wall of the studio. Nick's shoulders connected with an impact that seemed to shake the foundations. He roared with pain and threw an arm around Cooper's neck, wrestling him to one side and dragging him several steps along the corridor.

For several moments they struggled in silence to gain the upper hand; then Nick got a leg across Cooper's ankles, tripping him and slamming him head-first against the opposite wall. Cooper swore, and seemed to go slack in Nick's arms; but then he drove an elbow back hard into Nick's ribs, driving the breath out of him and making him release his hold. Nick stumbled back gasping, and Cooper turned to face him. They squared up, stood there in the narrow corridor, glaring into each other's eyes, both of them breathing hard now, arms out like a pair of professional wrestlers. There was a long angry silence, while they appraised each other, both of them looking for an opening.

Then Cooper shook his head and laughed ruefully, rubbing his hand across his stomach. 'Man, this is about the dumbest thing I ever heard of,' he observed. 'We's like to kill each other here.'

Nick maintained the icy glare for a few moments longer; then he also saw the absurdity of it and he laughed too. 'You're right,' he said, rubbing at his ear. 'The pair of us are getting too old for this kind of behaviour.'

'I mean . . . it's up to you. We can fight on if you want, or we can do the sensible thing and call it a draw. Whaddya say?'

Nick made an attempt to steady his breathing. His anger seemed to have dissipated in an instant. 'A draw sounds good to me,' he admitted. 'But we've got to talk about this interview thing . . .'

'Yeah, yeah.' Cooper waved a hand in dismissal. 'I think you made your point, bro. I was dicking around back there, and I guess it wasn't very professional. Listen, what say I go back in the studio and take another whack at it?'

'I'd appreciate that. And no more swearing, uh?'

Cooper gave Nick a long, thoughtful look. Then he nodded. 'Whatever you say. You know, Nick, that's quite a punch you got there. Amos 'n' Andy ever quit on me, you might consider applying for the job.' He turned away and began to walk back to the studio door.

Nick grinned. 'I think not,' he said. 'Seriously, Bobby, when we've finished up here, I'll understand it if you want to get yourself another PR man.'

Cooper glanced back at him. 'You kiddin'? I'm just

gettin' to appreciate the one I already got.' He pushed open the studio door and went inside, letting it swing shut behind him.

Nick composed himself, brushing back his ruffled hair with his fingers and straightening his tie. Taking a deep breath, he made his way back to the control room, where he joined Gabe Rothman by the glass partition. They watched as a smiling Bobby C. Cooper lowered himself back into his chair.

Rothman glanced at Nick in surprise. 'Shit, what did you say to him out there?'

Nick shrugged. 'It wasn't so much what I said,' he explained. 'More the way I said it.'

In the studio, Ray Wood faded down the music and the interview continued.

Chapter Twenty-Seven

Wart waited anxiously up on the first floor of the Westway Centre. Leaning on the smoked-glass and tubular-steel balustrade, he gazed down into the huge tiled rectangle that was Wallis Square. It was packed down there: hundreds of shoppers and their children gathered to gawk at the fountain. Wart knew that somewhere in their midst was Tommo – feigning an interest in the huge models of famous cartoon characters grouped around the spotlit fountain; but really he was keeping tabs on the entrance to the big shoe shop opposite. The woman and the little girl seemed to have been in there for hours.

Wart wished that Finn and Chaz would hurry it up. They must have had trouble finding a parking place for the stolen car; it was always a problem on Saturdays. He'd have felt happier if he could spot Tommo, but from this vantage point it was just a sea of heads – he could be anywhere.

The fountain looked pretty cool; Wart thought that he wouldn't mind changing places with Tommo. Down on the ground floor, you could hear the voices of various cartoon characters cutting through the backwash of syrupy Muzak – Elmer Fudd, Sylvester the Cat, Daffy Duck and Tweety-Pie. And if you looked up, towards the huge domed roof above the piazza, you could see cloudy, coloured swirls of light projected on to what looked like the underside of a flying saucer. Over the entrance of the shop responsible for all this customisation, a gigantic Bugs Bunny presided like a malevolent Roman emperor surveying his domain.

Wart thought it was all very sexy: a little chunk of Hollywood dropped into the middle of this grey drab city, lending it some much-needed colour. Wart liked cartoons, would have loved to exist in a world where you could drop a ten-ton weight on to somebody's head without doing them any permanent damage. What had happened to the newsagent wasn't at all like what happened in cartoons. Wart remembered the way his frail old body shook under the impact of the bullets – and one terrifying detail: the way a dark, wet hole had blossomed on his cheek, like the entrance to a tiny hell . . .

He closed his eyes, feeling suddenly nauseous.

'Hey, kid, wake up!'

Startled, Wart opened his eyes to see Finn and Chaz approaching him. They looked harassed, a little out of breath.

'Had to park miles away, 'Finn explained, as he stepped up to the balustrade. 'Where are they?'

'In there.' Wart pointed down to the entrance of the shoe shop. 'Been in there ages. Tommo's by the fountain somewhere, keepin' an eye on the door.'

'Good.' Finn reached into his pocket and took out an *A-Z* of Manchester. He handed it to Wart, together with a letter in a plain brown envelope. 'Now, you know what you've got to do? Just like we rehearsed, OK?'

Wart nodded, but glanced around in dismay.

'Problem?' Finn asked him.

'Well, we're not going to do it *here*, are we?'

'Why not?'

'Finn, there's just so many people! I thought we'd wait till she was somewhere quieter.'

Finn shook his head. 'Let me tell you somethin' about places like this, kid. Nobody ever sees anything. They're all wandering around down there wrapped up in their own little worlds. You could pull out a gun and shoot somebody; they wouldn't take a blind bit of notice.'

He glanced slowly around. 'Security men?' he asked.

'There was a guy here ten minutes ago, but he moved off up that way.' Wart gestured vaguely at the other end of the building.

'What about video cameras?' muttered Chaz. 'They're all over the place.'

Finn shrugged. 'They ain't gonna notice anything, not if we're quick.'

'Yeah, but if they look back through the tapes . . .'

'They won't. They'd only do that if it was *reported*. And, like I told you, nobody's gonna report this.'

'I hope you're right, man. I really do.'

'There they are now!' exclaimed Wart. He was about to point a finger, but Finn reached out a hand and checked him.

'I see them,' he says.

They were coming out of the shop now: mother and daughter, still hand in hand. Wart noticed for the first time how alike they were and realised that he was going to have a hard time getting the woman to let go of her child's hand. The little girl was clutching a plastic carrier bag with the name of the shoe shop printed on the side of it. Her mum had obviously bought her a new pair of shoes, and she wanted to carry them herself – show how grown-up she was. She looked a sweet girl, Wart thought. He had a sister just a year or two older. Now the girl was pointing excitedly at the fountain and pulling her mother closer to have a look at the cartoon characters.

Wart noticed Tommo at last: he was standing just ten yards away from his quarry, watching them intently. Then he tilted back his head to look up at Wart and the others, and his eyes widened slightly in recognition. He gave a barely perceptible nod.

'Zackly where we gonna do this thing?' asked Chaz.

'Depends where they go next,' murmured Finn. He pointed to a large double escalator off to the left of the fountain, leading up to and down from the floor on which they were standing.

'That'd be favourite,' he said. 'Chaz could wait around at the top there. And, Wart, you could distract her for a moment. That's all we'd need . . .'

'She ain't in any hurry,' observed Chaz.

This appeared to be true. The woman and the girl had edged closer to the fountain. The girl was laughing delightedly at the cartoon voices, and her mother was standing behind her, one hand on her daughter's shoulder.

'Good-lookin' bird,' observed Chaz. 'No wonder she's up the stick. I wouldn't mind a bit of that myself.'

Finn laughed. 'Do me a favour. You wouldn't know what to do with it!' He glanced around, then stiffened slightly. 'Watch out. Fuckin' uniform on the prowl.'

Wart tried not to stare. The security man was approaching them from across the way, strolling along in no particular hurry, a bored expression on his face. He was an ugly little man with a beer belly and a big arse. He looked faintly comical in his American cop style uniform. He glanced at the three boys suspiciously as he moved past, trying pathetically to play the hard man, but he didn't slow down. He moved past, and disappeared into the crowd behind them.

'Fuckin' jobsworth,' muttered Chaz. 'He was as soft as shite, you could tell.'

'Hey, they're on the move,' announced Finn.

Glancing down again, Wart saw that the woman and girl were moving away from the fountain and ... *yes*! They seemed to be heading towards the escalator.

'Right,' said Finn. 'Places, you two.'

Wart stuffed the *A-Z* into his pocket and hurried to his position. He headed along the side of the open rectangle, and kept on going until he reached a set of ornate cast-iron railings that bordered the next opening, some twenty yards further on. He waited there, trying to look nonchalant, but his heart was racing and his mouth was suddenly very dry. He'd kill for a can of Diet Coke.

He saw that Chaz was in position at the top of the escalators, standing with his back to the emergency-stop button.

Finn had remained where he was, to oversee the operation. He'd only pitch in if anything went wrong, but he'd assured Wart that nothing *would* go wrong this time, provided everybody did what was expected of him.

Timing was the thing, Wart told himself, it had to look natural. Problem was, from where he was standing Wart couldn't see the woman and girl; he couldn't tell how far up the escalator they were. But Finn was going to give him a signal when it was time to make his approach. He took the book from his pocket and opened it to the marked page. The envelope fell out and he stooped to pick it up with clumsy fingers.

As he straightened up he saw Finn remove his baseball cap, and he knew it was time. He began to walk towards the escalators. Chaz was watching him impassively, his mouth moving rhythmically as he chewed a piece of gum, and Wart wished he didn't have to have an audience for this. Supposing he fucked up again? But no, he wouldn't fuck up this time, he couldn't. He ran a selection of potential opening remarks through in his head as he walked.

Excuse me, missus . . . pardon me, missus. I'm sorry, missus, could you help me, please?

A head appeared over the metal horizon of the escalators, and Wart was still too far off. He was about to break into a run when he realised that this was a different woman: older, with shorter hair. She stepped on to solid ground and moved past Wart, not looking at him. Now he was closer, and two more heads were gliding into view: the woman and the girl.

Wart felt like his heart was going to explode in his chest – Chaz still gazing at him, a look on his face like there was a bad smell, like he was *expecting* Wart to fuck up.

Excuse me, missus . . . I was wonderin' if you could tell me somethin' . . .

Wart took a deep breath as the woman and the girl reached solid ground. They were still holding hands as they started to walk towards him. Wart opened his mouth to speak, and nothing came out: his voice just hitched in his throat. It was like his vocal chords were paralysed. He couldn't make a sound and now the woman was about to step past him. Finn would be furious! Wart made a supreme effort and something between a grunt and a cough burst out of him. The woman paused, looked down at him in surprise.

'I beg your pardon?' she said.

Wart held out the *A-Z* like a talisman. ''Scuse me, missus. I was . . . I was lookin' for Tib Street . . .'

The woman seemed amused by this. 'But we're in the Westway Centre!' she told him, as if somehow he hadn't noticed.

'Yeah, but . . . see, I couldn't find Tib Street – so I came in here to ask someone. Now I'm a bit lost.' He proffered the book again, doing his best to look helpless, willing her to reach out for it – to let go of the little girl's hand.

'Well, I'm really not very good with maps and things.'

'*Please*, missus! I got to meet my mum there, an' I'm goin' to be late. She'll be worried about me.'

The woman softened, smiled. Chaz was right, thought Wart. *She is a bit useful-looking*.

'All right,' she said. She let go of her daughter's hand to take the book from him, and Wart felt like cheering. She studied the open pages for a moment. 'Well, you seem to have the right area,' she observed.

Wart said nothing. He was trying not to look at Chaz, but out of the corner of his eye he couldn't help noticing the way the older boy stepped forward decisively.

'Now, look, here's where we are, the Westway Centre!'

'Uh-huh.' Wart moved a little closer, made out he was studying the page but really, he was seeing Chaz grab the little girl, one arm going around her waist, the other hand clamping over her mouth, her eyes bulging wide in surprise as Chaz lifted her clear of the ground, turned and stepped on to the 'down' escalator.

Wart experienced a powerful urge to run, the same feeling you got when you'd just put a stone through somebody's window, it was a panic that came over you, but he knew he had to stay put for a while yet, until Finn gave him the all-clear signal. The woman was still intent on the map, a sharp red fingernail tracing the jumble of streets and roads.

'Now, you see, here's Market Street – that's right out of the exit there. All you need to do is turn right, by Marks and Spencer . . .'

'Turn right, uh-huh.' Wart glanced anxiously towards Finn, but no, the hat was still off. He risked a glance down the escalator and saw that Chaz and the girl were only halfway down. Jesus, this was taking forever! The woman could turn, see her daughter, and hit the emergency stop button . . .

'And then you turn right again, I think. Yes, that's where the bookstalls are – you know them, don't you?'

'Er . . . bookstalls, sure.'

'So you carry on past them, up to the top of the street . . .'

Chaz was at the bottom of the escalator now, trying to look natural with his arms wrapped around the struggling girl, but people on the opposite escalator were staring at him in open suspicion. He stepped on to the ground floor and hurried off through the crowd towards the exit.

'. . . and make a left turn – that's Tib Street! It'll take you ten minutes, no more.' She handed back the book and he accepted it, noting as he did so that Finn was putting his hat back on.

The woman gave Wart a last smile and turned to take her daughter's hand. She looked down in dull surprise.

'Molly?' she said.

Wart took the envelope from his pocket. 'This is for you, missus,' he said and stuffed it into her hand. She glanced at him in surprise.

'What?' she said distractedly.

But now Wart was running away, heading off through the crowds, leaving the woman standing there alone at the top of the escalators. 'Wait!' he heard her shout, but he wasn't going to stop now, not till he was safely back at the regrouping point with the others.

In his haste to flee the scene, he collided with a middle-aged woman. Her carrier bag of groceries tore open, and apples and oranges went rolling across the tiles, but Wart wasn't about to slow down. He angled back on himself and went down a staircase, three steps at a time.

Out on the street, he tried to make himself slow down a little. He was gasping for breath now, like he'd just run a marathon. Out in the grey light of day everything seemed unreal, but he knew that he hadn't imagined what just happened. Still, he did OK this time. No cock-ups. Finn was going to be very pleased with him.

Helen stood at the top of the escalators, gazing frantically around. She felt stunned by the suddenness of Molly's disappearance but told herself, no, there was no need to panic; she'd catch sight of her daughter at any moment, looking into some shop window just a short distance away. For goodness sake, Helen had only let go of her hand for a few moments. She *couldn't* have gone very far, could she?

But turning around in a slow circle, Helen had to admit that she couldn't spot Molly anywhere. She glanced back down the escalator to the fountain; maybe her daughter had doubled back for another look at those cartoon characters . . .

Then Helen caught sight of the carrier bag lying at the bottom of the descending escalator, the name of the shoe shop emblazoned on the side of it. With an oath, Helen stepped on to the escalator and rode down, using the steps to make her journey quicker. As she reached the level, she picked up the bag.

The shoes were still inside – together with Lucy, Molly's precious doll.

She immediately knew that something was horribly wrong. Molly would never have discarded these items – not if she'd had any choice. And why had that young boy suddenly run away, without so much as a word? And this envelope? What did it all mean?

A powerful sensation of icy fear arose in the pit of Helen's stomach. Suddenly she knew with a cold, precise certainty what had happened. Molly had been snatched. Somebody had taken her! She tore open the envelope with trembling fingers and withdrew a single sheet of folded paper. Opening it, she studied the words for a moment, reading them but not really registering their meaning; noting only how they were printed in large, laborious letters, horrifically spelt – the work of a young child, surely? She looked quickly around again, hoping against hope to see Molly coming towards her; but knowing that she wouldn't, because the note, the note . . .

She tried to calm herself, to read the words through a second time, more slowly, allowing their full meaning to sink in.

WE HAVE GOT YOUR DORTER
IF YOU WANT TO SEE HER ALIFE AGAIN
DO NOT TRY GOEING TO THE POLICE
WE WILL NO ABOUT IT AND YOU WILL BE
SORRY
IF YOU TELL ANYWON ELS WE WILL NO
AND YORE DORTER WILL DYE
ONLY TELL YOUR HUSBIND
WE WILL CONTAC YOU TONITE
BE REDDY FOR OUR CALL

'Oh God,' whispered Helen. Her eyes filled with tears. 'Oh God, Molly. No, no ...'

'You all right, dear?'

An elderly gentleman, stepping off the escalator, had heard her involuntary cry. He had now paused beside her, concern on his face.

'Oh, I'm ... I'm fine ... Thank you. Do you know if there are any phones here?'

'Just down the hall, there.' He pointed. 'Are you sure you're OK?'

'Fine, thank you! Excuse me.' She began to stumble away from the old man, fighting to control the panic rising within her. She assured herself that this couldn't be happening, but knew at the same time that it was – that somebody had taken her daughter, that even now they might be doing unspeakable things to her.

She must force herself to function, otherwise she might just as well drop in her tracks and succumb to total hysterics. A phone. Find a phone, call Nick at *Metrosound*, or ask them to relay a message through to him somehow. Maybe *he* would know what to do ...

She plunged on into the crowded piazza, moving past the illuminated fountain where the huge grinning animals no longer seemed quite so cuddly, and where a recorded burst of manic laughter spilling from unseen speakers chilled her to the bone.

Chapter Twenty-Eight

Wart and Chaz marched the little girl up the stairwell that led to the Swamp. She was quieter now, temporarily more resigned to what was happening to her. Back in the car she struggled and cried and kept asking awkward questions, but now she seemed to have retreated into a sullen silence, and Wart was relieved about that.

Finn and Tommo had taken the car back into town, Finn saying something about picking up supplies, and meanwhile Wart and Chaz were to watch the little girl, see that she didn't try to escape, or come to any harm. Chaz complained loudly about this, telling Finn that he wasn't a bloody nursemaid, but Finn just gave him one of those looks, and Chaz quietened down, probably remembering the smack in the mouth he got before. He accepted the task with silent ill-humour.

But Wart had noticed that, once out of the car, Chaz became unnecessarily surly with the little girl, prodding her in the back whenever she dawdled, growling at her to shut up whenever she tried to speak. Wart couldn't help feeling sorry for her: she must be terrified by all this.

They climbed the last flight of steps, up to the fifth floor, and Chaz unlocked the door. He pushed the girl into the hallway, shepherded her along to the lounge, and kicked open the door.

The little girl stood looking around the room in dismay, like maybe she was expecting something better than this. Her face was already grimy with tears and her bottom lip quivered. Wart could tell she was about to start crying again. Chaz indicated the grubby mattress and sleeping bag in the corner of the room.

'Get on there,' he told her.

She looked at him defiantly for a moment.

'*Won't*!' she retorted. 'Want my mummy!'

'You'll see her soon enough,' said Chaz. Again he pointed at the mattress. 'Now get on there and shut up.'

She shrank from him as though he had hit her, went over to the mattress and sat down on it, pressing her back into the corner as though trying to fuse with the crumbling plaster.

'Want Lucy,' she said.

'Who's Lucy?' Chaz wanted to know.

'My *doll*. She was inna bag wiv' my new shoes.'

Wart looked at Chaz. 'What happened to the bag?' he asked.

'Dropped it, didn' she? Back at the Westway. Well, I wasn't fuckin' goin' back for it, was I?'

The little girl looked outraged.

'Umm!' she said. 'You *sweared*!'

'So what?' Chaz laughed unpleasantly. 'Just sit there and shut up, all right?' He glanced at Wart. 'You've got a sister, haven't you? Do something wiv' 'er before I lose me patience.'

Wart frowned. He went over to the mattress and sat down on the edge of it, gave the little girl what he hoped was a friendly smile.

'What's your name?' he asked her.

She pouted, looked down at her hands, shook her head.

'Go on, it's OK. You can tell me. My name is . . .' He paused, remembering that Finn had warned him not to use any names. 'My name's Brian,' he said.

Chaz sneered. 'Brian!' he exclaimed. 'Christ!' He pulled the canvas toolbag out from under an old blanket, and went to sit on an upturned wooden crate beside the French windows. He took out his cigarettes and lit one up.

The girl sniffed, wiped her nose on the sleeve of her coat.

'Molly,' she said. 'My name's Molly.'

'That's a nice name.' Wart felt self-conscious, knowing that Chaz was listening, but he pressed on. 'Well, listen, Molly, you're goin' to have to stay here wiv' us for a while, OK? Just till we sort somethin' out. Then you'll be able to go home.'

'Stay *here*?' Molly glanced fearfully around. 'You mean, like at night time? *Sleep* here?'

Wart shrugged. 'Yeah. It'll be all right.'

'But it's dirty and cold!'

'You were expecting Buckingham Palace?' asked Chaz.

'And I'm *hungry*!'

'You and me both. Stop complaining. You're doin' my head in!'

Wart glanced at Chaz admonishingly. 'Come on, she's only a kid, for Christ's sake.'

'You don't say? Fuck me, I thought she was Cindy Crawford! It's a pity we didn't grab her mum. At least we could have had some fun with her.'

'You sweared again!' protested Molly.

Chaz rolled his eyes towards the ceiling. 'Oh, this is gonna be fun,' he observed. 'It's like kidnapping Mary fuckin' Whitehouse!'

There was a long pause, then:

'I'm still hungry,' Molly reminded them.

'Don't worry,' Wart told her. 'There'll be something to eat just as soon as . . . when the boss gets back.'

'Him that was drivin' the car?' asked Molly. She seemed suddenly respectful. 'Him wiv' the black clothes?'

Wart was puzzled by this remark. *Yes*, he thought, *Finn was wearing black clothes today – but what had that got to do with anything?*

'Child Catcher,' whispered Molly, so quietly that Wart could hardly hear her.

He leaned closer. 'What?'

'Child Catcher. He come for me. Daddy said he w'unt, but he did. Now I got to wait for daddy come get me back again.'

Wart looked at Chaz. 'What's she on about?' he asked.

'Fuck knows. Who can ever figure out kids?' Chaz had unzipped the toolbag, and had taken out the automatic pistol. He held it up so that Molly could see it. 'You just pipe down, or I'll have to use this, OK?'

Molly shrank back against the wall, her eyes wide and staring.

'Don't,' said Wart. 'Can't you see you're frightening her?'

'*I'll* bloody frighten her in a minute,' snarled Chaz. He extended his arm and sighted the gun up on Molly's forehead. Then he made a shooting sound, blowing out air between his lips.

'Stop it,' pleaded Wart. 'It might go off! Besides, Fi – the boss told us not to play with the guns!'

'Quit bellyaching. You're as bad as she is.' Chaz lowered the pistol and slipped it into his jacket pocket. He inhaled on his cigarette and blew out a thick cloud of smoke, then turned his head to peer out of the French windows.

'Where's Finn got to?' he muttered; then winced when he realised what he'd said. 'Ah, fuck it! All this cops 'n' robbers stuff is bullshit anyway.'

Wart eyed Chaz warily, aware that he was working himself up into one of his tetchy moods. He was not particularly nice to know at times like that. Wart then glanced at Molly.

'Listen, why don't you try and get some sleep?' he suggested. 'You must be tired.'

'*Not* sleep!' protested Molly. 'Want my mummy.'

'You'll see her real soon. You just got to be patient. Here.' Wart took his Gameboy from his coat pocket and put it down on the mattress beside her. 'Play wiv' this, if you like.'

But Molly's lip was trembling again. 'Don't wanna!' she wailed. 'Want my mummy! I want . . . I want . . .' And then she was crying, *really* crying this time: a long, formless wail of misery interspersed with gasps for air.

Wart looked at her in dismay.

'Oh perfect,' said Chaz. 'Shut her the fuck up, Wart, before somebody hears her.'

'We're not supposed to use names!'

'Stuff that. Just shut her up. She's drivin' me crazy.'

Wart frowned. 'What am I supposed to do?' he protested.

'I don't know. I don't care. Just . . . just make her stop, OK? What do you do when your sister cries?'

'I go out and leave my mum to sort it.'

'Well . . . sort it yourself this time. Come on, do something – before *I* get up and take care of it.'

Wart tried putting a hand on Molly's arm, but she shook him off and cried with renewed ferocity.

'Don't cry,' pleaded Wart anxiously. He didn't want

Chaz to get up to her, there was no telling what he might do. 'Please, listen to me. Your Mum's gonna be here soon and . . . and there'll be nice things to eat. We'll have burgers and chips and milk shakes. We . . .'

'For Christ's sake!' yelled Chaz. He flicked the remains of his cigarette across the room, and got up off his box. 'What use are you, soft lad?'

He went over to Molly, kneeled beside her and grabbed her by the shoulders. Then he started shaking her vigorously like a terrier going at a rat.

'Hang on,' said Wart, 'I don't think you should—'

'Leave it! Somebody's got to do something with her, haven't they? She's just trying it on – see how far she can push us.'

He leaned close to shout in Molly's ear. 'Now listen to me, OK? You shut your whining mouth or you're gonna be sorry, understand me? I ain't puttin' up with any more of this shit, so—'

Molly went berserk. Now she was not crying so much as *screaming*, her eyes shut, her arms flailing as she went into a full-tilt, five-star temper tantrum. To Wart it looked like she was having some kind of fit.

'Bloody hell!' said Chaz. He slapped her about the head a couple of times, but that only seemed to make her worse. He looked quickly around the room and came to a decision. 'Open the French windows,' he told Wart.

Wart stared at him fearfully. 'What you gonna do?' he asked.

'Never mind. Open them, *now*!'

Wart got reluctantly to his feet. He crossed the room and unlatched the big windows. Stepping out on to the balcony, he glanced over the sagging wooden railing to the concrete pavement fifty feet below. He had hoped to see Finn and

Tommo down there but the weed-strewn forecourt was deserted.

He turned back and saw to his dismay that Chaz had picked up Molly by the arms and was carrying her towards the open window. The little girl kicked and struggled in his grasp, and she was still making a lot of noise.

'Chaz, no,' pleaded Wart. 'You can't!'

'I told you to shut it,' Chaz reminded him. He pushed past Wart and lifted Molly over the rail, holding her out at arm's length. She was still struggling furiously, not yet aware of what had happened to her.

'Now,' said Chaz triumphantly. 'Stop that noise or I'll let you fall.'

Molly opened her eyes and stopped struggling. She glanced down over one shoulder and her eyes widened in shock. Wart stepped closer to the railing. He could see Molly's legs making a cycling motion on the empty air. Chaz was grinning, enjoying the new-found sense of power he had established over her.

'That's enough,' pleaded Wart. He spoke quietly, not wanting to startle Chaz into releasing his hold. 'Pull her back up now.'

'Not till she tells me she won't make any more noise,' said Chaz through gritted teeth.

Wart could see that Chaz's arms were beginning to tremble; the girl was heavier than he had anticipated.

'No, no, no, no, no!' shrieked Molly. 'Lemme go!'

'That what you want?' Chaz asked her. 'That what you *really* want?' He pretended to let her fall a few inches, leaning his weight against the ancient wood of the balustrade. Wart heard it creak ominously, and saw drops of moisture ooze from it.

'Please, Chaz, pull her up now. I think she's learned her

lesson.' Wart was terrified by the wild look in Chaz's eyes, a look that said he didn't give a fuck any more – he'd drop her just to see what happened.

In his mind's eye, Wart saw Molly falling, her arms and legs flailing as she spun around in the empty air to shatter like ripe fruit on the paving slabs far below.

'Finn will kill us if anything happens to her!'

'Finn?' Chaz sneered. 'That wanker, what's *he* gonna do?' Then Molly gave a sudden wild kick and Chaz almost lost his grip on her wrists. He grunted, nearly overbalanced. The wooden rail gave a long creak of protest.

A car drew up outside the block's front entrance. Wart nearly cheered as the driver's door opened and Finn climbed out. Tommo got out of the passenger door. The two of them stood there, looking up at the balcony.

'What the fuck are you doing?' Finn shouted up.

Chaz gazed defiantly down at him. 'Just fooling around.'

'Pull her back up!' Finn told him. 'Before I have a bit of fun with *you*.'

'It's not like we *need* her or anything,' argued Chaz. 'I mean, we get the money whether she's alive or dead, right? And Wart went and blurted out all our names . . .'

'That's not true!' protested Wart.

'Pull her up,' said Finn calmly, and this time there was no mistaking the note of threat in his voice, hard and flinty like a handful of flung gravel. 'You drop that kid and I'll come up there and throw you down after her. That's a promise.'

Wart heard Chaz mutter something under his breath; but at last, with considerable effort, Chaz hauled Molly back over the rail and carried her into the room.

Wart remembered to breathe again and followed them

inside, as Chaz flung the little girl back on to the mattress. She scrambled into the corner and crouched like a cornered animal, staring at Chaz in dumb hatred.

'You shouldn't have done that,' Wart told him.

'Who says? Finn?' Chaz swaggered back to his seat on the wooden crate. 'Just 'cos you'd lick his arse if he told you to.'

'Yeah? Well I don't see you tellin' him where to get off.'

Chaz didn't say anything to that.

'You better put that gun back where you found it,' Wart told him.

'I'll do what I like with it.'

'Finn'll be angry if he finds out you took it.'

'Yeah? Who's gonna tell him? You?'

Wart shrugged, turned away. They heard the sound of a key in the door, then footsteps in the hall.

The door opened and Tommo stepped into the room, carrying a cardboard box full of fish and chips. He was followed by Finn who, incongruously, had a big furry teddy bear tucked under one arm.

'Fuck me!' exclaimed Chaz. 'Aren't you gettin' a bit old for that kind of thing?'

Finn didn't smile and Wart could see that he was angry.

'It's for the kid,' he said, unnecessarily. 'Thought it might keep her quiet.' He studied Molly for a moment, then moved towards her, holding out the teddy bear for her to take.

'Look,' he said. 'What about this, then?'

She cowered away from him, shaking her head. Her face was grimy with tears.

Wart and Tommo busied themselves unwrapping the food.

'Look,' said Finn. He crouched down and turned the

bear around to show her the metal zip in the back. 'What's in here, then?' he asked. He opened the zip and pulled out a pair of pyjamas with cartoon characters printed on them. 'Something for you to sleep in,' he explained, but she just kept right on shaking her head, her eyes staring as though fixed on something only she could see.

Finn shrugged. He stuffed the pyjamas back inside and pulled up the zip. 'It's a good bear,' he protested, to nobody in particular. 'Cost me nearly twenty notes.'

'Good old Uncle Finn!' sneered Chaz. 'You gonna read us all a bedtime story later on?'

Finn turned and threw the teddy bear at Chaz. He caught it, sat it on his lap. 'Maybe you forgot,' said Finn, getting to his feet. 'We weren't gonna use names.'

'Yeah, well after Wart went and blurted it out . . .'

'That ain't true!' said Wart. 'It was *him*!'

'It don't matter who it was.' Finn was pacing up and down now, and Wart could see that his temper was rising. He fixed Chaz with a challenging look. 'Maybe you'd like to tell me what you was doing out on the balcony, when I got here.'

Chaz sighed. 'It's just that the kid wouldn't stop skriking, would she? So I figured I'd scare her a bit, quieten her down.'

'By hangin' her off the fuckin' balcony?' Finn moved closer, stabbed an accusing index finger in Chaz's direction. 'You stupid pillock! You could've slipped. She could've died. No wonder she's in such a state!'

'Yeah, but—'

'Listen to me! And this goes for all of you.' He looked towards Wart and Tommo, and they stopped eating their chips for a moment. 'There've been enough cock-ups. I want this one to go *right*. I don't want this little girl to come to any harm. That's not what this is about. Far as I'm concerned, we've just borrowed her for a couple've nights, and she goes back to her mum and dad, safe and well, just as soon as we've got the money.'

'Yeah, but she knows our names!' said Chaz.

'OK, who's fault is that? We'll just have to take our chances, won't we? One thing we ain't is child killers. So we get the money, we split, and she gets dropped off in a safe place. All right? Anybody got a problem with that?' He looked around the room at the others, but nobody said a word.

Then he turned back to Chaz. 'As for you, pal, you're close to the edge. If you put one more foot wrong, you've had it. Hear me? *One* more thing.'

Chaz looked insulted. 'I already told you, it was Wart shot his mouth off, not me!'

'Yeah, but Wart wasn't the one hanging the kid off the balcony, was he? Don't forget Mason and his posse are still looking for us. Supposing one of them had chanced by. We—'

Finn broke off as he noticed the open toolbag lying by Chaz's feet. He gave a tut of irritation.

'You been foolin' around with them shooters?' he wanted to know. 'I thought I told you to leave the guns alone?' He stooped, picked up the bag and carried it back to its usual place on the other side of the room.

Chaz took the opportunity to unzip the teddy bear on his lap. He slipped the automatic out of his pocket and pushed it in amidst the folds of the pyjamas, then zipped it up again. Nobody saw him do it. He hadn't really thought this through; he just didn't want to further incur Finn's wrath by being caught with the gun on him.

'How about some of them chips?' he asked.

Tommo brought him a portion and exchanged them for the teddy bear. Chaz started eating greedily, and Tommo carried the bear over to Molly.

'Here,' he said. 'Play with this for a while.'

Chaz stopped eating. He looked at the bear doubtfully, realising that maybe he hadn't made such a smart move.

'Leave her,' he said. 'Can't you see she doesn't want it?'

As if to spite him, Molly reached out her arms and hugged the bear to her, burying her face against the thick nylon fur.

Chaz frowned but didn't say anything. He went back to eating his chips, uncomfortably aware that Finn was rummaging in the toolbag.

'Where's the Glock?' he asked.

Everyone looked at him. 'The what?' muttered Tommo.

'The automatic! It ain't here.' He glared accusingly at Chaz, but Chaz just shrugged.

'Well, don't look at me!' he protested. 'I ain't seen it.' He ignored the glance that Wart threw at him. 'Maybe we left it back at the newsagent's.'

'No, that's the one gun we didn't take with us. It was here, in this bag. Listen, Chaz, if you're holding out on me . . .'

'I told you, I ain't got it!' Chaz put his chips in his lap and extended his arms theatrically. 'Search me if you like!'

'Yeah, search him,' suggested Wart, feeling suddenly reckless. He was getting sick of Chaz's little games; it would be fun to see him caught out.

Finn got up and went over to pat Chaz's pockets, but he found nothing. Wart couldn't understand this; he saw Chaz put the gun in his pocket. He was aware that Chaz was grinning at him triumphantly now, pleased with the trick he'd pulled. Chaz put his tongue out, like some kid. Unfortunately Finn noticed this and thought it was directed at him.

'What the fuck's going on?' he snapped. He looked around at the others and was met by blank expressions. 'Listen, we're supposed to be a team, not a bunch of dumb kids. We can't afford to go misplacing equipment like that. Now, can somebody tell me what's happened to that shooter?'

Wart frowned, studied his fish and chips for a moment. Half of him wanted to grass on Chaz, but the other half couldn't allow himself to be a sneak. He shrugged, went on eating. Besides, grassing would be a mistake; he'd only have to pay for it sooner or later.

'I'm waiting,' said Finn quietly. He turned back to look at Chaz. 'Where is it?' he asked. 'Where've you hidden it?'

Chaz looked indignant. 'What makes you think it's got anything to do with me?'

'Because it's *always* you,' snarled Finn. The anger was bubbling to the surface now, reddening his cheeks. 'Always pushin' it, shootin' off at the mouth, seein' how much you can get away with. Then I leave you for ten minutes, and you're hangin' the girl off the fuckin' balcony, like some stupid kid! Tell me where it is before I get really pissed off!'

But Chaz, too, was losing his temper. 'Do me a favour, will you? Get off my fuckin' back! I'm sick of you pushin' me around.'

'Is that a fact?' Finn's voice had gone suddenly quiet, calm.

Wart knew that this always happened just before he lost

313

his rag, but Chaz didn't seem to be aware of it. He was talking indignantly now, scooping up handfuls of chips with his dirty fingers and cramming them into his mouth.

'Big fuckin' boss man,' he spluttered. 'Do this – do that – I'm in charge! Leadin' us into one shit-storm after another. But these two didn't see you the night Gibbo was killed, runnin' like a frightened rabbit, nearly shittin' in your pants you was so scared. Then you've got the nerve to come waltzin' around like you're Arnold bleedin' Schwarzenegger. And you can't see that you're finished around here. You're history!'

'You reckon?'

'Yeah, I reckon.' Chaz gestured at Wart and Tommo. 'Maybe you can get these two arseholes to do what you want, but not me, mate, I don't take no shit from nobody. And you—'

Retribution was swift. Finn took two quick strides across the room and kicked the crate from under Chaz. He went down hard on his backside, with a squawk of surprise, and Finn lashed a boot up hard between his legs. As Chaz doubled up with a scream of pain, Finn grabbed the remains of the chips and ground the hot food into Chaz's face, ignoring his squeals of protest.

'Sick of it are you?' cried Finn. 'Had enough, yeah? Well, good, 'cos so have I! So just fuck off out of it, why don't you?'

He grabbed Chaz by the collar of his jacket and hauled him upright. Chaz was whimpering, trying to claw the scalding sludge of potato and vinegar out of his eyes. Finn slapped him across the face a couple of times and propelled him towards the door.

It started to dawn on Chaz what was happening.

'What?' he grunted. 'Uh, Finn, what—?'

'You heard me! You're *out*.'

'Finn, for fuck's sake—'

'OUT!' Finn seemed incensed. He lashed another blow at Chaz's face, driving him backwards towards the door.

'But ... you can't throw me out, Finn! Not after all I've done for you ...'

'Sure I can! We don't need you – moaning and whining every five minutes. Get out before I kick your fuckin' head in.'

'Finn, please!' Chaz was desperate now. He started to cry, and the other two looked away, embarrassed to witness this. 'I ... I was only kiddin'. I'll do whatever you want ... I'll tell you where the shooter is. Please, don't push me out!'

'Too late, Chaz.' Finn aimed another kick at his balls and Chaz retreated into the hallway. Wart and Tommo watched in dismay. Up till now, Wart had been thinking that Finn would relent, but his face was still set in a furious scowl and it was clear he wasn't going to change his mind – not this time.

'PLEASE!' Chaz made a last desperate plea, his arms held out in supplication, and Finn punched him in the face: a powerful right cross that slammed him backwards down the hall, his mouth and nose pumping blood down the front of his shirt. Finn took him by the collar again and frog-marched him down the hallway.

Chaz stumbled along, still dazed by the blow. He was whining now, bubbles of red snot hanging from his nostrils.

'Fuck off,' Finn told him. He opened the door and flung Chaz out on to the walkway, pushing him so hard that he collided with the concrete balustrade and nearly toppled over it.

Chaz steadied himself with an effort, and turned slowly

back. He stared at Finn, his eyes bulging in a pale face splashed with blood. He pointed a shaking finger.

'You're fuckin' dead,' he said, almost matter-of-factly. 'I'll get you for this.' Then he turned aside and walked unsteadily off along the walkway.

'Don't come back!' Finn yelled after him. He stood there watching till Chaz was out of sight. Then he slammed the door and strode to the living room, where he surveyed the two remaining members of his gang.

'If you've got a problem with me bein' in charge, you'd better go with him,' he said. But there was deep silence as they sat gazing back at him in a mixture of awe and fear.

'Well?' he demanded. 'Nobody got anything to say?'

Another long silence; then a tiny voice whispered: 'I'm hungry.'

They looked at Molly in surprise. She was still crouching on the mattress, her arms around the teddy bear.

Finn snapped his fingers at Tommo.

'For God's sake, get her some fish 'n' chips,' he said. 'Let's start thinkin' like a team, 'stead of always lookin' after number one.'

He went into a corner and slumped down against the wall with a groan. The sudden explosion of anger had left him feeling strangely weak, and part of him wanted to run after Chaz and ask him to come back. But it was far too late for that and, anyway, Chaz would probably come back under his own steam, soon enough.

Tommo collected the two remaining portions of food. He took one across to Molly and laid it on the grubby mattress in front of her. Then he took the other package and handed it to Finn.

'What happens now?' he asked.

Finn took a deep breath to calm himself. 'Now, we wait

316

till tonight,' he said. 'Let her parents sweat it out for a few hours.' He took the cell phone from his pocket and set it on the floor beside him. 'Then, when we're ready,' he said, 'we give them a call.'

He unwrapped his food and started to eat.

Chapter Twenty-Nine

It was the longest night of their lives.

Nick and Helen sat side by side on the sofa in the lounge of their home, waiting, hoping, praying for the phone to ring. They didn't say much to each other for most of the time. Neither of them really knew what to say.

From the moment he'd received Helen's incoherent call, just as he was about to leave the *Metrosound* offices, he'd known who was responsible for kidnapping his daughter. He remembered the cold, cruel face of the teenager with the shotgun, the way the boy's eyes had examined him as though Nick's life meant nothing to him. Now that same boy held Molly's life in his hands, and Nick was terrified at the prospect. He'd left Cooper and Rothman without so much as a word, and had driven straight home at top speed. For an instant only, he'd considered calling the police – but had warned himself that any threat made by these kids must be taken seriously. They had already killed once. No, he daren't risk it.

He and Helen were instructed to sit tight and wait for further instructions. But it was gone eight o'clock, and still they'd heard nothing.

Nick glanced at Helen. Her eyes were strained, red from crying, and Nick knew that she blamed herself for her daughter's disappearance. 'If I'd only kept hold of her hand,' she kept saying, over and over. Nick had been quick to argue that it wasn't her fault so much as his. If only he hadn't gone into that newsagent's for cigarettes . . .

Backwards and forwards they batted their respective guilt, before accepting that, really, neither of them was responsible. They were victims of lousy luck, pure and simple. They'd drawn the short straw in some cosmic game of chance, and their forfeit was to have their most treasured possession taken away from them. But they couldn't, *mustn't* allow themselves to believe that she was gone forever. They'd get her back safe and sound, provided they kept their heads and didn't panic.

Nick put his arms around Helen, hugged her close.

'We mustn't go on torturing ourselves,' he whispered. 'Neither of us is to blame. It's nobody's fault.'

'I keep telling myself that, but when I think what could be happening to her. How *frightened* she must be . . .'

He reached down and squeezed one of her hands tightly. 'We have to believe that she's coming back to us. It's only a matter of time.'

She seemed to make an effort to get her emotions under control. 'Shall I make a cup of coffee?'

'That would be nice.' He didn't feel remotely interested in coffee, but it might be a good idea if Helen occupied herself with such a simple task.

She got up from the sofa and moved towards the kitchen, like some sleepwalker locked in a nightmare. She was halfway there when the phone in the hall trilled loudly, and she seemed to jerk awake.

Nick was up off the sofa and running through the door before he even had a chance to think about it. He reached the phone first and snatched up the receiver.

'Yes?'

'Nick? What the fuck's going on?' Terry's voice sounded distinctly peeved. 'I just got home and Maureen told me the phone hasn't stopped ringing all day. Apparently you didn't take Bobby to any of his afternoon appointments.'

'Yeah, look, Terry, something came up, and—'

'I just phoned Gabe Rothman at the Midland. He says that you received a phone-call at *Metrosound*, and just took off. Left them standing there. They didn't have the first idea what to do next, so they headed back to their hotel. Nobody knows what happened to you!'

'Terry, please. I'm expecting an important call any minute. I need you to clear the line.'

'Huh?'

'Get off the line, OK?'

A brief pause. 'Nick, are you all right? You sound really odd.'

'I'm fine but I have to hang up now.'

'Nick? Nick, wait a minute—'

'I'm sorry, Terry. I'll explain later.' Nick put down the phone and turned to Helen with an apologetic expression.

'That was Terry,' he said unnecessarily. 'He wanted to know what—'

The phone trilled again. Nick snatched it up, 'Look, Terry,' he snapped, 'please don't ring here again tonight!'

'Who the fuck's Terry?'

It was a different voice. Nick felt a quickening in his pulse as he recognised the hard Mancunian tones that only a day earlier had threatened to blow his head off.

'Oh,' he said. 'It's you.'

'That Mr Saunders?'

'Yes.' Nick gave Helen a meaningful look, and she stepped closer to the phone. 'Who am I speaking to?'

'It don't matter what my name is.'

'OK. Is Molly there with you? Is she safe?'

'She's just fine. Now listen, we—'

'I want to talk to her.'

'What for?'

'I need to know that she's all right.'

'OK, 'ang on a minute.' A pause as the phone was moved a short distance. Then the sound of somebody breathing into the mouthpiece, and somebody else in the background instructing, 'Go on, say somethin'.'

'Molly?' asked Nick.

'Daddy?' The sound of her voice sent a wave of relief right through him, and also a kind of shock. She sounded so close, she might almost be in the room with him.

He felt Helen's hand tighten on his arm.

'Hello, Button. You OK?'

'Yes, but ... it's cold and dirty here. An' they keep swearin' all the time.'

'All right, don't worry. I'm going to get you out of there, just as soon as I can.'

'You promise?'

'Yes.'

'Cross your heart 'n' hope to die?'

'In a ...' His voice caught in his throat, and he had to cough before he could manage the familiar reply. 'In a cellar full of rats,' he whispered.

She sniffed and then spoke again, her voice close to tears. 'Is Mummy there?'

'I'm right here, darling,' said Helen, and Nick gave her the handset; but kept his ear close so he could listen in.

'Mummy, I'm frightened.'

'There's no need to be, Molly. Think of it ... think of it as a game.'

'A game?'

'Yes, like hide-and-seek. You're going to stay hidden for a little while, and then we're going to come and find you.'

'It was the Child Catcher. Daddy said he wun't come for me, but he did. Daddy lied.'

'No, he didn't lie, darling. He was mistaken, that's all ... But he's just told you that he's going to come and get you out of there. Remember that, Molly. He's never broken a promise yet, has he?'

The child didn't answer that.

Nick could feel the sting of tears in his eyes, and he had to struggle to control his emotions. He took the receiver back from Helen.

'I'm going to get you out of there,' he told Molly. 'You've got to be a little bit patient. Now ... now give the phone back to the ... whoever's there. We'll see what has to be done.'

A scuffling sound. He could hear Molly protesting noisily in the background, and then the phone moved away from her, as if being carried into a different room. *A mobile, then*, thought Nick.

'OK, now you know she's safe. And she's gonna stay that way so long as you don't do nothin' stupid. You ain't told anyone about this, have you?'

'Nobody,' said Nick. 'Not a soul, I swear.'

'Good. OK, then, we'll talk money. We've set a fair price for your daughter. We want half of it up front in cash, and the other half when we hand her over to you. We want twenty thousand quid.'

Despite the situation, Nick felt a snort of laughter spring to his lips. 'Christ, is that all? What makes you think I've got that kind of money?'

A pause – then, 'You quibbling?'

323

'No, but I . . . that's a lot of cash to put my hands on. I don't know if I can get it.'

'Sure you can,' said the boy confidently. 'And no hanging around, neither. We want the first half tomorrow.'

'Tomorrow?' Nick could feel a sense of rising panic. His savings amounted to no more than a few thousand pounds and they were currently locked away in a high-interest building society account, requiring three months' notice to remove them. Tomorrow was Sunday. Even if he could swing some kind of loan from his bank, he couldn't realistically sort it out till Monday morning; and asking for it in cash would doubtless prompt some very tricky questions. He couldn't see his bank manager casually forking out a case full of used tenners.

'Look, that's just stupid. I mean, ten thousand in cash – how am I supposed to raise that at such short notice?'

'I don't care how you raise it. Just do it! We're in a big hurry here.'

'Yes, but you must appreciate, it's not as simple as that. Maybe by Monday, I could—'

'Tomorrow.' The voice was abrasive now, close to becoming angry. 'Don't tell me you can't afford it, pal! Luxury house in Didsbury, brand new BMW parked in the drive. You must be rollin' in it.'

'You want the BMW? You could sell that. You'd get a lot more than ten thousand for it.'

'Get serious. I ain't in a position to stick an advert in the *Manchester Evenin' News*, am I? I've got the filth lookin' for me and I've got . . . I've got other people on my back. In short, I've overstayed my welcome here. I want hard cash in me 'and, by tomorrow. Monday night, you bring me the second payment, and then I'll tell you where you can pick up your daughter.'

'You're going to have to give me more time! You surely don't believe that I keep cash like that lying around the house!'

'No, but a bloke like you can get money if he puts his mind to it. There's dozens of moneylenders operate out of this city. Go see them if you need to. And you're a friend of Bobby C. Cooper, aren't ya? If you're strapped for the readies, you'll 'ave to borrow it off him. He wouldn't let a friend go down. Look at all that dosh he gave to his mate in *No Quarter*.'

'That's a *film*,' protested Nick. 'Real life isn't quite so convenient.'

A pause, then the kid's voice was calmer, filled with cruel intent. '*Tomorrow*, Mr Saunders. If you don't bring it by then, you're gonna be very sorry. You've got a nice-lookin' daughter. You ever seen the damage you can do with a Stanley knife?'

Nick closed his eyes. 'Don't,' he whispered. 'Please, don't harm her. I'll get the money somehow. You can depend on it.'

'That's my boy. OK, listen up. Come to the Merton Estate tomorrow night. There's this big wall wiv' a painting on it, what you call a muriel; got this big black feller with his arms in the air . . .'

'I know it,' Nick assured him.

'Oh yeah, I forgot. You already been slummin' round my neck of the woods, ain'tcha? Be there for midnight. And come *alone*. If you ain't alone, I'll soon know about it – and so will your little girl.'

'Midnight,' muttered Nick. 'I'll be there.'

The phone on the other end of the line went dead. Nick put down the handset and turned back to face Helen. He could see by her face that she had heard everything. He'd been hoping she hadn't caught the bit about the Stanley knife.

'Ten thousand pounds,' she whispered. 'Nick, what are we going to do? We haven't got that kind of money.'

'I know. Or any way of getting it – not at such short notice . . .' He stepped past her and walked back into the lounge. 'Maybe if there was something we could sell . . .'

She followed him. 'There isn't time! He has to give us more time! You should have explained to him.'

'I tried. He wouldn't listen. Probably thinks our mattresses are stuffed with hundred-pound notes.' He felt his anger boiling up within him, and had to fight to hold it at bay. 'Christ, he's just a snot-nosed kid. He hasn't a clue how it works. If I could get my hands on him, I'd crush him like a fly!' He sighed, dropped on to the sofa, cradled his head in his hands. He just didn't know what to do. 'Maybe we have to call in the police,' he said.

'No!' Helen grabbed his arms, forced him to look up at her. 'You heard what he said. He'll hurt Molly, might even kill her.'

'He could be bluffing.'

'We daren't take that risk! He's already killed one man, what's he got to lose?'

Nick shook his head. 'There's got to be something we can do. If there was only somebody who could help us . . .'

Helen brightened, like she'd just had a brilliant idea. 'Ajay!' she said. 'He's loaded; ten thousand would be nothing to him. I could call him; he'd probably have cash from his various business premises. Maybe—'

'Forget it,' said Nick.

She reacted as though he'd spat in her face, flinching away from him in disgust.

'You bastard!' she cried. 'You selfish bastard! Just

because you're jealous of him? This is our daughter's life we're talking about!'

She raised her arms to strike at him, but he reached out and grabbed her wrists. 'Don't be stupid.' he told her. 'It's nothing to do with jealousy. I happen to know that Ajay flew out to Germany straight after the radio interview.'

'You . . . you're lying! You're just saying that because—'

'Helen, no! He got into a taxi for the airport just before I took your call. He had some kind of business meeting in Frankfurt. He won't be back in Manchester until Wednesday morning.' He glared at her. 'For Christ's sake, do you honestly think I'd let feelings like that get in my way? For Molly I'd make a deal with the devil himself!'

'I'm sorry.' Helen shook her head, trying to ward off another bout of tears. 'I don't know what I'm saying. I thought . . .' She broke off as she noticed the expression on Nick's face, a look of sudden inspiration. 'What?' she prompted him.

'The devil himself,' he murmured.

'What's that supposed to mean? Tell me!'

'Maybe that's the answer. The kid suggested it because he thinks we're friends, he doesn't know I hate the man . . . but maybe it's not a bad idea. He's got pots of cash lying around the place. He showed me a case full of big notes just the other day. And he's got plenty of traveller's cheques, if we need more.'

'Bobby Cooper? Do you think he might help?'

'Well, he's got all that money set aside to support his drug habit. Maybe . . . just maybe, I could persuade him to put it to a better use.'

'It's got to be worth a try.'

'Right.' Nick got up from the sofa and grabbed his mobile phone off the coffee table.

'I'll come with you,' said Helen.

'No. We need somebody here in case they phone again. If there are any developments, you can contact me on the mobile. If anybody else calls, get rid of them. Keep the line open. I'll phone you as soon as I have some news about the money.' He found his car keys and hurried towards the front door.

Helen followed him into the hallway. As he opened the door, she took his arm, restraining him for a moment.

'Nick,' she said. 'I'm sorry for doubting you. That business about Ajay. I . . .'

'It doesn't matter,' he said. 'For the record, I *would* have had to swallow an awful lot of pride before I could approach him for help.' He thought for a moment. 'Almost as much as I'm going to have to swallow chasing after Cooper.'

'But you'll do it?' she asked him anxiously.

'Of course. For Molly I'll do it. I made her a promise, didn't I?'

He went out of the door and walked towards the parked BMW. He unlocked the door and climbed in, then drove in the direction of town.

It was a little after eight-thirty and the darkness was gathering. The lights in the surrounding houses were clicking on one by one. He pictured himself punching Bobby C. Cooper earlier that day, and wished he'd been able to anticipate how much he might be needing the man's help before very much longer. Maybe he wouldn't have hit him quite so hard.

Chapter Thirty

Chaz walked through the gathering gloom to the Jamaica Pattie Shop, his hands in his pockets, his baseball cap pulled down over his eyes. His lips and nose were raw and swollen where Finn's last punch had connected, but it was nothing to the fierce, simmering anger that boiled in the cauldron of his chest. Finn had humiliated him in front of the others, kicked him out just for fooling around. Well, Chaz wasn't about to let him get away with that – no way. After spending the last few hours mulling it over, he'd decided on his course of action. He'd show that bigheaded fucker who should really be in control around here.

The lights were on in the café and he paused to peer through the yellowed net curtains. This place was, until recently, Finn's 'office'. Not surprisingly, the new 'management' had adopted it as their preferred hangout too. Chaz recognised a couple of black guys sitting at an alcove table. They were members of Otis Mason's posse. There was a white woman with them, a punky-looking blonde, and Chaz seemed to remember Finn saying something about meeting her earlier.

Chaz moved to the door and extended a hand to push it open – then hesitated as he considered the enormity of what he was about to do. He was going to grass Finn up!

Christ, not so very long ago he'd have died under torture rather than do such a thing. But Finn had just turned around and shat on one of his closest friends; he'd forfeited the right to be treated with any respect. And besides, what Chaz was planning to do was so sexy, even Finn would have had to applaud the audacity of it. Chaz made his mind up. He pushed open the door and stepped into the café.

It was pretty deserted in there. Julius, the elderly proprietor was standing around behind the counter, watching the time tick slowly away on the big, grease-spattered clock on the wall. He glanced at Chaz but his grizzled face showed no sign of recognition.

Chaz felt a momentary sense of betrayal, but told himself that Julius had lasted as long as he had by giving his allegiance to whoever happened to be ruling the roost. It was a good system and one Chaz might learn from.

Besides the three members of Mason's posse, the only others present were an elderly couple sipping their mugs of tea over in the corner. Reggae music thumped from a transistor radio, and by the door a fruit machine warbled and burbled to itself, sequences of coloured lights flickering on its glass front.

Chaz steered himself towards the three people in the alcove. One of the men glanced up at him. He had a long scar running down the left-hand side of his face, and Chaz remembered him from that night at the Nile Club.

The man grinned, said something to his companions. They turned their heads to study Chaz with insolence in their eyes.

'Well, well,' said the scarred man. 'What we got here?'

Chaz stepped up to the table, looking straight into the man's eyes to show that he wasn't afraid.

'I'm lookin' for Otis Mason,' he said.

The woman's red-painted lips curved into a mocking smile.

'Yeah? What you want with him, then?'

'That's *my* business,' said Chaz.

'No,' she corrected him, 'that's *my* business, sunshine. Otis is away at the moment, won't be back till Monday. He's left me in charge. If it's a deal you're lookin' for, you can talk to me.'

'It's a deal,' admitted Chaz. 'But it ain't the kind you're thinkin' of.'

'Carmel, dis kid's one of Finn McManus' bwoys,' said the scarred man. 'I 'member him from that night at the Nile Club. He ran like fuckin' Ben Johnson on steroids.'

'Yeah, tha's right!' said his companion, a stocky, well-muscled man with a shaved head. 'Didn' t'ink he was gonna stop runnin' till he reached the coast!'

Carmel looked more interested. 'One of Finn's boys? You wouldn't know where Mr McManus is now, would you?'

Chaz shrugged. 'I might,' he said.

Carmel studied Chaz for a moment, and he assumed that she was noticing the mashed lips and the bruises around his nose, putting two and two together and probably coming up with the right answer.

'I sense a falling out,' she said. 'McManus do that to you?'

'Could be.'

'Cagey fucker, aren't we?' Carmel indicated a vacant place on the other side of the table. 'Why don't you sit down with us, Mr . . . ?'

'Chaz. My name's Chaz.' He dropped into a seat next to the scarred man, then glowered across the table at Carmel, noting her bleached, spiked hair, the studded leather dog-collar she was wearing. Finn had been right, she looked awful, but only because she didn't make the best of herself. Could be quite a looker under all that thick make-up.

'Chaz, this is Linton.' She indicated the scarred man, then nodded at his companion. 'That's Kojak. As you may know, we're very keen to find Finn McManus. We've been lookin' for him everywhere, as a matter of fact. We heard about some place called the Swamp but nobody seems to know where that might be.'

'I do,' said Chaz smugly. 'In fact, I was there today.'

'That so?' Carmel smiled sweetly. 'Well, I tell you what, Chaz, old mate. Perhaps you'd like to give me one reason why we shouldn't start breakin' your fingers, one by one, till you give us the address?'

Chaz's smile faded. She'd said it dead-pan, but he was pretty sure she meant it.

'Ain't no need for aggro,' he assured her. 'Like I said, I've got a deal for you.'

Carmel frowned. 'Supposin' I told you I don't much care for deals?'

'You'll like this one.'

'Go on then, try me.'

Chaz took a deep breath. He knew this was the point where he had to sell them on the idea. If they didn't go for it, he'd be well and truly in the shit. They'd take him some place nice and quiet and rearrange the way his body fitted together. After a while, he would tell them what they wanted to know. So he had to prove to them now that it was worth their while doing things *his* way.

He leaned forward across the table. 'We kidnapped somebody this morning,' he said.

'What? Fuck off!'

'No, for real. A little girl. It was Finn's idea. He was desperate to make some money. He wants to get out of Manchester, head for the sticks, where nobody can find him.'

'Bit fuckin' extreme isn't it? He *that* scared of us?'

'More the filth than you. You probably heard about that hold-up at the newsagent's in Rusholme? That was us.'

Carmel looked genuinely impressed. 'Fuck, I saw that on the box. Some old geezer was blown away, wasn't he?'

'That's right. All that, and we still come away with peanuts. Then Finn gets this new idea, 'bout how we can make a lot of dosh real quick. At first I figured he was just talkin' big, you know, but he was dead serious. Backed into a corner, see. It was shit or bust. So, like I said, he's holding this kid to ransom. Her parents are loaded. Half the money's coming in tomorrow night. The price is twenty thousand quid.'

Carmel and her two companions exchanged glances. Then she sneered. 'I never heard such bollocks! Kidnapping? He wouldn't have the nerve to pull something like that. Christ, he ain't much more than a kid himself.'

'We did it all right,' Chaz insisted. 'Snatched the kid this mornin' from the Westway Centre. It was me that grabbed her, carried her out of there. Finn just gave the fuckin' orders; he's good at that. And then, when we've got her safe back at the Swamp, the bastard goes and cuts me out of the deal, just 'cos I was dickin' around with one of his shooters.'

Carmel looked at him. 'Never!' she said.

'Straight up. I think he's losin' it, meself. I mean, what kind of sense is that, chuckin' out your right-hand man?'

'No sense at all.'

'So here's what I think would be a real funny joke on him. We wait till he picks up the payment tomorrow night – that's ten thousand quid, don't forget. Then we follow him back to the Swamp and pay him a surprise visit. You get McManus, and I get the money.'

Kojak laughed. 'Oh sure, dread, that's a great deal for us! You really think we're gonna let you take it all?'

'No, 'course not! Remember, you'll still have the kid. You'll be able to collect the second payment for yourselves, even put the price up a bit, if you want. That's up to you.'

Carmel considered the idea for a moment.

'It's an interestin' proposition,' she admitted. 'But kidnapping, I don't know . . . I never did anything like that before.'

'Neither did I. But it's a piece of piss. Once you've got the kid, they're gonna give you anything you want to get 'er back again. And they daren't go to the police, in case you do somethin' to hurt her. Finn put it all down in a letter we gave to the kid's mam, 'bout how, if she went to the filth, she'd be sorry.'

Carmel looked impressed. 'He had it all figured out, didn't he?'

'I suppose,' said Chaz grudgingly. 'But he ain't figured on us jumpin' in there and taking it all away from him.'

'Yeah, but he ain't gonna give up without a fight,' observed Linton.

'What's your problem?' Chaz asked him. 'I'll set it up for you. All you got to do is walk in there, easy as pie, and rip him off.' He laughed. 'Fuck, I've even got a key for the front door!'

Carmel nodded. She seemed to be warming to the idea.

Chaz told himself that he was doing all right: he was going to walk out of there with his fingers intact, at any rate.

'Be a neat surprise for Otis,' Carmel told her companions. 'When he walks back in, I tell him I've got a surprise for him. Then I just hand him the kid's balls on a plate.'

Chaz laughed. 'That'd be funny,' he said. He didn't realise that she was talking literally.

'I dunno,' said Linton. 'Maybe we should wait till Otis gets back. There's only the three of us to do the job.'

Carmel gave him a scornful look.

'Don't be stupid,' she protested. 'It's happening tomorrow night. If we wait for Otis, we'll miss it. Besides, they're only fuckin' kids!' She glanced at Chaz. 'How many of them in there with McManus?'

'Two.' Chaz smirked. 'The youngest is only ten!' He thought for a minute. 'That's a good point. If we make a deal on this, I'd expect you to let Wart and Tommo walk out of there.'

'Them's his mates?' Carmel smiled. 'What kind of names are those? Wart and—?'

'Tommo. Well, they're just kids, like you say. I wouldn't want them wasted, you know?'

'Of course not. We wouldn't burn a couple of kids, would we boys?'

'You burned Gibbo. He was only twelve.'

Carmel scowled. 'Uh, yeah, I heard about that. But Otis told me the kid got in the way. It was a pure accident. Sure, he was lookin' to put McManus down, 'cos he'd not shown respect. That's fair enough, right? But Otis was sorry about what happened; he lost some sleep over that.'

Chaz nodded. 'I got your word, then?'

'Trust me,' said Carmel. 'I'll sort it for you.' She regarded Chaz for a moment from beneath lowered eyelashes. 'And I hope we can trust *you*. I mean, if I was to find out that you're tryin' to lay some kind of double cross on us...'

'Relax. You'll be able to judge for yourself – watch the guy handin' over the money to Finn. I know where and when they're makin' the drop, see. Meet me tomorrow night by the Rasta wall. You know where that is?'

Carmel nodded.

'We'll get there before him, say around eleven-thirty? Then once he's picked up the dosh, we'll trail him back to the Swamp and do the business.'

'Those kids armed?'

'They've got a few shooters, but they won't be expectin' nothin'. If we're quick, they won't even have time to make a move for 'em. Then I want to watch what you do to McManus. I wanna watch him suffer.'

'That's our speciality,' Carmel told him. 'You still haven't told me where this place is.'

'That's right. I figure I have to keep a little bit back. I'll show you where tomorrow night. Eleven-thirty. Be on time.' Chaz got up from the table and strolled towards the exit, more confident now that he knew his pitch had been accepted.

He paused by the door and looked back at them. 'One other thing. When it's over, I wouldn't mind comin' to work for your posse. I prefer to be on the winnin' team, know what I mean?'

Carmel smiled. 'Yeah,' she says. 'I know what you mean. Might be a small problem with your colour, though.'

Chaz frowned. 'You don't seem to have a problem,' he observed. 'And you're white.'

'I am?' Carmel glanced down at her hands in mock horror. 'Fuck, why didn't one of you guys *tell* me?'

Linton and Kojak threw back their heads and laughed. Carmel laughed too.

Then she turned back to face Chaz. 'OK, kid,' she said. 'Leave it with me. We'll talk about it, later.'

Chaz grinned through broken lips. He went out of the door into the darkness.

Carmel's smile vanished.

'Cheeky little fucker,' she muttered. She could hardly believe the balls of the kid, breezing in here with his big ideas and his arse hanging out of his trousers. She figured he was on the level, though. She had a natural aptitude for sniffing out lies, and that kid's story was so OTT, it *had* to be for real. She was almost glad that Otis was in Warrington, arranging for Cooper's big cocaine consignment. This would be her chance to prove that she could handle unexpected opportunities in his absence.

'Think the kid's on the level?' asked Linton.

'Yeah, I'd say so. But we'll see. We'll tool up properly before we go, take the automatic weapons, meet him as arranged, but keep our eyes open for a double cross. If we see this drop made, we'll know it's gospel, won't we? Then we'll go on into the place and waste 'em all.'

'All of them? I thought you said . . .'

'Fuck that. I want them *all* dead, including that smarmy little twat who just waltzed out of here. Everyone except for McManus. I've got somethin' special lined up for him, and I want him to live long enough to enjoy it.'

Linton grinned. 'You gonna necktie him?'

'I'm a big believer in tradition. Just 'cos Otis ain't here, it don't mean we should get lazy.'

'What about the little girl?'

Carmel shrugged. 'Kidnapping ain't our scene. I'll be happy with the ten thousand – the rest is too complicated. No, we'll burn her, too.'

Kojak frowned. 'I don't much like the idea of wastin' a little kid.'

Carmel grimaced. 'Don't be sentimental. I'll bet she's not so young that she can't remember your face and pick you out of a line-up. We can't afford to leave any witnesses – don't matter how old they are.' She looked at the two men in turn, but their expressions remained doubtful. 'Oh, fuck it, *I'll* do it if it bothers you.'

Linton was impressed by her businesslike attitude.

'Carmel,' he said, 'you are one real star, you know what I'm sayin'?'

She laughed. 'I'm getting there,' she admitted, feeling very pleased with herself now. 'Oh yes, I am most definitely on my way!'

Chapter Thirty-One

Nick parked the BMW outside the G-Mex Exhibition Centre and walked around the corner to the front entrance of the Midland Hotel. He passed through the revolving door and headed straight across the lobby to the lifts, where he rode up to the sixth floor. At this stage, he still wasn't sure how he would approach Cooper. He only knew that he couldn't leave the hotel without the money.

Nick stepped out of the lift and started along the corridor towards Cooper's suite, only to be intercepted there by the hulking shape of Andy, who was doing his usual diligent job of guarding the door.

'Mr Saunders,' he said. 'Hey, man, we wasn't expectin' you. I'm real sorry, but Bobby's kind've busy just now.'

'That's tough,' said Nick. 'Something important came up.'

'That may be so, but I've got instructions—'

'Stuff your instructions!' Nick tried to push past Andy but was brought up sharp by a huge hand on his shoulder.

'Now, look, Mr Saunders, I don't wanna have to get rough with you, but if you make me, I—'

'Get your hands off me!' protested Nick. 'Gabe Rothman said I was to have access to Bobby at all times.'

'I 'preciate that, but—'

Nick wasn't going to be dissuaded. He hooked one leg behind the big man's ankles and gave him a fierce shove in the chest. Caught totally unaware, Andy fell backwards and hit the carpet with a crash that shook the floor. Without waiting for further reaction, Nick turned and made a run for Cooper's door.

'Fuck it, come back here!' roared Andy indignantly, clambering to his feet.

Ignoring him, Nick threw open the door and went in, aware of Andy now thundering after him in hot pursuit. As Nick hurried into the room, he saw Amos get up off the sofa, a look of surprise on his face. He'd been reading a *Spiderman* comic, and was clearly unprepared for this unexpected visitation.

Nick gazed frantically around the room. Cooper didn't seem to be in evidence, but Nick noticed that the door to his bedroom was slightly ajar, so he headed in that direction.

'Hey, hold up homeboy!' yelled Amos. 'You can't go in there!' He made a lunge for Nick, just as Andy came crashing into the room. Nick ducked under Amos' outstretched arms and did a body-swerve that Maradona would have been proud of.

Andy went barrelling into Amos, with unstoppable momentum. The two bodyguards collided and went sprawling into a stainless-steel trolley loaded with food and drink. The din of breaking glass and crockery mingled with the outraged bellows of Amos as his partner's thirty-stone frame came crashing down on him.

Nick threw a frantic glance at the desolation he had caused, and told himself it was too late to worry about that now. He pushed open the bedroom door and stepped into darkness.

'Bobby?' he inquired, peering into the gloom. 'Bobby, I

need to talk to you.' He reached out a hand and snapped on the lights.

'Oh,' he said.

Cooper's face wore an expression of outrage, as he glared back at Nick over his bare shoulder. Nick had clearly caught him at an inconvenient moment. He was crouched on all fours on the bed, his ass sticking up in the air, his muscular arms supporting his naked body above the prone figure of the skinny blonde who lay beneath him.

She, too, was staring at Nick with an expression composed of equal parts surprise, embarrassment and sudden recognition. It was Maria Sweeny, clearly making good use of her boyfriend's business trip to Germany, and she seemed far from happy to be discovered there with a man she had previously claimed to hate.

Nick just stood staring at them, his mouth hanging open like a stranded fish.

Then Amos and Andy came scrambling through the doorway, clearly with the intention of dragging him back out by his hair if necessary. But they, too, froze in their tracks, aghast at their boss's humiliation.

There was a long, horrible silence which seemed to Nick to last forever. Then Cooper spoke with, under the circumstances, amazing self-control.

'I wonder if you guys would oblige me by steppin' back outside for a moment? Only, I ain't used to doin' this kinda shit for an audience, you know what I'm sayin'?'

'I'm sorry,' muttered Nick. 'I didn't realise . . .'

'Yeah, Nick. If you could just . . .'

'. . . only this is really important. I need to talk to you.'

'. . . wait outside for a minute.'

'It's a matter of life and—'

'Look, Nick. Just get the fuck out, OK?'

Amos and Andy scuttled obediently back towards the lounge, and Nick followed them, pulling the door closed behind him. Once they were all safely out of the way, the recriminations started.

'You know somethin'?' Andy glared at Nick. 'You are gettin' to be one big pain in the ass, my friend. Why didn' you listen to me, back there?'

'Jesus, I didn't know he was doing *that*, did I?'

'Hell, that's what I was tryin' to tell you! Now Bobby is gonna be real pissed with us, you know?'

Amos was glumly surveying the remains of the food and drink.

'Shit, just look at this mess! Bobby ordered it up special, too.' He stooped and tried to extricate a long-stemmed red rose from the remains of a squashed Black Forest gateau.

Nick could now see that what had been intended as a romantic post-coital champagne dinner was now reduced to a bilious-looking mess on the carpet. To add to his discomfort, he could hear Maria Sweeny's shrill tones issuing from the bedroom. She didn't sound best pleased.

'Oh shit,' said Andy. 'This is just perfect, man. He's liable to come out here and sack our asses off've this job.'

'I'm sorry,' Nick told him. 'Look, I'll take full responsibility.'

'Too fuckin' right, you will,' growled Amos.

The bedroom door opened and Cooper stepped out, dressed in his red silk kimono. He flung a remark over his shoulder.

'Quit bellyachin', woman. It ain't my fault! Now jes' sit tight while I sort this mess out.'

He slammed the door and stood glowering at the room's three other occupants. He then crossed his arms over his chest and took in a deep breath.

'Nick,' he said icily. 'This is an unexpected pleasure.'

Nick held out his hands in a gesture of apology. 'Bobby, I don't know what to say. I—'

Cooper had lifted a hand to silence him.

'Nick, I want you to 'magine yourself in my position. You're about to hump the ass off 've some gal. Not just any gal, no sir. This is the girlfriend of the guy who's currently employin' you, the guy who just paid a whole heap of dough to bring you into the country in the first place. So you want to keep things, you know, kind've low-key? Now, what do you think is the *last* thing you'd want to happen? Huh?'

'Well, I . . .'

'I'll tell you what. It would be three fuckin' crazy men runnin' into your bedroom like the Marx Brothers on acid, and switchin' on all the motherfuckin' lights, that's what! Now, I don't know, maybe I'm bein' kind've old-fashioned here, but there was a time when people used to wait till you was *available* to talk to 'em, you know what I'm sayin'?'

'Boss,' said Andy. 'It wasn't our fault. This sum'bitch just ran by me like—'

'Don't you say nothin'!' snapped Cooper indignantly. 'Christ, you're just the guy who's paid a fortune to protect my ass.' He pointed a finger at Amos. 'Same goes for you, cheesedick. If'n you cain't keep somebody like *him* out, what chance do I have when some crackhead with an Uzi steps outa the elevator? Huh?'

'Aww, that ain't fair, boss! We—'

'Just get back out into the hall, the pair of you. I'll deal with you later. Go on, move yo' asses!' Amos and Andy glumly did as they were told. 'And be careful out there!' Cooper shouted after them. 'Could be an eighty-year-old grandma comes lookin' for me and beats the shit out of the both of ya!'

The door closed behind them and Cooper began to pace agitatedly around the room. He didn't get very far before his bare feet encountered the demolished gateau, and he stood there staring down in shocked disbelief.

'Aww, shit, man, what is this?' he muttered.

'You'd better be careful,' Nick warned him. 'I think there's broken glass in that lot.'

Cooper rolled his eyes towards the ceiling. Then he moved carefully across to the sofa, leaving a trail of chocolaty footprints on the pile carpet. There he sat down with as much dignity as he could muster, and fixed Nick with a withering look.

'You ever wonder what you did to deserve somethin' bad?' he muttered. 'See, I'm thinkin' that when I took on this job, the las' thing I expected was somebody like *you* on my team. I mean, I don't know where you get off bein' the way you are, man.'

'Bobby, look, I need to talk—'

'Shut the fuck up a minute, will ya? I ain't finished.' Cooper ran his fingers through his close-cropped hair, and Nick realised that he was trying to keep his temper under control. 'Since I been here, you've been like the god-damned monkey on my back, you know that? You've insulted me, ordered me around, countermanded my instructions, punched me in the motherfuckin' guts ... Hell, I was beginnin' to think that you'd gone about as far as you could go. But no, I was underestimatin' you, Nick-O-Las. Now you've decided to *humiliate* me – come bustin' in on my most private moments. Jeez, why don't I just go take a shit now, and you can bust in on that, too. Then you'll have the full score!'

'Look, Bobby, I've said I'm sorry. You've every right to be angry with me—'

'Angry? I ain't fuckin' angry, I'm *freaked*!'

'OK, but if you'll just let me explain *why* I came busting in, I think you'll understand.'

Cooper raised his eyebrows, crossed his powerful arms, and sat back in the sofa. 'This I gotta hear,' he said.

'I need to borrow some money from you.'

Cooper gave a snort of laughter, as though he didn't believe what he was hearing. He searched Nick's face for some sign that he was kidding, but clearly didn't find what he was looking for.

'How much?' he asked incredulously.

'Ten thousand pounds. In cash.'

Cooper laughed again, with more conviction this time.

'Now I *know* you's puttin' me on,' he said. 'You think I'd lend you money after everythin' you've said to me? You think I'd lend you a goddamned *dime*?'

'You've got to,' Nick told him. 'The money's not for me; it's for my daughter.'

'Yeah? Don't tell me. She needs some kind've life-savin' operation. I think I saw this movie.'

'Bobby, she's been kidnapped. If I don't have half the ransom money by midnight tomorrow, she could die.'

For a moment Cooper allowed this information to sink in. He looked genuinely surprised.

'Excuse me?' he said. 'Did I fall asleep and wake up in the fuckin' *Twilight Zone*? Your daughter? Shit, man, I didn't even know you had a daughter.'

'Well, I do. She's four years old, and right now she must be very scared. She was abducted today while my wife was out shopping. She was taken by the same kids who did this.' He indicated the bruise on his cheek. 'I spoke to them on the phone less than an hour ago. They want ten thousand in cash by midnight tomorrow, and they don't seem to appreciate how difficult it is to get that kind of money at such short notice. You're the only person I can think of who might be able to help me.'

'Ten grand,' muttered Cooper. 'That's a lot of dough.'

'Not to you. You've probably made that much for a couple of hours' work.'

'Yeah, well, maybe I have. Don't mean I'm gonna hand it over to every asshole who wanders in off the street with some half-assed story.'

Nick stared at him. 'You don't believe me?'

'I ain't decided.'

'I swear to you, it's the truth. Come on, you surely know enough about me to appreciate I wouldn't make that up?'

'Well, I don't know that I *do*, Nick. I know you like to throw your weight around . . .' Cooper rubbed his stomach, as if it had just given him a twinge. 'I know you like to tell me how I should live my life. But I don't know much about yours. Maybe you got business debts need payin' off. Maybe you feel like takin' a vacation. Maybe you just wanna try and rip me off for the hell of it.'

'Bobby, I swear to God I'm on the level.' Nick pulled the mobile phone from his pocket. 'Here, if you want, you can phone my wife and talk to her about it. She'll confirm everything.'

Cooper waved away the phone. 'All right, let's suppose I do believe you. What do the cops have to say about it?'

'I haven't told them. I daren't. The kids said . . . they said they'd cut Molly with a knife if I went near the police . . .' Nick could feel his eyes filling with tears, and he struggled to control his emotions. 'Look, Bobby,' he said. 'I know we haven't always seen eye to eye—'

'Hah! You're a master of understatement, Nick-O-Las, you know that?'

Nick noted the despised version of his name, but figured this wasn't the time to object to it.

'I need your help, Bobby, and I'm prepared to do just about anything to get it. I'll sign an IOU, a series of blank cheques – anything you like. If you make me, I'll go even further . . .'

Cooper's eyes narrowed suspiciously.

'What's that supposed to mean?' he demanded.

'Well, I couldn't help noticing a familiar face there in the bedroom. That would cause problems, wouldn't it – if Ajay found out how you and Maria spent this afternoon?'

Cooper laughed. 'Hey, man, don't try and hit me with that crap. I couldn't give a shit what you say to ol' Sanji-Panjie. I'm disappointed in you, Nicky baby. Thought you had more class than that.'

'I'm desperate, Bobby. I'll do anything to save my daughter.'

Cooper thought for a moment, stroking his chin between thumb and forefinger. 'Anythin', huh? You really mean that?'

'Yes, of course.'

'Well, lemme see now. Supposin' I was to say you had to get down on your knees and lick this cake 'n' shit off 've my feet. How would that be?'

Nick scowled. 'You'd make me do that?'

'That ain't the question, Nicky. I asked if you'd be prepared to swallow your pride and *do* it.'

'I guess so. For Molly, yes, I would.'

'How about in front of a couple 've witnesses?'

'I—'

'Think about it real careful now!'

Nick thought about it. It would be humiliating, yes – but probably no worse than the humiliation Cooper himself had just suffered.

'Yes. Yes, I'd do anything for her.'

Cooper looked at Nick. 'Shit, you know, I believe you would. The kid means a lot to you, huh?'

'Of course she does. It'd be the same for any parent.'

'OK.' Cooper tilted back his head and shouted. 'Amos, Andy, get yo' asses in here, now!'

Oh shit, thought Nick. *The bastard's going to make me go through with it!*

The door opened and the two bodyguards shuffled into the room. Cooper was grinning malevolently at Nick.

'Boys,' he said. 'I want you to witness somethin' here.'

Nick steeled himself and stepped closer to Cooper's outstretched feet, assuring himself that this didn't *mean* anything: he could detach himself from the deed, observe it as though it was happening to somebody else – absolutely nothing to do with him. Molly was depending on him. He took a deep breath and dropped to his knees.

Amos and Andy stared at him. Then Cooper laughed. 'Hey, don't sweat it, Nick. I ain't gonna make you do that shit! Andy, go fetch the case that's got the stash money in it. I just want you boys to witness that I'm loanin' Nick here ten thousand pounds.'

Andy stared at his employer. 'Say what?' he gasped. 'Boss, you sure about this?'

'Sure I'm sure! What, you questioning my judgement now? Go get that case from Lionel's room. Take out everythin' except ten thousand, then bring it back to me.'

Amos and Andy hurried off to carry out his orders. Nick got back to his feet with a sigh of relief.

'Jesus,' he said. 'Thanks. I really believed—'

'Oh, don't think it didn't cross my mind neither. But you're a friend, Nick, and you don't do somethin' like that to a friend, right?'

'A friend?' Nick couldn't keep the note of surprise out of his voice. 'I'm sorry, but I wouldn't have dreamed you'd regard me as anything other than a pain in the arse.'

Cooper shook his head. He looked suddenly serious. 'Let me tell you somethin', Nick. I respect you, man, I really do. You know why? Because apart from Gabe Rothman, you're about the only other motherfucker that's ever had the balls to stand up to me.'

'Well, Bobby, I only—'

'I can respect that, you know? See, it's an occupational hazard with me. Ever since I got to be somebody, most everyone I meet has got their heads so far up my ass, I cain't make out what they're saying. "Yes, Bobby. No, Bobby. Whatever you say, Bobby!" Means I can act like a spoiled brat and ain't nobody gonna tell me no different.'

'I can see it could get annoying,' admitted Nick.

'Annoying? Man it drives me nuts! "Hey, Bobby, you wanna drive my car? That's OK. Hey, Bobby, you wanna fuck my wife. Real neat!" You know what I mean? I get that kind of shit day in, day out. Gabe'll cross me, up to a point, that's why he's still my manager. But you? You were prepared to take it one step further. Up at the radio station? Fuck, man, respect to that! I was lucky to walk out of there in one piece.'

Nick smiled. He moved over to the sofa and sat down beside Cooper.

'I appreciate this,' he said. 'Thanks. And whatever happens, I'm going to pay you back.'

'Aww, don't sweat it. It's only money. I found out a long

time ago, some things are worth more than that. I know it sounds dumb, but it's true. Listen, I was gonna ask, you want to take Amos 'n' Andy along with you on this gig? They ain't much for brains but they can be handy in a fight.'

Nick shook his head. 'I have to go alone,' he said. 'They're going to be watching me.' He thought for a moment. 'You realise this will be just half of the fee? I may have to come back for another ten thousand in two days' time.'

Cooper nodded. 'Just be sure and knock first.'

Nick grimaced. 'I'm really sorry. I had no idea . . .'

'Yeah, well, you didn't interrupt much. Shit, I wasn't enjoyin' it anyway.'

'Then why . . . ?'

Cooper grinned. 'Professional pride, I guess. Chick came sniffin' around this afternoon. It was obvious what she wanted.'

'But I thought she detested you.'

'Oh, she probably does. Only I gave her the magic words.'

'Magic words?'

'Yeah, goes like this: "I can get you into movies." Works every time.' He spread his hands in a 'so what' gesture and they both grinned.

Amos and Andy came back in, the latter carrying a black attaché case. He handed it to Nick with a resentful look.

'Could buy a lot of goodies with that much,' he observed, to nobody in particular.

'You dissin' me?' snapped Cooper. 'Don't forget, I ain't forgiven you two for lettin' this maniac loose on me.' He indicated the mess on the floor. 'Now, go get room service to clean this mess. And order some replacement dinner, I'm *hungry!*'

Amos and Andy trudged out of the room, throwing resentful glances at Nick.

Cooper studied him for a moment. 'Midnight tomorrow, huh? Anythin' else you need, homeboy? Like maybe a piece.'

'A piece of what?'

'No, man, I mean a *piece*. A gun. Figure I could get hold of one for you.'

Nick shook his head. 'No thanks. I wouldn't have the first idea how to use it.'

'So you're goin' in there unarmed?'

'I guess I am.'

'Well, I wish you luck, man. You let me know how it turns out, and if you need any more help, gimme a call.' Cooper got to his feet. 'I guess I'd better get back to Miss What's-her-name.'

'Sweeny,' Nick prompted him. 'Maria Sweeny.'

'Yeah. Well, it's like, you know, a guy's got his reputation to think about. Don't want the gal tellin' everyone that I couldn't cut it in the sack. I'll see you 'round, Nick.' He walked back to the bedroom, being careful to avoid the debris from the trolley. He closed the bedroom door carefully behind him.

Nick lifted the attaché case to his lap and unlatched it. Studying the bundles of money lying there, he told himself that it didn't seem so very much when all neatly laid out like this. With a sigh, he took the mobile phone from his pocket and called Helen.

The call was answered immediately: she must have been waiting by the phone.

'Helen, I've got the cash.'

'Oh, thank God!' He could hear her sobs of relief, but refrained from warning her that it was a little too early to

351

relax. Instead he assured her that everything would be OK now, and that he was coming straight home. Hanging up, he walked over to Cooper's drinks cabinet and helped himself to a large shot of brandy. He figured that, under the circumstances, Cooper would excuse him for not asking first.

As he sipped, he could hear the creaking of bedsprings from Cooper's room – starting slowly at first, and then picking up speed and volume. After a little while, he heard Maria Sweeny's voice, supplying an urgent accompaniment. 'Yes, yes, *yes*!' she was shrilling.

Nick shook his head, feeling uncomfortable at being here as that was going on in the next room. He drained the brandy in one final swallow, and set down the empty glass.

Then he picked up the attaché case and left the room, closing the door gently behind him.

Chapter Thirty-Two

In the dim glow of the battery-powered camping light, Finn can see the time on his digital watch. It's just gone three o'clock in the morning. He sits on the bare floor of the Swamp, with his back against the crumbling plaster of the wall, trying to talk himself out of falling asleep, and not doing a very good job of it.

He's not helped much by the sounds of Wart and Tommo snoring in their respective sleeping bags on the other side of the room. It's Finn's turn to watch Molly, to make sure she doesn't try and steal off into the night. It was his idea for them to take turns in watching her – one hour on, two hours off – because he doesn't want to put her through the discomfort of being tied up. But this is only his second spell on duty; he's been sitting here no more than fifteen minutes and he can already feel sleep creeping up on him like some stealthy enemy, ready to snatch him headlong into the world of dreams.

It wouldn't be so bad if the little girl would go to sleep too, but so far she's managed to resist that. She lies on the mattress cuddling the teddy bear, staring up wide-eyed at the ceiling. Through the day she's had bouts of crying and screaming, huddling into the corner of the room and wailing pitifully. But she seems to have finished with that now, and instead there's just that glum, mournful stare, enough to give you the creeps. She seems to be waiting for something. Maybe she thinks her old man is going to bust through the door at any moment like some cop-movie hero. She's told Finn earlier that her Dad has promised to come and get her, and Finn doesn't have the heart to tell her that – if all goes according to plan – there won't be so much as a sniff of her Dad for the next twenty-four hours.

Finn doesn't think the man would be stupid enough to try and pull some kind of stunt, but he has to remind himself that he doesn't know anything about Nick Saunders other than what can be gleaned from the contents of his wallet.

Finn sighs, takes out his cigarettes and lights one up. He's only got a few left, but smoking is the one thing guaranteed to keep sleep at bay. He's aware, as the Zippo flares, that Molly's head has swivelled sideways, to turn that accusing look directly upon him. He decides to try and ignore her, but she has other ideas.

'You shouldn' smoke,' she says after a lengthy pause.

He glances at her irritably.

'What?' he snaps.

'You shouldn' smoke. It's bad for you. My Daddy an' my Mummy gave up 'cos it was bad.'

'Well, bully for them. I bet they feel really pleased with 'emselves.' Finn inhales on his cigarette and blows out a cloud of smoke.

'It smells horrible,' persists Molly. 'An' it gives you lung cancer.'

'That's my problem. Can't you shut up and get some sleep?'

She shakes her head. 'Can't,' she says.

'Sure you can, if you try. Just close your eyes and take deep breaths. You must be tired by now.'

'I'm tired but . . .' She sighs, shakes her head. 'It isn't like home here.'

'No, but you could make it more like home, couldn't you? Supposin' you put your pyjamas on? You might feel more comfortable.' He makes a move to take the teddy bear from her, but she shrugs away from him, clutching it to her with renewed force.

'Don't wanna!' she protested. 'He's *my* teddy. You *gave* him to me.'

'Yes, but I only want to—'

'No, no, no, no, no!'

'All right, all right, it was just an idea.' He goes back to his cigarette, taking deep tokes on it, letting the nicotine jolt through his system. He keeps thinking about his outburst of temper earlier in the day, wishing that he hadn't kicked Chaz out like that, so close to them bringing off the ransom demand and everything. Maybe he should send Wart or Tommo to look for Chaz tomorrow, tell him he's forgiven, and he can come back and get his fair share of the money if he wants to . . . After all, he *has* earned it . . .

'I wanna do a wee,' Molly tells him.

'*Again?* This must be the fifth time tonight!'

'I can't help it. I wanna go!'

'OK, OK.' Finn pinches the end of his cigarette, to save it for later. Then he collects the camping light and leads the way out of the room into the hall. They climb the creaky wooden stairs to the top floor, where there's a decrepit bathroom and toilet. The bath has been smashed open at some point in time, but the toilet bowl, at least, is intact, even if it no longer flushes.

He hands Molly the lamp and she goes into the bathroom, struggling with the fastenings on her dungarees. Finn settles down in the darkness to wait for her.

'It smells horrible in here,' he hears her complain.

'Just get on with it,' he says. He fumbles in his pockets for the cigarette stub and the Zippo, and resumes his smoke. Now he finds himself thinking about Gibbo: poor, stupid Gibbo who'd have done just about anything for Finn, and who proved it in the most drastic and pointless way. Finn wonders if he knows anything about what's happening to the posse now – if he's up there somewhere, sitting on a cloud and looking down at this mess, wishing he was still a part of it.

Finn doubts that. He doesn't believe there's anything after death. That's why it's so important to live life to the full. That's why, if he brings this deal off successfully, he's going to take his share of the money and leave the Merton Estate far behind him.

'You don't ever look back,' he whispers to the darkness.

He hears Molly trying to pull the chain.

'I've already told you,' he says, 'the bloody thing doesn't work! Leave it, will you.'

There's a resentful silence. Then, after a few moments, she comes out of the bathroom, carrying the lamp in front of her.

'You're a *grump*,' she informs him, primly.

'A what?'

'A grumpy grump,' she elaborates. 'My Mummy says you should always pull the chain after the toilet.'

'Is that right? In our house we always used to lick the bowl.' He chuckles at the old joke, but Molly just looks puzzled. He flicks his cigarette stub away, gets to his feet and takes the lamp from her. Then he pushes her ahead of him back towards the stairs.

'Now, try and make that the last one tonight, will you?' he pleads. 'It ain't natural wanting to pee so much.'

They go down the stairs and back into the lounge where, in their sleep, Wart and Tommo are still snorting and grunting like wild animals. As he passes, Finn prods Tommo with his boot, and the boy's snoring stops for a few moments, before resuming as loud as ever.

Molly gets back on to the mattress and takes hold of the teddy bear. Finn settles down beside her and places an old parka over her to keep her warm.

'How about going to sleep now?' he suggests hopefully.

She shakes her head. 'Can't,' she says.

'What do you mean, *can't*? You haven't even tried yet! Just pretend you're at home and—'

'It's not like at home,' she says. 'It's dirty and smelly here.'

'Yeah, I know that. But if you close your eyes, you won't see it, will you?'

'I'll still *smell* it.'

'Yeah, but . . . look, what do you do at home when you can't get to sleep?'

'My Daddy tells me a story.'

He looks at her warily. 'Uh . . . well, what else do you do?'

'Nothin'. That's it. My Daddy finds a good story an' he tells it to me, an' I go to sleep.' She gives him a hopeful glance. 'Do you know any stories?' she asks.

'Me? Christ, no!'

'You must do. Everybody knows one story, don't they? Like, what your Daddy told you when you was little.'

'My old man? Only thing he ever read was the betting forecast. Me mam, though, there was this one story she used to tell me: *The Pied Piper*. You know that one?'

Molly shakes her head. 'Tell me,' she says.

'Oh, I don't really remember all of it,' he warns her.

'Tell me the bits you 'member, an' make up the other bits.'

Finn frowns, shrugs. 'OK, then.' He thinks for a minute, then settles himself down. 'Er ... well, it all starts in this foreign country somewhere.' He thinks about the few foreign locations he has visited himself, and selects one. 'In Torremolinos – that's in Spain, right? There's this town and they've got this problem with ...'

'What's it called?' asks Molly. 'This town?'

'Oh, er ... it's called, er ... Rat Town.'

'Rat Town? Why's it called that?'

'I'll tell you if you just shut up a minute!' Finn scowls. 'It's called Rat Town 'cos they got this real problem with rats runnin' everywhere. They keep gettin' into the babies' prams an' biting them or crappin' in people's food – stuff like that.'

'Ooh, horrible. You don't think there are any rats in here, do you?'

'Course not. Anyway, the people are gettin' real pissed off with it, as you can imagine. They keep complaining to the guys what runs the place. For some reason, I think they're called burghers ...'

'What, because they only eat hamburgers?'

'Well, more cheese-burgers, really. 'Cos, see, it's a big town for cheese, they have these big factories there an' the place always smells of Cheddar. That's what brought the rats there in the first place. Well, these cheese-burghers say, we gotta do somethin' about all these bleedin' rats, see? So they put an advert in the *Rat Town Evenin' News* askin' for somebody to come help 'em get rid of them. And this guy turns up, right, and he says, "I'm the Pied Piper, and I'll sort it for you."'

'Why's he called the *Pied* Piper?'

'Er ... well, 'cos he only eats pies. Steak and kidney, cheese and onion, meat and potato. Yeah, he tells 'em if they give him a lot of money—'

'How much?'

'Er ... twenty thousand quid. If they give him that much, he says, he'll get rid of the rats. So the cheese-burghers say, "Yeah, all right, we'll 'ave some of that." And they give him like a contract to do the job, you know? So then this Pied Piper bloke, he gets out this like synthesiser keyboard and starts playing a rap rhythm ...'

'Don't you mean a *rat* rhythm?'

'Well, yeah, it's like a rat rap, see, and all these rats come dancing out on to the street – you know like in the Bobby C. Cooper *Streetlife* video, where all those cartoon cats and dogs are givin' it some. These rats just think this music is the best they've ever heard. They're raving to the beat, you know, 'cos he's probably got a drum machine going as well and they all kind of dance along behind him and he leads 'em up into the hills and he's got, like, a bunch of friends waiting up there with automatic weapons and they start shooting all these rats and they're all, like, falling down and screamin' and some of 'em try to make a run for it but the Pied Piper, he whips out this, like, flame-thrower and he says "No Quarter", and he just wastes the whole bunch of 'em, an' they're all screamin' and running about on fire, and then they're all dead.'

'I don't think I like this story much,' says Molly, in a small, tired voice.

'Oh, well, it gets better now, 'cos the Pied Piper goes back to the cheese-burghers and he asks for his dosh, and they say, "Oh, we was only kiddin' about givin' you all that money. Here's a fiver. Go and get yourself some break-fast." Well, he's fuckin' furious, ain't he? So he whips out his synth again and starts givin' it some socks on another tune, and what do you think happens?'

Molly's reply is barely more than a murmur.

'All the kids come out dressed in their best gear and start ravin', and the Pied Piper, he leads 'em all up into the hills, where he's got this big cave, and it's all fitted out like a rave club, right. There's, like, really good lighting effects and a load of top DJs and they start, like, havin' this party, everyone dancin' up a storm. And the Pied Piper sends a ransom letter down to the cheese-burghers, sayin' that they gotta bring him the twenty thousand quid if they want to see their kids alive again. And this is the funny thing, 'cos I can never remember if the cheese-burghers pay up and get their kids back, or whether the Pied Piper just turns on his flame-thrower and incinerates the whole bunch of 'em . . .'

Finn glances down at Molly and sees that she has fallen asleep, the teddy bear clutched tight against her, her breathing slow and rhythmic. Finn smiles, pleasantly surprised that his first attempt at a bedtime story has gone so well. He's been forced to invent quite a lot of details, but he reckons that those were the best bits.

'I think maybe they paid the ransom,' he says quietly. 'I hope so, anyway.'

It occurs to him, not for the first time, that if things go wrong, he may have to be prepared to kill the little girl. He hopes it doesn't come to that. Despite all her moaning, there's something about her that he really likes. He glances at his watch, expecting to see that an hour has slipped by; but, no, it's barely fifteen minutes since he last looked.

He sighs, reaches for his cigarettes. Three-seventeen a.m., Sunday, and daybreak seems such a long way off. He remembers now the drawing of the Pied Piper in the old children's book his mother used to read from. Closing his eyes, he conjures the image back into his head, and now he can see that the guy wore this weird black-and-white suit and was playing what looked like a set of bagpipes. Of course, that was why he was called a piper! How come he'd forgotten that?

He shrugs, lights his cigarette, tells himself it doesn't matter. The story did what it was supposed to do and, anyway, Finn still prefers to picture him with a synthesiser.

Chapter Thirty-Three

On Sunday morning, the weather changed. Nick woke to the sight of dark grey clouds massing on the western horizon, and by the time he was washed and dressed it had begun to rain, gently at first but steadily worsening as the day unfolded.

Helen was already up, preparing a breakfast that neither of them would eat. They sat disconsolately at the dining table, sipping coffee, each lost in their individual thoughts. Nick had to try and persuade himself not to keep looking at his watch. He wondered if he was going to get through to midnight without losing his mind.

To add to his worries, he thought that Helen was looking ill. Neither of them had slept last night, and her eyes were strained and red. Every so often a look of discomfort flashed across her face, and she had to get up from where she was sitting and move about the room. At one point he went over to her and started massaging her shoulders, something she normally loved. But this time she shrugged irritably away from him, so he decided it best to give her some space.

He went off to his study to try and occupy his mind with some routine paperwork that needed taking care of; but, gazing at the sheets of printed figures on *Futures* stationery, he felt more than ever that any interest he had left for his company had been extinguished in the face of this crisis. Worse still, he doubted if he'd ever be able to rekindle it again. Putting the papers aside, he picked up a novel he'd been reading. He tried to resume where he'd left off but found himself reading the same paragraph over and over, unable to extract one iota of meaning from it.

The shrilling of the doorbell made him almost jump out of his skin, but at least this might provide a diversion from the monotony of waiting. As Nick walked out into the hallway, Helen came to the door of the kitchen.

'It's Terry,' she warned him. 'I recognised the car. Do you think we should try and get rid of him?'

He shook his head. 'That will just make him suspicious. I'll talk to him.'

'I'll make some coffee,' she said, and turned back into the kitchen. Nick continued down the hall and opened the door.

Terry stood there on the porch step, grim-faced and wearing a gaberdine trenchcoat, its collar turned up against the rain. He looked at Nick inquiringly.

'I think we need to talk,' he said.

'OK. You'd better come through to the study.' Nick gestured him into the house, but Terry paused to wipe his feet on the doormat. Then he stepped in and pulled the door shut behind him, glancing round expectantly.

'Where's Helen?' he asked.

'She's in the kitchen, brewing up.'

'And Molly?'

'She's er . . . at a friend's house. Children's party.'

Terry frowned, and Nick thought that he didn't look too convinced – but he followed Nick into the study. Nick indicated an armchair but Terry shook his head, clearly preferring to stay on his feet. He swung around and fixed his partner with a withering look.

'I think some explanation is in order, don't you?' he said. 'I still haven't the foggiest idea what happened to you yesterday.'

'Well, I came home,' Nick told him.

'I've managed to work that much out. The question is *why*?'

Nick indicated the bruise on his cheek.

'Came over all dizzy, didn't I? Realised that I was pushing it – coming back to work too soon. I came straight home and went to bed, OK?'

'No, it's not OK! You didn't think to phone the office and let us know what was happening? Christ, Nick, you've been in this business long enough to—'

'Maybe too long,' interrupted Nick.

Terry looked exasperated. 'What's that supposed to mean?'

'It means exactly what it says. I'm tired of PR, Terry. I'm tired of the whole sorry circus. Maybe it's time I moved on.'

There. He'd said it. He hadn't planned to announce this right now, but the opportunity had arisen and he'd taken it. What's more, it felt pretty good.

Terry stared at him. 'Move on? Have you gone barmy or something? *Futures* is on the point of really taking off. It's going to be a much easier ride from here on in. I can't *believe* you'd turn your back on it!'

'Believe it,' Nick told him. 'Oh, it isn't such a surprise, surely? You must have sensed I was getting disillusioned with it all. And you'll easily find a new partner, Terry – maybe somebody younger, with a bit more drive.'

Terry started to pace. There was a suspicious look on his face now, as though he sensed some ulterior motive.

'What's going on, Nick? That business last night, asking me to get off the phone . . . Who were you expecting a call from?'

'Nobody you'd know.'

'You've been head-hunted, haven't you? Somebody's made you a better offer.'

'Terry, don't be ridiculous! It's nothing like that.'

'Sure it is. Who *is* it? Brian Glasswell at Everdean and Monroe? I heard they were looking for a new senior partner . . .'

'Brian *who*?'

'Oh, don't come over all coy with me, Nick. It has to be something like that. Nobody in their right mind would pass up a position like yours unless they'd had a sniff of something better.'

'For God's sake, Terry, not everything is business, you know. It could be that I just want out of the rat-race.'

Terry didn't seem to have an answer to that. He stood staring at Nick in sheer disbelief.

Then Helen came into the room, carrying cups of coffee and a plate of biscuits on a tray. She set them down on Nick's desk.

'Helen, what do you have to say about this?' asked Terry.

She looked at him blankly. 'About what?'

'About Nick giving up his post at *Futures*.'

'Oh, that.' She shrugged dismissively. 'Well, he did mention that he might. I said I'd support any decision he made.'

'Well, *you* sound pretty bloody complacent about it! Maybe the two of you should have a serious talk.' He gestured at her swollen stomach. 'This could be a bad time to kiss goodbye to his kind of income. A new baby on the way, all the equipment and clothes you'll need to buy. And what about Molly? You wouldn't want her to suffer, would you?'

Helen reacted like he had struck her across the face. She flinched and her eyes filled with tears. One hand flew to her mouth to choke back a sob.

'Helen?' said Terry, bemused by her reaction.

'I'm sorry,' she mumbled. She turned and hurried out of the room.

Terry looked at Nick in astonishment. 'What did I say?' he demanded. 'Do you think I should go after her?'

'No, she'll be all right. Helen's a bit jumpy at the moment. Hormones, you know?'

Terry lifted a hand to run fingers through his curly hair. 'Look, just what the fuck is going on here? Why do I get the impression there's some dark secret that I alone am not in on?'

'Paranoia,' said Nick. 'Just drink your coffee, OK?'

Terry sighed. He went to the desk, picked up one of the cups, and sipped at it dutifully. He still looked baffled.

'One thing's for sure,' he said. 'You can't make a major decision like that off the cuff. We need to discuss all the repercussions. I'll schedule a full hour tomorrow morning, when we can sit down and . . .' His voice trailed off as he noticed the stubborn look on Nick's face. 'Oh God, Nick, you *are* coming in tomorrow, aren't you? Please don't tell me you're not. There's a mountain of work to catch up on.'

'I'm sorry, Terry. Look, perhaps it would be best if you just started looking for a replacement straight away. We can come to some arrangement where the new partner buys out my share in the company. Or *you* can buy me out, handle the whole shebang yourself. It's up to you. I won't make any problems, I promise.'

Terry seemed to be losing his temper. 'I just don't understand, Nick. You must have had a brainstorm or something. I mean, this is what we've worked for all these years, and you're just throwing it away. And you're dropping me right in the shit – you know that, don't you?'

Nick nodded. 'I guess so,' he said. 'But you'll handle that, Terry. You always did respond to a challenge.'

'And what about friendship? Isn't that worth something?'

'Ah, I wondered when we'd get around to that. But I'm not proposing to stop being your friend, Terry; just your business partner. And maybe that will make it easier to be your friend.'

Terry shot him an accusing look. 'What are you talking about?' he growled.

'Only that friendship seems to have been well down the agenda over the past six months. See, in my book a friend is somebody who sympathises with your problems. But what was the first thing you wanted to know after I'd been knocked out and robbed? That I was OK? That I wasn't too badly hurt or upset? No. You wanted to make sure that I'd be well enough to come in to work the next day. Sorry, Terry, but in my book that's not the reaction of a friend.'

'Oh, now, come on! You know the situation. We're up to our eyes in the biggest deal we've ever handled. OK, maybe I was a bit thoughtless; and if that's what prompted your resignation . . .'

'It's not,' Nick assured him. 'It's more the Biblical thing, you know? *To every thing there is a season*. I've worked in

PR, at one level or another, pretty much since I left school. It's time for a change.'

'And what do you suppose you'll do?'

'Take some time for myself. Get to know Molly better. Help Helen with the new baby . . .'

'And get to know what hunger's like, most probably. Thought about that?'

'Yes, I've thought of it. But this is *my* decision, Terry. You claim to be my friend, so can't you just respect that?'

Terry shrugged. 'All I see,' he said, 'is somebody throwing away a goldmine. And that strikes me as unbelievably stupid.'

Nick sighed. 'Maybe you'd better go now,' he said.

'Yes, maybe I better had.'

'We'll talk about this again in a few weeks' time. Preferably over a pint. Perhaps by then you'll have forgiven me.'

Terry gave him a cold, resentful look.

'I doubt it,' he said. 'I'll see myself out.'

He left the room, leaving his cup of coffee, barely touched, on the desk. Nick heard the front door open and close, and shortly afterwards the roar of Terry's car as it accelerated out of the drive.

Helen came to the door and looked in at him.

'I'm sorry,' she said. 'I nearly blew it. Do you think he guessed anything?'

'No,' said Nick. 'I don't think he can see anything but his work these days.' He held his arms out to her, and she came forward into his embrace.

'Nick, I'm so frightened,' she whispered. 'I can't even hear her name being mentioned without bursting into tears. Tell me she's going to be all right.'

'She's going to be fine,' he said; and wished he could believe that himself.

After Terry's departure, the house seemed eerily silent. The only sounds came from outside: the constant pattering of rain on the roof and the occasional rumble of distant thunder.

Grimly they settled down to wait.

The long day finally succumbed to darkness, but they didn't switch on the lights or draw the curtains. They sat side by side in the lounge, holding hands while the television blathered meaninglessly in the corner. The rain continued unabated. At six o'clock, Nick prepared another meal that they didn't feel like eating, but he made himself fork down a few mouthfuls, and urged Helen to do the same. He told her that he was going to leave the house at eleven-thirty on the dot. If he went any earlier, he'd arrive at his appointment before midnight and go crazy waiting in the car.

'May as well do that in the comfort of my own home,' he added.

At about nine o'clock, the telephone rang, and he went out into the hall to answer it. He picked up the receiver with some trepidation, and was surprised to hear Bobby Cooper's voice.

'Nick, my man, I was just phonin' to wish you the best o' luck for tonight.'

'Well, thanks, Bobby, I really appreciate that. You ... you haven't told anyone else about this, have you?'

'Not a soul, Nick. You's doin' this thing round midnight, ain't that so?'

'Yes, that's right.'

'And you're sure there's nothin' else you need?'

'Just some luck,' Nick told him. 'And that second payment for tomorrow night.'

'It'll be ready. I'll be thinkin' about ya, dude.' The line went dead.

Nick stood for a few moments, staring at the handset. He felt genuinely touched by this gesture, and decidedly guilty about some of the things he had said and thought about Cooper in the recent past. It only proved that people can surprise you from time to time.

He went back to the dark living room, to Helen and the television that they were both pretending to watch.

The hours creaked by like slow torture.

At about eleven-fifteen, Nick went upstairs to change his clothes. He put on a thick grey sweat-shirt, jeans and a pair of waterproof boots. He selected a green waxed jacket. Then he pulled Cooper's attaché case from under the bed and checked that the catches were fastened securely. He carried the case back downstairs.

Helen was still sitting in the darkened lounge. There was a brainless situation comedy on the television now, all lame jokes and canned laughter. She was staring at the screen as though this was her favourite programme.

Nick switched on the lights, then walked across to the window and pulled the curtains shut. Turning back to look at Helen, he said, 'I guess I'll be going then.'

She got up from her chair and they embraced.

'Be careful,' she whispered. 'And don't do anything to antagonise them. I wish I was coming with you.'

'I need you to stay here just in case they call again,' he said. 'Besides, in your condition . . .' He didn't say any more about that. 'Listen, if you need to contact me, you can use the mobile, but only if it's absolutely necessary. I'll call you just as soon as I've handed over the money. If all goes well, we'll have Molly back safe with us by tomorrow night.'

She gazed up at him for a moment and he could see the pain in her eyes.

'You don't think . . . Nick, you don't think she's already dead, do you?'

He flinched. She was voicing a fear he'd harboured all day, but hadn't dared to mention.

'She's going to be OK,' he said. 'Believe it.' He gave Helen a last kiss on the cheek, picked up the case, and headed for the door.

'Wait!' she exclaimed. 'Your phone.' She hurried across to the coffee table to pick up the mobile. As she straightened up and turned, an expression of pain flickered momentarily across her face, and she drew in her breath with a sharp hiss.

'You all right?' Nick asked her.

'I'm fine,' she assured him. 'Bloody Braxton Hicks' again. Here.' She handed him the mobile and he slipped it into his jacket pocket.

'See you later,' he said. He went into the hall, opened the front door. He stepped out into the pouring rain and hurried across the gravel drive to unlock the door of the BMW. Stowing the attaché case under the passenger seat, he climbed behind the wheel. The car started first time.

As he drove away, he saw Helen's figure silhouetted in the illuminated doorway, one hand raised to wave goodbye. He waved back but couldn't be sure she'd seen it, so he gave her a quick blast on the horn. Then he turned out on to the main road.

He resisted the urge to put his foot down.

He planned to get there for about ten to midnight. That ten minutes promised to be the longest wait of his life.

Chapter Thirty-Four

As Helen turned back into the hallway, she felt another spasm ripple through her womb, an abrupt tightening sensation that sent a jolt of pain through her.

She was forced to remain where she was for a moment, taking deep breaths until it subsided. She'd known for over an hour now that something more was happening to her than just Braxton Hicks' contractions. The baby was going to be a full month early, but she hadn't dared say anything to Nick that might dissuade him from keeping his grim appointment. Able to move at last, she closed the front door and walked back into the lounge, moving slowly because there was a dull ache in the small of her back. She felt suddenly sapped of energy.

She lowered her body carefully into an armchair and told herself that, if her last pregnancy was anything to go by, there were no immediate worries; the contractions would go on building gradually for hours yet. And if the worst came to the worst, well then she'd just have to ring for an ambulance and get herself admitted to hospital. On no account was she going to pester Nick at a time like this. He had enough on his plate. Molly was the priority now, and though the prospect of facing the birth without Nick was a daunting one, she knew she could handle it if she had to.

She tried to concentrate all her attention on the television screen, currently showing one of those funny adverts for Australian lager. Usually they made her laugh, but not tonight. Tonight she'd got nothing but troubles around her, and it seemed that things were going to get worse before they got better . . .

Another spasm hit her, more insistent this time, making her suck in her breath between clenched teeth.

Christ, that hurts!

She reached back a hand to try and massage the base of her spine, but the fullness of her own body made that difficult. She glanced at her wristwatch.

Bloody hell! Only ten minutes since the last spasm! She hadn't realised until now that she'd started timing them, must have done it unconsciously when she suffered the last pain. The sensation passed as quickly as before, and she relaxed into the chair, reminding herself of the different bits of advice Moira gave her at the parent-craft classes all those years ago.

The main thing, they always told her, was not to go into hospital too early. You were supposed to hold back until you were a least a few centimetres dilated. The suspicion had grown in Helen's mind that there was a kind of female machismo associated with that course: a woman was made to feel like a failure if she didn't perform a 'good' birth, that she was a spineless coward if she asked for anything stronger than gas and air. A female acquaintance had recently told Helen how she'd refused all pain relief when giving birth to her first child. Helen had congratulated her, naturally, and had felt distinctly inferior, remembering how, when she had Molly, she'd more or less begged them to slam in an epidural. This time, she'd promised herself, she was going to cope better with the pain.

'Greet every contraction with a smile,' Moira had always been fond of saying. 'Each one brings you a step closer to the birth of your child.'

Which had all seemed well and good until the time actually came for Molly to make her entrance into the world; at which point the epidural had started to wear off and all of that good advice had gone straight out the window. *'Greet every contraction with a scream'* would have been closer to the mark.

Helen remembered how, when it was all over, she'd said she'd never put herself through this hell again, not for anything; but here she was like some beached whale, all blown up and useless, unable to even climb a flight of stairs without feeling like she was attempting to conquer Everest.

Nature is so sneaky, she told herself, *the way she encourages you to forget about the pain and discomfort and remember only the good things*.

And there had been good things, that was for sure: her first sight of Molly's little face, bruised and crumpled and plastered with vernix, the dark blue eyes, that one day would turn mint green, widening in what looked like recognition as she was placed into her mother's arms; Nick, crying like a baby himself, as he and Helen marvelled at this new arrival, examining her tiny hands, feet, ears, unconsciously searching for defects but happily finding none.

And, after that, so many other delights. Molly's first words, her first steps, her first birthday as she delightedly blew out the solitary candle on a teddy-bear-shaped cake. Snapshots in a mental photo album, preserved just as surely as the many images captured on film and video.

And now Molly was in an unfamiliar place, guarded by

strangers who were barely more than children themselves.
What a terrible, hopeless world, when children ended up
playing such deadly adult games . . .

Helen felt something swell and pop abruptly inside her.
What the . . . ?

Warm water gushed down from between her legs,
soaking her feet and the fabric of her dress. She sat there,
staring down in disbelief, felt a wave of fear rising up within
her.

No, no, this can't be happening so soon! I'm not ready yet!

She'd anticipated a more gradual process, the way it was
with Molly: the contractions getting stronger and closer
together, until she felt it was time for Nick to drive her to
the hospital. Even then, the midwife had to break her
waters manually, an hour or so after arrival, in order to
speed things up a bit. Now everything had changed. Helen
knew that she was expected to contact the hospital the
moment her waters broke. Any delay now could be
dangerous.

Better pack a bag, she told herself.

She was just about to get up from the armchair when the
next contraction hit her with a force she could not have
anticipated. It was like a great steel gauntlet slowly
unclenching within her womb.

Mother of God, the pain!

It built slowly to what she thought (prayed!) was a peak,
then carried on building far beyond that point. She eased
herself forward off the chair, and dropped on to her hands
and knees. A ball of fire was blossoming deep inside her.
She squeezed her eyes shut and a long, shapeless moan
escaped from between her clenched teeth. Beads of sweat
popped on her brow and went trickling down her face. Just
when she thought she was going to lose control, the

contraction peaked and faded away, leaving her stunned and gasping for breath.

Now naked fear took its place.

The baby isn't going to wait another four hours, let alone four bloody weeks! He's ready to come now!

And she was all alone here. How the hell was she supposed to manage? There should be somebody with her. She couldn't handle this, she couldn't . . .

With a massive effort she got a grip on her panic.

Got to keep control, she told herself. *The phone. Get to the phone.*

She tried to clamber back to her feet, but couldn't seem to summon the necessary strength, so she abandoned the idea and started to crawl on hands and knees out to the hallway. It seemed to take forever to cover the distance to the door, and the effort was draining the strength from her limbs. She had to stop to rest for a moment, panting to try and control her breathing. Then she felt something stirring within her, and had to fight the panic.

Another one coming. Oh Jesus.

She started to scramble forwards, but then the pain returned, bubbling up like a scalding pool deep inside her. She stopped moving and abandoned herself to the worst pain she'd ever experienced in her life. She told herself grimly that she'd never grumble about going to the dentist again. She dug her fingers into the pile of the carpet, pressed her face to the floor, and screamed against the pain, but it kept right on growing, swelling, spreading until it threatened to envelop her, and she told herself that something was very badly wrong here. It shouldn't be as bad as this until the second stage, when the baby pushed out into the world.

Oh God, don't let that happen here, please!

She felt herself teetering on the brink of unconsciousness, sensed it opening like a dark, yawning chasm beneath her, and had to mentally pull herself back on to solid ground. She pummelled the floor with her clenched fists, hoping that this fresh pain in another part of her body might distract her, but it seemed to her that the carpet was becoming soft and viscous beneath her.

You mustn't faint now, you silly bitch! That won't help at all. You've got to hold on, just a few more seconds. Count, go on, count the pain away! One, two, three, four, five . . .

The contraction peaked and ebbed. She didn't waste any more time but continued to crawl towards the phone, sweat soaking her clothing now, and she knew she had to make the call before the next contraction slammed into her, otherwise she *was* going to faint and that would be the end of her *and* the baby. A wave of dizziness went through her, but she struggled on. Only now a really peculiar thing was happening: the hallway seemed to be getting longer, stretching out like melting toffee under her hands and knees. The phone appeared as a black speck on a table right off on the very edge of her horizon, an impossibly long distance away. She flung out an arm, and that too was melting, stretching across the intervening gap like a fleshy, pink tentacle. Her clumsy fingers brushed against the handset and it fell slowly to the carpet. She tried to pick it up, and her fingers couldn't grasp it. It was like trying to pick up a piece of smoke, so she abandoned that attempt and prodded instead at the call buttons with one bulbous finger that looked to her fuddled senses to be about twelve inches long.

What's happening to me? I'm hallucinating.

She was trying to hit the *nine* but her finger wouldn't go where she wanted it to. She hit one of the other buttons

instead – one of the larger preset selectors. She slammed
her smoky fist down on the smoky receiver, and tried again,
stabbing several times at the button she wanted. *Nine nine
nine*. Such a familiar number yet she'd never had occasion
to use it in her life, before now. She thought she might have
hit it right this time, but she couldn't be certain. She
lowered herself to the swaying floor, her cheek resting on
the undulating carpet, so that the mouthpiece was only a
few (inches?) away from her mouth.

Sounds came from the earpiece, a tiny insect-like voice,
buzzing questions at her, but she couldn't make out what it
was saying.

'Please,' she whispered. 'Please, I'm ...' She hesitated,
sensing the next contraction stirring like a sea beast on the
ocean floor, getting ready to rise to the surface. Quickly
now, there wasn't much time. 'My name is ...'

The pain coming back now, foaming, expanding, claim-
ing her totally, making her panic.

'Oh please,' she whispered. 'Please, help me. My ...
baby.'

The insect voice was buzzing furiously at her. But what
was it saying? Could that be ... her name? No, it must be
asking for the address. The address, of course.

But the pain ... the pain—

... and she was screaming into the phone now, some
crazy babble, she didn't know what she was saying, she
didn't care, she just wanted the pain to stop, oh please, to
stop now and let her get some rest ...

... and the carpet parted like a biblical sea and she sank
beneath its viscous surface, leaving the insect voice far
behind her ...

... and for an instant she saw Molly's tear-stained face
receding into blackness, her hand outstretched to take her

mother's hand in hers, but she was slipping backwards into the night, she was already so very far away and—
   Helen slept and there was no more pain.

Chapter Thirty-Five

The rain was still coming down in torrents as Nick drove on to the Merton Estate. Grey tower blocks loomed like spectres through the downpour as he motored slowly to the top of the road, peering ahead through the blurred windscreen for any signs of life. His headlights picked out a familiar shape standing in a layby: the rusting hulk of an ancient Datsun saloon. Beside it, the ground was still littered with glass from Terry's BMW.

Nick killed the lights and engine, and sat for a moment, gazing around him. As far as he could tell, there was nobody else about. The clock on the dashboard told him that it was nine minutes to twelve. He'd timed the journey well. He picked up the attaché case from under the seat beside him, opened the door and climbed out into the darkness. Rods of icy rain peppered his head and shoulders and he pulled up the collar of his jacket. Turning back, he secured the car doors and activated the alarm. It hadn't done Terry's car much good, but was all Nick could do for now – and, besides, this was no time to be worrying about a mere car. BMWs could be replaced. His daughter couldn't.

He set off along the narrow walkway leading between two blocks of flats, keeping his eyes skinned for any sign of trouble. It was probably just his imagination but he received the distinct impression that he was being watched. At least there was some shelter from the rain in the narrow alleyway, but very little light and he began to feel edgy, wishing he'd thought to bring some kind of weapon with him.

He moved past an open doorway: a derelict ground-floor flat that he remembered from his previous visit, its floor littered with used syringes and crumpled beer cans. He sensed, rather than saw, some kind of movement within. His heart seemed to leap into his throat and he tightened his grip on the handle of the attaché case. Supposing he got mugged before he could get the money to the kidnappers? What would happen to Molly then?

Now he heard a bronchial-sounding cough in the darkness.

'Who's there?' he demanded; and his voice seemed to echo hollowly off the towering buildings.

There was an abrupt scuffling as somebody moved to stand in the open doorway. It was an old black man, a Rastafarian judging by the greasy grey dreadlocks that were plastered to his skull by the rain. A ray of moonlight caught the edge of his thin face, and Nick winced. The man had recently been in some kind of fight: his left eye was just a scabbed and festering slit, and on his jaw another wound dripped with corruption. He was wearing a filthy rainslicker, which he clutched tight around his throat with one hand. His near-toothless mouth was curved in a manic leer.

'Babylon is all around us,' he croaked. 'Where you goin', mister? Would you walk alone into the spider's web? Would you offer your throat to the dogs of Babylon?'

Nick merely stared at the old man, aware that the hairs

382

on his scalp were prickling with fear. The Rasta man looked at him as though he knew everything about Nick, as though that one good eye could see into his deepest, darkest secrets.

'Pray, breddar! It's your only hope. Pray for de strength to overcome the powers of darkness. Prayer can make you invincible! The brood of Babylon t'ought he had vanquished me, but I alone am returned to tell thee of the true path.'

The old man started shuffling painfully forward now, one hand extended towards Nick in what looked like some kind of arcane ritual gesture. He began to speak in a voice that was more like a chant. 'Now dey took the demon, the one dey call Lucifer, Satan, Beelzebub, Plunderer, an' dey bound him wid chains and cast him down into de bottomless pit . . .'

Nick began to move slowly past the old man as he continued with his chant.

'. . . dey sealed him up so that he could no more have dominion over de lords of de earth . . .'

Nick turned and hurried on into the heart of the estate, but the Rasta's wailing voice seemed to follow him like the crying of a banshee.

'. . . and dere he must stay for a t'ousand years. But, after dat time, he must be let loose for a little while. He mus' walk abroad to seek the souls of men like you and me, mister! He got de taste for it, see? He got the taste of blood in his mouth!'

Nick kept moving. He emerged from the shadow of the tower block into more open ground, where the rain came at him with renewed ferocity, soaking into the fabric of his coat, plastering his hair to his skull. The old Rasta had unnerved him, jabbering at him like something out of a nightmare, and Nick struggled to hold down a mounting sense of dread.

Out of the rain the huge mural loomed ahead of him: the towering figure of a naked black man, fists raised in a gesture of triumph. Nick slowed down, gazing around to see if he could spot anybody, but the area seemed deserted. Now he was standing at the very centre of the connecting walkways – the spot where Alan Richards had been when those two kids had stolen his camera.

Nick gazed back up at the mural, just as a break in the clouds let moonlight illuminate it with a lurid glow. He gasped. It was crazy, but didn't that painted face up there look just like a younger, less haggard version of the Rasta he'd just encountered?

Nick shook his head. *No*, he told himself. *I'm letting my imagination run away with me*.

And, yet, the same intense eyes, the same ragged dreadlocks, the same high cheekbones . . .

'Mr Saunders?'

The voice, right behind him, spun him round with a grunt of surprise. The youth seemed to have appeared out of nowhere.

Nick recognised him instantly as the kid from the newsagent's, but this time he didn't appear to be armed. He wore a duffel-style leather jacket with its hood pulled up over his head, and he was examining Nick calmly with cold and calculating eyes.

'You brought the money?'

Nick nodded, lifted the case so the youth could see it. The boy extended a hand to take it, but Nick moved back a step, with a shake of his head.

'First,' he said, 'we talk. What's your name?'

The youth sneered. 'Think I'm gonna tell you that?'

384

'Why not? What harm can it do? Besides, I have to call you something, don't I? And you already know mine.'

The youth seemed to consider for a moment. Then he shrugged.

'OK, what the fuck. It's Finn.'

'Finn? What kind of name is that?'

'Only one I answer to.'

'All right, *Finn*, I need to know my daughter's safe and well.'

'She's fine,' said Finn dismissively. 'Now, what say you hand over the case?'

'I'm sorry, but that's not good enough. I want to see her.'

'Forget it. You'll see her tomorrow.'

'No way. For all I know, she could already be dead! I want to speak to her, *now*!'

Finn frowned. Then he reached into his pocket and took out a cell phone. He punched in a number and the call was answered almost immediately.

'It's me,' he said. 'Put the kid on a minute.' He handed the phone to Nick. 'And I do mean a minute,' he added.

Nick held the receiver to his ear. Almost immediately, he heard Molly's voice.

'Daddy? Izzat you?'

'Hello, Button. Are you all right?'

'Yes, but I don't like it here. Are you coming for me now?'

'Not just yet, darling. Soon. You have to be a little more patient, that's all.'

'But I want to come *home*! I miss you and Mummy and Lucy and . . . I'm hungry.'

'Haven't you had anything to eat?'

'Only greasy 'n 'orrible fish'n'chips. I want Mummy's special biscetti.' She still hadn't learned to pronounce the word 'spaghetti'.

'It's the first thing she'll make when we get you home,' he promised her.

'OK,' Finn interrupted him, 'that's enough Happy fuckin' Families. You know she's alive now.' He snatched the phone back from Nick and dropped it into his pocket.

Nick glared at him.

'OK, so she's still alive. But how do I know she will be when I bring the second payment?'

Finn shrugged. 'You'll just 'ave to trust me, won't you? Besides, do I *look* like a killer?'

Nick laughed bitterly.

'I suppose I have to say that you do, considering what happened to that shopkeeper.'

'Uh? Oh, right, the Paki.' Finn scowled. 'Yeah, well that was a mistake. One of my boys lost his bottle, that's all. I ain't never killed nobody.'

Nick lifted a hand to slick some strands of wet hair out of his eyes. 'You'll forgive me if I don't perform a dance of joy at that news? How do I know that one of your boys won't lose his bottle again?'

'I got 'em under control now. I don't even let 'em near guns without I say it's OK.'

'And what situation is Molly being kept in?'

'How d'you mean, like?'

'I mean, what circumstances?'

'She's in a flat, ain't she? Not far from here. It ain't the fuckin' Ideal Home Exhibition, right. She ain't got champagne and hot-water bottles; but she's got some decent scran and a place to kip. She won't come to no harm.'

386

'I hope not, for your sake.' Nick fixed Finn with a threatening look. 'If anything happens to her I'll make you sorry you were ever born.'

'Yeah, yeah. Hard man, right? What you gonna do, get the filth on to me?'

Nick shook his head.

'I'd take care of it myself,' he said flatly. 'Without a second thought.'

Finn shrugged. 'Right, I get the picture. Now, you gonna show me the money or what?'

Nick sighed. He kneeled down, unlatched the case, and lifted the lid to show Finn the contents.

'Jesus,' said Finn. He sounded pleasantly surprised, as though he hadn't really expected the money to be there. 'Looks nice all laid out like that, don't it? Is it all there?'

'It's there. Count it if you want to.'

'Nah, that's all right. I trust you. See, I told you if you put your mind to it, you'd get it.'

'Well, you can thank Bobby Cooper for that. I had to take your advice about borrowing from him.'

'Yeah?' Finn was clearly impressed by this news. He reached out a hand to trace his fingers across the surface of the neatly stacked bills. 'So this is Bobby's money? He's *touched* this?'

'I don't know about that. He has a couple of minders do that kind of stuff for him.'

Finn looked suddenly wistful.

'I heard about him comin' to Manchester, even filmin' right here on the estate. Had it all planned to find out where he was stayin' and go up there, try'n' meet him . . . but that was the night everythin' turned to shit.'

'You're a fan of his, then?'

Finn looked indignant. 'More'n just a fan!' he protested.

'Bobby's my main man, you know? And now he's given me ten thousand quid. Jesus, wait till I tell the others!' He seemed to get a sudden flash of inspiration. 'Hey, when you come tomorrow, maybe you could bring him with you?'

'I don't think he'd want to come.'

'Course he would! Bobby'd *love* this! In *No Quarter*, he makes this speech about how people've got to take what they want, no matter what the cost.' He slipped into a fair impersonation of Cooper's voice. 'You gotta take the world by the balls and squeeze till that motherfucker begs for mercy!' Finn laughed. 'He's the best, man!'

'That's just a film,' Nick reminded him. 'You think Cooper's like that in real life? No way. I've seen him nearly shit himself when a car backfired.'

Finn glared at him. 'Bollocks! You're just sayin' that.'

'No, I'm pointing out that *real* life isn't like what you see up on the screen. And in real life Cooper wouldn't want to have anything to do with a cheap little thug like you!'

Finn snapped the case shut and secured the latches.

'Don't push your luck,' he said. 'Remember, I've still got your kid.' He tried to pull the case out of Nick's grasp, but Nick hung on to it for a while, staring into the boy's hooded face.

'Look why don't we cut all this crap? Let me take Molly home now. I'll still bring you the second payment tomorrow, I promise.'

Finn laughed at the suggestion.

'You must think I'm simple!' he exclaimed. 'Yeah, you'd turn up all right . . . with a bunch of pigs on your tail.'

'No, I swear to you, I—'

'Forget it. You just gotta be a bit more patient, man. One more night, that's all. Then you'll get her back safe and sound. You've got my word on that.'

'Yeah? And what's that worth?'

'You'd be surprised. Now, let go of the fuckin' case. I gotta warn you, if I ain't back with my boys in another ten minutes, they got orders to start gettin' rough with the kid.'

Nick glared at him.

'You're lying,' he said.

'Maybe. Maybe not. Thing is, you really don't want to find out, do you?'

'You rotten little bastard,' said Nick. 'I hope to God you suffer one day, the way you've made me and my wife suffer. If there's any justice in the world, you will.' He let go of the case and got wearily to his feet. 'So what happens tomorrow?' he muttered.

Finn shook his head. 'I ain't decided yet. I'll phone you, let you know. What I'll do, right, is give you details of where to find your daughter *after* I'm gone. So don't turn up with the filth, 'cos if I get busted, my boys will know. They'll waste the kid before you've had a chance to even think about it. See, we ain't got nothin' to lose now, and they'll do whatever I tell 'em.'

Nick made a sound of disgust.

'How old are you?' he asked.

'What's that got to do with anythin'?'

'How old?'

Finn shrugged. 'I'm fourteen, 'en I?'

'Just tell me, how does a kid of fourteen get to be such an evil little shit?'

Finn looked amused by the question.

'I 'ad good teachers,' he said. 'Now, you wanna start walkin' back to your car, Mr Saunders?' He made a show of looking at his watch. 'Only, like I said, if I ain't back with the others in . . . eight minutes . . .'

'Yes, all right, all right!' Nick stabbed a finger at Finn.

'Tomorrow then. And like *I* said, if you harm her in any way . . .'

'Time's movin' on!'

Nick forced himself to turn around. He jammed his hands into his pockets and started walking back the way he had come. Once he glanced over his shoulder, to see that Finn had seemingly disappeared into thin air. There was nothing else to do but wait till tomorrow. As he moved along the walkway, four figures came towards him from out of the shadows, heads lowered against the driving rain. They seemed an incongruous bunch: a teenage boy, two big black youths, and a punky-looking white woman. Nick tensed himself for a possible confrontation but they ignored him, moved on into the night, walking quickly as if with a sense of purpose.

Nick hurried on into the narrow alley between the blocks of flats. To his left now the open doorway yawned, but if the old Rasta was still in there, he was keeping quiet. Nick quickened his pace, eager to get away from the place.

The BMW appeared to be unharmed. He unlocked the door and climbed into the driver's seat, aware now that his boots and the legs of his jeans were sodden. He took out his mobile phone, remembering that he had promised to call Helen the moment he'd handed over the money. He dialled his home number and the phone was picked up immediately, as though she'd been waiting beside it in the hallway.

'Helen, it's me. It's all—'

But it was Terry's voice that interrupted him.

'Nick? For Christ's sake, where have you been?'

'Terry? What the fuck are you doing there? Where's Helen?'

'She's down at the hospital having the baby.'

'What?' Nick felt like he'd suddenly woken from a bad

dream into a worse one. 'I don't understand. How did you . . . ?'

'Helen rang me. I don't think she meant to; she must have hit one of the presets by mistake. She wasn't making a whole lot of sense, half scared the bloody life out of me. I sent an ambulance and drove over myself. We had to break a window to get in to her.'

'Is she all right?'

'I guess so. Ambulance took her off forty, maybe forty-five minutes ago.'

'But she . . . she has another four weeks to go, she—'

'Not this time, mate. The baby was well on its way – may have already arrived. She was near hysterical when we found her. I wanted to phone your mobile, but for some reason she begged me not to. She made me promise to wait here until you phoned. I don't understand. Where *were* you?'

'I can't talk now, Terry. Withington Hospital?'

'Yeah, maybe if you head straight over there—'

Nick threw the phone on to the passenger seat. He could still hear Terry's voice shouting something from the earpiece, but the words were lost in the roar of the engine as Nick performed a reckless U-turn and pressed his foot down on the accelerator. He drove towards the entrance of the estate, and swung left on to the main road with a screech of tyres. He took off in the direction of the hospital, telling himself that, if he broke a few speed limits and jumped a couple of red lights, he could be there in fifteen minutes.

He just hoped that Helen could hang on that long.

Chapter Thirty-Six

Finn climbs the concrete stairs up to the Swamp, whistling tunelessly as he goes. He's feeling pretty pleased with himself, this time everything went like a dream, and here he is bringing home the bacon. He grins, anticipating the looks of awe on Wart's and Tommo's faces, proof positive that he knows what he's doing – that he has every right to be the leader of this crew.

He steps out on to the walkway and strolls along to the door, performing a few impromptu dance steps as he goes. And to think this money came from Bobby C. himself! It's almost a shame to spend it. What he figures he might do is get Saunders to bring the Rap Terminator with him tomorrow, and Finn will just ask him, cool as you please, to autograph one of the notes for him. Then he'll get it framed and never spend it, no matter how desperate he gets.

Finn takes out his keys and lets himself into the flat, closing the door behind him. He walks slowly along the hall and pushes the lounge door open with his foot. Then he jumps theatrically into the room, his free hand held out as if he's just stepped into an imaginary spotlight.

'Ta-daa!' he says. 'Ladies 'n' gennlemen, welcome to the Finn McManus Show!'

The three others in the room stare at him open-mouthed

in surprise. Tommo is sitting by the french windows. Wart sits on a crate on the other side of the room. Molly reclines on her mattress in the corner, still cuddling her teddy bear.

It's Tommo who finds his tongue first. 'It went OK then?'

'It went better than OK,' Finn assures him. 'It went like fuckin' clockwork!'

'What, you mean he paid up?'

'Sure he did.' Finn raises the attaché case and lets them all have a good look at it. 'What d'yer think's in here, me butties?' He walks across to the mattress and sits down beside Molly. 'What's more, all this dosh is a present from my Uncle Bobby.'

'Who?' mutters Wart.

'Uncle Bobby. As in Bobby C., the Sultan of Soul. That's where Molly's dad got the dosh!'

'Gerraway,' says Tommo.

'No, straight up. He just told me.' Finn nudges Molly with his elbow. 'Wanna see what your dad thinks you're worth?' he asks her.

She nods dumbly. She's got her thumb in her mouth and she's sucking on it greedily, like maybe she's hungry again. Finn unlatches the case and opens it, not letting the others see inside.

'Look,' he says.

Her eyes get big and round.

'How much do you figure is there?' he asks her.

She considers for a moment, then removes her thumb to answer the question. 'A hundred pounds?' she ventures.

He laughs. 'Nope. Not even close. There's ten thousand quid here. Loadsamoney!' Impulsively, he pulls out a thick wad of notes, removes the paper band and flings it up into the air.

Wart and Tommo jump to their feet, laughing delightedly, trying to snatch handfuls of the notes as they come drifting down in a blizzard of printed paper.

'Magic,' yells Wart. 'Absolute fuckin' magic!'

Finn opens another wad and throws that up in the air. Wart and Tommo react again with childlike glee. They're laughing fit to bust now, grabbing handfuls of tens and twenties, throwing them at each other, rubbing them into each other's faces, stuffing them down each other's neck. This is probably the most money they've ever seen in one lump, and the beauty of it is that there's no Gordie waiting to take the lion's share. This is all for them.

Now the room is full of fluttering scraps of paper and everybody is laughing – even Molly, who seems to have forgotten she's a hostage – as Wart and Tommo dance, and Tommo gives a tuneless rendition of *Singin' In The Rain* and ...

'Surprise, surprise,' says Chaz.

Everything stops dead, except the money, which continues to drift down past their astonished gazes. And there's Chaz, right enough, grinning at them from the doorway. Three other people are moving into the room behind him, and Finn feels his stomach drop as he recognises Carmel and two other members of Otis Mason's posse. He sits there next to Molly, the open case in his lap, knowing that his guns are zipped up in the canvas bag on the other side of the room; knowing that he's got no time to make a dive for them, even as he notes the two Uzis coming out from under the black guys' raincoats.

He looks imploringly at Chaz, and sees the boy's face lapse into a leering grin.

'You bastard!' says Finn. 'You grassed me up!'

Chaz shrugs. 'Well, come on, pal. You really think I was gonna let you get away with it?'

There's a silence then: a silence that's deep and pregnant with violence. Finn senses it, and sees from Chaz's expression that he is relishing this moment.

'Remember,' Chaz tells his companions. 'Just Finn.'

'Do it,' says Carmel; and Chaz glances at her uncertainly.

And then everything happens at once. Finn sees flames spurting from the two Uzis; sees Chaz react in outraged surprise, turning his head to shout 'NO!' at his companions; sees Wart's head explode like a ripe melon as a bullet hits him in the cheek, his body thrown clear across the room; sees Tommo open his mouth to yell, his body jerking convulsively, gouts of blood and stray banknotes exploding from his jacket; sees Chaz trying now to wrestle the gun from the bald-headed guy and receiving a punch in the face that sends him sprawling; sees Wart's feet and hands twitching madly as he hits the floorboards, clouds of dust rising from the impact; hears the smashing of glass and lifts his head to see Tommo crashing backwards through the French windows, jagged pieces of glass raining down around him as he falls.

All this in an instant, and then Finn reacts, dropping the attaché case and throwing an arm around Molly, hugging her against him as he backs into the corner of the room. She in turn hugs the bear – so it's the three of them huddled there. Finn isn't sure if his actions are protective or whether he's simply using her as a shield and—

Chaz suddenly lunges at Finn, wild-eyed, his arms outstretched as if to tear at his throat; only, no, his hands are scrabbling at, of all things, the teddy bear and—

The Uzis kick up their infernal yattering as the two killers

396

turn their weapons on Chaz, raking him with automatic fire, kicking the floorboards beneath him into flying splinters and punching bloody holes through the fabric of his jacket.

His hands turn into claws, his eyes bulging with shock and he looks imploringly up at Finn and says, 'In the bear—'

It's as far as he gets, because another burst of gunfire rakes his legs and buttocks and he rolls away with a scream of agony, his hands up to his face, his ruined legs flailing like he's trying to run on the spot and then quite suddenly he stops kicking and . . .

It's very quiet in the room.

The place stinks of gunfire, and swirls of grey smoke drift across the riddled floorboards towards the broken windows. The last of the banknotes settle gently on the ground.

Finn sits there stunned, hardly believing that so much can happen in the space of only a few seconds. A moment ago he was the leader of a posse. Now there's no posse left to lead. He looks at Wart, a ruined mannequin with a head like a latex Halloween mask. He glances towards the window, where only Tommo's blood-spattered trainers are visible, protruding into the room over a jagged border of broken glass. Finn turns his attention to Chaz, who now wears casuals liberally patterned with psychedelic red.

Through a numbing wave of shock, Finn ponders Chaz's final remark.

'*In the bear*.' Is that what he said?

Now Finn looks at the three people moving slowly across the room towards him. They're beaming down at him like benefactors, but he knows that they're here to kill him. Carmel's mouth is a smiling red gash.

'Mr McManus,' she says. 'We've found you at last.

We've been looking everywhere for you.' She kicks up a shower of banknotes with the toe of a motorcycle boot. 'Looks like you've been busy since I last saw you.' She reaches slowly into her jacket and pulls out a large pair of secateurs. 'There was something Otis wanted very much to give you. Kind of a present. He ain't here at the moment, so I'll have to do it on his behalf. Gonna give you a nice new necktie.'

Finn feels the warmth drain out of his body, like somebody's poked a hole in his gut. He can hear Molly whimpering as she huddles against him.

In the bear. In the bear. In the bear . . . The words go through Finn's mind like an incantation. What was it supposed to mean? And why was Chaz so eager to get hold of the toy? Picturing Chaz, yesterday afternoon, sitting on that wooden crate, the bear on his lap . . . and a few minutes later, no bear, but Chaz holding out his arms, saying, 'I haven't seen the gun. Search me if you like!' Christ, could it be? Could it possibly be . . . ?

Almost unconsciously, Finn's hand reaches up to the zip in the toy's back and eases it down. He plunges his right hand into the cavity and finds only the soft folds of a child's pyjamas . . .

'Hold him,' Carmel tells the others.

. . . but no, not just the pyjamas. There's something else tucked away in there, his fingers detect the hardness of it beneath the material. He twists his fingers, trying to find a path through the folds.

The two black men are moving forward now, the bald one reaching out to him one-handed. The scarred one grasps Molly by the shoulder and tries to prise her away but she resists, hugging herself hard against Finn and burying her face in his leather coat . . .

. . . and Finn's fingertips brush against cool metal, they've found the smooth contours of the Glock's hand-grip . . .

Carmel stepping closer now, making snipping motions with the secateurs. 'Come on, Finn,' she croons. 'Don't be shy. I'll leave you a pretty little stump.'

. . . his index finger hooking into the trigger guard now, and he feels a smile changing the shape of his mouth.

Carmel's own smile vanishes and she hesitates, her eyes narrowing in suspicion.

'What's so fuckin' funny?' she asks him.

'You are, you ugly bitch,' he says and squeezes the trigger.

Nothing happens.

It's a very bad moment. Carmel looks angry now. She's going to make him pay for that remark. But what went wrong? Surely the gun can't be empty?

You have to rack the slide to arm it! squeals a voice in his head and suddenly, he's in a complete panic, plunging his other hand into the bear in a frantic attempt to arm the weapon.

It must look comical, the bear jiggling in his lap like a ventriloquist's dummy. At any rate, Carmel and the black guys are laughing at him. At least they are until they hear a tell-tale metallic click and then their laughter dries up and they're too busy reacting, the guys trying to bring their Uzis back into play as Finn fires, several times, the muffled shots exploding the stuffed toy into fragments of cotton wadding and synthetic fur.

Kojak screams as the first two shots hit him point-blank in the guts, and he reels backwards. Linton has got the Uzi around and he steps back to fire but Finn's third shot hits him in the throat, throwing out a jet of crimson behind him.

His finger tightens on the trigger as he arches backwards and Finn feels a terrible impact smash into his left shoulder, slamming him back against the wall.

Bullets kick plaster chunks from just above his head and then punch a climbing pattern of holes up to the ceiling, as Linton's shoulders crash against the floorboards. He's already dead but the Uzi doesn't stop firing until its magazine is empty.

Finn finds himself sitting there with a torn furry rag hanging around his wrist, the gun now in plain view. Molly is still clinging to him, sobbing now, her face turned away. Finn's only dimly aware that he's hit, can feel a warm wetness pulsing down his chest, but for the moment he's more intent on Carmel.

She is standing there open-mouthed, the secateurs held uselessly in one hand. Kojak isn't dead yet; he's lying on his back, his body arching and his hands clutching at the two holes in his belly. He throws back his head and roars his pain, so Finn, almost casually, puts another bullet into him, up near the heart this time. Kojak gives a grunt of surprise, and his body sinks slowly back down to the horizontal.

Then everything is quiet again.

Finn studies Carmel, enjoying her plight. He can see that she doesn't know what to do now, whether to fling herself at him, die in a blaze of glory or go down on her knees and beg for mercy. Finn hopes she'll try the latter; he'd like to see her grovel.

'Well,' he says. 'Any last requests?'

She nods. 'Just one.' She pauses a moment as though thinking. Then 'Go fuck yourself!' she screams, and makes a run at him.

He shoots her in the forehead. The bullet makes a small

entry wound, barely more than the size of a five-pence coin, but the back of her head explodes in a splash of blood and bone fragments, and she's jerked backwards as though attached to an invisible wire. She crashes to the floor and goes into a kind of spastic fit, her arms and legs thrashing and kicking, while a stream of words come babbling out of her mouth: nonsense words, slurred and uncoordinated, like some kind of machine that's gone into overdrive. Then they stop abruptly, as if a plug has been pulled from a socket. As she stops kicking, a pool of blood begins to fan out from her shattered skull.

Finn finally registers the pain of his wound. It kicks him like a jolt from a cattle prod, coaxing an involuntary groan from his lips. He tries to move his left arm and finds that he can't, it hangs uselessly beside him like something that doesn't belong to him any more. He lets the pistol drop and eases himself away from Molly. She seems to have become almost catatonic. She has seen more in the last few minutes than anyone should see in a lifetime.

Finn reaches up and gingerly pulls the jacket back from the wound. Glancing behind him, he sees a telltale blood splash and a bullet hole in the wall. The shot has gone clean through him. He still has the scrap of teddy-bear fur hanging around his wrist, so he wads this and pushes it in against the wound, hissing and grinding his teeth against the fresh pain this causes him. He pulls the jacket back over the wound, then picks up the pistol and drops it into his pocket.

He gets to his feet and looks around the room in a kind of daze. The scene of carnage tells him that he daren't stay here any longer. Even in a lonely dump like this one, people will have heard those gunshots. He's got to get out of here.

He prods Molly with his foot, and she seems to wake from a deep sleep. She blinks up at him.

'Get your coat on,' he tells her. 'We're leaving now.' Molly stumbles over to the other side of the room, trying to avoid the bodies that litter the floor.

'Want my mummy!' she wails.

'You'll see her, soon. Come on, hurry it up!'

He kneels and latches the attaché case, one-handed. No use trying to pick up the scattered notes on the floor, many of them spattered with blood. Besides, he's still got more than his fair share.

Molly has put on her duffel-coat now. She stands there sobbing.

'Come on,' he urges her. 'Let's get out of here.'

'But what about them?' She gestures hopelessly around the room. 'Aren't they coming?'

He stares at her. 'Don't be stupid,' he tells her. 'Come on.'

She moves closer to him and reaches up to take the sleeve of his injured arm. 'Where we going?' she asks him.

'Somewhere else,' he says, and doesn't feel he needs to explain any further. He goes out through the open door into the hallway, but has to set down the case in order to open the front door. A wave of pain ripples through him, and he grits his teeth again to prevent himself from crying out.

It's still raining heavily out there, and maybe the noise of the downpour will have covered the sound of the shots. He can't take the risk though and, anyway, the last thing he wants to do is share a room with a bunch of stiffs. Finn curses his bad luck. A couple of inches higher and the bullet would have missed him completely. Still, he's not finished

yet, and he thinks he knows another place he can hide out –
provided he's got enough strength left to make it there.

'Come on,' he tells Molly; and they step out into the
night.

Chapter Thirty-Seven

Nick drove in through the entrance of the hospital car park, ignoring prominent signs advising him to stop and obtain a ticket from the Pay-and-Display. Gone midnight on a Sunday, the roads had been deserted and he hadn't stopped for many red lights, so he wasn't going to waste time looking for coins.

He motored past rows of parked cars and located a vacant slot near to the entrance of the maternity unit. He brought the BMW to a screeching stop and was out of the door an instant later, not even bothering to waste precious seconds locking it behind him.

He ran up the wheelchair ramp that led to the swing doors of the entrance. No need to ask for directions; he'd been here before in not much less of a panic. He turned left and ran the short distance along the deserted corridor until he reached a set of locked glass doors. He pushed a button set into the wall, then turned his head to look directly into the lens of the security camera mounted on the ceiling above him. He waited with growing impatience, but nothing happened.

'Come on, come on!' he hissed and pushed the button again. From somewhere within, he heard the muted shrilling of a bell. At last a flat, metallic voice sounded from a speaker grille beside the button.

'Yes?'

'It's Nick Saunders. My wife, she—'

That was as much as he needed to say. There was an abrupt buzzing tone and Nick was able to push open the glass doors. He strode through into Maternity and turned right, around the corner to the entrance of the delivery unit, remembering, as he did so, the last time he was here: how frightened and nervous he and Helen had been. He'd been looking forward to handling things better this time, but for reasons beyond his control he was now in a worse state than before.

Just inside the doors he was met by a woman he judged to be somewhere in her late thirties. She was small and plump, dressed in a pale blue smock. She had a pleasant, freckled face, a warm smile, and her wavy auburn hair was tied back in a ponytail.

'Mr Saunders,' she said, holding out a hand for him to shake. 'Pleased to meet you. I'm Jane Keating, the midwife attending your wife's delivery. For a minute there I thought we were going to have to do it without you.'

'I'm sorry.' Nick spread his hands in a gesture of apology. 'I couldn't get here earlier. It . . . it's been quite a night.'

'Well, you're here now. That's the main thing.'

'How's Helen doing?'

'She's doing fine. She's currently coming out of transition into second-stage labour.'

'My God, that means she's liable to drop the baby at any minute, doesn't it?'

Jane smiled at his anxiety. 'Calm down,' she advised him. She put a hand on his arm and gave it a gentle squeeze. 'Maybe it would be a good idea if you composed yourself a little before you go in to see her. I could get somebody to make you a cup of coffee or something . . .'

He shook his head. 'No thanks. I'd rather go straight in, if you don't mind.'

'Of course. But perhaps I'd better just quickly fill you in on what's happened so far . . .'

'Look, she *is* OK, isn't she?'

'She's fine. She's in considerable pain, though. The baby's lying in a posterior position, with its back against Helen's spine. That's putting a lot of pressure on a very sensitive area. Apparently, the contractions came on suddenly, and were very fierce from the word go. I wanted Helen to have an epidural as soon as she arrived, but she wouldn't consider it. Same went for pethidine. Said she wanted nothing stronger than gas and air.'

Nick frowned. 'She did tell me she was determined to have as natural a birth as possible. Last time out she opted for an epidural, and I think she feels that she failed in some way. The tutor at our parent-craft class . . .'

Jane rolled her eyes. 'I had a feeling they'd be involved somewhere,' she said caustically. 'Me, I don't go for all that Wonder Woman stuff. I'm two months pregnant myself, and when my time comes I'll have 'em slam in an epidural at the first twinge.' She sighed, shook her head. 'Still, if that's the way Helen wants it, who am I to argue? Anyway, if you're sure you want to go straight in . . . ?'

She took his silence as an affirmative and led him down the corridor to one of the delivery rooms. She pushed open the door and they stepped inside.

Helen lay on the bed, which had been raised into a sitting position. She was wearing a short, open-backed hospital nightdress. Her eyes were closed and there was an expression of intense concentration on her face. Beside the bed, a foetal monitor bleeped rhythmically, its twin sensors tracing scribbles of ink on a slowly unwinding spool of paper. As Nick stepped up to the bed, Helen opened her eyes and noticed him. An expression of relief replaced the look of concentration. She reached out to him and he took her in his arms.

'Nick,' she whispered. 'Thank God. Did you see Molly?'

He shook his head. 'I talked to her,' he said. 'On a mobile phone. She seemed fine. Said she was looking forward to her special biscetti.'

'Who's Molly?' asked Jane, brightly. 'Your little girl?'

Helen broke out of Nick's embrace and did her best to smile. 'Yes,' she said. 'Molly's four. She . . . she's staying with friends at the moment.'

'It's quite an upheaval for a little girl, isn't it? Is she hoping for a brother or a sister?'

'A brother,' said Helen. 'She's got it all planned.'

'That's a wonderful moment, when they first see the new arrival.' Jane turned away to busy herself at a work surface, arranging implements in a kidney-shaped bowl.

'Jane tells me you've refused any pain relief,' said Nick quietly. 'Why don't you try something?'

Helen shook her head adamantly.

'I don't deserve any,' she said grimly. 'If I'd only kept hold of Molly's hand . . .'

'Hey, that's crazy talk! I've already told you, nobody's to blame for what happened. Why do you want to punish yourself like that?'

'It's nothing to what Molly's going through, Nick. If anything happens to her—' She broke off in mid-sentence. 'Oh, oh,' she said. 'Here comes another one.' She grabbed hold of Nick's hand and then glanced down at it sadly. 'You won't let go of my hand, will you?'

Nick thought she sounded like a forlorn little child herself, and he felt desperately sorry for her. She was grimacing now as the pain started to build within her. With her other hand she took up the mouthpiece that dispensed gas and air, and the midwife came to the other side of the bed to put a comforting arm around her. Glancing at the monitor, Nick saw how the scribble of ink was veering to the left, to create a V-shaped ridge. Helen inserted the mouthpiece and started taking in big gulps of the mixture, while her other hand tightened its grip until Nick thought his knuckles might break under the pressure. As beads of sweat broke on Helen's forehead, Jane wiped them off with a cool flannel.

To Nick, this contraction seemed to last for ever. Finally the monitor's needle reached its peak and veered sharply back to the right. There was a corresponding relaxation in Helen's body. She let go of the mouthpiece and settled back on to the pillows with a sigh of relief. Then she gave Nick a look of mock accusation.

'Whose idea was it to have another kid?' she asked him.

'Yours,' he reminded her. 'And you're doing great. If you'd just take something to help ease the pain . . .'

'No way, José. We're doing this one *au naturel*. Moira would be proud of me.'

'Stuff Moira,' he said uncharitably.

He took the opportunity to remove his jacket and hang it up out of the way. Jane, meanwhile, had slipped on a disposable glove and was giving Helen an examination.

'You're fully dilated,' she announced. 'Contractions are coming about one in one, and lasting up to a minute, so it's going to be more or less continuous from here on in. I think we'll get you to start bearing down when the next one hits.'

'Goody gumdrops,' said Helen grimly. 'Still, it ought to be easier this time. The baby's only small, and everyone says that the second one—' She broke off again and grabbed for the mouthpiece. 'Fasten your seat belts,' she said.

Nick climbed on to the bed beside her and started massaging her back, where the worst of the pain seemed to be situated. He remembered from last time how useless this experience was going to make him feel, knowing that there was little he could do for Helen other than be here, hold her, massage her, offer her the occasional sip of water, the occasional word of encouragement. But the hard work of labour, the sheer exhausting slog of it, was all down to her.

'OK, let's try pushing now, shall we?' he heard the midwife say. 'Deep breath in and . . . *push!*'

And so it began, the contractions stepping up now until they almost merged with each other, Helen pushing for all she was worth, screaming against the pain it caused her. Her whole body was bathed in sweat as she devoted every ounce of energy to the effort of pushing her baby out into the world. But progress was painfully slow: an hour passed with no discernible advance, then a second began to tick by. Helen was now close to exhaustion and Nick noticed that the readout on the monitor indicating the child's heartbeat was beginning to fluctuate, dipping from around 140 to as low as 70.

Nick could tell that Jane wasn't happy with this; she kept going across to check the readout. Then she announced that she wanted to call in the consultant, just to get his opinion. She went off to fetch him.

Nick said nothing, not wanting Helen to worry any more than she was already; but, for the first time in this pregnancy, he allowed himself to consider the horrible possibility that the baby might die. That wasn't something he wanted to think about, but it was there at the back of his mind, like some dark curse he was unable to shake off.

Jane came back with a young, bespectacled consultant who she introduced as Dr Montgomery. He looked at the monitor for a few moments, observing how it reacted during a contraction. Then he put on a glove and did a quick examination, asking Helen to push with the next spasm.

At length he announced that he was loath to leave the baby in distress for very much longer. They'd give it another half-hour and see what progress was made. After that, they'd have to consider performing a Caesarean. Since that would need a general anaesthetic, Nick should prepare himself for the possibility that he might not be present at the actual birth.

This information seemed to galvanise Helen into renewed effort. Jane's demands became more urgent, and she took on the persona of a PT instructor.

'Come on, Helen, you're not trying hard enough! *Push!*'

'I *am* trying, goddamn it!' Helen gave it everything else she had, her body rigid in Nick's arms, her eyes squeezed shut, her head thrown back to scream at the ceiling. Another fifteen minutes slipped by and then—

'Yes!' cried Jane. 'I can see the crown, Helen! Come on, now. Next time I want you to push him out to me.'

But Helen was shaking her head, spattering Nick with droplets of her sweat.

'Can't,' she whispered. 'I'm finished . . .'

'No,' Nick urged her. 'You can do it. You can't give up when you're so close.'

'Sleep,' murmured Helen. 'Please, let me sleep . . .'

Helen's voice was drowsy now, slurred by too much gas and air, her eyelids flickering with fatigue.

Other people were filing into the room. Dr Montgomery was chatting to another doctor, this one a young woman.

There was also an assistant midwife and a couple of student doctors. In the cramped delivery room, it seemed like quite a crowd.

'I don't want them here!' murmured Helen.

'Ignore them,' said Nick. 'Pretend it's just you and me. We're doing this together.'

'Contraction coming,' Jane warned him. 'Come on, now, Helen. You've done the hardest bit. A couple more pushes and it will all be over. Give it everything you've got.'

Helen's eyes filling with tears now, her voice ragged with emotion.

'I can't. I haven't got the strength . . .'

'Helen, you can.' Nick grabbed her chin between thumb and forefinger and turned her face to look him in the eyes. 'Think of Molly,' he said.

He wasn't sure why he said that, but his instinct was clearly a good one. Helen's eyes focused and a look of determination came back to her face. She snatched a deep breath and began to push with all her remaining strength, gritting her teeth against the long moan that spilled out of her. Jane was hunched forward now between Helen's spread legs.

'The baby's coming,' she cried. 'Coming out now . . . the . . . the head's out! Next time, Helen, we'll be there.'

Helen relaxed with a groan, slumped back into Nick's arms.

'Here,' Jane urged her. 'Give me your hands.' She was guiding Helen's hands down to touch the tiny head that protruded from her body. A look of wonder came to Helen's face and her eyes brimmed with fresh tears.

Nick felt his own emotions stirring. Impossible to try and control them at a time like this; he went with them, let them swamp him in a great overpowering wave.

'Now, Helen,' said Jane, sternly. 'This is the last one, I promise. Get that shoulder free and I'll put the baby into your arms. Ready? Take a breath and . . .'

Helen pushed for the last time, and Nick felt rather than saw the baby slide out of her.

There was a moment of deep silence – so deep and black and impenetrable that Nick thought he would fall into it. Then a sudden, mewling, cat-like cry emerged, and Nick saw Jane's arms come up into view. She was holding the baby in her hands. He was tiny, no more than four or five pounds, wizened, splattered with blood and mucus and greasy white vernix – but undeniably alive and proclaiming his presence in this unfamiliar world.

'You have a boy,' he heard Jane say, and then his eyes filled with tears and he held Helen against him as she sobbed too. 'Just a moment. We're cleaning him up a bit . . . cutting the cord . . . There!' And Jane was placing the baby into Helen's arms. 'Only for a moment now,' she warned. 'He'll have to go straight to Special Care.'

'Special Care?' Nick felt his worries flooding back again, and tried to tell himself that there was nothing unusual about this. After all, the boy was four weeks premature. It was surely normal procedure.

'Don't worry,' Jane reassured him. 'Congratulations to you both. He's lovely.'

They both gave her a hug, acknowledging the special bond that now existed between them. The midwife smiled and went back to the routine jobs of managing the third stage and performing any necessary stitching, but Helen was barely aware of that now.

'Look at him,' she whispered. 'He's the picture of you, Nick.'

'Is he?' Nick looked at the strange little face, the dark

413

blue eyes that stared so intently back at him, the tiny smudge of a nose, the thatch of curly black hair that would almost certainly fall out within a few weeks. People could never see themselves in their children; it always needed somebody else to point out the similarities.

'Now we have one lookalike each,' said Helen. 'And Molly wanted a little brother, didn't she? I can't wait to see her face when she—' She broke off, couldn't continue with what she was saying.

'Tomorrow,' Nick assured her. 'I'll bring her here to you, I promise.'

Jane came to them now and gently prised the baby out of Helen's arms. 'The paediatrician's waiting to look at him,' she explained. 'We must get him into the Special Care Unit.'

'Oh, just a moment longer, please!'

'We daren't, Helen. He's premature. We've got to be sure he's all right. Don't worry, you'll be able to visit him whenever you like.' She took the baby and carried him across to the female doctor. She wrapped the baby in a piece of towelling, placed him in a perspex trolley, and immediately wheeled him out of the room.

'Go with him,' Helen urged Nick.

'But what about you?'

'I'll be fine. To tell you the truth, all I want to do is sleep. I can hardly keep awake now. Just go and . . . be with him. Make sure he's . . . make sure . . . will you?'

'Of course.' He put his arms around her and kissed her gently on the forehead. 'You're beautiful,' he told her. 'And so is the baby. I love you both, very much.'

'Love you . . . too. Look . . . after him . . .'

'I will.' He eased her back on to the pillows and she was asleep instantly – the deep, silent sleep of exhaustion.

Nick stood and stretched, gave a long sigh of relief. He turned to grin at Jane, who was working with the needle and catgut.

'Thanks for everything you've done for us,' he said. 'Somewhere there's a big box of chocolates with your name on it.'

She smiled. 'Got a bit rough back there, didn't it? Bet you're ready for that cup of coffee now.'

'Maybe I'd better call at the Special Care Unit first.'

'No, give them a few minutes to check the baby over. I've asked one of the nurses to bring you a drink in the parents' room. After you've had that, you just go down the corridor and through the entrance. SCBU's straight ahead of you, across the lobby. While you're gone, we'll get Helen into a recovery room, and then you can go with her on to the ward. Hey, you got a name for that baby yet?'

'We hadn't fixed on anything. He kind of took us by surprise.' Nick felt suddenly drained, and realised that a shot of caffeine was probably just what he needed. 'I'll see you later,' he told Jane, and went out into the corridor. There he experienced a sudden rush of unreality, closely followed by a feeling of elation. He now had the little boy he'd been hoping for. It hardly seemed possible.

He found a cup of hot, sweet coffee in the parents' room and gulped it down gratefully. It was only instant, but he couldn't remember when he'd last enjoyed a cup so much. He felt that he wanted to run madly around, telling every stranger he met that his wife had just had a baby, but the place seemed deserted, and what staff there were had plenty to occupy them. He thought about Molly and pictured her gazing down for the first time at her new brother. That was something to look forward to. Maybe even something to pray for.

He drained the last of his coffee and went back out into the corridor. He walked through the main entrance and pushed wearily through the doors of SCBU. The moment he entered, he felt the distinct conviction that something was wrong. He headed down to the end of the corridor and looked through a glass partition. The room beyond was small, packed with monitors and all manner of technological equipment. There were four incubators inside, all of them occupied by tiny pink shapes.

The paediatrician was standing by the nearest of them, talking to a nurse dressed in a pale blue smock. They both had grave expressions and Nick felt his apprehension rising. He stepped into the room and the women moved aside to allow him a clearer view of the incubator.

Behind the clear perspex, the baby lay on his back on a knitted blanket. They had cleaned him up, put a tiny nappy on him and connected him to sensors on his chest and on one leg. An air pipe was taped into one nostril, and his tiny sparrow chest was sucking in and out like some mechanical toy.

Nick glanced fearfully at the doctor.

'What's wrong?' he asked.

She smiled at him. She was an attractive young woman, maybe in her mid-twenties, with straight black hair and hazel eyes. But she looked strained and tired, and Nick found himself wondering how long she had been on duty. Her nameplate informed him that she was Dr Beth Chandler, Senior Paediatrician.

'There's no need to worry unduly,' she told him. 'We're just following procedure.'

'Yes, but an air pipe? That's hardly routine, is it?'

'It's a sensible precaution, that's all. I was a little bit concerned about his breathing.'

'His breathing? What's wrong with his breathing?'

'Please, Mr Saunders, there's no need to overreact. You must appreciate that your wife has just delivered a premature baby. He's going to need a little extra help to get started, that's all.'

'But you said something about his breathing.'

'Well, it seemed to me that he *was* struggling a little. It happens sometimes.'

Nick lifted a hand to rub his eyes. He felt a terrible weariness clawing at him.

'Yes, look, I'm sorry, Dr Chandler, but ... I'd appreciate it if you could level with me. He *is* going to be all right, isn't he?'

She seemed to consider the question carefully before replying.

'There's absolutely no reason to think otherwise,' she told him.

'Can't you give me a simple yes or no?'

She sighed. 'I'm afraid not. At least not at this stage. I think the first twenty-four hours will be crucial. After that, we'll have a much clearer idea.' She gestured at the banks of monitors and VDU screens around the room. 'You can rest assured that your son will get the very best attention possible.'

Nick looked at the tiny figure in the incubator, the little arms and legs moving, the toothless mouth opening in a silent cry. Nick had thought his worries in this area were now resolved. But, no, here were more complications. Worse, they were vague, shadowy, insubstantial. He didn't really know what the problem was, but was convinced that another hour of questioning Dr Chandler would not yield any clearer picture.

'What do I tell his mother?' he asked hopelessly.

'Best say nothing for the moment. Judging by the way she looked back there, she's liable to sleep through till morning at least. Let us monitor the baby for a while, see how he gets on. There's every chance there's really nothing to worry about. I'd just rather be sure, that's all. Look, I'll get one of the nurses to take a Polaroid snap of him. Your wife can keep it with her.'

Nick frowned. 'Could you ... I know this sounds strange, but could you ask her to take it from the other side, so you can't see that air pipe. The last thing Helen needs at the moment is further worry.'

'Of course. I understand.' Dr Chandler lifted a hand to gently squeeze his shoulder. 'Look, Mr Saunders, I hope I haven't given you the impression that the problem is serious. I'm sure he'll be fine. I just want to give him every possible chance.' She studied the baby for a moment. 'He's the image of you, isn't he?'

'That's what my wife said.'

'Is he your first?'

'No, I've a daughter, Molly. She's ... she's four years old. She ...'

Once again he felt it swelling up within him, like some rancid balloon filled with fear and dread. In his mind's eye was an image of Molly crouching in some cold, deserted place, alone and desperately afraid. The balloon burst and he was swamped with terror. He buried his face in his hands and began to weep. 'I'm sorry, doctor,' he gasped. 'I can't ... I can't seem to ...'

'It's all right,' she assured him hastily. 'Look, I have some things to attend to. Try not to worry.'

She went out of the room, leaving him standing beside the incubator. There was a tall stool nearby, so he went and sat down on it and allowed himself to cry away his fear.

After a little while he felt calmer. Then he sat looking at the tiny creature in the perspex box: his son, so small, so helpless. Nick told himself that he mustn't give up hope.

Before very much longer, he promised himself, he'd bring Molly herself into this strange, hot room, and he'd show her what her new brother looked like. Both of them would then be safe and well. Nick pictured this scene in his mind's eye, and that served to calm him even more.

He glanced at his watch.

It was four a.m., and morning still seemed so very far away.

Chapter Thirty-Eight

Finn has to keep stopping to take deep breaths. The pain in his shoulder seems to come and go like a tide within him, and when that tide's at its height, it's all he can do to keep from screaming.

He's now shuffling along the dark walkways of the estate, heading for the Crescents, where he thinks he'll find a place to lie low, provided the demolition crew hasn't finished knocking them down yet. The Crescents are three huge tenement blocks out on the oldest part of the estate. Great ugly heaps of concrete, visible from many of the more select areas of the city, they were originally earmarked for demolition when Manchester was deeply embroiled in its doomed Olympic bid. Now the work is finally being effected a good two years late.

Finn realises it's not an ideal hideout, but he can't think where else to go. He just needs somewhere he can sit for a couple of hours and plan his next move. He carries the heavy attaché case in his right hand and Molly hangs on to the sleeve of his useless left arm. She scuttles obediently along beside him, even though she could easily make a run for it now, if she wanted to. But after the carnage back at the Swamp she seems to have assigned Finn the role of her protector.

'Where we goin'?' she keeps asking him.

'You'll see,' he tells her through gritted teeth. He fights a rising sense of panic. It's only just dawning on him that the wound is serious; it's not like the movies, where people carry on regardless with several holes blown clean through them. Beneath the jacket, his sweat-shirt is sodden with blood, and every little move sets all his nerve endings jangling like alarm bells. What is he supposed to do now? What use is all this money to him if he can't make his run with it?

Across the road he sees the tall chainlink fence of the demolition site, and he crosses over, dragging Molly along with him. He follows the line of the fence, looking for an opening that other kids have made. Sites like this always figure prominently on the list of convenient places to rob. Kids snip their way in with bolt cutters.

Finn spots a half-dozen other breaks in the wire that the workmen have already repaired, but he knows that by the following night another one will have appeared; and after a short search he finds the latest of them. He stoops to lift the cut section of wire, and pain spasms through him like a flicker of flame, making him snatch in his breath with a gasp.

'What'sa matter?' Molly asks him innocently. She seems genuinely concerned, and he's not sure whether she even realises that he's been shot.

'Bit of a twinge,' he tells her. He ducks under the wire, then holds it up for her to scramble under. He straightens up and stands in the semi-darkness of the site, looking uncertainly around.

The Crescents loom vast against the moonlit sky. Two of them are nothing more than mounds of rubble, but the nearest section looks mostly intact, its blind windows climbing sightlessly towards heaven. A short distance away, yellow JCBs slumber in the moonlight like sleeping dragons. The criss-cross metal framework of a huge crane towers above Finn as he picks his way through the rubble. Glancing up, he sees the lozenge-shaped lead wrecking ball swinging gently on its length of chain, heavy enough to crush him flat if it dropped on him.

Finn tells himself that he'd better not stay here long. He just needs to rest for a while, maybe do a better job of patching up his wound, then phone to arrange a time and place to meet Molly's old man, with the second payment. Hand back the kid, then get the fuck out of there. Head for Cheshire and lose himself in some small village community . . .

The trouble is he can't see it happening any more. He can't picture it in his mind like he once could. Whenever he reaches into his mind's eye to pluck out an image of his future, he can only see himself right here on this stinking estate, and that scares him badly.

He leads Molly in through the open entrance of the nearest tenement. Concrete stairs lead upwards into the gloom, and he decides to climb, despite the extra effort it will cost him, he'll feel too vulnerable on the ground floor. He thinks of something that Bobby C. Cooper says in *No Quarter*.

'Always take the high ground, kid. Then, when them motherfuckers below look up at you, you can spit right down into their faces!'

Yeah, that's right. Bobby C. always knows what to do in these situations. He's the Rap Terminator, thinks Finn. He wishes to God that Bobby was with him right now. He begins to climb the steps, gritting his teeth against the pain that it causes him. Molly trails wearily after him. She's tired and needs sleep; she's had precious little of it over the past twenty-four hours. But Finn just keeps climbing upwards, zigzagging up flights that keep angling back on themselves.

Molly peers fearfully over the railing down into the stairwell. It's already a long way down, but Finn is still climbing, dragging himself upwards as though his life depends on it.

Finally they get to the eighteenth floor and then they can't go any higher, because the stairs here are choked with rubble. Finn feels cold rain spattering his head and shoulders. Looking up in dull surprise, he sees that there's no roof left on the building, it opens directly on to the night sky. They've already started demolishing the place. He realises they must start at the top and work down . . .

He grunts, tells himself it doesn't matter. They won't resume till daybreak, and by then he's out of here. He goes back down a flight, and kicks open the first door he comes to. He leads Molly into a dark, empty room, and uses his Zippo to illuminate the interior. It's been mostly stripped of anything useful, but there's still ghastly flock wallpaper on the walls and a cheap paper lampshade dangles from a length of flex above them. Finn stumbles across to the window and peers out through the shattered panes. The construction site is laid out below him: children's toys on a muddy brown quilt. Nobody's going to think of looking for him up here, he tells himself. And if anybody should come snooping, well, he's still got the gun.

He puts down the attaché case, moves to a corner of the room, and sits down with his back against the wall. He feels weary now and wonders how much blood he's lost. He reaches up a hand to probe gingerly beneath his leather jacket. Molly squats down a short distance away, peering at him in the dull moonlight that comes in through the window.

'What you doin'?' she asks him.

'Never mind,' he tells her. He lifts the jacket away from his left shoulder and pulls out the scraps of fake fur that he has pushed into the hole in his flesh. The pain makes his head spin and he groans, tilting back his head to stare at the ceiling. Then he finds himself holding a sodden ball of fabric that looks oily black in the moonlight. He glances sharply at Molly.

'Need summing to make a bandage with,' he tells her. He gestures at a filthy length of curtaining trailing from the corner of the window. 'Fetch me that, will you?'

She frowns but gets up and does as she's told, tugging at the curtain until it comes down in a cloud of dust. Molly makes a sound of disgust, shakes her head to get the flecks of plaster out of her hair.

'Ugh,' she says. 'Horrible!'

'Never mind. Bring it over here,' he tells her impatiently. She comes back and drops it into his lap. He attempts to tear a strip off it, but can't seem to make his left arm obey him; it flops and twists with a spastic life all of its own. He gets Molly to hold on to the end of the length of fabric and tugs with his right hand until he succeeds in ripping off a long, ragged piece. He shrugs off the jacket and man-oeuvres the fabric into position with his right hand.

'Come and tie this around my shoulder,' he tells Molly. 'Good 'n' tight.'

She looks doubtful about this but she does her best for him, looping the floral material around his shoulder a couple of times and performing a clumsy reef knot.

He keeps flinching as she does this, but he refrains from shouting at her. He daren't risk upsetting her now when he needs her help; and he *does* need her help. There's a powerful weariness tugging at him, turning his limbs to jelly, turning his thoughts to incoherent, fleeting images in his feverish head.

Sleep, he thinks. *Just till first light. I'll feel better then*. He gets his coat back on with an effort, then simply curls up on the floor, right where he is.

'Get some sleep,' he tells Molly. 'Jus' for an hour or so.'

She stares at him.

'Here?' she asks indignantly; but he is already breathing rhythmically, so she lies down on the bare floorboards beside him, huddling close to share his body warmth, because the temperature is falling and it's really very cold now.

Finn sleeps and dreams that he's with the others, the old crew: Gibbo, Tommo, Chaz and Wart. They are all back in the Swamp and they're dying in a hail of bullets, all of them, being blasted to shreds over and over again. Finn can only stand there and watch, unable to move a muscle. The bullets aren't coming anywhere near him. But it's funny, because the others are *enjoying* it; it's like some crazy knockabout game to them. The bullets smash away chunks of flesh and bone, and they just laugh all the more, throwing back their ruined faces and howling with mirth as the bullets deconstruct them before Finn's horrified gaze . . .

In his sleep, Finn whimpers and Molly, just on the edge of dreams herself, hugs closer to him, throwing one arm around his waist. The gesture seems to calm him a little and he settles into a deeper slumber.

They lie like babes in the wood, unaware of the hours ticking inexorably away as the sun slowly rises and the new day begins.

Chapter Thirty-Nine

The muted sound of a ringing phone cut through Nick's sleep. He tried to shrug it away, nestle deeper into his slumber, but the damned thing went right on trilling, and it seemed close to him, impossibly close . . .

He opened his eyes with a start and looked blearily around at the unfamiliar surroundings of a hospital side ward. He was slumped into an uncomfortable plastic-covered armchair, beside Helen's bed. She was in a deep sleep, her head thrown back on the pillow, her pale face a mask of exhaustion. For a moment, Nick didn't recall what he was even doing here. He had to puzzle it out, piecing together the various incidents of the early hours of that same morning. Then everything came at him in a rush, images piling one on top of the other, and the damned phone kept right on trilling in his ear.

What the fuck?

He realised that the sound was coming from the cell phone in the pocket of his waxed jacket, which was slung over the back of the chair. Blinking furiously, he fumbled for the machine, peering foggily around him as he did so. The last thing he recalled was talking to Helen as she drifted towards sleep, assuring her that the baby was going to be fine, stroking her hair and promising her that there was nothing to worry about . . .

As he lifted the phone he glanced at his watch. It was just after seven a.m. Who the hell would be phoning him at this time of the morning?

'Uh?' he grunted; then added, 'Nick Saunders speaking.'

There was a long pause, punctuated only by the sound of laboured breathing, then: 'Where the fuck you ... been, man? I been calling your home number. There ... weren't no answer!'

Nick frowned, tried to focus his thoughts. Something in Finn's panicked tone alerted him to the possibility of impending trouble.

'Finn? I wasn't expecting to hear from you so early. I'm er ... at the hospital. My wife—'

'It's just lucky for me I had your ... your card. Got your mobile number on it. I can't ...' The voice trailed off in what sounded like a moan of pain. Nick shook his head to dispel the last traces of sleep.

'Finn, what's wrong?' he demanded.

'Got trouble. Big trouble. I been shot.'

'What?' Nick glanced warily at Helen as she stirred in her sleep, as though somehow she had overheard that remark. Nick got stiffly out of the chair and moved away to stand by the door of the little room. He lowered his voice to a whisper. 'What do you mean, you've been shot?'

'The fuck you think I mean? Las' night, we had some visitors after ... you brought the money. Bastards put a bullet into my shoulder, did'n' they?'

'Christ.' Nick's mind raced. 'What ... what about Molly? Is she all right?'

'Yeah, yeah, she's fine. She's here with me now. Fast asleep.'

'Here? Where's here?'

A pause, then another low moan.

'Fuck, that *hurts*! We had to move to a . . . a new hideout, didn' we? I only meant to stay here an hour or so, but I fell asleep and now . . . now I can't even fuckin' stand up! I need you to come and get us out of here, pronto.'

Nick felt fear stirring within him. This sounded bad. He had to work hard to keep his voice matter-of-fact. 'Just tell me where you are, Finn. I'll come straight over.'

'The Crescents . . . on the Merton Estate. Better not hang about. There's demolition goin' on here. Reckon . . . reckon they could be starting up again soon.'

'Demolition? For fuck's sake, where exactly is this place?'

'Told ya. Merton Estate. The Crescents. Ask anyone, they'll tell ya.' Another pause while Finn seemed to fight to catch his breath. 'Listen, I want that other payment. Want you to bring it with you . . .'

'Don't be stupid, there isn't time for that! I'd have to drive into town and get it from Bobby Cooper.'

'So? Listen, you ain't gettin' out of it that easy! You . . .' The voice broke off and was replaced by a bout of coughing which terminated with another moan. 'You owe me another ten thousand. That was the deal, right?'

'Yes, but Finn, be *reasonable*!'

'Fuck that! I'm still callin' the shots, right? 'Nother thing. I want you to . . . bring Bobby Cooper with you. Need to talk to him. He'll know what to do. Bobby always knows.'

Finn shook his head.

'You're not thinking straight, Finn. We can take care of the money later. The priority right now is to get you and Molly out of danger. If I go and collect Bobby, I might be too late.'

'You've got time. If you . . . if you get your foot down . . .

Don't wanna see you turn up here without Bobby and the money. Nobody else mind! I see anybody else coming and . . . you're gonna be sorry. Remember I've got Molly here with me. And I've got a gun.'

Nick licked his dry lips.

'Listen, how badly are you hurt?'

'Not so . . . bad I can't use the gun. Now, you gonna stay talkin' all day? Or are you gonna . . . fetch Bobby?'

'I'm on my way,' said Nick grimly. He snapped the phone shut and turned to look at Helen. He considered waking her, but promptly abandoned the idea. The less she knew about this latest situation, the better. Instead, he went to get his jacket. Rummaging in the pockets, he found a Biro and a scrap of paper. He thought for a moment, horribly aware of time ticking inexorably away. Finally, he wrote a short message.

> HELEN,
> GONE TO FETCH MOLLY,
> NICK

He left the scrap of paper on the foot of the bed and went out of the room, shrugging on his jacket as he walked. He strode along the corridor and out through the ward's entrance, reminding himself that he had planned to visit the new baby in Special Care as soon as he woke. But there was no time even to put his mind at rest. Molly had to be his priority now.

He descended a flight of stairs at speed and turned left through the open glass doors which had been locked when he'd arrived earlier that morning. He ran along the corridor beyond, and swung right out of the main entrance to Maternity. The cold air of morning hit him like a shock of electricity, driving away the last of his fatigue, allowing his mind to crystallise into sharp focus.

Now, he thought. *Got to be quick. Can't afford to waste a second.*

He figured, at best, he had till nine a.m. That was the most likely time when the demolition crew would start work. Could be they'd kick off earlier than that, eight-thirty, maybe even eight a.m., but he didn't want to think about the possibilities too much.

The BMW stood pretty much alone in the car park. He reached for his keys, then remembered that, in his hasty arrival, he'd neglected to lock the doors. It was a minor miracle the damned thing hadn't been stolen. He got in behind the wheel, started up the engine, and hit the windscreen wipers to clear the fog of condensation. Then he reversed in a reckless half-circle, threw the gears back into first, and took off for the exit at speed.

He turned right on to the road and got his foot down, heading for Princess Park Way, the major road that would be his quickest route into town. At this hour there wasn't too much traffic about, and he figured that with luck, and a couple of jumped traffic lights, he could reach the Midland Hotel in about twenty minutes.

But getting there wasn't the problem. How was he supposed to persuade Bobby Cooper to forsake the comfort of his bed, give Amos and Andy the day off, and accompany him to the cold, inhospitable habitat of the Merton Estate to meet a young fan who was also a wanted killer? Nick couldn't see that Cooper was going to be overjoyed at the prospect, but it had to be effected one way or the other, even if it meant dragging him kicking and screaming to the appointment.

Frowning, Nick swung the car into the outside lane of

431

Princess Park Way and got the speed up to around seventy. *No point in sweating over Bobby's reaction now*, he told himself. *Cross that bridge when you get to it*. And meanwhile, keep praying that he could then get to the Crescents – wherever the hell they were – before it was too late.

Chapter Forty

Otis Mason was frankly a little pissed off by Cooper's attitude.

He'd arrived at the hotel at what, seven o'clock this morning, made a big effort to drive up from Warrington with the man's consignment and everything, only to discover that the big star was still in bed. Well, OK, that was one thing, but Mason had been waiting here now for thirty-five minutes and there was still no sign of the man emerging from his bedroom and, damn it, that was just *rude*.

Amos, who Mason found asleep in a chair out in the corridor and had to literally shake awake (Christ, some bodyguard!), was stumbling around the room with a scowl on his face like the proverbial sore-arsed bear, muttering about Mason's untimely arrival, saying how, *back home*, deals like this were always conducted after midday. Jesus, like Mason wasn't doing him any favours, you know?

When Mason asked for coffee, Amos grudgingly phoned down an order, and ten minutes later a flunky ferried some into the room, and *still* there was no sign of Cooper. Who did this guy think he was?

Amos switched on the television set and told Mason to amuse himself for a while. Cooper would be out presently.

So Mason stowed the attaché case full of coke and wash-rock and slumped dejectedly down in a chair in front of the screen, telling himself that he'd make the Yanks pay even more over the odds for this slight.

A news bulletin came on and Mason half watched it: the usual bollocks about the Government's latest disaster and which members of the royal family were having a bit on the side and...

...and then it got interesting. A report from Manchester's Moss Side, an outside broadcast: serious-faced news guy standing outside a familiar-looking block of flats. There were ambulances and police cars parked out in front of it, uniformed men keeping a sizable crowd of onlookers at bay. The reporter had a neatly trimmed moustache and was wearing a waxed jacket. The grim look on his face alerted Mason to the fact that whatever he was about to relate, it wasn't going to be a laughter riot. Mason picked up the remote and cranked up the volume a few notches.

'...are still sketchy but what is known is that a violent gun battle raged here in Van Dyke Plaza in the early hours of this morning, a gun battle which left six people dead. Neighbours reported hearing the sounds of automatic gunfire coming from one of the many empty flats in the block. When police attended the scene, they found the bodies of three white teenagers, two black youths, and a white woman. So far, none of the victims has been officially identified, but it's thought that the shoot-out may have been drug-related.'

Mason grinned. 'No shit?' he muttered – but he felt distinctly uneasy. Van Dyke Plaza was slap-bang in the middle of his turf, and he liked to know about any drug-related killing that went down there. And hadn't the guy said something about a white woman...?

'Many of the flats in the Plaza have been unoccupied for some time, and are in a semi-derelict condition. Neighbours explained to me how some of the flats have been appropriated as hideouts for crack gangs of youngsters who operate in the area . . .'

The camera cut now to the interior of what must have been the death flat, showing close-ups of bullet-holes in plasterboard walls, blood splashes on bare floorboards. On one wall, somebody had sprayed two words in big red letters: THE SWAMP.

Mason stiffened, gasped. The camera panned away from that, showing a litter of blood-spattered banknotes on the floor, then came to rest on something incongruous lying amidst the other rubble. Mason's eyes widened in recognition. It was a pair of secateurs.

A white woman. Oh Jesus, Mary and Joseph, a white woman!

'Witnesses reported a teenage boy and a little girl fleeing the scene of the crime – though at this stage, it's unclear if they were involved in the incident. Police have appealed for them to get in touch on a special phone number . . .'

A sudden heat filled Mason's head, and he found it difficult to snatch his breath. Carmel dead? He couldn't believe it. He didn't *want* to believe it. He thought of her in this very room, only a couple of nights back. So sexy, so alive, so much in control. What could have happened? What could have gone wrong? And a young man fleeing the scene. Mason knew with a powerful certainty exactly who that young man would turn out to be. A cold rage flooded his chest.

And then Cooper came out of the bedroom, wearing the familiar red kimono. He grunted at Mason and then moved past him to slump on the sofa.

435

'Shit, man, what time you call this?' he grumbled. 'I didn't get to bed much more'n an hour ago. You bring everything I wanted?'

'Uh?' Mason hardly registered the question. He felt numbed. 'Oh sure, she all dere. Jes' like you ask for.'

Cooper stared at him for a moment.

'You OK, man? For a black guy you look surprisingly pale around the gills.'

'Uh . . . I'm awright. Me jes' a little under de wedder.'

'Hell, I ain't surprised – comin' round here all hours! Now lemme see, we got the dough stashed in Lionel's room. He ain't gonna be too happy 'bout havin' his beauty sleep disturbed. Tell you what, I'll get Amos to—' He broke off in surprise at the sound of violent hammering on the door. 'Who the fuck's that?' he muttered. He threw an accusing glance at Mason. 'I sure hope you wasn't followed, bro.'

Mason shook his head.

'No way!' he growled.

Cooper nodded to Amos.

'See who that is,' he said. 'And get rid of 'em.'

Amos moved across to the door and opened it. Immediately, a figure pushed past him into the room. Mason glanced up in surprise. It was a white guy, the Suit that he remembered from the day of the fashion shoot, the one that almost frogmarched him the fuck out of there. He looked frantic now, panicked by something.

'Bobby!' he yelled. 'Bobby, get dressed. You've got to come with me!'

'Nick? Whoah, hold up there, what's the problem?'

'Finn's been shot. He's moved to a new hideout. He's taken Molly with him!'

Mason stiffened at the mention of the familiar name.

He shook off his numbness and started paying more attention.

'He wants me to bring you along with the second payment. Says he needs to talk to you...' Only now did Nick notice Mason sitting there. He regarded him doubtfully for a moment, then carried on regardless, probably figuring it was too late to worry about being overheard. 'He told me if I didn't bring you and the money, he'll shoot Molly!'

'The fuck you say.' Cooper thought about it for only a few moments. Then he nodded. 'I'll get dressed,' he said. 'You can get Amos 'n' Andy ready. Tell 'em to bring a little personal insurance along...'

But Nick was shaking his head. You could see he didn't like that idea.

'Just you and me, Bobby – that's what he wants. We daren't take anyone else.'

Cooper hesitated at this news. A new expression came to his face now. Watching him, Mason could see that he was scared. The big movie star was scared shitless.

'Hey now, Nick, just a minute here! This kid is armed, right? He's already blown somebody away. Now, what we could do, you know, is get the boys to follow us at a distance – maybe creep up on the kid while we keep him talking...'

Again Nick shook his head.

'I can't take the risk, Bobby. I *daren't*. He says he'll kill Molly, and frankly I believe him.'

'Yeah, but, man ... all this hero stuff. I don't know if I...'

'You've got to do this, Bobby. To Finn you *are* a hero. That's the Bobby C. Cooper he'll expect to see – the one from *No Quarter*. Maybe you're the only person who can talk him into throwing down his gun and coming out of there.'

'Shit, man, I don't know . . .'

'Bobby, *please*! There isn't much time. We'll talk about it in the car, OK?'

Cooper considered it for a few moments more. Then he nodded.

'I'll get dressed,' he said.

He started towards the bedroom, and Nick called after him.

'I've been thinking. Can you dress like you do in *No Quarter*? That might help.'

Cooper shrugged. 'Yeah, I guess I can do that,' he said. 'Amos, go to Lionel's room. Get me another ten thousand.'

'Boss, you ain't really gonna—'

'Jump to it, lard-ass! I already tol' ya about questioning me, didn' I?'

Amos scowled, but he turned and hurried out of the room.

Cooper glanced at Mason.

'Otis, you gonna have to wait a little longer for your money. What we got here is an emergency.'

Mason nodded, made a dismissive gesture.

'Sure t'ing, star. Don' you worry on my account.'

'Do me a favour, will ya? Empty out the stuff from that attaché case. We're gonna need it to put the money in.'

'Sure t'ing, boss!'

Cooper smiled grimly, then hurried into the bedroom to get dressed. He was trying to act cool, but Mason could see that he was really nervous. Mason unlatched the attaché case and started heaping the packages of cocaine on to a coffee table. He watched as Nick paced restlessly up and down, impatient to get on the move again.

'Dis Finn bwoy you mention,' said Mason quietly. 'He an Irish-born fucker, name a Finn McManus, right?'

'I don't know his surname.'

'He got your lickle girl, dat what you say?'

Nick frowned, nodded. 'That's right.'

'An' where is he holed up now?'

Nick stopped pacing. Mason could see that he didn't really want to discuss this, but he really had no option. He was looking at Mason inquiringly now.

'You know the Merton Estate, don't you?' he muttered.

Mason nodded. 'I ought to. It's me turf, you nah?'

'There's a place I have to find. The Crescents? You know where they are?'

'Yeah, I know. I'll lead you dere meself.'

'No, I'll just have to take directions off you. I can't risk—'

'Relax, mon, no problem! Me hear what's goin' down. I'll just show you de quickest route dere. You can follow me. I'll keep well clear of de place. Don' worry, me got no wish to be involved wid dat nutter. Me jus' want to help.'

Nick seemed reassured.

'Thanks,' he said. 'Look, I really appreciate it.'

Cooper came out of the bedroom. He was dressed up in his trademark outfit of studded black biker's jacket, beret and shades. He spread his arms wide in a theatrical gesture. 'How do I look?' he asked.

Like de fuckin' imposter you is, thought Mason grimly. He was vaguely surprised to discover that he no longer cared about the big score he'd been planning to make from the American movie star. Suddenly, money didn't seem important – not half as important as avenging Carmel. But at least now he knew where to find Finn McManus. The little bastard had already been shot once. Mason just hoped he'd stay alive long enough to know what it felt like to have his dick cut off.

Amos came back into the room carrying a large brown Jiffy bag stuffed with money. Mason got up from his chair and handed him the empty attaché case, watched as Andy arranged the stacks of bills inside it, then latched it shut. Nick took the case from Andy, then turned to look hopefully at Mason.

'Ready?' he asked.

Mason grinned. 'Why sure,' he said. 'Come on along with me. I'll show you where dat bwoy is hidin'. After dat, man, it's up to you.'

Chapter Forty-One

Nick felt a little better to be on the move again. It was now just after eight o'clock and he sat hunched behind the wheel of the BMW, guiding it through the increasingly busy streets as he did his best to keep close on the tail of Otis Mason's car, a flashy red Chevrolet.

Beside Nick, in the passenger seat, Bobby C. Cooper looked far from happy. He was cradling the attaché case on his lap, clinging to it as though it was a life preserver. There was a film of sweat on his forehead and he kept fidgeting in his seat, reaching out from time to time to fiddle with the dial of the radio, as though unhappy with what he found on the pre-sets.

In the end, it became so irritating that Nick reached out and switched the radio off.

'Man,' muttered Cooper, 'I caint believe I let you talk me into this shit.'

Nick glanced at him, suddenly curious, wondering how the guy could be such a walking contradiction of his streetwise image.

'I already told you,' he said in what he hoped was a reassuring tone, 'this is just a kid we're dealing with: fourteen years old. And he worships you. He isn't going to let anything happen to you.'

'Yeah, yeah, tell me about it.' Cooper didn't seem in the

least bit reassured; on the contrary, he was as jumpy as a firecracker.

Up ahead, the Chevy took an unannounced left turn and Nick was obliged to throw the wheel hard around in order to follow suit, the BMW's tyres producing the shriek of rubber on tarmac.

Cooper threw out his hands to grab the dashboard.

'Fuck, man, where'd you learn to drive?' he snapped. 'You're gonna kill us!'

'Bit of a sharp turn, that's all. I don't get it. You know that sequence in *No Quarter* – where you drive the petrol tanker?'

Cooper snorted dismissively. 'You mean, where my *stunt double* drives the petrol tanker?'

'Yes, but it couldn't *all* have been a double. In the close-ups it was you.'

Cooper gave him a disparaging look. 'In the close-ups I was in a studio, sitting in front of a back-projection screen! Shit, man, I don't even have a driving licence!'

Nick stared at him.

'Well it certainly *looked* real.'

'Magic of the movies, Nick. They can make anything look real. They can...' His voice trailed off and an expression of worry was back on his face. 'Shit, the lights!'

The Chevrolet was going through a set of lights on amber, as though Mason had forgotten that somebody was supposed to be following him. Nick bit back a curse and stamped down on the accelerator pedal, reminding himself that he daren't risk losing the other vehicle.

The BMW shot out into a busy intersection, and vehicles to left and right of it were obliged to slam on their brakes. Horns blared a noisy protest, but the car was through and speeding after the Chevrolet.

'Fuck,' muttered Cooper. 'You do any more moves like that, boy, we gonna need more absorbent seats in here!'

He looked so outraged that Nick almost laughed at him.

'It wasn't my fault, it's this idiot in front. Seems to have forgotten about us back here. It's almost like he's trying to shake me off his tail.'

He got the BMW back up behind the Chevy, and tucked it in right on the red car's bumper. Then he glanced at Cooper again.

'I still don't get it,' he said. 'OK, so you don't drive. But, you know, growing up on the wild streets of East LA . . .'

Cooper scowled. 'How about maybe the wild streets of Washington DC?' he muttered.

Nick could hardly believe his ears.

'You're kidding me!' he said.

'Do I look like I'm joking?' Cooper's expression was grim. 'All that shit in my bio sheets? Made up by the press office at my first record company. Me, I come from a nice, respectable, upper-middle-class family in one of the better suburbs of Washington. My old man was a criminal lawyer, retired now of course. My home life was, well, I'd guess you'd call it comfortable, you know? Picture somethin' like *The Cosby Show* and you'll get the general idea.'

Nick shook his head. 'I don't believe it.'

'Take it from me. The closest I ever got to the mean streets was lookin' at 'em from the window of a stretch limo. Hell, Bobby C. Cooper ain't even my real name.'

'It isn't?'

'Nope.'

'So what is?'

'You don't wanna know.'

'Yes, I do.'

'Well it's ... Hell, if you really wanna know, it's Quentin. Quentin Appleby.'

'*Quentin Appleby*?'

Cooper gave Nick a sharp look.

'And believe me, homeboy, you mention that to anybody else and you're dead meat.'

'Point taken. But, Bobby, those songs you write ... I trust you *do* write your songs? I mean, you haven't got a ghost writer tucked away in a cupboard somewhere?'

'Oh, I ain't that much of a phoney! Sure I write my own songs! See, I did what any self-respectin' middle-class kid woulda done in my position. I rebelled. Bought myself a synth and started rappin' in the garage with a bunch've friends. Later on, I started makin' tapes on a home studio system the old man bought me.'

'Some rebellion,' observed Nick drily.

'Yeah, well sure, I appreciate that I was lucky to have that kinda help when I started out. If I'd been some poor trash from the wrong side of the tracks, I'd probably be doin' time for armed robbery now.' He shrugged. 'I just got lucky, I guess.' Nick was shaking his head again, and Cooper fixed him with a look. 'What?' he demanded.

'Well, I'm just thinking about some of the lyrics. What's that one? "Cut the crap, motherfucker, move to the beat. Listen to the lessons that they teach on the street?"'

Cooper grimaced. 'You have no idea how *shitty* that sounds in an English accent,' he complained. 'Anyway, what am I supposed to write about. Sittin' by the pool watchin' the houseboy skim scum off the surface? Yeah, I can see all the brothers gettin' down to that one. Ladies and gen'lemen, here he is, the Rap Terminator himself ... Quentin Appleby!' He shook his head, spread his hands in a matter-of-fact gesture. 'Nick, it's just play-acting, is all. I was doin' it long before I ever got into the movie business.'

Nick nodded. 'That's all I'm asking you to do now, Bobby. Be the character in *No Quarter*. Special matinée, one appearance only.'

'Well, I'll try to—'

Cooper broke off as the Chevrolet made another unannounced turn, and once again Nick had to take prompt action to follow suit. It was only as he was halfway through the turn that he realised they had entered a one-way street.

'For Christ's sake,' he muttered. 'What's this maniac trying to do?'

Up ahead, a horn blared, as a car approaching down the street swerved to avert a head-on collision with the Chevrolet – then had to repeat the manoeuvre to avoid the BMW. Nick saw the driver's horrified expression as he swept by only inches from the BMW's right wing.

Nick glanced at Cooper and saw that his eyes were closed and that his lips were moving rhythmically, as though he was rapping to himself or, more probably, praying.

The Chevrolet hung a sharp right turn out on to a major road and Nick followed, without waiting for an available space. Tyres shrieked as other cars were obliged to take prompt evasive action.

'Sonofabitch,' muttered Cooper.

The phone in Nick's pocket trilled and he fumbled for it, left-handed, and flipped it open.

'Yes?' he barked; then felt his stomach tighten at the awful sounds he heard coming from the earpiece. Crashing sounds, a full-throated grinding roar: the unmistakable noise of demolition. Then, shouting above that, Finn's voice sounding desperate, terrified.

'Where are you, man? Where the fuck are you? They started, didn' they? They're knockin' it down! They're—'

The rest of the sentence was lost in an ear-splitting din that sounded like worlds colliding.

'Finn?' Nick yelled into the phone. 'Finn, you all right? Talk to me! FINN!'

The noise settled. Then . . .

'Yeah, OK, here. Where are you?'

'We're on our way. Not far now. I've got the money with me. And Bobby Cooper, just like you asked. Is Molly OK?'

'Yeah, but . . . dunno how much longer we can—'

Another crash, the sound obliterating everything, Nick having to wait for another silence.

'Finn, you've got to get to a window! Show yourself. Then they'll hold off till we—'

'No way! They see me, and that'll be it. They'll . . . send for the cops. You got to get in here and pull us out . . . without lettin' them know about it.'

'Are you crazy? How the hell are we supposed to do that?'

'Bobby will think of a way.'

'Bobby? Finn, you've got to think this through!'

'Bobby will sort it.' Finn's voice stronger now, more assertive. 'Don't forget, I've still got the kid here with me. If this lot comes down on us—'

The end of the sentence was buried by noise again – but there had been no need to finish it, anyway.

Nick waited impatiently for the noise to subside. 'Finn, we're close to the estate now. We'll be with you in maybe ten minutes. I'll put Bobby on the line. You'd like to talk to him, wouldn't you?'

'Sure thing!'

'OK, hold on.' Nick thrust the phone at Cooper, and gave him a look.

Cooper nodded. He reached into his coat pocket, took out his mirrored shades, and put them on. It was weird, but this simple action seemed to transform him. He took the phone and spoke into the mouthpiece, his voice deeper now, more authoritative.

Nick marvelled at the transformation, even as he struggled to keep up with the Chevrolet, which now seemed to be going faster than ever. Up ahead, Nick could see the looming grey tower blocks of the Merton Estate, jagged peaks like the stumps of gigantic rotting teeth against the morning sky.

'Hey, bro,' growled Cooper. 'How's she hangin'? Them motherfuckers puttin' the heat on ya? All right, listen up. This here's what Bobby C. wants you to do . . .'

From the earpiece, quite audible now to Nick, the sounds of debris crashing down – then, after a heart-stopping pause, Finn's voice gasping some kind of reply.

'Yeah, kid, I hear you. Don't sweat it, now. Where are you 'zackly? Up high? And they's workin' from the top to the bottom, huh? OK, what I want you to do is start movin' down the floors.' A pause, a frantic reply. 'Whaddya mean, you cain't move? *Sure* you can! Well *crawl* if you have to . . . And listen, Finn, the brothers always takes care of women, right? So that little gal that's with you, I want you to send her right out of there, OK?'

Another pause. A crash. A silence. Then the buzzing sound that was Finn's voice, its tone changed now to one of protest.

'OK, you don't wanna do that, I can dig it. But keep her with you, kid – know what I'm sayin'? Anythin' happens to her and you're fucked, boy. You'll be lookin' at a major rap. Now, quit jawin' and get movin'! Get the little girl to help you down the stairs if you have to . . . Kid, stop arguin' with me and just do it! Hey, listen, I gotta hang up now. I think we're here.'

Nick saw that the Chevrolet was slowing to a halt alongside a high chainlink fence. As he pulled up behind the Chevy, he became aware that the sounds bleeding from the earpiece now coincided with the noises he could hear coming from the demolition site away to his left. He grabbed the attaché case from Cooper's lap and scrambled out of the car.

'Come on!' he yelled.

The skinny drugs dealer was already getting out of his car, as Nick and Cooper approached.

'You didn't exactly make it easy, did you?' Nick chided. 'I nearly lost you two or three times.'

Mason made an apologetic gesture.

'Me jest anxious t'get here, sport,' he said. He indicated an area of fence that had been cut open to make an unofficial entrance. 'Way in dere,' he observed. 'But looks like y' might be too late.'

Nick stood at the fence a moment, staring across the stretch of muddy wasteland. The last remaining tower block was coming down fast, but the demolition work was taking place out of sight on the far side of the building. He could see the metal framework of a crane jutting above it and occasionally a great cloud of dust would drift away from the impact of an unseen swinging lead ball. Dead ahead, he could see the open rectangle of the tower's main entrance.

He grabbed Cooper by the arm.

'Look, Bobby, we can get in *there* without anyone seeing us!'

448

Cooper grimaced.

'Oh great,' he muttered.

'Come on. There's not much time.' Nick ducked under the wire and pulled Cooper after him. He then paused, glanced back at Mason. 'Thanks for your help,' he said.

'Don' mention it, sport. Me say a little prayer for ya.'

Nick turned and led the way across the demolition site, breaking into a run. Cooper trailed reluctantly after him.

'Promise me one thing,' he gasped.

'What's that?'

'If I die in this place, don't tell anyone my real name.'

'It's a deal.'

'And we're really goin' in there?'

'We're going in.'

'Shit. That's what I was afraid you'd say!'

They continued in silence.

Mason stood at the fence and watched them crossing the site, weaving and stumbling across the chunks of building rubble that littered their route. He shook his head. Fuck it, man, he'd done his best to shake them off back there. Bad luck the white guy was parked right alongside the Chevy outside the hotel, or he could have left them standing, could have had time to go in and do what he needed to do without the complications of having witnesses. Now, most likely, he'd have to take them both out too . . .

A big cloud of dust rose on the far side of the building, and Mason told himself that maybe he wouldn't need to do anything, since all four of them would be buried under a mountain of rubble, and no bodies found for months to come. But he still hoped that wouldn't happen, not before he'd had a chance to hit McManus, hurt the little fucker, listen to him screaming for mercy, pay him back once and for all for his lack of respect – and for what'd happened to Carmel. Had to be sure this time, though. McManus was a slippery little twat; if there was a hole the size of a bee's ass he'd wriggle out of it. Mason was surprised to find that he no longer cared about the consequences of going in there. There was a cold, powerful rage building within him that only the spilling of blood was going to satisfy.

He strode over to the Chevy and unlocked the boot, took out the pump-action shotgun he kept in a hidden compartment: a twelve-gauge Remington, its barrel and stock sawn off to make it easy to conceal. He took a pair of secateurs from the boot, too, and dropped them into the pocket of his long leather coat. Just in case he had the opportunity. As he closed the boot and turned away from the car, he found himself humming a familiar tune, a blast from the past, Isaac Hayes' theme from *Shaft*. Motherfuckers didn't write them like that any more.

He ducked under the wire, pumped a round into the breech of the shotgun, and started to walk towards the block of flats. He was still humming, every step of the way.

Chapter Forty-Two

Nick climbed the concrete staircase, moving slowly upwards into a noisy hell of raining plaster dust and falling masonry, hampered by the attaché case he was carrying. He was aware of Cooper close on his heels, who was swearing rhythmically with every step, close to losing his nerve but hanging on in there just the same.

Nick couldn't blame him for being scared. Every so often the staircase would shudder beneath them as some mighty impact rocked the building to its very foundations, and a din of noise would come echoing down the stairwell, closely followed by chunks of brick and concrete that went crashing off the metal balustrades and tumbled down the stairwell to the ground floor that was currently, what, thirteen stories below? The problem was that Nick didn't know exactly how high up Finn and Molly were now positioned. When they'd talked on the phone, Finn had said something about being up at the very top, but Nick prayed to God that he'd had the sense and the strength to move down, away from the present source of the destruction . . .

He reached the top of the current flight, and angled back on himself to start up the next one, peering anxiously ahead through a thickening fog of dust particles. It was getting increasingly hard to breathe up here.

451

He glanced at Cooper, and his companion gave him a wild-eyed look saying more than words ever could. His hair and skin were plastered white and he seemed to have aged forty years since coming through the entrance door below. Nick shrugged and continued to climb.

Please let her be all right, he prayed.

Then he had a terrible vision, flashing through his mind like the stroke of a knife. He saw himself returning to the hospital burdened with the news of Molly's death. Then he saw himself passing through the entrance of the Special Care Baby Unit only to find Helen sobbing beside the incubator, grieving for the tiny, still form that lay inside it . . .

No, no, stop this right now!

He couldn't allow himself such dark thoughts! He had to believe that Molly was still alive up there in that inferno of noise and dust and falling debris; that he could get her out of here alive . . .

A fresh impact caused the concrete to lurch beneath his feet, and he fell forward on to the staircase. An instant later a huge lump of plaster hit the railing to the right of his head. It exploded, peppering his face with stinging fragments. He flung up an arm to shield himself from further harm, but the worst of it was already over. He felt a big hand catch his arm and help him to his feet.

'You all right?' Cooper asked with concern.

Nick nodded, spat out a mouthful of grit.

'I'm fine.'

'Better keep back from that stairwell, there's all kinds of traffic comin' down.'

Nick stepped back from the balustrade and continued upwards, aware now of a source of light several floors above: rays of sunlight vainly trying to pierce the fog of

452

dust. That was the open top of the building, he realised, the sides of which were fragmenting down around them like the crumbling shell of a gigantic boiled egg relentlessly battered by some giant's spoon. Suddenly he felt, with a powerful conviction, that Molly could not have survived such an onslaught – up there somewhere, her broken body must be lying buried beneath heaps of debris.

No, she's alive! She's got to be!

Nick shook his head, continued to climb. He wouldn't let himself give in now, while the faintest hope remained. He crested the flight of stairs, angled back around towards the next one – then hesitated. Though he could see only a half-dozen steps up into the curtain of dust, he thought he had sensed a movement there, something within that greyness, something displacing those dense particles.

His pulse quickened, and he started up the steps at a run. About halfway up, they came into view, huddled at the top of that flight: two small figures caked with grime and plaster dust.

Finn looked to be in a bad way. He was slumped forward, his head hanging in exhaustion, his sweat-soaked hair falling into his eyes. A large red stain soaked his leather jacket at the chest; and a more recent wound – a deep gash in his forehead – trickled blood down his face. One hand gripped the handle of a black attaché case; the other, Nick noticed, still held a heavy-looking automatic pistol.

Molly crouched beside him, tugging frantically at his arm, trying to coax him down the steps; but he just kept shaking his head, his eyes squeezed shut, his face a mask of agony as he fought to control his breathing. Molly could easily have left him before now, Nick realised, yet she seemed genuinely concerned for the boy, doing her utmost to persuade him to move.

All this Nick registered in an instant. Then he opened his mouth to yell.

But a further impact hit the building with a resonance blotting out everything else. Part of the staircase of the flight above instantly collapsed in an explosion of shattered concrete and tangled metal; and the steps beneath Nick seemed to give an involuntary twist, throwing him sideways against the balustrade.

He threw out his right hand to steady himself, making an instinctive grab for the railing, but misjudging it badly. His two middle fingers locked in the fancy wrought-ironwork and took the full weight of his falling body, bending back on themselves with a dull snap, like two rotten twigs.

Pain flickered like a jolt of electricity up the length of Nick's arm. He screamed and almost fainted.

Then Cooper had an arm around him and was easing him back from the balustrade, was relieving Nick's good hand of the attaché case. The two broken fingers flopped uselessly.

'Oh Jesus,' he heard Cooper hiss under his breath. Then Cooper was slapping at Nick's face to bring him back to full consciousness.

'Nick! Nick, you OK?'

Nick gave a moan through gritted teeth, and dropped to his knees on the staircase. Fresh dust was bucketing down from above, so he could no longer see Molly or Finn. Terrified, he yelled in their direction. 'Molly? Molly, it's dad! I'm here, baby!'

His words seemed lost in the din that now seemed so close: the rumbling of a powerful engine, the grinding of gears and cables, the relentless slamming of lead against concrete. It seemed as though the whole place would come down on his head at any second.

Then he heard Molly's voice calling out to him.

The dust began to recede, and again he saw the two figures struggling on the staircase: Molly wide-eyed, open-mouthed in recognition, and trying to come down towards him; but Finn, alerted by Nick's yell, had dropped the case he was carrying and thrown one arm tight around the girl's neck, hugging her against him and pressing the gun barrel to her head.

Nick stared at the tableau, horrified. He began to struggle up the staircase.

'Finn!' he gasped. 'Finn, it's all right. It's Nick and Bobby C. We've come to get you out of here.'

'Keep back!' Finn's eyes stared blindly out from a mask of fresh blood, looking like he didn't know what was happening to him. Molly struggled to pull free, but he jabbed the gun tighter against her head, and she froze.

'Finn, it's *me*!' pleaded Nick. He indicated the attaché case that Cooper was holding up for inspection. 'We brought you the money, see? Now we're going to get you out of here . . .'

But Finn merely shook his head, releasing clouds of plaster dust.

'No way, motherfucker! Always take the high ground! Then you can spit down in their faces!' He threw back his head and gave a deranged laugh.

Nick and Cooper exchanged glances. The boy had lost it. Whatever had happened to him up in that roaring devastation had now unhinged him completely. He no longer seemed to know who he was.

'Listen to me,' pleaded Nick. 'You have to—'

Another section of the staircase above them was smashed into oblivion. As Nick felt a corresponding lurch beneath him, the din threatened to burst their eardrums. Glancing to his left, he saw to his horror that a six-inch split had opened up between the stairs and the wall, with lengths of exposed steel reinforcing rods vainly struggling to hold the two together. As he stared they began to bend beneath the weight of the staircase, tilting over into the sick-making void of the open well. Meanwhile, large blocks of debris continued crashing down behind the two youngsters, raining chunks of plaster on to their heads.

But Finn seemed oblivious to it. He was still laughing wildly.

Nick waited for the noise to die down before he tried again.

'Finn, Bobby's here with me. Bobby C. Cooper!'

At last Finn's eyes widened in recognition.

'Bobby C.?' he said hopefully; but his grip on Molly didn't relax.

Taking the initiative, Cooper stood up and moved a step closer. Somehow he'd managed to slap a confident grin on his face, and even Nick had to admit that he looked every inch the hero in his scuffed black leathers.

'Hey, homeboy,' Cooper growled. 'What's happening?'

Finn looked confused by this question. Then his face collapsed into an expression of misery, his bottom lip trembling. Suddenly he looked exactly what he was: a hurt, confused and frightened child.

'They shot me, Bobby,' he said, in a tone of outraged disbelief. 'They hurt me bad.'

'It ain't over till it's over,' Bobby assured him, and Nick recognised another line from *No Quarter*. 'Now get yo' ass down these stairs, pronto, 'fore this place comes down on all our heads.' He started to take another step forward, but Finn's gun snapped suddenly upwards to point straight at Cooper's chest.

'That's close enough!' Finn warned. 'I'm holdin' the high ground. Ain't that what you told me, Bobby?'

'Shit, boy, there ain't gonna *be* no high ground left soon. Now, put down the piece and let's get outa here!'

'No, I'm stayin'. I'm done for anyway.'

'Who says? That ain't much more'n a flesh wound. We'll get you to a medic and—'

An impact, the worst yet, threw Cooper down on his hands and knees – and made the flight of steps tilt crazily at a forty-five-degree angle. Nick felt himself slide up against the metal railings, and he was treated to a terrifying view of other flights zigzagging down the stairwell towards the ground so many floors below. Cooper slammed into him, and the two of them clung together grimly, waiting for the din to fade.

Then Cooper clambered back to his feet, gripping one-handed to the railing to keep himself upright.

'Boy, I'm gettin' tired of this!' he yelled. 'You wanna stay here, fine, but the little gal comes with me, OK? Now let her come down here, 'fore I climb up there and stick that toy pistol up yo' ass.'

Finn just stared at him. 'A hundred cops won't take me,' he said calmly. 'I'm the king of the castle.'

Cooper gave a snort of exasperation, then began to climb, hauling himself upwards along the tilted staircase.

Then a voice behind him brought him to a stop.

'Dat's far enough, actor mon! De bwoy's already spoken for!'

Nick gaped over his shoulder in astonishment.

Otis Mason appeared on the flight below, a stubby sawn-off shotgun held threateningly in his big hands. His eyes glared at them from beneath the brim of his black fedora.

'What the fuck are you doing in here?' gasped Nick. 'I thought you were waiting outside.'

'Well, y' t'ought wrong! Me an' Finny here, we got somethin' to settle.' He came around the bend to the twisted foot of the next flight up, the weird angle making him unsteady in his platform shoes. He recovered his balance, then motioned with the barrel of the shotgun for Cooper to step out of the line of fire.

'You's blockin' me view,' he said calmly.

'You can't shoot!' cried Nick. 'You'll hit my daughter!'

Mason sucked on his teeth and shrugged his shoulders. 'Some days are like dat,' he observed, matter-of-factly. Again he gestured with the shotgun. 'Simple rule of combat. Take out de armed fucker first. You bwoys ain't packin', so you can wait your turn. Lie down, actor mon, lessen you're lookin' to jump de queue.'

Nick fully expected Cooper to comply with this order, but he remained where he was, wearing a defiant sneer. He was still playing his most famous role, and playing it to the hilt.

'Fuck you,' Cooper said.

Mason shrugged. 'Well, sooner or later, it make no difference.' He cocked the hammer of the shotgun, holding it at waist level.

Cooper's eyes widened in surprise.

'Bye bye, star,' said Mason.

'NO!' yelled Nick.

The explosion erupted from the wrong direction. It came through the wall to Nick's left: a huge, dark shape smashing through concrete, cutting a ragged swathe through the already weakened staircase and swinging straight towards Cooper's back. He threw himself down beside Nick with an oath, and the lead ball – reaching the lowest point of its swinging circuit – cleared their heads by a matter of inches. It began to rise towards the level where Mason was standing.

Mason had only just time to register what was happening. Nick saw an expression of surprise appear on his face an instant before the lozenge-shaped weight struck him in the chest, mashing the sawn-off shotgun upwards into his face, flattening his nose, shattering his teeth. One hand made an instinctive grab at the swinging cable as the weight's impetus lifted him from the floor, carrying him backwards a short distance. Then, reaching the end of its swing, the wrecking ball fell back again with Mason's lanky body still attached to it like a ragged scarecrow. His finger must have twitched involuntarily on the trigger of the shotgun, which discharged itself, blowing the top of his head out through the crown of his fedora in a crimson spray.

Nick hugged the steps as he felt the slipstream of the wrecking ball fan his hair. He took a glancing blow on his shoulder from one of Mason's platform shoes.

Then the weight smashed back through the hole it had made, peeling the Yardie's body off and sending it tumbling down the outside of the building, the black leather coat flapping like the wings of a huge bat.

Nick and Cooper exchanged astonished glances.

'*Somebody* must've seen that?' pleaded Cooper.

As if in answer to his question, the sound of the crane's engine stopped abruptly. Far below, they heard somebody shouting in alarm. Then everything was suddenly, eerily silent.

459

Nick and Cooper turned back to look up the tilting stairs, as the latest clouds of dust began to thin. To his horror, Nick saw that only six steps away they culminated in a ragged break.

'Oh my God,' he whispered. 'Molly.'

But then Cooper grabbed his arm, pointing urgently into the receding dust.

'Look!' he said.

A few feet further on, a small section of stair platform still clung tenaciously to the wall, supported on exposed metal rods. On it were crouched Finn and Molly looking amazed to be still alive. The adjoining length of balustrade was gone, and a few inches to Finn's left side, where his attaché case had stood a few moments earlier, there was a terrifying drop down the open maw of the stairwell.

Nick began to scramble forward. Jarring his broken fingers against one of the steps, he stifled a moan and nearly blacked out with pain. He was shaking his head clear, ready to try again when Cooper grabbed him, held him back.

'I'll do it,' he said. 'The kid'll talk to me.'

Before Nick could protest Cooper was dragging himself upwards, groping for handholds on the balustrade. Nick felt the whole staircase dip ominously beneath them, and glancing to the side, he could see that the reinforcing rods were fighting a losing battle to support the weight of the stairs.

'We don't have much time,' he warned Cooper, and was surprised by the calmness in his own voice.

Cooper had clawed his way to the very edge of the drop, and now he pulled himself into a kneeling position. But Nick couldn't stay inactive. He edged out after Cooper, until he was crouching just behind him. There was a gap of some three feet to the little platform on which Molly and Finn were perched.

'OK,' said Cooper quietly. 'Kid, I think we've all jerked around with this long enough, don't you? I want you to let go of the gal now. Let her jump across to me.'

Finn obeyed as though nothing was any longer of importance to him. His hand dropped from around Molly's neck, the gun trailing forgotten on the step, his head sunk in apparent defeat.

'Molly,' said Cooper. 'I want you to stand up real easy now.'

The little girl slowly did as she was told, her wide eyes constantly straying to the void at her side.

'Don't look down there, honey,' Cooper advised her. Both he and Nick were horribly aware of how the platform swayed on its metal bars as she finally got herself upright.

'OK, that's good. You stay still just a moment, Molly. What I want you to do next is jump over here to me and your daddy. Think you can do that?'

Molly shook her head, her bottom lip quivering.

'I'll fall,' she said.

'No you won't, honey. Look, it ain't but a couple of feet to where I am! It'll be just like ... what's that game you play in school, where they chalk squares on the floor?'

Molly frowned. 'Hopscotch?' she ventured.

'Yeah, sure, that's the one. Be just like that. You must've jumped twice as far before. It's just 'cos it feels funny bein' way up here, right?'

Molly looked at Nick imploringly.

'Daddy, I can't,' she pleaded.

'Yes you can, Button,' he said, his voice snagging in his throat. He knew that there was no other choice now. The flimsy platform wasn't going to stay in place for very much longer. She was going to have to make the leap. 'Just do what Bobby says, and you'll be all right.'

She nodded, then stepped closer to the edge to inspect the gap. But a small chunk of concrete crumbled beneath the toe of her shoe, almost making her lose her footing. She threw out her arms to regain her balance, then stepped back, shaking her head.

'I'll fall,' she said again.

'Listen,' Nick told her. 'You know where we're going straight after this? We're going to the hospital to see your new baby brother!'

She looked at him doubtfully. 'But he isn't here yet.'

'He is, I promise you. He arrived early. It's a boy, just like you wanted. Soon as we're out of here we can go and visit him.'

She thought about that for a moment – then new determination flooded her face. Molly took another step back, and she stood there for what seemed a long time, as if judging the distance. Then she ran forward and launched herself into the air. But just as she did another piece of concrete broke away beneath her step, making her mistime her jump.

Nick's heart leapt into his throat as he saw her flailing through space, a terrified expression on her face, legs pumping around as though she was trying to run on the air itself. Her feet just touched the edge of the lower stairs, but she hadn't allowed for their odd tilt, and her awkward landing pitched her sharply to one side, throwing her headlong against the twisted metal balustrade.

Cooper made a frantic grab and caught her around the waist, but this effort almost caused him to lose his own balance. The two of them teetered for a moment, and with panic Nick noticed that the balustrade had worked loose in its moorings and was buckling under their combined weight.

He threw himself forward, and helped to tug them both off the railings, ignoring the pain in his broken fingers.

Then Molly was sobbing in his arms, her cheek pressed to his. 'Daddy, daddy, daddy,' she whispered fiercely.

'It's OK, baby,' he comforted her, stroking her grimy, matted hair. 'Everything's fine now.'

'Take her out of here,' suggested Cooper. 'I'm gonna try get the boy across now.'

Nick eased down the steps a little, still clutching his daughter, to give Cooper some more room.

Cooper turned back to Finn, who still sat slumped blankly on his concrete platform. 'OK, soldier. Now it's your turn. I want you on your feet.'

Finn shook his head.

'What's the point?' he muttered. 'It's all gone to fuck now. I dropped the money. And they must know I'm here. They'll be waiting for me.'

'So? You think it's better to die than to serve a little time? That's bullshit, man! C'mon, jump across here before that thing gives way.'

Finn lifted his head and glared across at Cooper.

'You don't understand!' yelled Finn, striking himself on the forehead. 'I've killed people! They'll lock me up and throw away the fuckin' key.' He suddenly became animated, scrambling to his feet, the movement causing the platform to dip and sway alarmingly. He brandished the pistol across the narrow space that separated him from Cooper.

'Whaddya say, Bobby? You and me, eh? The two of us, we'll wait for 'em here, fight 'em off together!'

'Grow up,' Cooper told him. 'That's just for the movies. See the situation for what it is. You gave it your best shot, and you lost. There's no shame in that. But the law's the law, and you have to take what's comin' to you. Now, I'm askin' you, boy. Come across here and let's get you out alive.'

Finn's anger seemed to erupt and he glared at Cooper in disgust.

'You're a fuckin' phoney!' he roared. 'I don't believe this! I respected you, man. I thought you had something. But you're just make-believe.'

Cooper shrugged. 'Well, maybe I am. Now, if you're so pissed about it, why don't you jump across here and talk to me face to face?'

'Bollocks!' yelled Finn. 'You're just trying to get me to chicken out!' He was suddenly incensed by the injustice of it all. 'I bought all your records, man – went to see your film six fuckin' times. I *believed* in you!' He flung the pistol at Cooper's head, but the big man ducked it easily, and it went clattering away down the twisted stairs.

Now Finn was stripping off his leather jacket. He flung it into the stairwell, and it went flapping down like a dying bird.

'What are you doin', man?' demanded Cooper, but Finn didn't seem to hear him.

'I used to think you was God. I used to lie in bed at night and wonder what it was like to *be* you.' Now Finn was stripping off his bloody sweatshirt, and that too went flying after the jacket.

'For Christ's sake,' said Cooper quietly. 'Kid, what are you—?' He broke off in shock when he saw the bloody open wound in Finn's shoulder. 'This is bullshit,' he continued. 'All that heroic stuff you're talkin' about? It's just for the movies. It ain't *real*.'

'No?' Finn looked at Cooper for a long, silent moment,

making no attempt to hide his disdain. 'How would you know?'

He stepped to the edge of the concrete platform and looked down into the stairwell.

'Oh God,' said Cooper, realising the boy's intention. 'Don't do this. Please.'

'I'll show you something *real*,' Finn told him. 'I'll show you how we do it round here.' He raised a fist in the air in a Black Power salute and tilted back his head to yell to the heavens.

'No Quarter!' he shouted.

'Kid, wait!' Cooper stretched out an arm across the empty space, in the vain hope of stopping the boy: this boy he'd only just met for the first time; this boy who was about to do something unthinkable.

'Fuck you,' said Finn.

He stepped off the jagged edge of the platform and into the stairwell. His body hurtled downwards in eerie silence, then struck a balustrade some six floors down, cartwheeled, and went spinning madly onwards to oblivion.

Cooper made a low groaning noise and buried his face in his hands. Leaning out over the sagging balustrade, he was in danger of falling himself.

Nick set Molly down for a moment and scrambled up to him, dragging him back from the edge. Then he turned Cooper around and pulled him close, hugging him tightly. There were tears in the big man's eyes and his powerful shoulders shook.

Nick held him for several moments while he cried. Then he pulled back to look Cooper in the eyes.

'For what it's worth,' he said, 'the boy was wrong. You *are* a hero, Bobby. Don't let anybody tell you different.'

Bobby reached up a hand to wipe at his eyes. Then he

managed a feeble grin. 'I *was* pretty good, wasn't I?' he admitted. 'Just not good enough to stop that poor kid from throwing his life away . . .'

The staircase gave a long, splintering creak as the reinforcing rods finally began to lose their fight. Nick slapped Cooper urgently on the shoulder.

'Come on,' he said. 'Let's get the fuck out of here.' He turned back and gathered Molly into his arms, then noticed the attaché case, still lying on the steps just below them. 'Don't forget that,' he added.

Cooper frowned, shook his head. He clambered down to the case, unlatched it and, hefting it by the handle, threw it over the balustrade. The case went hurtling down, spilling its contents: bundles of notes bouncing off the railings and bursting open, clouds of paper money trailing on the air.

Nick stared at Cooper, bemused. 'Why?' he asked.

'It was the boy's money,' said Cooper grimly. 'I'd say he earned it.'

They clambered carefully down the lopsided staircase to a lower section, where they could walk more easily. Nick paused and lifted Molly up into his arms, to give her another comforting hug. Cooper threw a last glance down the stairwell to where Finn's shattered body was waiting, fourteen floors below.

Then the three of them continued the long climb back down, moving slowly through drifting clouds of banknotes that took a long, long time to reach the ground.

Epilogue

Nick brought the BMW to a halt in the hospital car park and climbed out, opening the door gingerly with his damaged right hand. He walked stiffly around to the passenger side, and helped Molly out. Leaving the doors open, he lifted her into his arms and limped towards the entrance to Maternity.

He felt like he could sleep for a hundred years, and Molly too was close to exhaustion, but this was just another promise that he'd made her – and had to keep. He'd left Cooper back at the demolition site, to explain things to the police when they arrived. It was going to take all his acting powers to handle that particular scene. For now, all Nick could do was hope that everything here was all right.

People turned to stare at them as Nick pushed through the swing doors, but he was too tired to care about that. He knew that he was caked from head to foot in filth and blood and dust, just as Molly was, but there would be plenty of time to take care of that later. He plodded along the short stretch of corridor, but had only taken a few steps when the voice made him stop in his tracks. He turned his head and found himself looking into a common room, where a television set was playing to a small group of patients. It was an outside broadcast from an all-too-familiar location:

a demolition site in Moss Side. A rumpled-looking announcer was delivering an ill-prepared introduction to camera.

'. . . still not sure of the exact details, but it's now known that two men died here today in a building undergoing demolition. Also that a young girl was earlier being held captive here, and that American rap superstar Bobby C. Cooper was involved in her rescue. I'm going to try and have a few words with Mr Cooper himself.'

The broadcaster was moving to his right now, to where a press of reporters and photographers were gathered in front of the partially destroyed tower block. In the background were police cars and ambulances, and several bemused-looking workmen stood around grinning sheepishly at the camera. In the midst of the furore, Bobby Cooper was doing his best to field a flurry of questions from frantic reporters.

'Mr Cooper, we understand that you saved a young girl's life today?'

'Shit, I didn't do nothin' that any other red-blooded man wouldn't do! Little gal was in trouble, that's all. She needed some help, so what was I gonna do – walk away?'

'She was being held hostage here?'

'Yeah, kinda thing. The gal's father's a personal friend of mine. That's how I got involved.'

'And where is the child now?'

'I hope she's where she oughta be, with her momma and her baby brother.'

'Mr Cooper. A hero on film – a hero in real life?'

'Hey, don't lay that on me! I tol' you, I did what I had to do, that's all.'

'Do you regret the deaths of the other two men that died here today?'

'Man, more than you'll ever know. I regret it when anybody dies.'

'But don't your own films promote violence?'

'They used to. My next film's a comedy. I just decided.' Then he paused, looked straight at the camera, and grinned. 'Whaddya think, Nick? Figure I could cut it as the next Eddie Murphy?'

Nick laughed involuntarily and felt his scalp prickle. It was a surreal moment. The people watching the television were all turning in their seats, staring at him open-mouthed.

Nick muttered an apology, turned away, and carried on along the corridor.

'Could he really see you standing there?' asked Molly. It was the first time she had spoken since leaving the tower block.

Nick didn't know how much her ordeal had affected her, or how much of it she had shut out. He would only discover that in time.

'No,' he assured her. 'It just seemed that way.'

'He's a *nice* man, Uncle Bobby.'

'*Uncle* Bobby?' Nick raised his eyebrows, unsure at what stage Bobby C. Cooper had been taken on board as her honorary relative. He turned right and started climbing the stairs that led up to the wards, telling himself how refreshing it was to find a set of concrete steps that stayed solid and dependable beneath the feet.

'Where's Mummy?' asked Molly eagerly.

'She's up here in a special ward,' he told her. 'See, because the baby came early he ... had to have a little help.'

'Is he poorly, then?'

Nick smiled vaguely and wished he could give a more

positive answer. 'Right here,' he said, and pushed through the swing doors into the Special Care Unit. He headed slowly and painfully along the corridor to the familiar room at the very end. There he paused to look in through the glass partition. His heart sank as he recalled the vision he'd experienced back in the awful confusion of the tower block, and he wondered fearfully if it was some kind of premonition.

Helen was sitting in a wheelchair beside the incubator. She was dressed in a hospital bathrobe, and she'd turned away from him, her shoulders blocking his view of the incubator. But he could see that her face was buried in her hands – how her shoulders moved up and down as she sobbed.

Ah well, then, he thought sadly, but something forced him into the room.

'Helen?' he said.

She turned to look at him in surprise, and he saw from the expression on her face that her tears were simply tears of relief.

'Nick,' she whispered. 'I just talked to Dr Chandler. Everything's fine now. The baby's breathing's improved. He's going to be . . .'

Her voice trailed off as she registered the small, filthy figure clutched in Nick's arms.

'Molly!' she cried. 'Oh, Molly. Thank God!'

Then Molly was scrambling out of Nick's grasp, was running to her mother's open arms.

'The Child Catcher's dead,' Nick heard his daughter say. 'He can't ever hurt me again.'

Then the two of them were hugging, both of them sobbing now, and for a long moment Nick was forgotten. He moved closer to the incubator and gazed in at his son, the child still impossibly small – but stronger now, he could tell: the tiny arms defiantly shadow-boxing at the world, his legs cycling on empty air; and, best of all, his chest rising and falling in a strong, regular rhythm.

Then suddenly Molly was beside Nick, raising herself on tiptoe to look in at the brother she'd wanted for so long.

'He's not very big,' she observed.

'He'll soon grow,' said Nick confidently; and he reached out his good hand to stroke Helen's hair. There'd be time to tell her everything that'd happened when he had pieced it all together for himself. When he had slept for a good long while.

'What are we going to call him?' asked Molly.

He thought for a moment. It was a good question. The baby's early arrival had caught them unprepared.

'I've always thought Quentin was a nice name,' he said.

There was a deep silence. He turned and saw that both Helen and Molly were looking at him with expressions of horror and puzzlement respectively.

He smiled at their reactions, thought about what he had just said. Suddenly it seemed the funniest thing he had ever heard in his life. His smile became a chuckle, then a full-throated roar of laughter. Having started, he found that he couldn't stop. He had to put one hand on the side of the incubator to support himself.

'Nick?' asked Helen at last, a worried tone in her voice.

'I'm sorry. Excuse me. I can't—' He threw back his head and brayed with laughter.

A couple of nurses passing along the corridor outside aimed disapproving glances at him.

Helen was smiling now, amused but clearly puzzled.

'Oh, I'm sorry,' he gasped. 'Excuse me. I'll just ... I'll just pop outside for ... for a moment.' He gestured helplessly as he felt a fresh wave of giggles bearing down on him.

He limped out to the corridor and found himself an old armchair tucked into a corner. He sat down and let the tears of laughter roll down his cheeks. He laughed until his jaw ached and his stomach hurt. He couldn't remember when he had last laughed this way. When he was a kid he supposed. When he was maybe Finn's age.

That did it for him. The laughter subsided and was replaced by a powerful weariness, settling over him like an all-pervading tide, pulling at his senses – easing him down into the unfamiliar territory of sleep. He shrugged deeper into the chair and stretched out his legs, closed his eyes. He'd just take forty winks he decided. What the hell, it couldn't hurt. And he was tired now. So very tired . . .

In seconds he was in a deep and satisfying slumber, and for the first time in ages there were no bad dreams to haunt him . . .